P9-DOG-778

The Edgar Award Book

The Edgar Award Book

Edited By

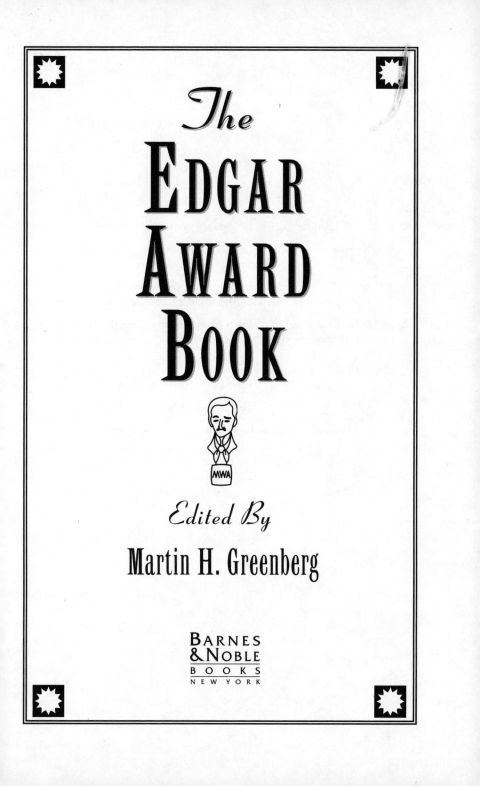

Martin H. Greenberg

BARNES
& NOBLE
BOOKS
NEW YORK

The acknowledgments appearing on pages 465–467 constitute
an extension of this copyright page.

This edition published by Barnes & Noble, Inc.,
by arrangement with Mystery Writers of America

1996 Barnes & Noble Books

Text design by Jim Sarfati, Rocket Design

ISBN 0-76070-130-X

Printed and bound in the United States of America

M 9 8 7 6 5 4 3 2 1

FG

CONTENTS

INTRODUCTION

THESE DAYS WHEN many publishers seem reluctant to issue single-author collections of short stories, even those by bestselling mystery writers, the anthology has become more important than ever as a place to preserve fine mysteries. An anthology finds its place in libraries, both public and private, and has a permanence far greater than the passing issues of even the best magazines. I realized this quite early in my writing career when I discovered that my stories adapted for television were invariably chosen from anthologies rather than from their original magazine appearances.

In order to help preserve and publicize some of the best mystery short stories of our time, the Mystery Writers of America (MWA) has issued two previous anthologies of its Edgar Award winners, one in 1980 and another in 1990. This third anthology differs from the first two in that it is not limited solely to winning stories.

It is a regrettable fact of life that the runners-up for honors and awards are often forgotten. Oscar nominees, Miss America alternates, and election losers can fade from memory all too quickly, and the public may lose sight of the qualities that brought them within a shade of winning. In many cases, only the whim of a few judges or voters makes the final difference between two equally worthy nominees.

Literary awards are no different. The Edgars are presented each spring by the MWA for outstanding achievements in various categories during the previous year. They are as prone to occasional misjudgment as any other awards, even though a winner is chosen by a committee of five professionals with experience or a special interest in the category they are judging. Still, it seems the fairest way to choose the winners and ensures that the committee members are all familiar with the works.

The anthology is designed in part to reintroduce readers to almost two dozen fine short stories that were nominated for the MWA Edgar Awards during the past thirty years. The selection includes seven winners and sixteen runners-up. Frederick Forsyth's "There Are No Snakes in Ireland" walked off with the Edgar in 1983, and Ruth Rendell's "The New Girl Friend" won the prize the following year. John Lutz's "Ride the Lightning" received the Edgar in 1986, Donald E. Westlake's "Too Many Crooks" in 1990, Wendy Hornsby's "Nine Sons" in 1992, Benjamin M. Schutz's "Mary, Mary, Shut the Door" in 1993, and Lawrence Block's "Keller's Therapy" in 1994.

We'll leave it to the readers to decide whether an Edgar should have been awarded to any of the sixteen stories that failed in their bids for the top prize. It's interesting to note that P. D. James's 1969 nomination came relatively early in her career, when she'd published only three novels. Evan Hunter's tale "The Last Spin" is virtually unknown, though some believe it to be one of his finest short stories. It first appeared in the magazine *Manhunt* in 1956.

Three authors included here—Joyce Carol Oates, Harlan Ellison, and Paul Theroux—are not usually thought of as mystery writers at all, though each has ventured into crime and murder more than once. The Oates story "Do with Me What You Will" became part of her 1973 novel of the same name. Theroux's "The Imperial Icehouse" was collected in *World's End and Other Stories* (1980). "Mefisto in Onyx," by Harlan Ellison, first appeared in *Omni* magazine.

Although I did not perform the final selection of the stories for this volume, I remember many of them quite vividly from my first reading and have reprinted nearly half of them in my own anthologies over the years. Ruth Rendell made a startling breakthrough with "The New Girl Friend," stretching the boundaries of the psychosexual tale. It was first published in *Ellery Queen's Mystery Magazine.* Brian Garfield's "Scrimshaw" and Clark Howard's "Challenge the Widow-Maker," which share nothing but their Hawaiian settings, are both memorable in their own ways. And certainly Wendy Hornsby's "Nine Sons" is not a story one is likely to forget.

Lawrence Block's stories about a hit man named Keller, which have appeared in *Playboy* and elsewhere since 1990, often seem like novels in miniature. "Keller's Therapy," included here, covers weeks of narrative time and settings in New York, White Plains, and Tucson. In contrast, Bill Pronzini's story "Incident in a Neighborhood Tavern" is just what the title suggests: a single incident in a single setting, with the mystery quickly and cleverly solved by his Nameless Detective.

Readers will find other contrasts here as well, from Michael Z. Lewin's gritty "The Reluctant Detective" to Donald E. Westlake's lighter "Too Many Crooks." The protagonist in Joseph Hansen's "McIntyre's Donald" is an old man, whereas Liza Cody's "Spasmo" deals with a ten-year-old boy. Included are classic Grand Masters such as Dorothy Salisbury Davis and Stanley Ellin, along with relative newcomers from the 1980s such as Gabrielle Kraft and Benjamin M. Schutz. Some authors, such as Robert Barnard and Ed Gorman, are regular contributors to mystery magazines and anthologies, while others have produced only a handful of tales in the short form.

There are stories here of every type—private eye and cozy, suspenseful and mysterious, action packed and atmospheric. I can only assure you these are stories worth remembering, and adding to your permanent library.

—Edward D. Hoch
1996

BREAKFAST TELEVISION

Robert Barnard

THE COMING OF Breakfast Television has been a great boon to the British.

Caroline Worsley thought so anyway, as she sat in bed eating toast and sipping tea, the flesh of her arm companionably warm against the flesh of Michael's arm. Soon they would make love again, perhaps while the consumer lady had her spot about dangerous toys, or during the review of the papers, or the resident doctor's phone-in on acne. They would do it when and how the fancy took them—or as Michael's fancy took him, for he was very imperative at times—and this implied no dislike or disrespect for the breakfast-time performer concerned. For Caroline liked them all, and could lie there quite happily watching any one of them: David the doctor, Jason the pop-chart commentator, Selma the fashion expert, Jemima the problems expert, Reg the sports round-up man, and Maria the link-up lady. And of course Ben, the link-up man.

Ben, her husband.

It had all worked out very nicely indeed. Ben was called for by the studio at four-thirty. Michael always waited for half an hour after that, in case Ben had forgotten something and made a sudden dash back to the flat for it. Michael was a serious, slightly gauche young man, who would hate to be caught out in a situation both compromising and ridiculous. Michael was that rare thing, a studious student—though very well-built too, Caroline told herself appreciatively. His interests were work, athletics, and sex. It was Caroline who had initiated him into the pleasures of regular sex. At five o'clock his alarm clock went off, though as he told Caroline, it was rarely necessary. His parents were away in Africa, dispensing aid, know-how and Oxfam beatitudes in some godforsaken part of Africa, so he was alone in their flat. He put his tracksuit on, so that in the unlikely event of his being seen in the corridor he could pretend to be going running. But he never had been. By five past he was in Caroline's flat, and in the bedroom she shared with Ben. They had almost an hour and a half of sleeping and love-making before breakfast television began.

Not that Michael watched it with the enthusiasm of Caroline. Sometimes he took a book along and read it while Caroline was drawing in her breath in horror at combustible toys, or tut-tutting at some defaulting businessman who had left his customers in the lurch. He would lie there immersed in *The Mechanics of the Money Supply* or *Some Problems of Exchange-Rate Theory*—something reasonably straight-forward, anyway, because he had to read against the voice from the set, and from time to time he was conscious of Ben looking directly at him. He never quite got used to that.

It didn't bother Caroline at all.

'Oh look, his tie's gone askew,' she would say, or: 'You know, Ben's much balder than he was twelve months ago—I've never noticed it in the flesh.' Michael seldom managed to assent to such propositions with any easy grace. He was much too conscious of balding, genial, avuncular Ben, grinning out from the television screen, as he tried to wring from some graceless pop-star three words strung together consecutively that actually made sense. 'I think he's getting fatter in the face,' said Caroline, licking marmalade off her fingers.

* * *

'I am not getting fatter in the face,' shouted Ben. 'Balder, yes, fatter in the face definitely not.' He added in a voice soaked in vitriol: 'Bitch!'

He was watching a video of yesterday's love-making on a set in his dressing-room, after the morning's television session had ended. His friend Frank, from the technical staff, had rigged up the camera in the cupboard of his study, next door to the bedroom. The small hole that was necessary in the wall had been expertly disguised. Luckily Caroline was a deplorable housewife. Eventually she might have discovered the sound apparatus under the double bed, but even then she would probably have assumed it was some junk of Ben's that he had shoved there out of harm's way. Anyway, long before then . . .

Long before then—what?

'Hypocritical swine!' yelled Ben, as he heard Caroline laughing with Michael that the Shadow Foreign Secretary had really wiped the floor with him in that interview. 'She told me when I got home yesterday how well I'd handled it.'

As the shadowy figures on the screen turned to each other again, their bare flesh glistening dully in the dim light, Ben hissed: 'Whore!'

The make-up girl concentrated on removing the traces of powder from his neck and shirt-collar, and studiously avoided comment.

'I suppose you think this is sick, don't you?' demanded Ben.

'It's none of my business,' the girl said, but added: 'If she is carrying on, it's not surprising, is it? Not with the hours we work.'

'Not surprising? I tell you, I was bloody surprised! Just think how you would feel if your husband, or bloke, was two-timing you while you were at the studio.'

'He is,' said the girl. But Ben hadn't heard. He frequently didn't hear other people when he was off camera. His comfortable, sympathetic-daddy image was something that seldom spilled over into his private life. Indeed, at his worst, he could slip up even on camera: he could be leant forwards, listening to his interviewees with appearance of the warmest interest, then reveal by his next question that he hadn't heard a word they were saying. But that happened very infrequently, and only when he was extremely preoccupied. Ben was very good at his job.

'Now they'll have tea,' he said. 'Everyone needs a tea-break in their working morning.'

Tea . . .

Shortly after this there was a break in Caroline's delicious early-morning routine: her son Malcolm came home for a long weekend from school. Michael became no more than the neighbour's son, at whom she smiled in the corridor. She and Malcolm had breakfast round the kitchen table. It was on Tuesday morning, when Malcolm was due to depart later in the day, that Ben made one of his little slips.

He was interviewing Cassy Le Beau from the long-running pop group The Crunch, and as he leaned forward to introduce a clip from the video of their latest musical crime, he said:

'Now, this is going to interest Caroline and Michael, watching at home—'

'Why did he say Michael?' asked Caroline aloud, before she could stop herself.

'He meant Malcolm,' said their son. 'Anyway, it's bloody insulting, him thinking I'd be interested in The Crunch.'

Because Malcolm was currently rehearsing Elgar's Second with the London Youth Orchestra. Ben was about two years out of date with his interests.

'Did you see that yesterday morning?' Caroline asked Michael, the next day.

'What?'

'Ben's slip on *Wake Up, Britain* yesterday.'

'I don't watch breakfast telly when I'm not with you.'

'Well, he did one of those "little messages home" that he

does—you probably don't remember, but there was all this publicity about the families when *Wake Up, Britain* started, and Ben got into the habit of putting little messages to Malcolm and me into the programme. Ever so cosy and ever so bogus. Anyway, he did one yesterday, as Malcolm was home, only he said "Caroline and Michael". Not Malcolm, but Michael.'

Michael shrugged.

'Just a slip of the tongue.'

'But his own *son*, for Christ's sake! And for the slip to come out as *Michael!*'

'These things happen,' said Michael, putting his arm around her and pushing her head back on to the pillow. 'Was there a Michael on the show yesterday?'

'There was Michael Heseltine on, as usual.'

'There you are, you see.'

'But Heseltine's an ex-cabinet minister. He would *never* call him Michael.'

'But the name was in his head. These things happen. Remember, Ben's getting old.'

'True,' said Caroline, who was two years younger than her husband.

'Old!' shouted Ben, dabbing at his artificially-darkened eyebrows, one eye on the screen. 'You think I'm old? I'll show you I've still got some bolts left in my locker.'

He had dispensed with the services of the make-up girl. He had been the only regular on *Wake Up, Britain* to demand one anyway, and the studio was surprised but pleased when Ben decided she was no longer required. Now he could watch the previous evening's cavortings without the damper of her adolescent disapproval from behind his shoulder.

And now he could plan.

One of the factors that just had to be turned to his advantage was Caroline's deplorable housekeeping. All the table-tops of the kitchen were littered with bits of this and that—herbs, spices, sauces, old margarine tubs, bits of jam on dishes. The fridge was like the basement of the Victoria and Albert Museum, and the freezer was a record of their married life. And on the window-ledge in the kitchen were the things he used to do his little bit of gardening . . .

Ben and Caroline inhabited one of twenty modern service flats in a block. Most of the gardening was done by employees of the landlords, yet some little patches were allotted to tenants who expressed an interest. Ben had always kept up his patch, though (as was the way of such things) it was more productive of self-satisfaction than of fruit or veg. 'From our own garden', he would say, as he served his guests horrid little bowls of red currants.

Already on the window-ledge in the kitchen there was a little bottle of paraquat.

That afternoon he pottered around in his mouldy little patch. By the time he had finished and washed his hands under the kitchen tap the paraquat had found its way next to the box of tea-bags standing by the kettle. The top of the paraquat was loose, having been screwed only about half way round.

'Does you good to get out on your own patch of earth,' Ben observed to Caroline, as he went through to his study.

The next question that presented itself was: when? There were all sorts of possibilities—including that the police would immediately arrest him for murder, he was reconciled to that—but he thought that on the whole it would be best to do it on the morning when he was latest home. Paraquat could be a long time in taking effect, he knew, but there was always a chance that they would not decide to call medical help until it was too late. If he was to come home to a poisoned wife and lover in the flat, he wanted them to be well and truly dead. Wednesday was the day when all the Breakfast TV team met in committee to hear what was planned for the next week: which ageing star would be plugging her memoirs, which singer plugging his forthcoming British tour. Wednesdays Ben often didn't get home till early afternoon. Wednesday it was.

Tentatively in his mental engagements book he pencilled in Wednesday, May 15.

Whether the paraquat would be in the teapot of the Teasmade, or in the tea-bag, or how it would be administered, was a minor matter that he could settle long before the crucial Tuesday night when the tea-things for the morning had to be got ready. The main thing was that everything was decided.

May 15—undoubtedly a turning-point in her life—began badly for Caroline. First of all Ben kissed her goodbye before he set off for the studio, something he had not done since the early days of his engagement on Breakfast Television. Michael had come in at five o'clock as usual, but his love-making was forced, lacking in tenderness. Caroline lay there for an hour in his arms afterwards, wondering if anything was worrying him. He didn't say anything for some time—not till the television was switched on. Probably he relied on the bromides and the plugs to distract Caroline's attention from what he was going to say.

He had taken up his textbook, and the kettle of the Teasmade was beginning to hum, when he said, in his gruff, teenage way:

'Won't be much more of this.'

Caroline was watching clips from a Frank Bruno fight, and not giving him her full attention. When it was over, she turned to him:

'Sorry—what did you say?'

'I said there won't be much more of this.'

A dagger went to her heart, which seemed to stop beating for minutes. When she could speak, the words came out terribly middle-class-matron.

'I don't quite understand. Much more of what?'

'This. You and me together in the mornings.'

'You don't mean your parents are coming home early?'

'No. I've . . . got a flat. Nearer college. So there's not so much travelling in the mornings and evenings.'

'You're just *moving out?*'

'Pretty much so. Can't live with my parents for ever.'

Caroline's voice grew louder and higher.

'You're not living with your parents. It's six months before they come home. You're moving out *on me*. Do you have the impression that I'm the sort of person you can just move in with when it suits you, and then flit away from when it doesn't suit you any longer?'

'Well . . . yes, actually. I'm a free agent.'

'You *bas*tard! You *bas*tard!'

She would have liked to take him by the shoulder and shake him till the teeth rattled in his head. Instead she sat there on the bed, coldly furious. It was 7.15. The kettle whistled and poured boiling water on to the tea-bags in the teapot.

'Have some tea or coffee,' said Ben on the screen to his politician guest, with a smile that came out as a death's head grin. 'It's about early morning tea-time.'

'It's someone else, isn't it?' finally said Caroline, her voice kept steady with difficulty. 'A new girlfriend.'

'All right, it's a new girlfriend,' agreed Michael.

'Someone younger.'

'Of course someone younger,' said Michael, taking up his book again, and sinking into monetarist theory.

Silently Caroline screamed: *Of course someone younger*. What the hell's that supposed to mean? They don't come any older than you? Of course I was just passing the time with a crone like you until someone my own age came along?

'You're moving in with a girl,' she said, the desolation throbbing in her voice.

'Yeah,' said Michael, from within his Hayek.

'Tea all right?' Ben asked his guest.

Caroline sat there, watching the flickering images on the screen, while the tea in the pot turned from hot to warm. The future spread before her like a desert—a future as wife and mother. What kind of life was that, for God's sake? For some odd reason a future as *lover* had seemed, when she had thought about it at all, fulfilling, traditional and dignified. Now any picture she might have of the years to come was turned into a hideous, mocking, negative image, just as the body beside her in the bed had turned from a glamorous sex object into a boorish, ungrateful teenager.

They were having trouble in the *Wake Up, Britain* studio, where the two anchor people had got mixed up as to who was introducing what. Caroline focused on the screen: she always enjoyed it when Ben muffed something.

'Sorry,' said Ben, smiling his kindly-uncle smile. 'I thought it was Maria, but in fact it's me. Let's see . . . I know it's David, our resident medico, but actually I don't know what your subject is today, David.'

'Poison,' said David.

But the camera had not switched to him, and the instant he dropped the word into the ambient atmosphere Caroline (and one million other viewers) saw Ben's jaw drop, and an expression of panic flash like lightning through his eyes.

'I've had a lot of letters from parents of small children,' said David, in his calm, everything-will-be-all-right voice, 'about what to do if the kids get hold of poison. Old medicines, household detergents, gardening stuff—they can all be dangerous, and some can be deadly.' Caroline saw Ben, the camera still agonizingly on him, swallow hard and put his hand up to his throat. Then, mercifully, the producer changed the shot at last to the doctor, leaning forward and doing his thing. 'So here are a few basic rules about what to do in that sort of emergency . . .'

Caroline's was not a quick mind, but suddenly a succession of images came together: Ben's kiss that morning, his smile as he offered his guest early morning tea, a bottle of paraquat standing next to the box of tea-bags in the kitchen, Ben's dropping jaw at the sudden mention of poison.

'Michael,' she said.

'What?' he asked, hardly bothering to take his head out of his book.

She looked at the self-absorbed, casually cruel body, and her blood boiled.

'Oh, nothing,' she said. 'Let's have tea. It'll be practically cold by now.'

She poured two cups, and handed him his. He put aside his book, which he had hardly been reading, congratulating himself in his mind on having got out of this so lightly. He took the cup, and sat on the bed watching the screen, where the sports man was now introducing highlights of last night's athletics meeting from Oslo.

'Boy!' said Michael appreciatively, stirring his tea. 'That was a great run!'

He took a great gulp of the tea, then hurriedly put the cup down, turned to look at Caroline, and then choked.

Caroline had not taken up her tea, but sat there looking at the graceless youth. Round her lips there played a smile of triumphal revenge—a smile that the camera whirring away in the secrecy of the study cupboard perfectly caught for Ben, and for the criminal court that tried them, ironically, together.

Keller's Therapy

Lawrence Block

"I HAD THIS DREAM," Keller said. "Matter of fact, I wrote it down, as you suggested."

"Good."

Before getting on the couch, Keller had removed his jacket and hung it on the back of a chair. He moved from the couch to retrieve his notebook from the jacket's inside breast pocket, then sat on the couch and found the page with the dream on it. He read through his notes rapidly, closed the book and sat there, uncertain of how to proceed.

"As you prefer," said Breen. "Sitting up or lying down, whichever is more comfortable."

"It doesn't matter?"

And which was more comfortable? A seated posture seemed natural for conversation, while lying down on the couch had the weight of tradition on its side. Keller, who felt driven to give this his best shot, decided to go with tradition. He stretched out, put his feet up.

He said, "I'm living in a house, except it's almost like a castle. Endless passageways and dozens of rooms."

"Is it your house?"

"No, I just live here. In fact, I'm a kind of servant for the family that owns the house. They're almost like royalty."

"And you are a servant."

"Except I have very little to do and I'm treated like an equal. I play tennis with members of the family. There's this tennis court in the back."

"And this is your job? To play tennis?"

"No, that's an example of how they treat me as an equal. I eat at the same table with them, instead of with the servants. My job is the mice."

"The mice?"

"The house is infested with mice. I'm having dinner with the family, I've got a plate piled high with good food, and a waiter in black tie comes in and presents a covered dish. I lift the cover and there's a note on it, and it says, 'Mice.'"

"Just the single word?"

"That's all. I get up from the table and follow the waiter down a long hallway, and I wind up in an unfinished room in the attic. There are tiny mice all over the room—there must be twenty or thirty of them—and I have to kill them."

"How?"

"By crushing them underfoot. That's the quickest and most humane way, but it bothers me and I don't want to do it. But the sooner I finish, the sooner I can get back to my dinner, and I'm hungry."

"So you kill the mice?"

"Yes," Keller said. "One almost gets away, but I stomp on it just as it's running out the door. And then I'm back at the dinner table and everybody's eating and drinking and laughing, and my plate's been cleared away. Then there's a big fuss, and finally they bring back my plate from the kitchen, but it's not the same food as before. It's—"

"Yes?"

"Mice," Keller said. "They're skinned and cooked, but it's a plateful of mice."

"And you eat them?"

"That's when I woke up," Keller said. "And not a moment too soon, I'd say."

"Ah," Breen said. He was a tall man, long-limbed and gawky, wearing chinos, a dark-green shirt and a brown corduroy jacket. He looked to Keller like someone who had been a nerd in high school and who now managed to look distinguished in an eccentric sort of way. He said "Ah" again, folded his hands and asked Keller what he thought the dream meant.

"You're the doctor," Keller said.

"You think it means I'm the doctor?"

"No, I think you're the one who can say what it means. Maybe it just means I shouldn't eat Rocky Road ice cream right before I go to bed."

"Tell me what you think the dream means."

"Maybe I see myself as a cat."

"Or as an exterminator?"

Keller didn't say anything.

"Let's work with this dream on a superficial level," Breen said. "You're employed as a corporate troubleshooter, except that you use another word for it."

"They tend to call us expediters," Keller said, "but troubleshooter is what it amounts to."

"Most of the time there is nothing for you to do. You have considerable opportunity for recreation, for living the good life. For tennis, as it were, and for nourishing yourself at the table of the rich and powerful. Then mice are discovered, and it is at once clear that you are a servant with a job to do."

"I get it," Keller said.

"Go on, then. Explain it to me."

"Well, it's obvious, isn't it? There's a problem and I'm called in and I have to drop what I'm doing and go and deal with it. I have to take abrupt, arbitrary action, and that can involve firing people and closing out entire departments. I have to do it, but it's like stepping on mice. And when I'm back at the table and I want my food—I suppose that's my salary?"

"Your compensation, yes."

"And I get a plate of mice," Keller made a face. "In other words, what? My compensation comes from the destruction of the people I have to cut adrift. My sustenance comes at their expense. So it's a guilt dream?"

"What do you think?"

"I think it's guilt. My profit derives from the misfortunes of others, from the grief I bring to others. That's it, isn't it?"

"On the surface, yes. When we go deeper, perhaps we will begin to discover other connections. With your having chosen this job in the first place, perhaps, and with some aspects of your childhood." He interlaced his fingers and sat back in his chair. "Everything is of a piece, you know. Nothing exists alone and nothing is accidental. Not even your name."

"My name?"

"Peter Stone. Think about it, why don't you, between now and our next session."

"Think about my name?"

"About your name and how it suits you. And"—a reflexive glance at his wristwatch—"I'm afraid that our hour is up."

Jerrold Breen's office was on Central Park West at 94th Street. Keller walked to Columbus Avenue, rode a bus five blocks, crossed the street and hailed a taxi. He had the driver go through Central Park, and by the time he got out of the cab at 50th Street, he was reasonably certain he hadn't been followed. He bought coffee in a deli and stood on the sidewalk, keeping an eye open while he drank it. Then he walked to the building where he lived, on First Avenue between 48th and 49th. It was a prewar high rise with an art deco lobby and an attended elevator. "Ah, Mr. Keller," the attendant said. "A beautiful day, yes?"

"Beautiful," Keller agreed.

Keller had a one-bedroom apartment on the 19th floor. He could look out his window and see the UN building, the East River, the borough of Queens. On the first Sunday in November he could watch the runners streaming across the Queensboro Bridge, just a couple of miles past the midpoint of the New York Marathon.

It was a spectacle Keller tried not to miss. He would sit at his window for hours while thousands of them passed through his field of vision, first the world-class runners, then the middle-of-the-pack plodders and finally the slowest of the slow, some walking, some hobbling. They started in Staten Island and finished in Central Park, and all he saw was a few hundred yards of their ordeal as they made their way over the bridge and into Manhattan. The sight always moved him to tears, though he could not have said why.

Maybe it was something to talk about with Breen.

It was a woman who had led him to the therapist's couch, an aerobics instructor named Donna. Keller had met her at the gym. They'd had a couple of dates and had been to bed a couple of times, enough to establish their sexual incompatibility. Keller still went to the same gym two or three times a week to raise and lower heavy metal objects, and when he ran into her, they were friendly.

One time, just back from a trip somewhere, he must have rattled on about what a nice town it was. "Keller," she said, "if there was ever a born New Yorker, you're it. You know that, don't you?"

"I suppose so."

"But you always have this fantasy of living the good life in Elephant, Montana. Every place you go, you dream up a whole life to go with it."

"Is that bad?"

"Who's saying it's bad? But I bet you could have fun with it in therapy."

"You think I need to be in therapy?"

"I think you'd get a lot out of therapy," she said. "Look, you come here, right? You climb the stair monster, you use the Nautilus."

"Mostly free weights."

"Whatever. You don't do this because you're a physical wreck."

"I do it to stay in shape. So?"

"So I see you as closed in and trying to reach out," she said. "Going all over the country, getting real estate agents to show you houses that you're not going to buy."

"That was only a couple of times. And what's so bad about it, anyway? It passes the time."

"You do these things and don't know why," she said. "You know what therapy is? It's an adventure, it's a voyage of discovery. And it's like going to the gym. Look, forget it. The whole thing's pointless unless you're interested."

"Maybe I'm interested," he said.

Donna, not surprisingly, was in therapy herself. But her therapist was a woman, and they agreed that he'd be more comfortable working with a man. Her ex-husband had been very fond of his therapist, a West Side psychologist named Breen. Donna had never met the man, and she wasn't on the best of terms with her ex, but . . .

"That's all right," Keller said. "I'll call him myself."

He'd called Breen, using Donna's ex-husband's name as a reference. "I doubt that he even knows me by name," Keller said. "We got to talking a while back at a party and I haven't seen him since. But something he said struck a chord with me and, well, I thought I ought to explore it."

"Intuition is always a powerful teacher," Breen said.

Keller made an appointment, giving his name as Peter Stone. In his first session he talked about his work for a large and unnamed conglomerate. "They're a little old-fashioned when it comes to psychotherapy," he told Breen. "So I'm not going to give you an address or telephone number, and I'll pay for each session in cash."

"Your life is filled with secrets," Breen said.

"I'm afraid it is. My work demands it."

"This is a place where you can be honest and open. The idea is to uncover the secrets you've been keeping from yourself. Here you are protected by the sanctity of the confessional, but it's not my task to grant you absolution. Ultimately, you absolve yourself."

"Well," Keller said.

"Meanwhile, you have secrets to keep. I respect that. I won't need your address or telephone number unless I'm forced to cancel an appointment. I suggest you call to confirm your sessions an hour or two ahead of time, or you can take the chance of an occasional wasted trip. If you have to cancel an appointment, be sure to give twenty-four hours' notice. Or I'll have to charge you for the missed session."

"That's fair," Keller said.

He went twice a week, Mondays and Thursdays at two in the afternoon. It was hard to tell what they were accomplishing. Sometimes Keller relaxed completely on the sofa, talking freely and honestly about his childhood. Other times he experienced the 50-minute session as a balancing act: He yearned to tell everything and was compelled to keep it all a secret.

No one knew he was doing this. Once, when he ran into Donna, she asked if he'd ever given the shrink a call, and he'd shrugged sheepishly and said he hadn't. "I thought about it," he said, "but then somebody told me about this masseuse—she does a combination of Swedish and shiatsu—and I have to tell you. I think it does me more good than somebody poking and probing at the inside of my head."

"Oh, Keller," she'd said, not without affection. "Don't ever change."

It was on Monday that he recounted the dream about the mice. Wednesday morning his phone rang, and it was Dot. "He wants to see you," she said.

"Be right out," he said.

He put on a tie and jacket and caught a cab to Grand Central and a train to White Plains. There he caught another cab and told the driver to head out Washington Boulevard and to let him off at the corner of Norwalk. After the cab drove off, he walked up Norwalk to Taunton Place and turned left. The second house on the right was an old Victorian with a wraparound porch. He rang the bell and Dot let him in.

"The upstairs den, Keller," she said. "He's expecting you."

He went upstairs, and 40 minutes later he came down again. A young man named Louis drove him back to the station, and on the way they chatted about a recent boxing match they'd both seen on ESPN. "What I wish," Louis said, "is that they had, like, a mute button on the remote, except what it would do is mute the announcers but you'd still hear the crowd noise and the punches landing. What you wouldn't have is the constant yammer-yammer-yammer in your ear." Keller wondered if they could do that. "I don't see why not," Louis said. "They can do everything else. If you can put a man on the moon, you ought to be able to shut up Al Bernstein."

Keller took a train back to New York and walked to his apartment. He made a couple of phone calls and packed a bag. At 3:30 he went downstairs, walked half a block, hailed a cab to JFK and picked up his boarding pass for American's 5:55 flight to Tucson.

In the departure lounge he remembered his appointment with Breen. He called to cancel the Thursday session. Since it was less than 24 hours away, Breen said, he'd have to charge him for the missed session, unless he was able to book someone else into the slot.

"Don't worry about it," Keller told him. "I hope I'll be back in time for my Monday appointment, but it's always hard to know how long these things are going to take. If I can't make it, I should at least be able to give you the twenty-four hours' notice."

He changed planes in Dallas and got to Tucson shortly before midnight. He had no luggage aside from the piece he was carrying, but he went to the baggage-claim area anyway. A rail-thin man with a broad-brimmed straw hat held a hand-lettered sign that read NOSCAASI. Keller watched the man for a few minutes and observed that no one else was watching him. He went up to him and said, "You know, I was figuring it out the whole way to Dallas. What I came up with, it's Isaacson spelled backward."

"That's it," the man said. "That's exactly it." He seemed impressed, as if Keller had cracked the Japanese naval code. He said, "You didn't check a bag, did you? I didn't think so. The car's this way."

In the car the man showed Keller three photographs, all of the same man, heavyset, dark, with glossy black hair and a greedy pig face. Bushy mustache, bushy eyebrows and enlarged pores on his nose.

"That's Rollie Vasquez," the man said. "Son of a bitch wouldn't exactly win a beauty contest, would he?"

"I guess not."

"Let's go," the man said. "Show you where he lives, where he eats, where he gets his ashes hauled. Rollie Vasquez, this is your life."

Two hours later the man dropped Keller at a Ramada Inn and gave him a room key and a car key. "You're all checked in," he said. "Car's parked at the foot of the staircase closest to your room. She's a Mitsubishi Eclipse, pretty decent transportation. Color's supposed to be silver-blue, but she says gray on the papers. Registration's in the glove compartment."

"There was supposed to be something else."

"That's in the glove compartment, too. Locked, of course, but the one key fits the ignition and the glove compartment. And the doors and the trunk, too. And if you turn the key upside down, it'll still fit, because there's no up or down to it. You really got to hand it to those Japs."

"What'll they think of next?"

"Well, it may not seem like much," the man said, "but all the time you waste making sure you got the right key, then making sure you got it right side up—"

"It adds up."

"It does," the man said. "Now you have a full tank of gas. It takes regular, but what's in there's enough to take you upward of four hundred miles."

"How're the tires? Never mind. Just a joke."

"And a good one," the man said. "'How're the tires?' I like that."

* * *

The car was where it was supposed to be, and the glove compartment held the Registration and a semiautomatic pistol, a .22-caliber Horstmann Sun Dog, loaded, with a spare clip lying alongside it. Keller slipped the gun and the spare clip into his carry-on, locked the car and went to his room without passing the front desk.

After a shower, he sat down and put his feet up on the coffee table. It was all arranged, and that made it simpler, but sometimes he liked it better the other way, when all he had was a name and address and no one to smooth the way for him. This was simple, all right, but who knew what traces were being left? Who knew what kind of history the gun had, or what the string bean with the NOSCAASI sign would say if the police picked him up and shook him?

All the more reason to do it quickly. He watched enough of an old movie on cable to ready him for sleep. When he woke up, he went out to the car and took his bag with him. He expected to return to the room, but if he didn't, he would be leaving nothing behind, not even a fingerprint.

He stopped at Denny's for breakfast. Around one he had lunch at a Mexican place on Figueroa. In the late afternoon he drove into the foothills north of the city, and he was still there when the sun went down. Then he drove back to the Ramada.

That was Thursday. Friday morning the phone rang while he was shaving. He let it ring. It rang again as he was showering. He let it ring. It rang again just as he was ready to leave. He didn't answer it this time, either, but went around wiping surfaces a second time with a hand towel. Then he went out to the car.

At two that afternoon he followed Rolando Vasquez into the men's room of the Saguaro Lanes bowling alley and shot him three times in the head. The little gun didn't make much noise, not even in the confines of the tiled lavatory. Earlier he had fashioned an improvised suppressor by wrapping the barrel of the gun with a space-age insulating material that muffled the gun's report without adding much weight or bulk. If you could do that, he thought, you ought to be able to shut up Al Bernstein.

He left Vasquez propped in a stall, left the gun in a storm drain half a mile away, left the car in the long-term lot at the airport. Flying home, he wondered why they had needed him in the first place. They'd supplied the car and the gun and the finger man. Why not do it themselves? Did they really need to bring him all the way from New York to step on the mouse?

"You said to think about my name," he told Breen. "The significance of it. But I don't see how it could have any significance. It's not as if I chose it."

"Let me suggest something," Breen said. "There is a metaphysical principle which holds that we choose everything about our lives, that we select the parents we are born to, that everything which happens in our lives is a manifestation of our wills. Thus, there are no accidents, no coincidences."

"I don't know if I believe that."

"You don't have to. We'll just take it as a postulate. So assuming that you chose the name Peter Stone, what does your choice tell us?"

Keller, stretched full length upon the couch, was not enjoying this. "Well, a peter's a penis," he said reluctantly. "A stone peter would be an erection, wouldn't it?"

"Would it?"

"So I suppose a guy who decides to call himself Peter Stone would have something to prove. Anxiety about his virility. Is that what you want me to say?"

"I want you to say whatever you wish," Breen said. "Are you anxious about your virility?"

"I never thought I was," Keller said. "Of course, it's hard to say how much anxiety I might have had back before I was born, around the time I was picking my parents and deciding what name they should choose for me. At that age I probably had a certain amount of difficulty maintaining an erection, so I guess I had a lot to be anxious about."

"And now?"

"I don't have a performance problem, if that's the question. I'm not the way I was in my teens, ready to go three or four times a night, but then, who in his right mind would want to? I can generally get the job done."

"You get the job done."

"Right."

"You perform."

"Is there something wrong with that?"

"What do you think?"

"Don't do that," Keller said. "Don't answer a question with a question. If I ask a question and you don't want to respond, just leave it alone. But don't turn it back on me. It's irritating."

Breen said, "You perform, you get the job done. But what do you feel, Mr. Peter Stone?"

"Feel?"

"It is unquestionably true that peter is a colloquialism for the penis, but it has an earlier meaning. Do you recall Christ's words to Peter? 'Thou art Peter, and upon this rock I shall build my church.' Because Peter *means* rock. Our Lord was making a pun. So your first name means rock and your last name is Stone. What does that give us? Rock and stone. Hard, unyielding, obdurate. Insensitive, unfeeling—"

"Stop," Keller said.

"In the dream, when you kill the mice, what do you feel?"

"Nothing. I just want to get the job done."

"Do you feel their pain? Do you feel pride in your accomplishment, satisfaction in a job well done? Do you feel a thrill, a sexual pleasure, in their deaths?"

"Nothing," Keller said. "I feel nothing. Could we stop for a moment?"

"What do you feel right now?"

"I'm just a little sick to my stomach that's all."

"Do you want to use the bathroom? Shall I get you a glass of water?"

"No, I'm all right. It's better when I sit up. It'll pass. It's passing already."

Sitting at his window, watching not marathoners but cars streaming over the Queensboro Bridge, Keller thought about names. What was particularly annoying, he thought, was that he didn't need to be under the care of a board-certified metaphysician to acknowledge the implications of the name Peter Stone. He had chosen it, but not in the manner of a soul deciding what parents to be born to and planting names in their heads. He had picked the name when he called to make his initial appointment with Jerrold Breen. "Name?" Breen had demanded. "Stone," he had replied. "Peter Stone."

Thing is, he wasn't stupid. Cold, unyielding, insensitive, but not stupid. If you wanted to play the name game, you didn't have to limit yourself to the alias he had selected. You could have plenty of fun with the name he'd had all his life.

His full name was John Paul Keller, but no one called him anything but Keller, and few people even knew his first and middle names. His apartment lease and most of the cards in his wallet showed his name as J. P. Keller. Just Plain Keller was what people called him, men and women alike. ("The upstairs den, Keller. He's expecting you." "Oh, Keller, don't ever change." "I don't know how to say this, Keller, but I'm simply not getting my needs met in this relationship.")

Keller. In German it meant cellar, or tavern. But the hell with that. You didn't need to know what it meant in a foreign language. Change a vowel. Killer.

Clear enough, wasn't it?

On the couch, eyes closed, Keller said, "I guess the therapy's working."

"Why do you say that?"

"I met a girl last night, bought her a couple of drinks and went home with her. We went to bed and I couldn't do anything."

"You couldn't do anything?"

"Well, if you want to be technical, there were things I could have done. I could have typed a letter or sent out for a pizza. I could have sung *Melancholy Baby.* But I couldn't do what we'd both been hoping I would do, which was to have sex."

"You were impotent?"

"You know, you're very sharp. You never miss a trick."

"You blame me for your impotence," Breen said.

"Do I? I don't know about that. I'm not sure I even blame myself. To tell you the truth, I was more amused than devastated. And she wasn't upset, perhaps out of relief that I wasn't upset. But just so nothing like that happens again, I've decided to change my name to Dick Hardin."

"What was your father's name?"

"My father," Keller said. "Jesus, what a question. Where did that come from?"

Breen didn't say anything.

Neither, for several minutes, did Keller. Then, eyes closed, he said, "I never knew my father. He was a soldier. He was killed in action before I was born. Or he was shipped overseas before I was born and killed when I was a few months old. Or possibly he was home when I was born or came home on leave when I was small, and he held me on his knee and told me he was proud of me."

"You have such a memory?"

"No," Keller said. "The only memory I have is of my mother telling me about him, and that's the source of the confusion, because she told me different things at different times. Either he was killed before I was born or shortly after, and either he died without seeing me or he saw me one time and sat me on his knee. She was a good woman, but she was vague about a lot of things. The one thing she was completely clear on was that he was a soldier. And he was killed over there."

"And his name?"

Was Keller, he thought. "Same as mine," he said. "But forget the name, this is more important than the name. Listen to this. She had a picture of him, a head-and-shoulders shot, this good-looking young soldier in a uniform and wearing a cap, the kind that folds flat when you take it off. The picture was in a gold frame on her dresser when I was a little kid.

"And then one day the picture wasn't there anymore. 'It's gone,' she said. And that was all she would say on the subject. I was older then, I must have been seven or eight years old.

"Couple of years later I got a dog. I named him Soldier, after my father. Years after that, two things occurred to me. One, Soldier's a funny thing to call a dog. Two, whoever heard of naming a dog after his father? But at the time it didn't seem the least bit unusual to me."

"What happened to the dog?"

"He became impotent. Shut up, will you? What I'm getting to is a lot more important than the dog. When I was fourteen, fifteen years old, I used to work after school helping out this guy who did odd jobs in the neighborhood. Cleaning out basements and attics, hauling trash, that sort of thing. One time this notions store went out of business, the owner must have died, and we were cleaning out the basement for the new tenant. Boxes of junk all over the place, and we had to go through everything, because part of how this guy made his money was selling off the stuff he got paid to haul. But you couldn't go through all this crap too thoroughly or you were wasting time.

"I was checking out this one box, and what do I pull out but a framed picture of my father. The very same picture that sat on my mother's dresser, him in his uniform and his military cap, the picture that disappeared, it's even in the same frame, and what's it doing here?"

Not a word from Breen.

"I can still remember how I felt. Stunned, like *Twilight Zone* time. Then I reach back into the box and pull out the first thing I touch, and it's the same picture in the same frame.

"The box is full of framed pictures. About half of them are the soldier, and the others are a fresh-faced blonde with her hair in a pageboy and a big smile on her face. It was a box of frames. They used to package inexpensive frames that way, with photos in them for display. For all I know they still do. My mother must have bought a frame in a five-and-dime and told me it was my father. Then when I got a little older, she got rid of it.

"I took one of the framed photos home with me. I didn't say anything to her, I didn't show it to her, but I kept it around for a while. I found out the photo dated from World War Two. In other words, it couldn't have been a picture of my father, because he would have been wearing a different uniform.

"By this time I think I already knew that the story she told me about my father was, well, a story. I don't believe she knew who my father was. I think she got drunk and went with somebody, or maybe there were several different men. What difference does it make? She moved to another town, she told people she was married, that her husband was in the service or that he was dead, whatever she told them."

"How do you feel about it?"

"How do I feel about it?" Keller shook his head. "If I slammed my hand in a cab door, you'd ask me how I felt about it."

"And you'd be stuck for an answer," Breen said. "Here's a question for you: Who was your father?"

"I just told you."

"But *someone* fathered you. Whether or not you knew him, whether or not your mother knew who he was, there was a particular man who planted the seed that grew into you. Unless you believe yourself to be the second coming of Christ."

"No," Keller said. "That's one delusion I've been spared."

"So tell me who he was, this man who spawned you. Not on the basis of what you were told or what you've managed to figure out. I'm not asking the part of you that thinks and reasons. I'm asking the part of you that simply knows. Who was your father? What was your father?"

"He was a soldier," Keller said.

Keller, walking uptown on Second Avenue, found himself standing in front of a pet shop, watching a couple of puppies cavorting in the window.

He went inside. One wall was given over to stacked cages of puppies and kittens. Keller felt his spirits sink as he looked into the cages. Waves of sadness rocked him.

He turned away and looked at the other pets. Birds in cages, gerbils and snakes in dry aquariums, tanks of tropical fish. He felt all right about them; it was the puppies that he couldn't bear to look at.

He left the store. The next day he went to an animal shelter and walked past cages of dogs waiting to be adopted. This time the sadness was overwhelming, and he felt its physical pressure against his chest. Something must have shown on his face, because the young woman in charge asked him if he was all right.

"Just a dizzy spell," he said.

In the office she told him that they could probably accommodate him if the he was especially interested in a particular breed. They could keep his name on file, and when a specimen of that breed became available. . . .

"I don't think I can have a pet," he said. "I travel too much. I can't handle the responsibility." The woman didn't respond, and Keller's words echoed in her silence. "But I want to make a donation," he said. "I want to support the work you do."

He got out his wallet, pulled bills from it, handed them to her without counting them. "An anonymous donation," he said. "I don't want a receipt. I'm sorry for taking your time. I'm sorry I can't adopt a dog. Thank you. Thank you very much."

She was saying something, but he didn't listen. He hurried out of there.

" 'I want to support the work you do.' That's what I told her, and then I rushed out of there because I didn't want her thanking me. Or asking questions."

"What would she ask?"

"I don't know," Keller said. He rolled over on the couch, facing away from Breen, facing the wall. " 'I want to support the work you do.' But I don't know what their work is. They find homes for some animals, and what do they do with the others? Put them to sleep?"

"Perhaps."

"What do I want to support? The placement or the killing?"

"You tell me."

"I tell you too much as it is," Keller said.

"Or not enough."

Keller didn't say anything.

"Why did it sadden you to see the dogs in their cages?"

"I felt their sadness."

"One feels only one's own sadness. Why is it sad to you, a dog in a cage? Are you in a cage?"

"No."

"Your dog. Soldier. Tell me about him."

"All right," Keller said. "I guess I could do that."

A session or two later, Breen said, "You have never been married?"

"No."

"I was married."

"Oh?"

"For eight years. She was my receptionist. She booked my appointments, showed clients to the waiting room. Now I have no receptionist. A machine answers the phone. I check the machine between appointments and take and return calls at that time. If I had had a machine in the first place, I'd have been spared a lot of agony."

"It wasn't a good marriage?"

Breen didn't seem to have heard the question. "I wanted children. She had three abortions in eight years and never told me. Never said a word. Then one day she threw it in my face. I'd been to a doctor, I'd had tests and all indications were that I was fertile, with a high sperm count and extremely motile sperm. So I wanted her to see a doctor. 'You fool. I've killed three of your babies already, so why don't you leave me alone?' I told her I wanted a divorce. She said it would cost me."

"And?"

"We've been divorced for nine years. Every month I write an alimony check and put it in the mail. If it were up to me, I'd burn the money."

Breen fell silent. After a moment Keller said, "Why are you telling me all this?"

"No reason."

"Is it supposed to relate to something in my psyche? Am I supposed to make a connection, clap my hand to my forehead and say, 'Of course, of course! I've been so blind!'"

"You confide in me," Breen said. "It seems only fitting that I confide in you."

Dot called a couple of days later. Keller took a train to White Plains, where Louis met him at the station and drove him to the house on Taunton Place. Later, Louis drove him back to the train station and he returned to the city. He timed his call to Breen so that he got the man's machine. "This is Peter Stone," he said. "I'm flying to San Diego on business. I'll have to miss my next appointment and possibly the one after that. I'll try to let you know."

He hung up, packed a bag and rode the Amtrak to Philadelphia.

No one met his train. The man in White Plains had shown him a photograph and given him a slip of paper with a name and address on it. The man in question managed an adult bookstore a few blocks from Independence Hall. There was a tavern across the street, a perfect vantage point, but one look inside made it clear to Keller that he couldn't spend time there without calling attention to himself, not unless he first got rid of his tie and jacket and spent 20 minutes rolling around in the gutter.

Down the street Keller found a diner, and if he sat at the far end, he could keep an eye on the bookstore's mirrored front windows. He had a cup of coffee, then walked across the street to the bookstore, where two men were on duty. One was a sad-eyed youth from India or Pakistan, the other the jowly, slightly exophthalmic fellow in the photo Keller had seen in White Plains.

Keller walked past a wall of videocassettes and leafed through a display of magazines. He had been there for about 15 minutes when the kid said he was going for his dinner. The older man said, “Oh, it’s that time already, huh? OK, but make sure you’re back by seven for a change, will you?”

Keller looked at his watch. It was six o’clock. The only other customers were closeted in video booths in the back. Still, the kid had had a look at him, and what was the big hurry, anyway?

He grabbed a couple of magazines and paid for them. The jowly man bagged them and sealed the bag with a strip of tape. Keller stowed his purchase in his carry-on and went to find a hotel.

The next day he went to a museum and a movie and arrived at the bookstore at ten minutes after six. The young clerk was gone, presumably having a plate of curry somewhere. The jowly man was behind the counter and there were three customers in the store, two checking the video selections, one looking at the magazines.

Keller browsed, hoping they would clear out. At one point he was standing in front of a wall of videos and it turned into a wall of caged puppies. It was momentary, and he couldn’t tell if it was a genuine hallucination or just some sort of flashback. Whatever it was, he didn’t like it.

One customer left, but the other two lingered, and then someone new came in off the street. The Indian kid was due back in half an hour, and who knew if he would take his full hour, anyway?

Keller approached the counter, trying to look a little more nervous than he felt. Shifty eyes, furtive glances. Pitching his voice low, he said. “Talk to you in private?”

“About what?”

Eyes down, shoulders drawn in, he said, “Something special.”

“If it’s got to do with little kids,” the man said, “no disrespect intended, but I don’t know nothing about it. I don’t want to know nothing about it and I wouldn't even know where to steer you."

"Nothing like that," Keller said.

They went into a room in back. The jowly man closed the door, and as he was turning around, Keller hit him with the edge of his hand at the juncture of his neck and shoulder. The man's knees buckled, and in an instant Keller had a loop of wire around his neck. In another minute he was out the door, and within the hour he was on the northbound Metroliner.

When he got home, he realized he still had the magazines in his bag. That was sloppy. He should have discarded them the previous night, but he'd simply forgotten them and never even unsealed the package.

Nor could he find a reason to unseal it now. He carried it down the hall and dropped it into the incinerator. Back in his apartment, he fixed himself a weak scotch and water and watched a documentary on the Discovery Channel. The vanishing rain forest, one more goddamned thing to worry about.

"Oedipus," Jerrold Breen said, holding his hands in front of his chest, his fingertips pressed together. "I presume you know the story. He killed his father and married his mother."

"Two pitfalls I've thus far managed to avoid."

"Indeed," Breen said. "But have you? When you fly off somewhere in your official capacity as corporate expediter, when you shoot trouble, as it were, what exactly are you doing? You fire people, you cashier divisions, close plants, rearrange lives. Is that a fair description?"

"I suppose so."

"There's an amplified violence. Firing a man, terminating his career, is the symbolic equivalent of killing him. And he's a stranger, and I shouldn't doubt that the more important of these men are more often than not older than you, isn't that so?"

"What's the point?"

"When you do what you do, it's as if you are seeking out and killing your unknown father."

"I don't know," Keller said. "Isn't that a little farfetched?"

"And your relationships with women," Breen went on, "have a strong Oedipal component. Your mother was a vague and unfocused woman, incompletely present in your life, incapable of connecting with others. Your own relationships with women are likewise out of focus. Your problems with impotence—"

"Once!"

"Are a natural consequence of this confusion. Your mother is dead now, isn't that so?"

"Yes."

"And your father is not to be found, and almost certainly deceased. What's called for, Peter, is an act specifically designed to reverse this pattern on a symbolic level."

"I don't follow you."

"It's a subtle point," Breen admitted. He crossed his legs, propped an elbow on a knee, extended his thumb and rested his bony chin on it. Keller thought, not for the first time, that Breen must have been a stork in a prior life. "If there were a male figure in your life," Breen went on, "preferably at least a few years your senior, someone playing a paternal role vis-à-vis yourself, someone to whom you turn for advice and direction."

Keller thought of the man in White Plains.

"Instead of killing this man," Breen said, "symbolically, I am speaking symbolically throughout, but instead of killing him as you have done with father figures in the past, you might do something to *nourish* this man."

Cook a meal for the man in White Plains? Buy him a hamburger? Toss him a salad?

"Perhaps you could think of a way to use your talents to this man's benefit instead of to his detriment," Breen went on. He drew a handkerchief from his pocket and mopped his forehead. "Perhaps there is a woman in his life—your mother, symbolically—and perhaps she is a source of great pain to your father. So instead of making love to her and slaying him, like Oedipus, you might reverse the usual course of things by, uh, showing love to him and slaying her."

"Oh," Keller said.

"Symbolically, this is to say."

"Symbolically," Keller said.

A week later Breen handed Keller a photograph. "This is called the thematic apperception test," Breen said. "You look at the photograph and make up a story about it."

"What kind of story?"

"Any kind at all," Breen said. "This is an exercise in imagination. You look at the subject of the photograph and imagine what sort of woman she is and what she is doing."

The photo was in color and showed a rather elegant brunette dressed in tailored clothing. She had a dog on a leash. The dog was medium-sized, with a chunky body and an alert expression. It was the color that dog people call blue and that everyone else calls gray.

"It's a woman and a dog," Keller said.

"Very good."

Keller took a breath. "The dog can talk," he said, "but he won't do it in front of other people. The woman made a fool of herself once when she tried to show him off. Now she knows better. When they're alone, he talks a blue streak, and the son of a bitch has an opinion on everything from the real cause of the Thirty Years' War to the best recipe for lasagna."

"He's quite a dog," Breen said.

"Yes, and now the woman doesn't want people to know he can talk, because she's afraid they might take him away from her. In this picture they're in a park. It looks like Central Park."

"Or perhaps Washington Square."

"It could be Washington Square," Keller agreed. "The woman is crazy about the dog. The dog's not so sure about the woman."

"And what do you think about the woman?"

"She's attractive," Keller said.

"On the surface," Breen said. "Underneath, it's another story, believe me. Where do you suppose she lives?"

Keller gave it some thought. "Cleveland," he said.

"Cleveland? Why Cleveland, for God's sake?"

"Everybody's got to be someplace."

"If I were taking this test," Breen said, "I'd probably imagine the woman living at the foot of Fifth Avenue, at Washington Square. I'd have her living at Number One Fifth Avenue, perhaps because I'm familiar with that building. You see, I once lived there."

"Oh?"

"In a spacious apartment on a high floor. And once a month," he continued, "I write an enormous check and mail it to that address, which used to be mine. So it's only natural that I would have this particular building in mind, especially when I look at this particular photo." His eyes met Keller's. "You have a question, don't you? Go ahead and ask it."

"What breed is the dog?"

"As it happens," Breen said, "it's an Australian cattle dog. Looks like a mongrel, doesn't it? Believe me, it doesn't talk. But why don't you hang on to that photograph?"

"All right."

"You're making really fine progress in therapy," Breen said. "I want to acknowledge you for the work you're doing. And I just know you'll do the right thing."

A few days later Keller was sitting on a park bench in Washington Square. He folded his newspaper and walked over to a dark-haired woman wearing a blazer and a beret. "Excuse me," he said, "but isn't that an Australian cattle dog?"

"That's right," she said.

"It's a handsome animal," he said. "You don't see many of them."

"Most people think he's a mutt. It's such an esoteric breed. Do you own one yourself?"

"I did. My ex-wife got custody."

"How sad for you."

"Sadder still for the dog. His name was Soldier. Is Soldier, unless she's changed it."

"This fellow's name is Nelson. That's his call name. Of course, the name on the papers is a real mouthful."

"Do you show him?"

"He's seen it all," she said. "You can't show him a thing."

"I went down to the Village last week," Keller said, "and the damnedest thing happened. I met a woman in the park."

"Is that the damnedest thing?"

"Well, it's unusual for me. I meet women at bars and parties, or someone introduces us. But we met and talked, and then I ran into her the following morning. I bought her a cappuccino."

"You just happened to run into her on two successive days."

"Yes."

"In the Village?"

"It's where I live."

Breen frowned. "You shouldn't be seen with her, should you?"

"Why not?"

"Don't you think it's dangerous?"

"All it's cost me so far," Keller said, "is the price of a cappuccino."

"I thought we had an understanding."

"An understanding?"

"You don't live in the Village," Breen said. "I know where you live. Don't look surprised. The first time you left here I watched you from the window. You behaved as though you were trying to avoid being followed. So I took my time, and when you stopped taking precautions, I followed you. It wasn't that difficult."

"Why follow me?"

"To find out who you are. Your name is Keller, you live at Eight-six-five First Avenue. I already knew what you were. Anybody might have known just from listening to your dreams. And paying in cash, and the sudden business trips. I still don't know who employs you, crime bosses or the government, but what difference does it make? Have you been to bed with my wife?"

"Your ex-wife."

"Answer the question."

"Yes, I have."

"Jesus Christ. And were you able to perform?"

"Yes."

"Why the smile?"

"I was just thinking," Keller said, "that it was quite a performance."

Breen was silent for a long moment, his eyes fixed on a spot above and to the right of Keller's shoulder. Then he said, "This is profoundly disappointing. I hoped you would find the strength to transcend the Oedipal myth, not merely reenact it. You've had fun, haven't you? What a naughty boy you've been. What a triumph you've scored over your symbolic father. You've taken this woman to bed. No doubt you have visions of getting her pregnant, so that she can give you what she cruelly denied him. Eh?"

"Never occurred to me."

"It would, sooner or later." Breen leaned forward, concern showing on his face. "I hate to see you sabotaging your therapeutic progress this way," he said. "You were doing so *well.*"

From the bedroom window you could look down at Washington Square Park. There were plenty of dogs there now, but none were Australian cattle dogs.

"Some view," Keller said. "Some apartment."

"Believe me," she said. "I earned it. You're getting dressed. Are you going somewhere?"

"Just feeling a little restless. OK if I take Nelson for a walk?"

"You're spoiling him," she said. "You're spoiling both of us."

On a Wednesday morning, Keller took a cab to La Guardia and a plane to St. Louis. He had a cup of coffee with an associate of the man in White Plains and caught an evening flight back to New York. He took another cab directly to the apartment building at the foot of Fifth Avenue.

"I'm Peter Stone," he said to the doorman. "Mrs. Breen is expecting me."

The doorman stared.

"Mrs. Breen," Keller said. "In Seventeen-J."

"Jesus."

"Is something the matter?"

"I guess you haven't heard," the doorman said. "I wish it wasn't me who had to tell you."

"You killed her," he said.

"That's ridiculous," Breen told Keller. "She killed herself. She threw herself out the window. If you want my professional opinion, she was suffering from depression."

"If you want *my* professional opinion," Keller said, "she had help."

"I wouldn't advance that argument if I were you," Breen said. "If the police were to look for a murderer, they might look long and hard at Mr. Stone-hyphen-Keller, the stone killer. And I might have to tell them how the usual process of transference went awry, how you became obsessed with me and my personal life, how I couldn't dissuade you from some insane plan to reverse the Oedipus complex. And then they might ask you why you employ an alias and just how you make your living. Do you see why it might be best to let sleeping dogs lie?"

As if on cue, Nelson stepped out from behind the desk. He caught sight of Keller and his tail began to wag.

"Sit," Breen said. "You see? He's well trained. You might take a seat yourself."

"I'll stand. You killed her and then you walked off with the dog."

Breen sighed. "The police found the dog in the apartment, whimpering in front of the open window. After I identified the body and told them about her previous suicide attempts, I volunteered to take the dog home with me. There was no one else to look after him."

"I would have taken him," Keller said.

"But that won't be necessary, will it? You won't be called upon to walk my dog or make love to my wife or bed down in my apartment. Your services are no longer required." Breen seemed to recoil at the harshness of his own words. His face softened. "You'll be able to get back to the far more important business of therapy. In fact," he indicated the couch, "why not stretch out right now?"

"That's not a bad idea. First, though, could you put the dog in the other room?"

"Not afraid he'll interrupt, are you? Just a little joke. He can wait in the outer office. There you go, Nelson. Good dog . . . oh, no. How *dare* you bring a gun. Put that down immediately."

"I don't think so."

"For God's sake, why kill me? I'm not your father, I'm your therapist. It makes no sense for you to kill me. You have nothing to gain and everything to lose. It's completely irrational. It's worse than that, it's neurotically self-destructive."

"I guess I'm not cured yet."

"What's that, gallows humor? It happens to be true. You're a long way from cured, my friend. As a matter of fact, I would say you're approaching a psychotherapeutic crisis. How will you get through it if you shoot me?"

Keller went to the window, flung it wide open. "I'm not going to shoot you," he said.

"I've never been the least bit suicidal," Breen said, pressing his back against a wall of bookshelves. "Never."

"You've grown despondent over the death of your ex-wife."

"That's sickening, just sickening. And who would believe it?"

"We'll see," Keller told him. "As far as the therapeutic crisis is concerned, well, we'll see about that, too. I'll think of something."

The woman at the animal shelter said, "Talk about coincidence. One day you come in and put your name down for an Australian cattle dog. You know, that's quite an uncommon breed in this country."

"You don't see many of them."

"And what came in this morning? A perfectly lovely Australian cattle dog. You could have knocked me over with a sledgehammer. Isn't he a beauty?"

"He certainly is."

"He's been whimpering ever since he got here. It's very sad. His owner died and there was nobody to keep him. My goodness, look how he went right to you. I think he likes you."

"I'd say we're made for each other."

"I believe it. His name is Nelson, but you can change it, of course."

"Nelson," he said. The dog's ears perked up. Keller reached to give him a scratch. "No, I don't think I'll have to change it. Who was Nelson, anyway? Some kind of English hero, wasn't he? A famous general or something?"

"I think an admiral."

"It rings a muted bell," he said. "Not a soldier but a sailor. Well, that's close enough, wouldn't you say? Now, I suppose there's an adoption fee and some papers to fill out."

When they handled that part she said, "I still can't get over it. The coincidence and all."

"I knew a man once," Keller said, "who insisted there was no such thing as a coincidence or an accident."

"Well, I wonder how he would explain this."

"I'd like to hear him try," Keller said. "Let's go, Nelson. Good boy."

SPASMO

Liza Cody

IT WAS NANNY who told me the rotten news. Nanny and rotten news seem to go together if you ask me.

'Magnus's mother has been to see your mother,' she said. 'Poor Magnus has chicken-pox, so you can unpack that suitcase, Andrew. Your trip to Cowes is off.'

She isn't my Nanny. She's Annabel's. She has a black hairy mole on her chin, and I hate her.

'It's very bad luck,' Nanny went on. 'But don't look at me like that. And don't throw your suitcase on the floor . . . now you'll have to pick everything up.'

She didn't understand.

'Temper!' she said. 'If you carry on like that, Andrew, I'll have to tell your father.'

Nobody understood.

I would have to have my tenth birthday party in the rumpus-room with the girls. The summer holiday was ruined. No yacht. No Cowes. No Magnus. It was absolutely and completely spasmo.

Nobody cared.

It was all right for Annabel—she's only six, and as long as she can feed sugar to the milkman's horse every morning she's happy. Little sisters are spasmo. So are big ones: Claire was going to the south of France. *Her* friends didn't go and get chicken-pox. They were all too old for that, and too superior.

Magnus, I thought, was a spasmo, spotty piece of elephant dung. If he was ill, bad luck, but why did he have to ruin everything for me?

'Don't kick the rug,' my mother said. 'It's Persian. Don't be so selfish, Andrew. Think of poor Magnus.'

Was Magnus thinking of me? Was Magnus's mother? If she chose to stay in London to nurse spotty Magnus instead of taking me sailing she was worse than everyone.

'It's spasmo,' I said. I must have said that several times already because Ma fixed me with a glittering stare and exclaimed, 'If you say that word once more, Andrew, just once more, I'll send you to the Science Museum again . . . with Annabel.'

I should have known better. Ma was always at her most unreasonable on do-days, and I must have known it was a do-day because not only did we have extra help in the house, but Nanny had been co-opted into the kitchen to make pastry.

'She has cold hands,' Ma explained. 'That's why her pastry is better than anyone else's.'

You didn't have to tell Claire, Annabel or me about Nanny's cold hands; we had suffered from them most of our lives, but what that had to do with pastry was what Father described as a 'female mystery'. He seemed to know a lot about female mysteries and I wanted him to explain. But he never had the time. We didn't see a lot of Father that year because he was in the Government.

'He wanted something in Dominions,' I heard Ma tell one of her friends. 'And he's not the most cultural man, but I expect he'll accept all the same.'

Of course he did: it made him more important. But, although it was something to tell the others at school, secretly I thought he was important enough already. All my life I have suffered because of Father being important.

'Don't disturb your father, Andrew,' Nanny would say, 'he's an important man.'

'Spasmo,' I said.

'And don't say that word. It's not the sort of thing the son of an important man should say.'

'Spasmo, spasmo, spasmo,' I said, under my breath.

'Go to your room!' ordered Ma. She was counting silver ice buckets for the do. What did she need ice buckets for? All she had to do was look at the champagne the way she looked at me and you'd be able to skate on it.

'It's your own silly fault,' Claire said. 'You think people have nothing better to do than listen to you.'

I might have guessed I'd get no sympathy from Claire. She's always sucking up to Ma.

'What's this one for, anyway?' I asked. 'We had a do only last week.'

'Don't call it a do,' Claire said. 'It's a reception.'

'What for?'

'Don't you listen to anything? It's for the Berlin Dance Company.' Claire was excited. I could tell because she was nibbling her fingernails and then trying not to. Now that she was sixteen she had to have long fingernails. You wouldn't think Claire could get any sillier, but she did.

'The exquisite Kezia Lehmann!' Claire said, and sat on her hands. 'They say she's the youngest prima ballerina ever to dance at the Coliseum.'

That was not really Kezia's name. It's just that I could never remember it afterwards, and anyway everyone seemed to pronounce it differently. At the time I was not even listening properly.

'Ooh, a belly dancer,' I said to annoy Claire.

'Everyone says she's exquisite,' Claire said dreamily. She wasn't listening either.

'Spasmo,' I said. Magnus could have made one of his rude jokes which would really have got Claire going. That might have been fun. But Magnus had boring chicken-pox and Claire ignored me.

'A bus-load of boring belly dancers,' I said, and pranced around the room. 'Another boring foreigner. I bet she's a Jew.'

'You're not supposed to say that,' Claire said primly. And she added something po-faced about toleration and talent.

It was the dullest reception ever. It's always the same. You stand by the window with a pathetic glass of lemonade while all Father's secretaries drink champagne and try to make conversation with hoards of people who don't know enough to speak English. Ma and Father shake hands with everyone and look as if they are having a wonderful time. Claire, Annabel and I are supposed to help distribute the food, and let me tell you, at some of these do's it's like feeding a pack of hounds. These foreigners are so greedy there's never anything left over for supper. I don't know why Ma and Father make us come.

I considered slipping away to chew a mouthful of toothpowder. I could work up a good froth and then make my entrance doing an impression of a rabid dog. That might wake the foreigners up.

Actually I quite like the Germans. Their soldiers really look like soldiers. I'd like to have a pair of boots like a German officer. Just think, if Magnus and I went back to school in boots instead of those horrible lace-up shoes, the big boys would have to watch out. Even Father says the Germans are not a bad lot really.

Claire appeared at my shoulder. 'That's her,' she said, tearing at a hangnail.

'Who?'

'Kezia.'

'She doesn't look very exquisite to me,' I said. She was no taller than I was and she wore a grey thing that looked like a schoolgirl's dress.

'Everyone says her extensions are spectacular,' Claire informed me. She pointed her right toe. Claire was wearing stockings instead of socks that summer, and her legs looked funny.

'She hasn't got any extensions as far as I can see,' I said. In the grey dress Kezia looked as flat-chested as Annabel.

'Not only are you ignorant,' Claire said icily, 'but you are also a filthy-minded little toad.' She went away.

I looked around, and it seemed that everyone was looking at

Kezia. A lot of them were pretending not to, but somehow she was the centre of an invisible circle. She wasn't saying anything, but Ma smiled at her as if she had done something very clever. It was so unfair. How could Ma look like that at someone who couldn't even speak English? And why was a country like Germany interested in anything as spasmo as ballet?

'You are not interested in the ballet, I think?' someone said, and I turned around. He was tall, and he looked as if he might be good at something decent like cricket. Except he was a German and they don't play cricket.

I was about to say ballet was spasmo, but I stopped myself.

'Girls are interested in ballet,' I said instead. I did not want any stranger thinking I could be keen on anything my sister was stupid enough to find interesting.

'Ah, the manly sports,' he said, and smiled. He was quite friendly really—for a foreigner. And he was the only one not swooning over Kezia Lehmann.

'You should come to my country, perhaps. *Our* young men are better entertained.'

'Sailing?' I asked. I am big for my age and I didn't mind if he thought I was a young man. It was about time. He wouldn't make me have my birthday party in the rumpus-room with the girls.

'Of course, sailing,' he said. 'And much, much more.'

'Could I have a pair of boots?' I asked. He was being much more friendly than Father who hadn't spoken a word to me all evening.

While we watched, Annabel wormed her way into the circle around Kezia with a plate of smoked salmon sandwiches.

I was thinking how funny it would be if I had switched the smoked salmon for ham. Everyone knows that if Hebrews see ham they fall writhing to the floor and all their teeth drop out.

I was going to tell my joke to the nice German but he had started talking to someone else.

Kezia refused a sandwich but she smiled at Annabel, and—I could hardly believe it—Annabel curtsied. All the grown-ups smiled in that boring way they have when little girls are being exceptionally sick-making. Annabel, taking advantage as usual, wanted to know how to curtsy properly, and Kezia showed her. All the grown-ups clapped their hands. Claire pushed forward. It was absolutely disgusting and shameful to see what fools my family made of themselves in public.

Just then one of Father's secretaries, who was standing right behind me, said, 'Such purity of line, do you notice, even when she's only showing that sweet child how to curtsy.'

She thought Annabel was a sweet child! That's how much she knew.

'They say she is on borrowed time,' someone else said.

'They say her family is being held hostage to her good behaviour. Utterly tragic.'

That was the limit—what did she know about tragic? 'They say she goes like a stoat too,' I said loudly. That is what Magnus says about girls he doesn't like and it's very funny. But I never expected the reaction it got coming from me.

Everyone stopped talking. Father spun round, took three steps towards me and smacked me on the ear. I was stunned. You shouldn't hit children on the head: Father says so himself. But he did it, right in front of a roomful of people. Tears filled my eyes. He didn't even notice. He grabbed my elbow and dragged me to the door.

'What for?' I cried. 'What have I done? I like stoats.'

Everyone was watching. 'Out,' Father said in his quietest voice. 'You've disgraced yourself once too often, Andrew. And this time you've disgraced us too.'

I caught sight of Claire, bright red in the face, looking as if she were about to burst into tears. What did she have to cry about, I thought as I stumbled through the door. Trust Claire to act as if she were the centre of attention. Although, at that moment, I could have done with a little less myself.

'What have I done?' I repeated. 'I only said . . .'

'I know exactly what you said,' Father almost whispered, 'and unfortunately so does everyone else. Go straight to your room.'

'But what am I going to do? It's spasmo in my room all by myself.'

Father looked as if he might hit me again. He said, 'A public insult deserves a public apology. You can think about that, all by yourself in your room. Because, believe me, Andrew, there *will* be an apology.' He just turned his back and walked away, leaving me in the hall.

'I hate you,' I shouted. 'You're a bully. You shouldn't hit boys.' The back of his neck went pink but he didn't come back.

I went upstairs, but I didn't go to my room. I sat on the gallery floor and watched through the balusters. When those silly women went to the downstairs powder room, I saw them go. I know what they do in there. They can't fool me with that 'powdering my nose' act. Even that spasmo Kezia has to have a wee. I thought about it and it made me feel a bit better. I thought about writing a letter to *The Times* and telling them about an important man who beat up his children. That made me feel good too. Magnus would have to take notice. His mother might take me away to live with her. She's a lot nicer than my mother because she doesn't have any stupid daughters to distract her. Magnus's mother understands me. It's so unfair. Magnus has a far better time than I do. It's probably because his father isn't important. When Magnus wants something he gets it, and his parents listen to him when he talks.

When I grow up, I thought, I'm going to join the Socialist Party and become a spy. I could make a floor plan of Father's study, and I'm good at listening behind doors. I bet if I told those Germans downstairs what I knew about Father's job they'd sit up and pay attention. You don't think all those men downstairs are what they say they are, do you? Half of them are spies and secret policemen. Everyone knows that. I could give them the key to Father's safe and they'd be so grateful they'd have a pair of boots made specially for me.

German secret policemen are funny. They wear black suits with baggy knees and look like wrestlers. I bet they're very strong. I'd like to see Father go a round or two with one of them. That'd teach him something. Bullies are always cowards.

I was beginning to feel quite happy again. I screwed my wet handkerchief into a ball. I was about to throw it at one of the maids as she passed beneath me with a tray of glasses, but just then Claire came out of the reception room.

She was saying, 'You can come up to my room if you like. I've got a lovely mirror. It's much better than downstairs.'

Annabel appeared too, tugging that awful Kezia by the hand. 'See my room too!' she squealed. 'I've got a camel. A big camel. It's the biggest one you ever saw.' And all three of them made for the stairs. That made me move in a hurry. I scuttled backwards and hid behind the curtains. Magnus and I call girls the 'Lower Breed', along with servants and foreigners. That made Kezia a 'Lower Breed' on two counts. Apologize to her! I'd rather eat cold fat.

But a good spy is supposed to take risks, so after a while I tiptoed along the passage to Claire's door and peeped in. There were my two sisters consorting with the enemy. She was sitting on Claire's bed with Annabel beside her and Annabel's disgusting camel on her knee. She was pretending it could speak German, chattering away in gobbledegook, and making Annabel scream with laughter. What really made me sick was Claire, who was kneeling behind her, brushing her hair. Downstairs you couldn't see her hair because it was all screwed up in a knot. But now it stretched all the way down her back and Claire was making it shine like black oil. Claire said, 'I wish I had long hair. It's beautiful. I wish you could stay here for ever. I'd brush your hair every day.'

Kezia said, 'I wish too, I could stay for ever.' She looked sad. Girls are always trying to make you feel sorry for them, but they can't fool me.

'It must be quite difficult for you,' Claire said, brushing, brushing, brushing the long black hair. It made me feel funny looking at that hair, and I didn't like it. So I didn't hear what Kezia said next.

But Annabel squeaked, 'Why can't you stay with us? You could have Nanny's room, next to mine.'

Well, if that meant Nanny leaving I could almost support the idea. Nanny is definitely a 'Lower Breed', but she doesn't act as if she knows it. Except Nanny would never leave. In fact I think she will live forever just to spite me.

'Is it your family?' Claire asked. What did Claire care about families? She is such a hypocrite.

'Everything depends on me,' Kezia said, and I nearly laughed out loud. Girls think they are so important.

'I must go down now,' she went on. 'I am watched, you see.'

You didn't have to tell me that. Everyone downstairs had been gawping at her. I made ready to slip away down the passage. But Claire said, 'I wish there was something I could do to help.'

A silence followed that, so I sneaked another look. Claire and Kezia were looking at each other and saying nothing. You'd have thought they were best friends or something, except that girls don't have proper friends the way boys do. And besides, they had only just met. But Claire is like that: one minute she knows nothing about a subject like ballet, and the next she's a world expert. You should have heard her when she got that craze for Vegetarianism and Bernard Shaw.

'I think you are sincere,' Kezia said next, and I had to stuff my handkerchief in my mouth. Anyone who thinks Claire is sincere must have a brain smaller than a mouse dropping.

'There is something you can do,' she said. 'It is a small thing, and for you there is no risk.'

'What is it?' Claire asked, eyes wide.

'I have written a letter,' Kezia replied in a whisper. 'There are friends of my family who are refugees in America. Perhaps they can help us. I cannot send this letter because I am always watched and I must never be a disloyal German.'

That finished me off. The girl must have cracked. 'Disloyal to letter boxes,' I said to myself and went down the passage where I could laugh without being heard.

If there's anything that is totally spasmo it's girls.

From my place on the gallery I could keep a watch on Claire's door and on what was happening in the hall below. People were beginning to leave. Not the foreigners, though. They always stay till there's nothing left to eat or drink.

Father came out. He was saying goodbye to a wrinkled old man, all smiles and handshakes. But then he turned towards the stairs and his face went grim and cold. Obviously he had remembered me. I made straight for the curtains, and he went by me without noticing. He walked past Claire's room and turned the corner. He was looking for me.

When he was out of sight I pushed the curtains aside and ran downstairs. If I could stay hidden until Kezia and the rest of the foreigners had gone, I would be all right. Father's study was locked, so I dashed to the kitchen. I don't think Father has been in the kitchen in his life.

But I had forgotten about Nanny. She caught me on my way to the back door. 'Can't you see we're all busy, Andrew?' she said. 'No one has time to attend to you. You're supposed to be making your guests feel welcome.'

'They're not my guests,' I told her. 'They're all spasmo.'

'Don't you use that word,' she said. 'Now get along and behave yourself.' She forced me back into the hall, where I was bound to run into Father.

There was nothing for it: I would have to run away. I had nearly got to the front door when Father appeared at the top of the stairs.

'Andrew!' he shouted in that horrible voice which means you're supposed to do what he says instantly. But I opened the door and bumped into one of the German secret policemen who was smoking on the top step.

'Help me,' I said. 'He'll kill me if he catches me out here.'

'Kill?' the German said, like a parrot.

'Andrew!' called my father from inside.

I had a brilliant idea. 'He's going to kill me,' I said, 'and I want to change sides.'

'Sides?' The German was so stupid.

'You know, be a refugee,' I said.

'Who wishes to become a refugee?' A tall thin man came out of the shadows at the bottom of the stone steps. I ran down to meet him, but when I got there I saw that he had narrow eyes and a mean mouth and I didn't like him one bit. I tried to run past him but he grabbed the collar of my coat.

'Who wishes to become a refugee?' he repeated. His voice was mean too: mean and foreign.

'Not me!' I cried, trying to pull away. 'It wasn't me. It was Kezia. It's all her fault.'

'Kezia?' His eyes were so narrow they looked like gun-slits. He pinched my arm.

'That hurts!' I shouted.

'What have you done with Kezia Lehmann?' He pinched my arm harder—just above the elbow where it really hurts.

'Let go of me!' I yelled. 'You've got it all wrong. It's that ballet dancer. She's upstairs with my sisters. She wants to stay for ever . . . she's, she's disloyal.'

'Andrew!' Father appeared above me on the top step and I wrenched myself out of the man's nasty fingers. I ran away as fast as I could along the pavement. I can run as fast as Magnus when I try. I expected Father to chase me, but when I reached the corner and looked back he was just standing there talking to the thin man. They seemed to be arguing. I'll never go back, I thought. He's not a proper father: he'd rather talk to a foreigner than come and find his own son.

I had to walk all the way to Magnus's house in the dark because I didn't have any money. And by the time I got there I was very cold and hungry. You would have thought Magnus's mother would have been nice to me but I bet Father had already telephoned and told her lies about me, because she made me wait in the hall until Nanny came to collect me in a taxicab. Father didn't even send the car. It was humiliating.

Of course I was sent to bed without any supper. What else would you expect after the rotten day I'd had? But anyway, the foreigners wouldn't have left much. I don't see why we can't have a proper meal after a do. They go to all that trouble to feed strangers and then expect their own family to do without.

There was one good thing, though: in all the fuss I hadn't had to apologize to Kezia. I'd got out of that because by the time I got home she was gone. There was no one there but the family. Ma had gone to bed with a headache, and Father was shut up in his study making telephone calls. That was quite a relief too.

Claire wouldn't speak to me. I tried to tell her about the horrible man on the doorstep but she wouldn't listen.

The next day I overheard her telling Mother about how that spasmo ballet company had cancelled the rest of their performances and gone home. She said it was tragic because of Kezia, and the way she went on you'd have thought it was all my fault.

The way I see it—if I had saved the world from a lot of boring belly dancers I ought to be congratulated.

But nobody ever sees things the way I do. It was going to be a rotten summer. Totally spasmo.

Old Friends

Dorothy Salisbury Davis

THE TWO WOMEN had been friends since childhood, their mothers friends before them. Both were in their late twenties; neither had married. Amy intended not to, although she was beginning to lose some of the vehemence with which she declared that purpose. Virginia was still saying that she was waiting for the right man to come along. She admitted herself to be an old-fashioned girl. One of the sadnesses in her life was that the men she liked most were already married. It made her furious when Amy would say, "Happily?"

"I suppose you think I should have an affair," Virginia said.

"Yes, as a matter of fact, it would be good for you."

"How do you know?"

"Well, let me put it this way," Amy would say, and the same conversation had occurred in some form or other a number of times, "it would be better than a bad marriage just for the sake of being married."

"According to you," Virginia would say, "there are no good marriages."

"Not many, and I don't know of a single one that came with a guarantee."

One might have thought that it was Amy who had grown up in the broken home. Her parents had only recently celebrated their thirty-fifth wedding anniversary. Whereas Virginia's mother had divorced her third husband, each of whom had left her better off financially than had his predecessor. She and Virginia were often taken for sisters. But so were Virginia and Amy. Or, to make Virginia's own distinction, she was always being taken for Amy's sister.

At one time they had worked for the same New York publishing house, Virginia as an assistant art director, Amy as an assistant to the senior editor. Amy's father, a retired executive of the firm, had arranged interviews for both girls after they finished college. The jobs, he insisted, they had got for themselves. Virginia stayed with hers. More than anything in the world, except possibly a husband who loved and respected her, she wanted her independence of her mother. Amy, to cap the interminable subject, once suggested that was why Virginia wanted a husband, to protect her from her mother.

"I am perfectly capable of protecting myself."

And that of course, Amy realized in time, was her friend's trouble. Nobody could do anything for her. She resented anyone's attempting it. Which made her yearning for a husband suspect: what Virginia really wanted, Amy decided, was a baby. This insight, as well as others just as profound if true, had slipped beyond Amy's conscious reckoning of her friend's character long before the weekend Amy reneged on the invitation to the country.

Sometimes months went by when they did not see each other. Amy, on inheriting an ancient cottage from an aunt, gave up her regular job for freelance writing, copy editing, and restoring the cottage. While not far from the city and not actually isolated, the cottage retained a rare privacy. It had settled deeper and deeper into the ground with the decades, and the mountain laurel that surrounded it was as snug as a shawl.

Knowing Virginia to be a Sunday painter, Amy thought of her whenever there was a change in nature. Such a change had come that week with the sudden November stripping of the leaves. The light took on a special quality and the long grass in the meadow quivered glossily golden in the sun and turned silver under the moon. She called Virginia on Thursday.

"Well, now, I would like to," Virginia said, mulling over the invitation aloud. "I half promised Allan—I don't know if I've told you about him, the architect?—I didn't actually commit myself. Thank you, Amy. I'd love to come."

Amy was on the point of saying she could bring Allan, the architect, and then it occurred to her that he might be an invention of Virginia's, part of that same old face-saving syndrome which, when they saw too much of one another, made their friendship dreary. She almost wished she had not called. However, they discussed the bus schedule and settled on a time for Virginia's arrival.

"If I miss that one, I'll take the next," Virginia said. There was always a little hitch to allow room for independence.

That very afternoon Amy received a call from Mike Trilling, one of the few men with whom she had ever been deeply in love. A newspaper correspondent, Mike had been sent overseas just when they had become very happy together. If he had asked it, she would have followed him, but he had not asked it, and she had been a long time getting over the separation. Except that she was not over it. She knew that the moment she heard his voice.

Her end of the conversation was filled with pauses.

Finally Mike said, "Are you still hung up on me?"

"What humility! Yes, damn you."

"You don't have to swear at me. I've got the same problem—once in love with Amy, here I am again. I'd come out for the weekend if you'd ask me."

"All right, you're invited."

"I'll rent a car and be there early tomorrow evening. We can have dinner at The Tavern. Is the food as good as it used to be?"

"I'll fix us something. It's not that good. You can bring the wine." She refrained from saying that he could take the bus, an hour's trip. There was no better way to put a man off than to try to save his money for him.

She postponed the decision on what to say to Virginia, and while she cleaned house she let her memory of the times she and Mike had been together run full flood. She washed her hair and dried it before the blaze in the fireplace. Mike loved to bury his face in her hair, to discover in it the faint fragrance of wood smoke; he loved to run his fingers through it on the pillow and give it a not altogether gentle tug, pulling her face to his.

She could not tell Ginny that Mike was the reason she was asking her to postpone until the following weekend. It would be unkind. Anyone else might understand, but Ginny would understand even more than was intended: she would reexamine the whole of her life in terms of that rejection. Amy did not call her until morning.

"Ginny, I've had the most tremendous idea for a story. I was up half the night thinking about it, afraid to lose it, or that it wouldn't be any good in the morning. But it's a good one and I want to dash it off fresh. Will you come next week instead? I know you understand . . ." She made herself stop. She was saying too much.

"Of course," Virginia said, and her voice had that dead air of self-abnegation. "I envy you."

"Bless you for understanding," Amy said. "The same time next weekend. I'll be watching for you."

Once off the phone she gave herself up to the pleasure of anticipation. Almost a year had passed since she and Mike were last together. She had had a couple of brief encounters since, but no one had taken his place. She had worked. She had done a lot more work with Mike away than when he was around. They had not corresponded. He had called her on New Year's Eve. Collect, because he was at a friend's house and the British would not accept his credit-card charge. She had not asked him about the friend. She did not propose to ask any questions now.

At first it seemed like old times, their sitting before the fire with martinis, Mike on the floor at her feet, his head resting on his arm where it lay across her knees. His hair had begun to thin on the very top of his head. She put her finger to the spot, a cold finger, for she had just put down her glass.

Mike got up and sat in the chair opposite hers, brushing back his hair, something almost tender in the way he stroked the spot.

"I'm wicked, aren't I?" she said, carrying off as best she could what she knew to have been a mistake.

"Tell me about that," he said, purposely obtuse.

"Naughty, I mean."

"Oh, nuts. With the British, every other word is 'naughty.' Aren't I the naughty one?" He mimicked someone's accent. "It's such a faggoty word."

"I guess it is," Amy said.

He fidgeted a moment, as though trying to get comfortable in the chair, then got up and gave one of the logs a kick. "It's not easy—getting reacquainted when so much has happened in between."

"Oh?" In spite of herself.

He looked around at her. "I've been working bloody hard. Five months in Cyprus."

"I know."

"Does nobody in America read history?"

"I suspect the trouble is that nobody listens to those who read history."

"Did you follow my dispatches?"

"Every word, my darling."

Things went a little better. He looked at his glass. "I can't drink martinis like I used to. What kind of vermouth did you use?"

The phone rang and Amy, on her way to answer it, said, "Try putting in more gin."

It was Virginia, of all people. "I won't disturb you except for a minute."

"It's all right. I'm taking a break." She was afraid Mike might put on a record.

"I want to ask a favor of you, Amy. I got myself into a predicament. When Allan called a while ago, I decided I didn't want to talk to him, so I said I was on my way to spend the weekend with you. I don't think he'll call, but in case he does, would you tell him I've gone on a long walk or something like that?"

Amy drew a deep breath and tried to think of something to say that would not expose the extent of her exasperation. The most natural thing in the world would have been: Ginny, the reason I asked you not to come—

"I don't think he will call."

"Okay, Ginny. I'll tell him."

"Get his number and say I'll call him back."

"I'll tell him that," Amy said. It was all a fantasy, and in some way or other Virginia thought she was getting even. If there was an Allan and if these little exchanges did occur, she would then have to call Virginia back and tell her that Allan had telephoned her.

"Was that Virginia?" Mike said.

"Yes."

"Hasn't she hooked herself a man yet?"

"You damn smug—" Amy exploded, possibly because she was annoyed with both Virginia and him. But Virginia, being the more vulnerable and absent, got such loyal defense in the argument that ensued, she would have been stunned. Indeed, it might have changed her whole picture of herself.

Mike and Amy did reach a rapprochement. After all, it was his remembering Amy's complaints about her friend in the old days that had provoked his comment: she should blame herself, not him. After the second martini they were laughing and talking about old intimacies, and how they had used to put the third martini on ice for afterward. Such good memories and the kisses which, if they weren't the same, were better than most, sufficed to get them into the bedroom. There, alas, nothing went the same as it had used to.

"Damn it," Mike kept saying, "this never happens to me."

"It's all right," Amy said over and over again, although well aware he had used the present tense.

Later, watching him stoop to see himself in her dressing-table mirror while he knotted his tie, she said, "Bed isn't everything."

"That's right."

"But it's a lot," she said and threw off the blankets.

By the time she finished in the bathroom, he had gone back to the living room where he stood before the fire and stared into it. A fresh log was catching on, the flames like little tongues darting up the sides. He had not brought the martini pitcher from the kitchen.

"You can't go home again," she said.

"I guess not." He could at least have said that it was fun trying. But what he said was, "Amy, let's not spoil a beautiful memory."

"Oh, boy. I don't believe you said it. Not Mike Trilling."

"All right. 'You can't go home again' wasn't exactly original either. We aren't going to make it, Amy, so why don't I just take off before we start bickering again? No recriminations, no goodbyes, no tears."

Her throat tight as a corked bottle, she went up the stairs and got his coat and overnight bag.

On the porch they did not even shake hands—a turn and a quickly averted glance lest their eyes get caught, and a little wave before he opened the car door. When he was gone, she remembered the wine. It was as well she had forgotten it. A "thank you" for anything would have humiliated them both.

Returning to the house she felt as sober as the moon and as lonely. There was a whispery sound to the fire, and her aunt's Seth Thomas floor clock ticked with the slow heavy rhythm of a tired heart. Most things break: the phrase from somewhere she could not remember kept running through her mind. The old clock rasped and struck once. Hard though it was to believe, the hour was only half-past eight.

She called Virginia.

Her friend took her time picking up the phone. "I wasn't going to answer. I thought it might be Allan. Did he call me there?"

"Not so far, dear. Ginny, you could make the nine-thirty bus and come on out. The story isn't ready yet. I always start too soon. I'm botching it terribly."

"Thank you, but I don't think I will, Amy. I want to stay home by myself now where I can think things out comfortably. I'm a mess, but since I know it, I ought to be able to do something about it."

"You sound awfully down. Do come and see me."

"Actually, I'm up. Have a nice weekend, Amy."

Have a nice weekend: that was the *coup de grace*. Amy went to the kitchen and got out the martini jug. She closed the refrigerator door on an eight-dollar steak. The cat, her paws tucked out of sight where she sat on the table, opened her eyes and then closed them again at once.

Amy returned to the living room by way of the dining-room door. As she entered, she discovered a man also coming into the room, he by the door to the vestibule. She had not locked up after Mike's departure.

"Hello. I did knock," he said, " but not very loudly. I thought I'd surprise you."

"You have, and now that I'm surprised, get the hell out of here before I call my husband."

"Funny. Ginny didn't tell me about him. In fact, she said you didn't want one."

"You're Allan."

He had stopped. They both had, in their tracks, on seeing one another. They now moved tentatively forward. He was handsome in an odd way: his quick smile and his eyes did not seem to go together. The eyes, she would have sworn, took in everything in the room while not seeming to look directly at anything, even at her when they came face to face.

"Yes, I'm Allan. So Ginny's told you about me? I'm surprised, though come to think of it, I shouldn't be. She's told me a lot about you, too. Where is she?"

Damn Ginny. "She's gone for a walk." She regretted at once having said that. Now it was reasonable for him to expect to wait for her return. "Don't you think, Mr.—" She stopped and waited.

"Just Allan," he said, which she did not like either, the familiarity of it. No. The anonymity: it was more like that.

"Mr. Allan, don't you think if Ginny wanted to see you, she would have arranged it?"

"It takes two to make an arrangement, Amy." His eyes, not really on hers anyway, slipped away to the glass where Mike had left it. Her glass was on the side table near which she stood, the martini pitcher in her hand. He might well have arrived in time to have seen Mike leave.

He then said, "Should I confess something to you, Miss Amy—I guess that's what you'd like me to call you, but it certainly rings strange against the picture Ginny gave me of you—let me tell you the reason I crashed this party. I wanted to see the cottage, and I wasn't sure I'd ever get an invitation, leaving it to Ginny. It's pre-Revolutionary, isn't it?"

"Yes."

"Don't you need an architect?"

That disarmed her—he was a man with humor at least. "Will you have a drink?" She swirled the contents of the pitcher. "A martini?"

"Thank you."

"I'll get a glass."

A few steps took him to the table where Mike's glass sat. "If this was Ginny's glass, I don't mind using it."

No more lies. She hardly knew now which were hers and which were Ginny's. "It wasn't Ginny's glass," she said.

He brought it to her anyway. "Whose ever it was, it won't poison me."

All the same, those eyes that just missed hers saw everything that passed through her mind. She wanted to escape them, however briefly, in the time it would take to get a glass from the other room. "That's ridiculous," she said. "Sit down, Allan. That chair is better for your long legs than this one."

His movements were such that she thought him about to take the far chair as she had suggested, but she had no more than stepped into the dining room than he was behind her.

"What a marvelous old room!"

Of all six rooms this was the plainest, with nothing to recommend it except the view of the garden and that was not available at night. One end of it had been chopped off in the nineteen-twenties to provide space for a bathroom. She took a glass from the cupboard.

"May I see the kitchen?" he asked, throwing her a quick, persuasive smile.

"Why not?" This time she stepped aside and let him go on by himself. The kitchen was straight ahead, not to be missed. He had an athlete's build as well as one's lightness of step, she observed as he passed her.

"Puss, puss, puss," he said, seeing the cat. She came wide-awake, stood up, and preened herself for him.

Amy kept trying to tell herself that it was she who was behaving oddly, letting her imagination run wild. She tried to think what he and Ginny would be like together. They were similar in a way she could not put her finger on. Then she had it: Ginny never seemed quite able to hit the nail on the head. God knows, he was direct enough, but his eyes slipped past what he was presumably looking at.

Well, he had made it to the kitchen and if there was something there he wanted—a knife or a hammer—there was no preventing his getting it. She turned into the vestibule, that entrance to it opposite the bathroom, with the purpose of making sure the shotgun was in its place alongside the porch door, more or less concealed by her old Burberry coat and the umbrella stand. She could not see it where she stood, but that did not mean it was not there. For just an instant she thought of making a dash to the front door.

"Amy?"

They very nearly collided, him coming in as she turned back.

"Is the kitchen fireplace a replica of the old one?"

"Probably."

"Afterwards I'll show you where I think the old one was." He caught her hand as though he were an old friend and led her back to the living room. When she tried to remove her hand he gave it a little squeeze before letting go.

She poured the drinks shakily. "I should have got more ice."

"Are you afraid of me?"

"Certainly not," she said.

"I'm harmless enough. You'd have to know that for a fact from Ginny's having anything to do with me."

She laughed, thinking how obviously so that was. If she knew Ginny. Sometimes she felt that she knew Ginny so well she could not possibly know her at all. Maybe there were two Ginnies. "Cheers."

The drink was strong enough, but it was going tepid.

"Would you allow me to get more ice and give these another stir?" he asked.

"I would allow it." She poked up the embers under the half-burned log. The sparks exploded and vanished. Ginny ought to have come even if she didn't believe the story about the story. It was funny how sure she had been that Allan was imaginary. Nor could she remember anything Ginny had ever told her about him. Had she told her anything? Or had Amy simply turned it off, doubting that there was a real live Allan?

He returned with the pitcher and the glasses, having taken them also to the kitchen. They now were white with frost. He poured the drinks, touched her glass with his, and said, "What else would you allow?"

Harmless? She said, trying to strike a pose of propriety without overdoing it: "I'd allow as how—I wouldn't allow much."

He shrugged. "No offense."

"None taken."

He started to shuffle across to the chair she had appointed his, then turned back. "What's much?" Having again amused her, he bent down and kissed her as she was reasonably sure he had never kissed Ginny. "Perfectly harmless," he said and trotted over to the chair while neatly balancing the glass so that he did not spill a drop. "Does she often take long walks at this time of night?"

"As a matter of fact she does."

"And if I'm not mistaken, we're at the full moon." He helped make the lie more credible. Knowingly? "Has Ginny talked about me?"

"Well now," Amy said, avoiding a direct answer, "I almost suggested that she bring you out for the weekend."

"How intuitive of me then to be here."

"I suppose Ginny has given you a complete dossier on me?"

"We do talk a lot," he said in a sly, wistful, almost hopeless way that again amused her. "Have you anything to suggest I do about it?"

She knew exactly what he meant. "A marriage proposal?"

"That's a bit drastic."

"It sounds archaic when you set it off and listen to it by itself—a marriage proposal."

"Or the title to a poem by Amy Lowell," he said. "You weren't by any chance named after her?"

"Good God, no."

"She did like a good cigar, didn't she?" he said, deadpan.

Amy sipped her drink and gave a fleeting thought to Mike, to the steak in the refrigerator, to the Haut Brion '61. And to the rumpled bed in the room back of the fireplace.

He put his glass on the table and got up with a sudden show of exuberance. "Shall I bring in more wood? I saw the pile of it outside."

"Not yet." Amy put the one log left in the basket onto the fire. While she swept in the bits of bark and ash, he came and stood beside her, bent, studying the fire, but stealing glimpses of her face. He touched his fingers lightly to a wisp of hair that had escaped one of the braids she wore in a circle round her head. "Your hair must be very long and beautiful."

"I've been told so."

"Ginny said it was."

"I wasn't thinking of Ginny."

"I wasn't either. Except in the way you hang onto somebody in the dark."

When they had both straightened up, he waited for her to face him, and then he lifted her chin, touching it only with the backs of his fingers as though to take hold of it might seem too bold. He kissed her. It was a long kiss which, nonetheless, didn't seem to be going anywhere until she herself thrust meaning into it. She had not intended to, but then the situation was not one open to precise calculations. He tasted of licorice as well as gin.

He drew back and looked at her. At that proximity his eyes did not seem to have the disconcerting vagary. He was, despite these little overtures, agonizingly shy: the realization came in a flash. Someone had prescribed—possibly a psychiatrist—certain boldnesses by which he might overcome the affliction. *Miss Amy*: that was closer to his true self.

He said, averting his eyes once more, "Ginny said we'd like one another . . . even though you don't like men."

"What?"

"She thinks you don't care much for men."

"What kind of woman does she think I am then? The kind who gets paid?"

Color rushed to his face. He backed off and turned, starting back to his chair in that shuffling way—a clown's way, really, the "don't look at me but at what I'm doing" routine which reinforced her belief in his shyness.

"I don't want another drink," she said, "but if you do, help yourself. I say what's on my mind, Allan. People who know me get used to it. By the sound of things, Ginny speaks hers too on occasion. I'd never got that picture of her."

"I shouldn't have blabbed that."

"No, you shouldn't." She started from the room, thinking: God save me from middle-aged adolescents.

"Where are you going?"

"To the bathroom for now. Then I'll decide where else."

She had not reached the door when he caught her from behind and lifted her from her feet, holding her close against him, her arms pinned to her sides. He kissed the back of her neck and then with his teeth he removed, one by one, her plastic hairpins and let them drop to the floor. "Please don't be so fierce," he said, his mouth at her ear. She felt the dart of his tongue there, but so tentative, as though he were following a book of instructions.

"Put me down. Your belt buckle's hurting me."

Her feet on the floor, she faced him. "I don't have to be fierce at all," she said and loosened the braids, after which she shook out that abundance of rich brown hair.

He ran his tongue round his lips. "It's just too bad that Ginny's going to be walking in."

"She's not."

"She's not?" he repeated. Something changed in his face, which was certainly natural with that bit of news. "I don't believe you," he said, the smile coming and going.

She motioned to him with one finger as much as to say, wait, and going to the phone, she dialed Virginia's number. With each ring Amy felt less sure of herself, less sure of Ginny. Then, after the fourth ring, came the gentle slow-voiced, "Hello."

Amy held the phone out toward Allan. He simply stared, his head slightly to the side. It could not have been more than a second, but it did seem longer before Ginny repeated more clearly, "Hello?"

He was about to take the phone. Amy broke the connection, pressing her finger on the signal, then returning the phone to its cradle.

"I don't get it," he said.

"It was a change of plan. That's all."

"And not anything to do with me?"

"My dear man, I wasn't even sure you were real."

"Maybe I'm not," he said, and smiled tentatively. It seemed flirtatious.

Amy threw her head back. "There's one way to find out."

He gave a funny little shudder, as though a chill had run through him. Or better, something interestingly erotic. He wet a finger and held it up as to the wind. Unerringly he then pointed to the closed door of the bedroom back of the fireplace. He motioned her to move on ahead of him. Had he looked in through, say, a part of the drapes at her and Mike? Or had Virginia told him that Amy slept downstairs? There did not seem to be much Ginny had not told him. With interpretations.

"Don't turn on the lights," he said.

Amy was not surprised. "We can always turn them off again."

"No." And then: "I'm able to see you in the dark."

A good trick. She said nothing. It was beginning to irritate her that Ginny had said she did not like men. Liking sex and liking men deserved a distinction, true. But she did not think it one Ginny was likely to make. And she had loved Mike. She had. Now it was over, ended. Nothing was beginning; nothing was about to be born. Except that you couldn't really tell. That was what was so marvelous about an encounter such as this: you couldn't really tell.

She bent down to remove her slippers. She felt his hand running lightly over her bare shoulder, sweeping the hair before it. A jolting pain struck at the base of her skull. Then came nothingness.

She awoke to the sound of voices and with a headache worse than any she had ever suffered. A woman's voice said that she was coming to. Like hell, she wanted to say; not if she could help it, not with all this pain. There was other pain besides that of her head, and with the awareness of it she began to realize what had happened. She tried to put her hand between her thighs. Someone gently pulled it away.

"Amy?"

She opened her eyes to the familiar ceiling beam with its ancient knot, the eye of the house. She turned her head far enough to see Virginia's round and worried face. "What are you doing here?"

A woman in a white uniform hovered alongside Ginny. She was filling a hypodermic needle from a medicine bottle. When Ginny glanced up at her, she moved away.

"On the phone," Ginny said. "I couldn't hear anything except the clock, but I'd know its tick anywhere. Remember when we were kids: 'take a *bath*, take a bath, take a *bath*, take a bath . . .' I decided I'd better catch the next bus out."

Amy gave her hand a weak squeeze. At the door of the room were two uniformed policemen, one of whom she thought she remembered having once talked out of giving her a speeding ticket. "How did *they* get in on the act?"

"I called the ambulance," Ginny said, and leaning close, she murmured, "You were"—she couldn't bring herself to say the exact word—"molested."

"I guess," Amy said.

One of the policemen said, "When you're strong enough we need the full story, miss. Did you recognize the intruder?"

The intruder. In a way he was, of course. She took a long time in answering. "Is there any way I can be sure he'll get psychiatric attention?"

The cops exchanged glances. "The first thing is to identify him so we can bring him in."

"And then I have to swear out a complaint against him?"

"If you don't, ma'am, some other woman may not get the chance to do it."

"To some extent it was my own fault," she said, not much above a whisper.

The cop made a noise of assent. Neither he nor his partner seemed surprised. "All the same, we better get him in and let the shrinks decide what happens to him. Okay?"

She thought of telling them of the point at which she had been knocked out and decided against it for the time being. "Okay," she said.

"Can you give us a description? Race, age, height, color of his eyes—"

"Ginny, I'm sorry. It was your friend Allan."

"Oh."

It was a little cry, scarcely more than a whimper.

"Would you give them his name and address? You won't have to do anything else."

"But, Amy, I can't. I mean, actually I've never seen Allan. He calls me and we just talk on the telephone."

GRAFFITI

Stanley Ellin

UP TO THAT exchange with Veszto in the Faculty Club dining room, Halas had never really given much thought to the subject of graffiti. After all, these testimonials to marker-pens and spray-can paints smeared over walls, monuments, buses, subway cars—especially those subway cars—were a fact of life in New York City. A bit of an eyesore perhaps, but one easily outweighed by all the glories of this spectacular city itself. Halas, who knew a good many of the world's cities at first hand, adored New York City.

Of course, to give Veszto his due in that heated exchange at lunch, the man obviously could not help having been born a cheapskate, *ein Geizhals*, *un avare*—observe there the root of "avaricious"—so the knowledge that those graffiti recently applied to the hood of his almost brand-new Buick could only be erased at great expense had to strike him through the heart like a javelin. And, of course, by some regrettable genetic twist, he was one of your darkly brooding Hungarians with no capacity to take life's little jokes with a touch of humor, no *joie de vivre* in him at all. In spirit at least, thought Halas, who overflowed with *joie de vivre*, the man was hardly what you could even call a Hungarian.

And getting down to the nitty-gritty, Veszto was afflicted with a consuming envy. Granted that he was a brilliant physicist, a consultant in the national space program, a full professor at the university which, as it added more and more to its vast properties around Washington Square, was also moved to lure to its roster such shining stars as this Doctor Bela Veszto.

But, as sourpuss Veszto was well aware, where he was a star in this firmament Janos Halas was undeniably a superstar. Janos Halas himself, that mesmerizing savant, lecturer, author, that master of comparative philology, who almost singlehanded had overturned clumsy Nineteenth Century German scholarship in philology and had come up with the common basis of all human language. The Halas Linguistics, no less.

No mere professor either, but Distinguished Professor of Linguistics, with a secretary and an office for life.

Oh, yes. Enter any academic gathering in the world, never mind how prestigious its attenders, and observe that when Doctor Janos Halas was announced he was the one they all craned their heads to see, the one they all murmured over in awe. A pet of *The New York Times* itself, judging from the amount of print it now and again bestowed on him.

An especially bitter pill for that viperish cheapskate Veszto to swallow every time it happened. Viperish in his insults, calculatingly cheap in the way he had wrathfully stalked out of the dining room overlooking his bill for lunch—what a convenient oversight—thus sticking Halas with the bill.

"Sick with envy," Halas told his wise and wonderful Klara that evening, recounting the tale of the stormy lunch. "But this time he was at his absolute worst. Do you know what he had the temerity to say to my face?"

"What?" asked Klara, who, after thirty years of marriage to her adored Janos, was well rehearsed in her lines.

"That my opinion on any subject is irrelevant, because I am not a scientist but a fantasist. Because linguistics is not a science but only a stewpot of unverifiable theories."

"And then?"

"And then I pointed out to him that my flawless mastery of

two dozen languages certainly suggested more than a talent for cooking up unverifiable theories and he said yes, it did suggest I might do very well teaching at Berlitz."

"And all this because of the graffiti?" said Klara.

"Because I didn't sympathize with him in his agony over that miserable automobile. You should have heard him carry on about the horrors of this city. Obviously, it is an abomination operated only for the benefit of *Lumpenproletariat* who go around marking up people's Buicks. So much for the most magnificent metropolis ever conceived by flawed humanity. In my judgment, a real worm's-eye view of it."

"And naturally you presented this judgment to him."

"Naturally."

Klara sighed. "Janos, why do you sit with him at lunch? There are other tables in that dining room, aren't there?"

"Why?" said Halas. "But, darling, Bela Veszto is my oldest friend. You know we played together in the streets of Budapest as children. That he was my schoolmate in the university at Prague. And if he's envious of me to the point of sometimes being insulting—"

"Yes?"

"Well, I can't be small-minded. I understand his feelings, and I forgive him for them."

No need to mention then and there that Veszto would have to suffer a little for venting those feelings so nastily. Would have to be stirred up a little by some mischievous baiting before the sun had set again.

So Halas was in a benignly mischievous mood when he left the house next morning to walk the mile downtown to the university. The October weather was crisp and clear; nowhere in the world was there more satisfying, more inspiring weather than this marvelous city offered during autumn. And the street itself made a pleasant prospect, a tree-shaded street in the East Thirties—the Murray Hill section—with facing rows of handsome old brownstones and graystones. The Halas residence was a four-storied graystone, one of the perquisites the grateful university, its owner, had provided at a nominal rental, and it offered all that could be desired for civilized living.

Which, come to think of it, was something that dried-up Veszto refused to appreciate. The joy of strolling among the endless variety of humanity in these streets. Of savoring the theaters, the concert halls, the museums and galleries, the exotic restaurants laid on in such profusion for the truly civilized. All wasted on a Veszto who fled the city in panic at every opportunity to take solitary refuge in his rustic hideout in Connecticut where he could sit and watch the grass grow. A scientist? A monk who had found the wrong vocation, that's what he was.

Well, that misplaced monk would have an interesting time of it at lunch today.

Graffiti, of all things. How the devil could anyone get so emotional about it?

Halas, about to cross the street, stopped short. Then he changed course and headed for the subway station on Park Avenue.

He let a couple of trains go by while he strolled the length of the platform studying the marker-pen and spray-can work adorning its walls. He missed another, so caught up was he by his examination of its gaudily spray-painted exterior as it unloaded and loaded passengers. Interesting. Really interesting. As any subject was when one put his mind to it. And the interior of the car he finally did enter was most rewarding of all, its walls, ceilings, even windows so thick with glossy black, illegible marker-pen messages that it made for an almost dizzying effect.

Dizzying. And inspiring.

In his office, at ease behind his desk, Halas considered how best to apply this inspiration to the forthcoming lunch. Across the room, Mrs. Gerard, his appointed secretary, attended to his mail, which arrived each morning by the bushel. It was her job to answer whatever of it she could and to then deliver the remainder to Klara who, in her study next to his on the third floor of the graystone, not only dealt with it, but copyread his manuscripts, saw to his accounts, arranged his travel itineraries, and kept house, contracting for whatever help was needed. The perfect wife. Not that she would altogether approve the entertainment he planned for Veszto. She had this unfortunate instinct for peacemaking. And if, God forbid, that instinct ever became prevalent among mankind, what a dreary world this would be.

At lunchtime, Halas delayed his arrival in the dining room so that Veszto would already be at the table and in no position to avoid unwanted company. Sure enough, there was Veszto well into his bargain-basement entrée—he always ordered the lowest-priced item on the menu—and, happy sight, there was Weissenfels of the psychology department deep in conversation with him. For all his many honors, Weissenfels remained *echt* Viennese, a roly-poly little man with deceptively innocent eyes behind those thick glasses and with a fondness for a good joke. His presence here and now, Halas felt, could only have been provided by a kindly and approving heaven.

Weissenfels greeted Halas warmly. Veszto looked for an instant as if he were ready to pack it in on the spot, but most likely because this would mean a waste of good money he decided to remain where he was, finishing his meal in stony silence. Weissenfels took all this in at a glance and, without actually doing so, gave the impression that he was settling back to enjoy whatever was forthcoming. Unlike dear Klara, Weissenfels had no unhealthy peacemaking instinct.

Halas concentrated on his menu, ordered luxuriously, then turned to Weissenfels. "My old friend Bela and I had a little contretemps yesterday. You see, his car—"

"Yes," said Weissenfels. "He was telling me about the car. And the contretemps."

"Then will you kindly inform him now that I regret the episode? That I apologize for what I had to say and the way I said it?"

Weissenfels looked disappointed that the curtain was apparently coming down before the action on stage had even warmed up. He said to Veszto, "You heard that, of course?"

"Heard it," said Veszto coldly, "and don't believe a word of it."

"In that case," Halas told him, "I withdraw the apology."

Veszto's lip curled. "That's more like it."

"At the same time, Bela," Halas said with intense sincerity, "get it into that thick head that I am truly grateful to you. Yesterday, without intending to, you led me to an absolute revelation. One of the most amazing insights into linguistics that anyone has ever known. And no matter what you think of it, linguistics does happen to be my discipline, my life's work, my *raison d'être.*"

Veszto frowned. "What the devil are you talking about?"

"What do you think?" Halas said impatiently. "Graffiti, my friend. Graffiti. The subject you got into such a sweat about yesterday."

"Ah, yes. Your favorite art form."

"Art? Art has nothing to do with it, Bela. Those spray-can decorations I've been examining are an offense to the eye."

Veszto raised an eyebrow. "Oh?"

"I acknowledge it. Idiot swoops and swirls in the most atrocious colors. Infantile, electronic-age Art Nouveau. Pathetic."

Weissenfels regarded Halas with honest curiosity. "You mean you've been studying graffiti? Seriously?"

Halas turned to him and gave him a broad and meaningful wink. "Very seriously, Doctor. Last evening and this morning. In subway cars."

Weissenfels caught on at once. He managed to conceal a smile. "That's the place for it," he said.

"It is. And let us dismiss that spray-can foolishness. Forget it. But"—Halas held up a commanding forefinger—"in the marker-pen script we have a different story. A most meaningful and exciting one."

Weissenfels, definitely sent by heaven, put on an expression of intense interest. Veszto glowered.

"Script?" he snarled. "You call those scrawls by some slobbering vandal a script?"

"Yes, Bela. And the marvelous discovery I made by close examination—the discovery I owe to you—is that this script appears to be the simulation of a written language. Try to read it, and you find you can't. Those dashing loops and lines seem meaningless."

Veszto snorted. "And have you considered," he demanded scathingly, "that this is because they are the hopeless efforts of illiterates to shape letters they can vaguely recognize but cannot duplicate?"

"That was my original hypothesis, Bela. It doesn't hold water."

"Nonsense."

"Bela," Halas said in a tone of stern reproof, "keep in mind that you're in my province now. My department. I don't give you lessons in physics. Please do not give me lessons in linguistics."

"I see. And graffiti is now in that department?"

"It well may be. Now try to keep an open mind while I explain." Halas pressed his hand to his chest. "Will you do me that small favor?"

Veszto shrugged broadly. "Sure. Go right ahead, maestro. Consider my mind wide open." He returned to the chicken leg on his plate, carefully prying off the last bits of meat from it with his knife.

Halas leaned forward and lowered his voice. "Very well, now listen carefully. Those apparently meaningless scrawls are not meaningless. I traveled a considerable distance back and forth examining samples of them closely. It suddenly struck me, Bela—a veritable thunderclap—that I was looking at a fine and flowing calligraphy, highly sophisticated, with breaks and rhythms indicating that what we had here was an authentic language."

Veszto's fork, on its way to his mouth, remained poised in the air. "A language? What language?"

The waitress brought Halas his soup and Weissenfels his coffee. Halas dipped into the soup, grateful for the chance to recharge imagination. A fantasist, was he? All right, Bela, let's see just how good a fantasist. He shook his head at Veszto. "At this point, my dear Bela, a language unknown to me. Incomprehensible to me."

"Oh? Well, in that case, my dear Janos—"

"No, no. Think, Bela, think. No matter how incomprehensible a script may be to you—Chinese, Arabic, Cyrillic, whatever—when you see it you know it represents a language, don't you?"

"Well—"

"For that matter, if you, as a superb physicist, are faced by some mathematical formula which uses totally unfamiliar symbols, you would still know at once that this is a mathematical formula. Admit it."

"Well, yes," Veszto said unwillingly, "but—" and then seemed lost in troubled thought. Ready to sound the retreat, Halas surmised. Beautiful. The danger now was that Weissenfels, his round face unnaturally scarlet, was obviously struggling against open laughter. Halas narrowed his eyes at him warningly and returned to the shaken Veszto.

"Those graffiti are a language, Bela. In fact, tomorrow I am taking my camera into the subway—"

"Wait, Janos. A language? A sophisticated calligraphy? Produced by juvenile delinquents?"

"Of course not. I told you to forget that element with their spray-cans of disgusting colors. I am talking about a different element entirely. One capable of writing those lines of script. Of communicating with each other through those lines." He shrugged regretfully. "One would like to think that those are passages of magnificent poetry, but that would be, well, an indulgence in fantasy. No, I must accept the cold reality that those are probably messages."

"Messages," Veszto echoed.

"Yes, Bela. And unpleasant messages at that. You know how often you've catalogued for me the disasters that afflict this city. Those wildfires devastating whole blocks. Floodwaters suddenly erupting from broken pipes under the pavements. Cornices of buildings suddenly tumbling on people's heads. God knows how many other calamities each day. And my response to you, my dismissal of all this, was wrong, Bela. Unjust. Unscientific. Because of the evidence now in hand convinces me that these endless disasters are no accidents."

"The evidence." Veszto squinted at Halas's solemn face. "Those lines of graffiti?"

"Exactly. Messages, plans, instructions exchanged by an invisible force among us conspiring to destroy this city by first destroying its population's morale. Agents of some galactic power out there whose designated prey we are. You see, Bela—"

Weissenfels could contain himself no longer. He sputtered helplessly, choking with laughter, pounding a fist on the table. Veszto gaped at him, then suddenly released from the spell, he glared at Halas. "Buffoon!"

"Now, Bela—"

"*Szamár!*" snarled Veszto, his face drained of all color. "*Disznó!*"

He stood up so violently that his chair almost went over backwards. Every face in the dining room turned his way as he plunged through the door. Then, as Halas glanced around, eyebrows raised, all faces politely turned away. And, Halas saw, there on the table was Veszto's lunch bill. So he had gotten away with it again, bad temper evidently becoming a profitable way of life. Halas picked up the bill, but Weissenfels, now under fair control, plucked it from his hand.

"No, I insist," Weissenfels said. He wiped the tears of mirth from his eyes. "I owe you this much at least for the entertainment. But you know, of course, that you really are a monster."

"Am I? Well, answer this question, Doctor. Did our friend ever inform you that your discipline—the field of psychology—was nonsense? That you yourself were no scientist at all but a spinner of fantastic and unprovable theories?"

"As a matter of fact, yes. But since he also charged Freud, Jung, and Adler with the same sin, I couldn't be too offended."

"Very generous of you."

"And very politic. After all, I work with him on the Faculty Coordinating Committee, and he could make life there difficult. Which," said Weissenfels, "reminds me that the committee meets tomorrow morning. I have a feeling a little soothing syrup in advance is prescribed. Too bad. I'd love to tell this story around, but he'd be let to know at once who it came from." Weissenfels shook his head in wonder. "Oh, Lord. Invisible invaders from outer space. Astral linguistics. And the way he sat there with his mouth open—"

"Being spoonfed the fantasy he so detests—"

"Yes, indeed. Of course," said Weissenfels, straight-faced, " I can only hope it is fantasy, Doctor. Otherwise, you must realize the dreadful danger you're in. I mean, once those invaders know you're onto their precious secret—"

"And shared it with you and our humorless colleague—"

"True. That makes three of us. Well, I suppose all we can do is bear up bravely under the strain."

"I'm sure we'll manage to," said Halas.

That evening, despite a powerful temptation to do so, he refrained from telling dear Klara about his triumph. He had the feeling that this time—especially since an outsider had witnessed the scene—he might have gone a bit too far in his teasing, and if he had that feeling Klara would have it even more acutely. She, angelic but deluded creature, somehow managed to find Bela Veszto pathetic. So next thing—it had happened before—there might be a surprise dinner party announced, a large and extravagant peacemaking dinner party, at which Doctor Bela Veszto would turn up as one of the guests and would sit there stuffing himself with expensive viands and treating his host, who had paid for them, with icy indifference.

And yet, what good friend had advised Veszto not to park that car on the streets overnight but to rent space in a garage, never mind the expense? Naturally, none other than the foresighted Janos Halas.

And how had Veszto responded to this wisdom? "But how generous you are with other people's money, aren't you, Halas?"

The devil with him. This time there would be no peacemaking dinner party, because Klara was not going to be given any reason for one.

Case closed.

So when Klara, with unclouded brow and affectionate good humor, woke him next morning he felt distinctly pleased with himself that he had not confided in her, had exercised an almost noble self-restraint. And, thought Halas, since there's no sense depending on virtue to be its own reward, he'd make sure of that reward tonight by taking himself and Klara to a supremely good restaurant for dinner and then to a show. Something frivolous.

Altogether a promising day. The weather was again crisp and clear, the seminar scheduled for the afternoon would bring around the table a dozen of his most fervent acolytes—including two of the prettiest graduate students in the university—and then would come that gormandizing dinner and a lighthearted entertainment. Altogether promising.

Until, after bidding dear Klara a loving farewell, he stepped through the outside door of the house and closed it behind him.

Graffiti.

Disgusting glossy black scrawls made by marker-pen fouling the stone wall beside the door. Several feet of that hitherto pristine gray wall—a lovely soft-toned Wedgwood gray—defaced by those loops and lines and cross-strokes. Halas backed up to get the whole view, and indeed the further he backed up, the more horrid the view. He took notice that people walking by glanced at it with distaste. An aristocratic-looking woman with a small aristocratic-looking dog on a leash slowed down to shake her head at the sight. It was that kind of block, after all.

Halas looked up and down the street. As far as he could see, it was still that kind of block, no trace of any such vandalism marring any other building in sight. Only this one. As if the home of Doctor Janos Halas had been singled out for desecration by some drooling delinquent.

Singled out?

But, of course, thought Halas, stunned by sudden enlightenment. And if he had gone a little too far in his teasing of Veszto, well, dear Bela had gone the whole distance in this vindictive and sophomoric response. On the other hand, it did make a comic picture: a man of Veszto's years and academic stature prowling around in the dark hours to filthy this wall. And probably foaming at the mouth with rage as he did so.

And the sweetest revenge now, Halas told himself, would be to react as Veszto would never expect him to. Overlook all this. Be blind to it. The wall should be promptly cleaned—it was just a matter of phoning Mrs. Gerard, the faithful secretary, to have the university put a maintenance man on it—and then, when meeting Veszto, to wear a bland and untroubled face. Make no complaint, no accusation, don't mention this business at all, it never happened. While all Veszto could do was grind his teeth in frustration.

Dear Bela. Some people never learned not to play games with really clever opponents.

Halas walked back into the house, and from high above Klara called, "Janos? Did you forget something?"

"Just a phone call, darling."

Not bothering to take off hat or coat, Halas used the phone in the hallway near the foot of the staircase. Mrs. Gerard, who was rarely made breathless by anything, answered his greeting breathlessly.

"Yes, Doctor. I was expecting you'd call as soon as you heard. Isn't it awful? I was just talking to Doctor Weissenfels's assistant, and he practically—"

"Mrs. Gerard!"

"Yes, Doctor?"

"What the devil is this all about?"

"Then you don't know? Oh, it's awful. It seems that last night Doctor Weissenfels got together with Doctor Veszto for a drink at some café near where Doctor Veszto lives. I mean, lived."

"Lived?"

"Yes. Because there was this terrible explosion—the police think it was a gas leak in the kitchen there—and they were both killed. Some other people were hurt, but they were killed. Both of them."

"Veszto and Weissenfels are dead?"

"Isn't it horrible? It was on the television news this morning. And Doctor Weissenfels's assistant was just telling me all—Doctor? Are you there, Doctor Halas?"

Halas put down the phone. His heart was hammering furiously, a cold sweat was enveloping him. So it wasn't poor Bela coming around to do mischief in the dark. How stupid, how unkind, to even suspect it might have been.

But Bela had been at that lunch table yesterday. And Weissenfels. How Weissenfels had laughed. How quickly both of them had been wiped out just like that. And Janos Halas, the third one at that table? Given a few hours dispensation? Thank God at least that he hadn't repeated to Klara one word of the story he had told at the table. Otherwise, she could would walk out of the house on her way to do her shopping and suddenly—

What is this, Halas asked himself in astonishment. He pulled out his handkerchief and mopped his dripping forehead. Grotesque, the direction his thoughts were taking. Next thing he'd be reporting flying saucers to the police. All because of a thundering coincidence.

So he had told that story to Bela and Weissenfels. So, poor souls, they had suddenly died in an accident, the kind that could happen to anyone. A coincidence.

To believe for even one instant that invisible and malevolent beings were closing in because he had given their secret away was ridiculous.

But those fresh graffiti marking that wall outside?

"A coincidence!" Halas cried out, and when Klara called down, "What is it, dear?" he shouted back angrily, "It's nothing! Nothing at all! Absolutely nothing!"

Passionately shouting it out, he knew, like an exorcism.

MEFISTO IN ONYX

Harlan Ellison

ONCE. I ONLY went to bed with her once. Friends for eleven years—before and since—but it was just one of those things, just one of those crazy flings: the two of us alone on a New Year's Eve, watching rented Marx Brothers videos so we wouldn't have to go out with a bunch of idiots and make noise and pretend we were having a good time when all we'd be doing was getting drunk, whooping like morons, vomiting on slow-moving strangers, and spending more money than we had to waste. And we drank a little too much cheap champagne; and we fell off the sofa laughing at Harpo a few times too many; and we wound up on the floor at the same time; and next thing we knew we had our faces plastered together, and my hand up her skirt, and her hand down in my pants . . .

But it was just the *once*, fer chrissakes! Talk about imposing on a cheap sexual liaison! She *knew* I went mixing in other peoples' minds only when I absolutely had no other way to make a buck. Or I forgot myself and did it in a moment of human weakness.

It was always foul.

Slip into the thoughts of the best person who ever lived, even Saint Thomas Aquinas, for instance, just to pick an absolutely terrific person you'd think had a mind so clean you could eat off it (to paraphrase my mother), and when you come out—take my word for it—you'd want to take a long, intense shower in Lysol.

Trust me on this: I go into somebody's landscape when there's *nothing else* I can do, no other possible solution . . . or I forget and do it in a moment of human weakness. Such as, say, the IRS holds my feet to the fire; or I'm about to get myself mugged and robbed and maybe murdered; or I need to find out if some specific she that I'm dating has been using somebody else's dirty needle or has been sleeping around without she's taking some extra-heavy-duty AIDS precautions; or a co-worker's got it in his head to set me up so I make a mistake and look bad to the boss and I find myself in the unemployment line again; or . . .

I'm a wreck for weeks after.

Go jaunting through a landscape trying to pick up a little insider arbitrage bric-a-brac, and come away no better heeled, but all muddy with the guy's infidelities, and I can't look a decent woman in the eye for days. Get told by a motel desk clerk that they're all full up and he's sorry as hell but I'll just have to drive on for about another thirty miles to find the next vacancy, jaunt into his landscape and find him lit up with neon signs that got a lot of the word *nigger* in them, and I wind up hitting the sonofabitch so hard his grandmother has a bloody nose, and usually have to hide out for three or four weeks after. Just about to miss a bus, jaunt into the head of the driver to find his name so I can yell for him to hold it a minute Tom or George or Willie, and I get smacked in the mind with all the garlic he's been eating for the past month because his doctor told him it was good for his system, and I start to dry-heave, and I wrench out of the landscape, and not only have I missed the bus, but I'm so sick to my stomach I have to sit down on the filthy curb to get my gorge submerged. Jaunt into a potential employer, to see if he's trying to lowball me, and I learn he's part of a massive cover-up of industrial malfeasance that's caused hundreds of people to die when this or that cheaply-made grommet or tappet or gimbal mounting underperforms and fails, sending the poor souls falling thousands of feet to shrieking destruction. Then just *try* to accept the job, even if you haven't paid your rent in a month. No way.

Absolutely: I listen in on the landscape *only* when my feet are being fried; when the shadow stalking me turns down alley after alley tracking me relentlessly; when the drywall guy I've hired to repair the damage done by my leaky shower presents me with a dopey smile and a bill three hundred and sixty bucks higher than the estimate. Or in a moment of human weakness.

But I'm a wreck for weeks after. For weeks.

Because you can't, you simply can't, you absolutely *cannot* know what people are truly and really like till you jaunt their landscape. If Aquinas had had my ability, he'd have very quickly gone off to be a hermit, only occasionally visiting the mind of a sheep or a hedgehog. In a moment of human weakness.

That's why in my whole life—and, as best I can remember back, I've been doing it since I was five or six years old, maybe even younger—there have only been eleven, maybe twelve people, of all those who know that I can "read minds," that I've permitted myself to get close to. Three of them never used it against me, or tried to exploit me, or tried to kill me when I wasn't looking. Two of those three were my mother and father, a pair of sweet old black folks who'd adopted me, a late-in-life baby, and were now dead (but probably still worried about me, even on the Other Side), and whom I missed very very much, particularly in moments like this. The other eight, nine were either so turned off by the knowledge that they made sure I never came within a mile of them—one moved to another entire country just to be on the safe side, although her thoughts were a helluva lot more boring and innocent than she thought they were—or they tried to brain me with something heavy when I was distracted—I still have a shoulder separation that kills me for two days before it rains—or they tried to use me to make a buck for them. Not having the common sense to figure it out, that if I was *capable* of using the ability to make vast sums of money, why the hell was I living hand-to-mouth like some over-aged grad student who was afraid to desert the university and go become an adult?

Now *they* was some dumb-ass muthuhfugguhs.

Of the three who never used it against me, my mom and dad, the last was Allison Roche. Who sat on the stool next to me, in the middle of May, in the middle of a Wednesday afternoon, in the middle of Clanton, Alabama, squeezing ketchup onto her All-American Burger, imposing on the memory of that one damned New Year's Eve sexual interlude, with Harpo and his sibs; the two of us all alone except for the fry-cook; and she waited for my reply.

"I'd sooner have a skunk spray my pants leg," I replied.

She pulled a napkin from the chrome dispenser and swabbed up the red that had overshot the sesame-seed bun and redecorated the Formica countertop. She looked at me from under thick, lustrous eyelashes; a look of impatience and violet eyes that must have been a killer when she unbottled it at some truculent witness for the defense. Allison Roche was a Chief Deputy District Attorney in and for Jefferson County, with her office in Birmingham. Alabama. Where near we sat, in Clanton, having a secret meeting, having All-American Burgers; three years after having had quite a bit of champagne, 1930s black-and-white video rental comedy, and black-and-white sex. One extremely stupid New Year's Eve.

Friends for eleven years. And once, just once; as a prime example of what happens in a moment of human weakness. Which is not to say that it wasn't terrific, because it was; absolutely terrific; but we never did it again; and we never brought it up again after the next morning when we opened our eyes and looked at each other the way you look at an exploding can of sardines, and both of us said *Oh Jeeezus* at the same time. Never brought it up again until this memorable afternoon at the greasy spoon where I'd joined Ally, driving up from Montgomery to meet her halfway, after her peculiar telephone invitation.

Can't say the fry-cook, Mr. All-American, was particularly happy at the pigmentation arrangement at his counter. But I stayed out of his head and let him think what he wanted. Times change on the outside, but the inner landscape remains polluted.

"All I'm asking you to do is go have a chat with him," she said. She gave me that look. I have a hard time with that look. It isn't entirely honest, neither is it entirely disingenuous. It plays on my remembrance of that one night we spent in bed. And is just *dis*honest enough to play on the part of that night we spent on the floor, on the sofa, on the coffee counter between the dining room and the kitchenette, in the bathtub, and about nineteen minutes crammed among her endless pairs of shoes in a walk-in clothes closet that smelled strongly of cedar and virginity. She gave me that look, and wasted no part of the memory.

"I don't *want* to go have a chat with him. Apart from he's a piece of human shit, and I have better things to do with my time than to go on down to Atmore and take a jaunt through this crazy sonofabitch's diseased mind, may I remind you that of the hundred and sixty, seventy men who have died in that electric chair, including the original 'Yellow Mama' they scrapped in 1990, about a hundred and thirty of them were gentlemen of color, and I do not mean you to picture any color of a shade much lighter than that cuppa coffee you got sittin' by your left hand right this minute, which is to say that I, being an inordinately well-educated African-American who values the full measure of living negritude in his body, am not crazy enough to want to visit a racist '*co*-rectional center' like Holman Prison, thank you very much."

"Are you finished?" she asked, wiping her mouth.

"Yeah. I'm finished. Case closed. Find somebody else."

She didn't like that. "There *isn't* anybody else."

"There has to be. Somewhere. Go check the research files at Duke University. Call the Fortean Society. Mensa. *Jeopardy*. Some 900 number astrology psychic hotline. Ain't there some semi-senile Senator with a full-time paid assistant who's been trying to get legislation through one of the statehouses for the last five years to fund this kind of bullshit research? What about the Russians . . . now that the Evil Empire's fallen, you ought to be able to get some word about their success with Kirlian auras or whatever those assholes were working at. Or you could—"

She screamed at the top of her lungs. *"Stop it, Rudy!"*

The fry-cook dropped the spatula he'd been using to scrape off the grill. He picked it up, looking at us, and his face (I didn't read his mind) said *If that white bitch makes one more noise I'm callin' the cops.*

I gave him a look he didn't want, and he went back to his chores, getting ready for the after-work crowd. But the stretch of his back and angle of his head told me he wasn't going to let this pass.

I leaned in toward her, got as serious as I could, and just this quietly, just this softly, I said, "Ally, good pal, listen to me. You've been one of the few friends I could count on, for a long time now. We have history between us, and you've *never,* not once, made me feel like a freak. So okay, I trust you. I trust you with something about me that causes immeasurable goddam pain. A thing about me that could get me killed. You've never betrayed me, and you've never tried to use me.

"Till now. This is the first time. And you've got to admit that it's not even as rational as you maybe saying to me that you've gambled away every cent you've got and you owe the mob a million bucks and would I mind taking a trip to Vegas or Atlantic City and taking a jaunt into the minds of some high-pocket poker players so I could win you enough to keep the goons from shooting you. Even *that*, as creepy as it would be if you said it to me, even *that* would be easier to understand than *this*!"

She looked forlorn. "There isn't anybody else, Rudy. *Please*."

"What the hell is this all about? Come on, tell me. You're hiding something, or holding something back, or lying about—"

"I'm not lying!" For the second time she was suddenly, totally, extremely pissed at me. Her voice spattered off the white tile walls. The fry-cook spun around at the sound, took a step toward us, and I jaunted into his landscape, smoothed down the rippled Astro-Turf, drained away the storm clouds, and sug-

gested in there that he go take a cigarette break out back. Fortunately, there were no other patrons at the elegant All-American Burger that late in the afternoon, and he went.

"Calm fer chrissakes down, will you?" I said.

She had squeezed the paper napkin into a ball.

She was lying, hiding, holding something back. Didn't have to be a telepath to figure *that* out. I waited, looking at her with a slow, careful distrust, and finally she sighed, and I thought, *Here it comes.*

"Are you reading my mind?" she asked.

"Don't insult me. We know each other too long."

She looked chagrined. The violet of her eyes deepened. "Sorry."

But she didn't go on. I wasn't going to be outflanked. I waited.

After a while she said, softly, very softly, "I think I'm in love with him. I *know* I believe him when he says he's innocent."

I never expected that. I couldn't even reply.

It was unbelievable. Unfuckingbelievable. She was the Chief Deputy D.A. who had prosecuted Henry Lake Spanning for murder. Not just one murder, one random slaying, a heat of the moment Saturday night killing regretted deeply on Sunday morning but punishable by electrocution in the Sovereign State of Alabama nonetheless, but a string of the vilest, most sickening serial slaughters in Alabama history, in the history of the Glorious South, in the history of the United States. Maybe even in the history of the entire wretched human universe that went wading hip-deep in the wasted spilled blood of innocent men, women and children.

Henry Lake Spanning was a monster, an ambulatory disease, a killing machine without conscience or any discernible resemblance to a thing we might call decently human. Henry Lake Spanning had butchered his way across a half-dozen states; and they had caught up to him in Huntsville, in a garbage dumpster behind a supermarket, doing something so vile and inhuman to what was left of a sixty-five-year-old cleaning woman that not even the tabloids would get more explicit than *unspeakable;* and somehow he got away from the cops; and somehow he evaded their dragnet; and somehow he found out where the police lieutenant in charge of the manhunt lived; and somehow he slipped into that neighborhood when the lieutenant was out creating roadblocks—and he gutted the man's wife and two kids. Also the family cat. And then he killed a couple of more times in Birmingham and Decatur, and by then had gone so completely out of his mind that they got him again, and the second time they hung onto him, and they brought him to trial. And Ally had prosecuted this bottom-feeding monstrosity.

And oh, what a circus it had been. Though he'd been *caught*, the second time, and this time for keeps, in Jefferson County, scene of three of his most sickening jobs, he'd murdered (with such a disgustingly similar m.o. that it was obvious he was the perp) in twenty-two of the sixty-seven counties; and every last one of them wanted him to stand trial in that venue. Then there were the other five states in which he had butchered, to a total body-count of fifty-six. Each of *them* wanted him extradited.

So, here's how smart and quick and smooth an attorney Ally is: she somehow managed to coze up to the Attorney General, and somehow managed to unleash those violet eyes on him, and somehow managed to get and keep his ear long enough to con him into setting a legal precedent. Attorney General of the state of Alabama allowed Allison Roche to consolidate, to secure a multiple bill of indictment that forced Spanning to stand trial on all twenty-nine Alabama murder counts at once. She meticulously documented to the state's highest courts that Henry Lake Spanning presented such a clear and present danger to society that the prosecution was willing to take a chance (big chance!) of trying in a winner-take-all consolidation of venues. Then she managed to smooth the feathers of all those other vote-hungry prosecutors in those twenty-one other counties, and she put on a case that dazzled everyone, including Spanning's defense attorney, who had screamed about the legality of the multiple bill from the moment she'd suggested it.

And she won a fast jury verdict on all twenty-nine counts.

Then she got *really* fancy in the penalty phase after the jury verdict, and proved up the *other* twenty-seven murders with their flagrantly identical trademarks, from those other five states, and there was nothing left but to sentence Spanning—essentially for all fifty-six—to the replacement for the "Yellow Mama."

Even as pols and power brokers throughout the state were murmuring Ally's name for higher office, Spanning was slated to sit in that new electric chair in Holman Prison, built by the Fred A. Leuchter Associates of Boston, Massachusetts, that delivers 2,640 volts of pure sparklin' death in 1/240th of a second, six times faster than the 1/40th of a second that it takes for the brain to sense it, which is—if you ask me—much too humane an exit line, more than three times the 700 volt jolt lethal dose that destroys a brain, for a pus-bag like Henry Lake Spanning.

But if we were lucky—and the scheduled day of departure was very nearly upon us—if we were lucky, if there was a God and Justice and Natural Order and all that good stuff, then Henry Lake Spanning, this foulness, this corruption, this thing that lived only to ruin . . . would end up as a pile of fucking ashes somebody might use to sprinkle over a flower garden, thereby providing this ghoul with his single opportunity to be of some use to the human race.

That was the guy that my pal Allison Roche wanted me to go and "chat" with, down to Holman Prison, in Atmore, Alabama. There, sitting on Death Row, waiting to get his demented head tonsured, his pants legs slit, his tongue fried black as the inside of a sheep's belly . . . down there at Holman my pal Allison wanted me to go "chat" with one of the most awful creatures made for killing this side of a hammerhead shark, which creature had an infinitely greater measure of human decency than Henry Lake Spanning had ever demonstrated. Go chit-chat, and enter his landscape, and read his mind, Mr. Telepath, and use the marvelous mythic power of extra-sensory perception: this nifty swell ability that has made me a bum all my life, well, not *exactly* a bum: I do have a decent apartment, and I do earn a decent, if sporadic, living; and I try to follow Nelson Algren's warning never to get involved with a woman whose troubles are bigger than my own; and sometimes I even have a car of my own, even though at that moment such was not the case, the Camaro having been repo'd, and not by Harry Dean Stanton or Emilio Estevez, lemme tell you; but a bum in the sense of—how does Ally put it?—oh yeah—I don't "realize my full and forceful potential"—a bum in the sense that I can't hold a job, and I get rotten breaks, and all of this despite a Rhodes scholarly education so far above what a poor nigrah-lad such as myself could expect that even Rhodes hisownself would've been chest-out proud as hell of me. A bum, mostly, despite an *outstanding* Rhodes scholar education and a pair of kind, smart, loving parents—even for foster-parents—shit, *especially* for being foster-parents—who died knowing the certain sadness that their only child would spend his life as a wandering freak unable to make a comfortable living or consummate a normal marriage or raise children without the fear of passing on this special personal horror . . . this astonishing ability fabled in song and story that I possess . . . that no one else seems to possess, though I know there must have been others, somewhere, sometime, somehow! Go, Mr. Wonder of Wonders, shining black Cagliostro of the modern world, go with this super nifty swell ability that gullible idiots and flying saucer assholes have been trying to prove exists for at least fifty years, that no one has been able to isolate the way I, me, the only one has been isolated, let me tell you about *isolation*, my brothers; and here I was, here was I, Rudy Pairis . . . just a guy, making a buck every now and then with nifty swell impossible ESP, resident of thirteen states and twice that many cities so far in his mere thirty years of landscape-jaunting life, here was I, Rudy Pairis, Mr. I-Can-Read-Your-Mind, being asked to go and walk through the mind of a killer who scared half the people in the world. Being asked by the only living person, probably, to whom I could not say no. And, oh, take me at my word here: I *wanted* to say no. *Was*, in fact, saying no at every breath. What's that? Will I do it? Sure, yeah sure, I'll go on down to Holman and jaunt through this sick bastard's mind landscape. Sure I will. You got two chances: slim, and none.

All of this was going on in the space of one greasy double cheeseburger and two cups of coffee.

The worst part of it was that Ally had somehow gotten involved with him. *Ally!* Not some bimbo bitch . . . but *Ally*. I couldn't believe it.

Not that it was unusual for women to become mixed up with guys in the joint, to fall under their "magic spell," and to start corresponding with them, visiting them, taking them candy and cigarettes, having conjugal visits, playing mule for them and smuggling in dope where the tampon never shine, writing them letters that got steadily more exotic, steadily more intimate, steamier and increasingly dependant emotionally. It wasn't that big a deal; there exist entire psychiatric treatises on the phenomenon; right alongside the papers about women who go stud-crazy for cops. No big deal indeed: hundreds of women every year find themselves writing to these guys, visiting these guys, building dream castles with these guys, fucking these guys, pretending that even the worst of these guys, rapists and woman-beaters and child molesters, repeat pedophiles of the lowest pustule sort, and murderers and stick-up punks who crush old ladies' skulls for food stamps, and terrorists and bunco barons . . . that one sunny might-be, gonna-happen pink cloud day these demented creeps will emerge from behind the walls, get back in the wind, become upstanding nine-to-five Brooks Bros. Galahads. Every year hundreds of women marry these guys, finding themselves in a hot second snookered by the wily, duplicitous, motherfuckin' lying greaseball addictive behavior of guys who had spent their sporadic years, their intermittent freedom on the outside, doing *just that:* roping people in, ripping people off, bleeding people dry, conning them into being tools, taking them for their every last cent, their happy home, their sanity, their ability to trust or love ever again.

But this wasn't some poor illiterate naive woman-child. This was *Ally*. She had damned near pulled off a legal impossibility, come *that* close to Bizarro Jurisprudence by putting the Attorneys General of five other states in a maybe frame of mind where she'd have been able to consolidate a multiple bill of indictment *across state lines*! Never been done; and now, probably, never ever would be. But she could have possibly pulled off such a thing. Unless you're a stone court-bird, you can't know what a mountaintop that is!

So, now, here's Ally, saying this shit to me. Ally, my best pal, stood up for me a hundred times; not some dip, but the steely-eyed Sheriff of Suicide Gulch, the over-forty, past the age of innocence, no-nonsense woman who had seen it all and come away tough but not cynical, hard but not mean.

"I think I'm in love with him." She had said.

"I *know* I believe him when he says he's innocent." She had said.

I looked at her. No time had passed. It was still the moment the universe decided to lie down and die. And I said, "So if you're certain this paragon of the virtues *isn't* responsible for fifty-six murders—that we *know* about—and who the hell knows how many more we *don't* know about, since he's apparently been at it since he was twelve years old—remember the couple of nights we sat up and you *told* me all this shit about him, and you said it with your skin crawling, *remember*?—then if you're so damned positive the guy you spent eleven weeks in court sending to the chair is innocent of butchering half the population of the planet—then why do you need me to go to Holman, drive all the way to Atmore, just to take a jaunt in this sweet peach of a guy?

"Doesn't your 'woman's intuition' tell you he's squeaky clean? Don't 'true love' walk yo' sweet young ass down the primrose path with sufficient surefootedness?"

"Don't be a smartass!" she said.

"Say again?" I replied, with disfuckingbelief.

"I said: don't be such a high-verbal goddamned smart aleck!"

Now *I* was steamed. "No, I shouldn't be a smartass: I should be your pony, your show dog, your little trick bag mind-reader freak! Take a drive over to Holman, Pairis; go right on into Rednecks from Hell; sit your ass down on Death Row with the rest of the niggers and have a chat with the one white boy who's been in a cell up there for the past three years or so; sit down nicely with the king of the fucking vampires, and slide inside his garbage dump of a brain—and what a joy *that's* gonna be, I can't believe you'd ask me to do this—and read whatever piece of boiled shit in there he calls a brain, and see if he's jerking you around. *That's* what I ought to do, am I correct? Instead of being a smartass. Have I got it right? Do I properly pierce your meaning, pal?"

She stood up. She didn't even say *Screw you, Pairis!*

She just slapped me as hard as she could.

She hit me a good one straight across the mouth.

I felt my upper teeth bite my lower lip. I tasted the blood. My head rang like a church bell. I thought I'd fall off the goddam stool.

When I could focus, she was just standing there, looking ashamed of herself, and disappointed, and mad as hell, and worried that she'd brained me. All of that, all at the same time. Plus, she looked as if I'd broken her choo-choo train.

"Okay," I said wearily, and ended the word with a sigh that reached all the way back into my hip pocket. "Okay, calm down. I'll see him. I'll do it. Take it easy."

She didn't sit down. "Did I hurt you?"

"No, of course not," I said, unable to form the smile I was trying to put on my face. "How could you possibly hurt someone by knocking his brains into his lap?"

She stood over me as I clung precariously to the counter, turned halfway around on the stool by the blow. Stood over me, the balled-up paper napkin in her fist, a look on her face that said she was nobody's fool, that we'd known each other a long time, that she hadn't asked this kind of favor before, that if we were buddies and I loved her, that I would see she was in deep pain, that she was conflicted, that she needed to know, *really* needed to know without a doubt, and in the name of God—in which she believed, though I didn't, but either way what the hell—that I do this thing for her, that I just *do it* and not give her any more crap about it.

So I shrugged, and spread my hands like a man with no place to go, and I said, "How'd you get into this?"

She told me the first fifteen minutes of her tragic, heart-warming, never-to-be-ridiculed story still standing. After fifteen minutes I said, "Fer chrissakes, Ally, at least *sit down*! You look like a damned fool standing there with a greasy napkin in your mitt."

A couple of teen-agers had come in. The four-star chef had finished his cigarette out back and was reassuringly in place, walking the duckboards and dishing up All-American arterial cloggage.

She picked up her elegant attaché case and without a word, with only a nod that said let's get as far from them as we can, she and I moved to a double against the window to resume our discussion of the varieties of social suicide available to an unwary and foolhardy gentleman of the colored persuasion if he allowed himself to be swayed by a cagey and cogent, clever and concupiscent female of another color entirely.

See, what it is, is this:

Look at that attaché case. You want to know what kind of an Ally this Allison Roche is? Pay heed, now.

In New York, when some wannabe junior ad exec has smooched enough butt to get tossed a bone account, and he wants to walk his colors, has a need to signify, has got to demonstrate to everyone that he's got the juice, first thing he does, he hies his ass downtown to Barney's, West 17th and Seventh, buys hisself a Burberry, loops the belt casually *behind*, leaving the coat open to suh-*wing*, and he circumnavigates the office.

In Dallas, when the wife of the CEO has those six or eight upper-management husbands and wives over for an *intime*, *faux*-casual dinner, sans placecards, sans *entrée* fork, *sans cérémonie*, and we're talking the kind of woman who flies Virgin Air instead of the Concorde, she's so in charge she don't got to use the Orrefors, she can put out the Kosta Boda and say *give a fuck*.

What it is, kind of person so in charge, so easy with they own self, they don't *have* to laugh at your poor dumb struttin' Armani suit, or your bedroom done in Laura Ashley, or that you got a gig writing articles for *TV Guide*. You see what I'm sayin' here? The sort of person Ally Roche is, you take a look at that attaché case, and it'll tell you everything you need to know about how strong she is, because it's an Atlas. Not a Hartmann. Understand: she could *afford* a Hartmann, that gorgeous imported Canadian belting leather, top of the line, somewhere around nine hundred and fifty bucks maybe, equivalent of Orrefors, a Burberry, breast of guinea hen and Mouton Rothschild 1492 or 1066 or whatever year is the most expensive, drive a Rolls instead of a Bentley and the only difference is the grille . . . but she doesn't *need* to signify, doesn't *need* to suh-*wing*, so she gets herself this Atlas. Not some dumb chickenshit Louis Vuitton or Mark Cross all the divorcee real estate ladies carry, but an Atlas. Irish hand leather. Custom tanned cowhide. Hand tanned in Ireland by out of work IRA bombers. Very classy. Just a state understated. See that attaché case? That tell you why I said I'd do it?

She picked it up from where she'd stashed it, right up against the counter wall by her feet, and we went to the double over by the window, away from the chef and the teen-agers, and she stared at me till she was sure I was in a right frame of mind, and she picked up where she'd left off.

The next twenty-three minutes by the big greasy clock on the wall she related from a sitting position. Actually, a series of sitting positions. She kept shifting in her chair like someone who didn't appreciate the view of the world from that window, someone hoping for a sweeter horizon. The story started with a gang-rape at the age of thirteen, and moved right along: two broken foster-home families, a little casual fondling by surrogate poppas, intense studying for perfect school grades as a substitute for happiness, working her way through John Jay College of Law, a truncated attempt at wedded bliss in her late twenties, and the long miserable road of legal success that had brought her to Alabama. There could have been worse places.

I'd known Ally for a long time, and we'd spent totals of weeks and months in each other's company. Not to mention the New Year's Eve of the Marx Brothers. But I hadn't heard much of this. Not much at all.

Funny how that goes. Eleven years. You'd think I'd've guessed or suspected or *some*thing. What the hell makes us think we're friends with *any*body, when we don't know the first thing about them, not really?

What are we, walking around in a dream? That is to say: what the fuck are we *thinking*!?!

And there might never have been a reason to hear *any* of it, all this Ally that was the real Ally, but now she was asking me to go somewhere I didn't want to go, to do something that scared the shit out of me; and she wanted me to be as fully informed as possible.

It dawned on me that those same eleven years between us hadn't really given her a full, laser-clean insight into the why and wherefore of Rudy Pairis, either. I hated myself for it. The concealing, the holding-back, the giving up only fragments, the evil misuse of charm when honesty would have hurt. I was facile, and a very quick study; and I had buried all the equivalents to Ally's pains and travails. I could've matched her, in spades; or blacks, or just plain nigras. But I remained frightened of losing her friendship. I've never been able to believe in the myth of unqualified friendship. Too much like standing hiphigh in a fast-running, freezing river. Standing on slippery stones.

Her story came forward to the point at which she had prosecuted Spanning; had amassed and winnowed and categorized the evidence so thoroughly, so deliberately, so flawlessly; had orchestrated the case so brilliantly; that the jury had come in with guilty on all twenty-nine, soon—in the penalty phase—fifty-six. Murder in the first. Premeditated murder in the first. Premeditated murder with special ugly circumstances in the first. On each and every of the twenty-nine. Less than an hour it took them. There wasn't even time for a lunch break. Fifty-one minutes it took them to come back with the verdict guilty on all charges. Less than a minute per killing. Ally had done that.

His attorney had argued that no direct link had been established between the fifty-sixth killing (actually, only his 29th in Alabama) and Henry Lake Spanning. No, they had not caught him down on his knees eviscerating the shredded body of his final victim—ten-year-old Gunilla Ascher, a parochial school girl who had missed her bus and been picked up by Spanning just about a mile from her home in Decatur—no, not down on his knees with the can opener still in his sticky red hands, but the m.o. was the same, and he was there in Decatur, on the run from what he had done in Huntsville, what they had *caught* him doing in Huntsville, in that dumpster, to that old woman. So they *couldn't* place him with his smooth, slim hands inside dead Gunilla Ascher's still-steaming body. So what? They could not have been surer he was the serial killer, the monster, the ravaging nightmare whose methods were so vile the newspapers hadn't even *tried* to cobble up some smart-aleck name for him like The Strangler or The Backyard Butcher. The jury had come back in fifty-one minutes, looking sick, looking as if they'd try and try to get everything they'd seen and heard out of their minds, but knew they never would, and wishing to God they could've managed to get out of their civic duty on this one.

They came shuffling back in and told the numbed court: hey, put this slimy excuse for a maggot in the chair and cook his ass till he's fit only to be served for breakfast on cinnamon toast. This was the guy my friend Ally told me she had fallen in love with. The guy she now believed to be innocent.

This was seriously crazy stuff.

"So how did you get, er, uh, how did you . . . ?"

"How did I fall in love with him?"

"Yeah. That."

She closed her eyes for a moment, and pursed her lips as if she had lost a flock of wayward words and didn't know where to find them. I'd always known she was a private person, kept the really important history to herself—hell, until now I'd never known about the rape, the ice mountain between her mother and father, the specifics of the seven-month marriage—I'd known there'd been a husband briefly; but not what had happened; and I'd known about the foster homes; but again, not how lousy it had been for her—even so, getting *this* slice of steaming craziness out of her was like using your teeth to pry the spikes out of Jesus's wrists.

Finally, she said, "I took over the case when Charlie Whilborg had his stroke . . ."

"I remember."

"He was the best litigator in the office, and if he hadn't gone down two days before they caught . . ." she paused, had trouble with the name, went on, ". . . before they caught Spanning in Decatur, and if Morgan County hadn't been so worried about a case this size, and bound Spanning over to us in Birmingham . . . all of it so fast nobody really had a chance to talk to him . . . I was the first one even got *near* him, everyone was so damned scared of him, of what they *thought* he was . . ."

"Hallucinating, were they?" I said, being a smartass.

"Shut up.

"The office did most of the donkeywork after that first interview I had with him. It was a big break for me in the office; and I got obsessed by it. So after the first interview, I never spent much actual time with Spanky, never got too close, to see what kind of a man he *really* . . ."

I said: "Spanky? Who the hell's 'Spanky'?"

She blushed. It started from the sides of her nostrils and went out both ways toward her ears, then climbed to the hairline. I'd seen that happen only a couple of times in eleven years, and one of those times had been when she'd farted at the opera. *Lucia di Lammermoor.*

I said it again: "Spanky? You're putting me on, right? You call him *Spanky*?" The blush deepened. "Like the fat kid in *The Little Rascals* . . . c'mon, I don't fuckin' be*lieve* this!"

She just glared at me.

I felt the laughter coming.

My face started twitching.

She stood up again. "Forget it. Just forget it, okay?" She took two steps away from the table, toward the street exit. I grabbed her hand and pulled her back, trying not to fall apart with laughter, and I said, "Okay okay okay . . . I'm *sorry* . . . I'm really and truly, honest to goodness, may I be struck by a falling space lab no kidding 100% absolutely sorry . . . but you gotta admit . . . catching me unawares like that . . . I mean, come *on*, Ally . . . *Spanky*!?! You call this guy who murdered at least fifty-six people Spanky? Why not Mickey, or Froggy, or Alfalfa . . . ? I can understand not calling him Buckwheat, you can save that one for me, but *Spanky*???"

And in a moment *her* face started to twitch; and in another moment she was starting to smile, fighting it every micron of the way; and in another moment she was laughing and swatting at me with her free hand; and then she pulled her hand loose and stood there falling apart with laughter; and in about a minute she was sitting down again. She threw the balled-up napkin at me.

"It's from when he was a kid," she said. "He was a fat kid, and they made fun of him. You know the way kids are . . . they corrupted Spanning into 'Spanky' because *The Little Rascals* were on television and . . . oh, shut *up*, Rudy!"

I finally quieted down, and made conciliatory gestures.

She watched me with an exasperated wariness till she was sure I wasn't going to run any more dumb gags on her, and then she resumed. "After Judge Fay sentenced him, I handled Spa . . . *Henry's* case from our office, all the way up to the appeals stage. I was the one who did the pleading against clemency when Henry's lawyers took their appeal to the Eleventh Circuit in Atlanta.

"When he was denied a stay by the appellate, three-to-nothing, I helped prepare the brief when Henry's counsel went to the Alabama Supreme Court; then when the Supreme Court refused to hear his appeal, I thought it was all over. I knew they'd run out of moves for him, except maybe the Governor; but that wasn't ever going to happen. So I thought: *that's that.*

"When the Supreme Court wouldn't hear it three weeks ago, I got a letter from him. He'd been set for execution next Saturday, and I couldn't figure out why he wanted to see *me.*"

I asked, "The letter . . . it got to you how?"

"One of his attorneys."

"I thought they'd given up on him."

"So did I. The evidence was so overwhelming; half a dozen counselors found ways to get themselves excused; it wasn't the kind of case that would bring any litigator good publicity. Just the number of eyewitnesses in the parking lot of that Winn-Dixie in Huntsville . . . must have been fifty of them, Rudy. And they all saw the same thing, and they all identified Henry in lineup after lineup, twenty, thirty, could have been fifty of them if we'd needed that long a parade. And all the rest of it . . ."

I held up a hand. *I know,* the flat hand against the air said. She had told me all of this. Every grisly detail, till I wanted to puke. It was as if I'd done it all myself, she was so vivid in her telling. Made my jaunting nausea pleasurable by comparison. Made me so sick I couldn't even think about it. Not even in a moment of human weakness.

"So the letter comes to you from the attorney . . ."

"I think you know this lawyer. Larry Borlan; used to be with the ACLU; before that he was senior counsel for the Alabama Legislature down to Montgomery; stood up, what was it, twice, three times, before the Supreme Court? Excellent guy. And not easily fooled."

"And what's *he* think about all this?"

"He thinks Henry's absolutely innocent."

"Of all of it?"

"Of everything."

"But there were fifty disinterested random eyewitnesses at one of those slaughters. Fifty, you just said it. Fifty, you could've had a parade. All of them nailed him cold, without a doubt. Same kind of kill as all the other fifty-five, including that schoolkid in

Decatur when they finally got him. And Larry Borlan thinks he's not the guy, right?"

She nodded. Made one of those sort of comic pursings of the lips, shrugged, and nodded. "Not the guy."

"So the killer's still out there?"

"That's what Borlan thinks."

"And what do *you* think?"

"I agree with him."

"Oh, jeezus, Ally, my aching boots and saddle! You got to be workin' some kind of off-time! The killer is still out here in the mix, but there hasn't been a killing like Spannings' for the three years that he's been in the joint. Now *what* do that say to you?"

"It says whoever the guy *is*, the one who killed all those people, he's days smarter than all the rest of us, and he set up the perfect freefloater to take the fall for him, and he's either long far gone in some other state, working his way, or he's sitting quietly right here in Alabama, waiting and watching. And smiling." Her face seemed to sag with misery. She started to tear up, and said, "In four days he can stop smiling."

Saturday night.

"Okay, take it easy. Go on, tell me the rest of it. Borlan comes to you, and he begs you to read Spanning's letter and . . . ?"

"He didn't beg. He just gave me the letter, told me he had no idea what Henry had written, but he said he'd known me a long time, that he thought I was a decent, fair-minded person, and he'd appreciate it in the name of our friendship if I'd read it."

"So you read it."

"I read it."

"Friendship. Sounds like you an' him was *good* friends. Like maybe you and I were good friends?"

She looked at me with astonishment.

I think *I* looked at me with astonishment.

"Where the hell did *that* come from?" I said.

"Yeah, really," she said, right back at me, "where the hell *did* that come from?" My ears were hot, and I almost started to say something about how if it was okay for *her* to use our Marx

Brothers indiscretion for a lever, why wasn't it okay for me to get cranky about it? But I kept my mouth shut; and for once knew enough to move along. "Must've been *some* letter," I said.

There was a long moment of silence during which she weighed the degree of shit she'd put me through for my stupid remark, after all this was settled; and having struck a balance in her head, she told me about the letter.

It was perfect. It was the only sort of come-on that could lure the avenger who'd put you in the chair to pay attention. The letter had said that fifty-six was not the magic number of death. That there were many, *many* more unsolved cases, in many, *many* different states; lost children, runaways, unexplained disappearances, old people, college students hitchhiking to Sarasota for Spring Break, shopkeepers who'd carried their day's take to the night deposit drawer and never gone home for dinner, hookers left in pieces in Hefty bags all over town, and death death death unnumbered and unnamed. Fifty-six, the letter had said, was just the start. And if she, her, no one else, Allison Roche, my pal Ally, would come on down to Holman, and talk to him, Henry Lake Spanning would help her close all those open files. National rep. Avenger of the unsolved. Big time mysteries revealed. "So you read the letter, and you went . . ."

"Not at first. Not immediately. I was sure he was guilty, and I was pretty certain at that moment, three years and more, dealing with the case, I was pretty sure if he said he could fill in all the blank spaces, that he could do it. But I just didn't like the idea. In court, I was always twitchy when I got near him at the defense table. His eyes, he never took them off me. They're blue, Rudy, did I tell you that . . . ?"

"Maybe. I don't remember. Go on."

"Bluest blue you've ever seen . . . well, to tell the truth, he just plain *scared* me. I wanted to win that case so badly, Rudy, you can never know . . . not just for me or the career or for the idea of justice or to avenge all those people he'd killed, but just the thought of him out there on the street, with those blue eyes, so blue, never stopped looking at me from the moment the trial began . . . the *thought* of him on the loose drove me to whip that case like a howling dog. I *had* to put him away!"

"But you overcame your fear."

She didn't like the edge of ridicule on the blade of that remark. "That's right. I finally 'overcame my fear' and I agreed to go see him."

"And you saw him."

"Yes."

"And he didn't know shit about no other killings, right?"

"Yes."

"But he talked a good talk. And his eyes was blue, so blue."

"Yes, you asshole."

I chuckled. Everybody is somebody's fool.

"Now let me ask you this—very carefully—so you don't hit me again: the moment you discovered he'd been shuckin' you, lyin', that he *didn't* have this long, unsolved crime roster to tick off, why didn't you get up, load your attaché case, and hit the bricks?"

Her answer was simple. "He begged me to stay a while."

"That's it? He *begged* you?"

"Rudy, he has no one. He's *never* had anyone." She looked at me as if I were made of stone, some basalt thing, an onyx statue, a figure carved out of melanite, soot and ashes fused into a monolith. She feared she could not, in no way, no matter how piteously or bravely she phrased it, penetrate my rocky surface.

Then she said a thing that I never wanted to hear.

"Rudy . . ."

Then she said a thing I could never have imagined she'd say. Never in a million years.

"Rudy . . ."

Then she said the most awful thing she could say to me, even more awful than that she was in love with a serial killer.

"Rudy . . . go inside . . . read my mind . . . I need you to know, I need you to understand . . . Rudy . . ."

The look on her face killed my heart.

I tried to say no, oh god no, not that, please, no, not that, don't ask me to do that, please *please* I don't want to go inside, we mean so much to each other, I don't *want* to know your landscape. Don't make me feel filthy, I'm no peeping-tom, I've *never* spied on you, never stolen a look when you were coming out of the shower, or undressing, or when you were being sexy . . . I never invaded your privacy, I wouldn't *do* a thing like that . . . we're friends, I don't need to know it all, I don't *want* to go in there. I can go inside anyone, and it's always awful . . . please don't make me see things in there I might not like, you're my friend, please don't steal that from me . . .

"Rudy, *please*. Do it."

Oh jeezusjeezusjeezus, again, she said it again!

We sat there. And we sat there. And we sat there longer. I said, hoarsely, in fear, "Can't you just . . . just *tell* me?"

Her eyes looked at stone. A man of stone. And she tempted me to do what I could do casually, tempted me the way Faust was tempted by Mefisto, Mephistopheles, Mefistofele, Mephostopilis. Black rock Dr. Faustus, possessor of magical mind-reading powers, tempted by thick, lustrous eyelashes and violet eyes and a break in the voice and an imploring movement of hand to face and a tilt of the head that was pitiable and the begging word *please* and all the guilt that lay between us that was mine alone. The seven chief demons. Of whom Mefisto was the one "not loving the light."

I knew it was the end of our friendship. But she left me nowhere to run. Mefisto in onyx.

So I jaunted into her landscape.

I stayed in there less than ten seconds. I didn't want to know everything I could know; and I definitely wanted to know *nothing* about how she really thought of me. I couldn't have borne seeing a caricature of a bug-eyed, shuffling, thick-lipped darkie in there. Mandingo man. Steppin Porchmonkey Rudy Pair . . .

Oh god, what was I thinking!

Nothing in there like that. Nothing! Ally wouldn't *have* anything like that in there. I was going nuts, going absolutely fucking crazy, in there, back out in less than ten seconds. I want to block it, kill it, void it, waste it, empty it, reject it, squeeze it, darken it, obscure it, wipe it, do away with it like it never happened. Like the moment you walk in on your momma and poppa and catch them fucking, and you want never to have known that.

But at least I understood.

In there, in Allison Roche's landscape, I saw how her heart had responded to this man she called Spanky, not Henry Lake Spanning. She did not call him, in there, by the name of a monster; she called him a honey's name. I didn't know if he was innocent or not, but *she* knew he was innocent. At first she had responded to just talking with him, about being brought up in an orphanage, and she was able to relate to his stories of being used and treated like chattel, and how they had stripped him of his dignity, and made him afraid all the time. She knew what that was like. And how he'd always been on his own. The running-away. The being captured like a wild thing, and put in this home or that lockup or the orphanage "for his own good." Washing stone steps with a tin bucket full of gray water, with a horsehair brush and a bar of lye soap, till the tender folds of skin between the fingers were furiously red and hurt so much you couldn't make a fist.

She tried to tell me how her heart had responded, with a language that has never been invented to do the job. I saw as much as I needed, there in that secret landscape, to know that Spanning had led a miserable life, but that somehow he'd managed to become a decent human being. And it showed through enough when she was face to face with him, talking to him without the witness box between them, without the adversarial thing, without the tension of the courtroom and the gallery and those parasite creeps from the tabloids sneaking around taking pictures of him, that she identified with his pain. Hers had been not the same, but similar; of a kind, if not of identical intensity.

She came to know him a little.

And came back to see him again. Human compassion. In a moment of human weakness.

Until, finally, she began examining everything she had worked up as evidence, trying to see it from *his* point of view, using *his* explanations of circumstantiality. And there were inconsistencies. Now she saw them. Now she did not turn her prosecuting attorney's mind from them, recasting them in a way that would railroad Spanning; now she gave him just the barest possibility of truth. And the case did not seem as incontestable.

By that time, she had to admit to herself, she had fallen in love with him. The gentle quality could not be faked; she'd known fraudulent kindness in her time.

I left her mind gratefully. But at least I understood.

"Now?" she asked.

Yes, now. Now I understood. And the fractured glass in her voice told me. Her face told me. The way she parted her lips in expectation, waiting for me to reveal what my magic journey had conveyed by way of truth. Her palm against her cheek. All that told me. And I said, "Yes."

Then, silence, between us.

After a while she said, "I didn't feel anything."

I shrugged. "Nothing to feel. I was in for a few seconds, that's all."

"You didn't see everything?"

"No."

"Because you didn't want to?"

"Because . . ."

She smiled. "I understand, Rudy."

Oh, do you? Do you really? That's just fine. And I heard me say, "You made it with him yet?"

I could have torn off her arm; it would've hurt less.

"That's the second time today you've asked me that kind of question. I didn't like it much the first time, and I like it less *this* time."

"You're the one wanted me to go into your head. I didn't buy no ticket for the trip."

"Well, you were in there. Didn't you look around enough to find out?"

"I didn't look for that."

"What a chickenshit, wheedling, lousy and *cowardly* . . ."

"I haven't heard an answer, Counselor. Kindly restrict your answers to a simple yes or no."

"Don't be ridiculous! He's on Death Row!"

"There are ways."

"How would *you* know?"

"I had a friend. Up at San Rafael. What they call Tamal. Across the bridge from Richmond, a little north of San Francisco."

"That's San Quentin."

"That's what it is, all right."

"I thought that *friend* of yours was at Pelican Bay?"

"Different friend."

"You seem to have a lot of old chums in the joint in California."

"It's a racist nation."

"I've heard that."

"But Q ain't Pelican Bay. Two different states of being. As hard time as they pull at Tamal, it's worse up to Crescent City. In the Shoe."

"You never mentioned 'a friend' at San Quentin."

"I never mentioned a lotta shit. That don't mean I don't know it. I am large, I contain multitudes."

We sat silently, the three of us: me, her, and Walt Whitman. *We're fighting*, I thought. Not make-believe, dissin' some movie we'd seen and disagreed about; this was nasty. Bone nasty and memorable. No one ever forgets this kind of fight. Can turn dirty in a second, say some trash you can never take back, never forgive, put a canker on the rose of friendship for all time, never be the same look again.

I waited. She didn't say anything more; and I got no straight answer; but I was pretty sure Henry Lake Spanning had gone all the way with her. I felt a twinge of emotion I didn't even want to look at, much less analyze, dissect, and name. *Let it be*, I thought. Eleven years. Once, just once. *Let it just lie there and get old and withered and die a proper death like all ugly thoughts.*

"Okay. So I go on down to Atmore," I said. "I suppose you mean in the very near future, since he's supposed to bake in four days. Sometime very soon: like today."

She nodded.

I said, "And how do I get in? Law student? Reporter? Tag along as Larry Borlan's new law clerk? Or do I go in with you? What am I, friend of the family, representative of the Alabama State Department of Corrections; maybe you could set me up as an inmate's rep from 'Project Hope.' "

"I can do better than that," she said. The smile. "Much."

"Yeah, I'll just bet you can. Why does that worry me?"

Still with the smile, she hoisted the Atlas onto her lap. She unlocked it, took out a small manila envelope, unsealed but clasped, and slid it across the table to me. I pried open the clasp and shook out the contents.

Clever. Very clever. And already made up, with my photo where necessary, admission dates stamped for tomorrow morning, Thursday, absolutely authentic and foolproof.

"Let me guess," I said, "Thursday mornings, the inmates of Death Row have access to their attorneys?"

"On Death Row, family visitation Monday and Friday. Henry has no family. Attorney visitations Wednesdays and Thursdays, but I couldn't count on today. It took me a couple of days to get through to you . . ."

"I've been busy."

". . . but inmates consult with their counsel on Wednesday and Thursday mornings."

I tapped the papers and plastic cards. "This is very sharp. I notice my name and my handsome visage already here, already sealed in plastic. How long have you had these ready?"

"Couple of days."

"What if I'd continued to say no?"

She didn't answer. She just got that look again.

"One last thing," I said. And I leaned in very close, so she would make no mistake that I was dead serious. "Time grows short. Today's Wednesday. Tomorrow's Thursday. They throw those computer-controlled twin switches Saturday night midnight. What if I jaunt into him and find out you're right, that he's absolutely innocent? What then? They going to listen to me? Fiercely high-verbal black boy with the magic mind-read power?

"I don't think so. Then what happens, Ally?"

"Leave that to me." Her face was hard. "As you said: there are ways. There are roads and routes and even lightning bolts, if you know where to shop. The power of the judiciary. An election year coming up. Favors to be called in."

I said, "And secrets to be wafted under sensitive noses?"

"You just come back and tell me Spanky's telling the truth," and she smiled as I started to laugh, "and I'll worry about the world one minute after midnight Sunday morning."

I got up and slid the papers back into the envelope, and put the envelope under my arm. I looked down at her and I smiled as gently as I could, and I said, "Assure me that you haven't stacked the deck by telling Spanning I can read minds."

"I wouldn't do that."

"Tell me."

"I haven't told him you can read minds."

"You're lying."

"Did you . . . ?"

"Didn't have to. I can see it in your face, Ally."

"Would it matter if he knew?"

"Not a bit. I can read the sonofabitch cold or hot, with or without. Three seconds inside and I'll know if he did it all, if he did part of it, if he did none of it."

"I think I love him, Rudy."

"You told me that."

"But I wouldn't set you up. I need to know . . . that's why I'm asking you to do it."

I didn't answer. I just smiled at her. She'd told him. He'd know I was coming. But that was terrific. If she hadn't alerted him, I'd have asked her to call and let him know. The more aware he'd be, the easier to scorch his landscape.

I'm a fast study, king of the quick learners: vulgate Latin in a week; standard apothecary's pharmacopoeia in three days; Fender bass on a weekend; Atlanta Falcon's play book in an hour; and, in a moment of human weakness, what it feels like to have a very crampy, heavy-flow menstrual period, two minutes flat.

So fast, in fact, that the more somebody tries to hide the boiling pits of guilt and the crucified bodies of shame, the faster I adapt to their landscape. Like a man taking a polygraph test gets nervous, starts to sweat, ups the galvanic skin response, tries to duck and dodge, gets himself hinky and more hinky and hinkyer till his upper lip could water a truck garden, the more he tries to hide from me . . . the more he reveals . . . the deeper inside I can go.

There is an African saying: *Death comes without the thumping of drums.*

I have no idea why that one came back to me just then.

Last thing you expect from a prison administration is a fine sense of humor. But they got one at the Holman facility.

They had the bloody monster dressed like a virgin.

White duck pants, white short sleeve shirt buttoned up to the neck, white socks. Pair of brown ankle-high brogans with crepe soles, probably neoprene, but they didn't clash with the pale, virginal apparition that came through the security door with a large, black brother in Alabama Prison Authority uniform holding onto his right elbow.

Didn't clash, those work shoes, and didn't make much of a tap on the white tile floor. It was as if he floated. Oh yes, I said to myself, oh yes indeed: I could see how this messianic figure could wow even as tough a cookie as Ally. *Oh my, yes.*

Fortunately, it was raining outside.

Otherwise, sunlight streaming through the glass, he'd no doubt have a halo. I'd have lost it. Right there, a laughing jag would *not* have ceased. Fortunately, it was raining like a sonofabitch.

Which hadn't made the drive down from Clanton a possible entry on any deathbed list of Greatest Terrific Moments in My Life. Sheets of aluminum water, thick as misery, like a neverending shower curtain that I could drive through for an eternity and never really penetrate. I went into the ditch off the I-65 half a dozen times. Why I never plowed down and buried myself up to the axles in the sucking goo running those furrows, never be something I'll understand.

But each time I skidded off the Interstate, even the twice I did a complete three-sixty and nearly rolled the old Fairlane I'd borrowed from John the C Hepworth, even then I just kept digging, slewed like an epileptic seizure, went sideways and climbed right up the slippery grass and weeds and running, sucking red Alabama goo, right back onto that long black anvil pounded by rain as hard as roofing nails. I took it then, as I take it now, to be a sign that Destiny was determined the mere heavens and earth would not be permitted to fuck me around. I had a date to keep, and Destiny was on top of things.

Even so, even living charmed, which was clear to me, even so: when I got about five miles north of Atmore, I took the 57 exit off the I-65 and a left onto 21, and pulled in at the Best Western. It wasn't my intention to stay overnight that far south—though I knew a young woman with excellent teeth down in Mobile—but the rain was just hammering and all I wanted was to get this thing done and go fall asleep. A drive that long, humping something as lame as that Fairlane, hunched forward to scope the rain . . . with Spanning in front of me . . . all I desired was surcease. A touch of the old oblivion.

I checked in, stood under the shower for half an hour, changed into the three-piece suit I'd brought along, and phoned the front desk for directions to the Holman facility.

Driving there, a sweet moment happened for me. It was the last sweet moment for a long time thereafter, and I remember it now as if it were still happening. I cling to it.

In May, and on into early June, the Yellow Lady's Slipper blossoms. In the forests and the woodland bogs, and often on some otherwise undistinguished slope or hillside, the yellow and purple orchids suddenly appear.

I was driving. There was a brief stop in the rain. Like the eye of the hurricane. One moment sheets of water, and the next, absolute silence before the crickets and frogs and birds started complaining; and darkness on all sides, just the idiot staring beams of my headlights poking into nothingness; and cool as a well between the drops of rain; and I was driving. And suddenly, the window rolled down so I wouldn't fall asleep, so I could stick my head out when my eyes started to close, suddenly I smelled the delicate perfume of the sweet May-blossoming Lady's Slipper. Off to my left, off in the dark somewhere on a patch of hilly ground, or deep in a stand of invisible trees, *Cypripedium calceolus* was making the night world beautiful with its fragrance.

I neither slowed, nor tried to hold back the tears.

I just drove, feeling sorry for myself; for no good reason I could name.

Way, way down—almost to the corner of the Florida Panhandle, about three hours south of the last truly imperial barbeque in that part of the world, in Birmingham—I made my way to Holman. If you've never been inside the joint, what I'm about to say will resonate about as clearly as Chaucer to one of the gentle Tasaday.

The stones call out.

That institution for the betterment of the human race, the Organized Church, has a name for it. From the fine folks at Catholicism, Lutheranism, Baptism, Judaism, Islamism, Druidism . . . Ismism . . . the ones who brought you Torquemada, several spicy varieties of Inquisition, original sin, holy war, sectarian violence, and something called "pro-lifers" who bomb and maim and kill . . . comes the catchy phrase Damned Places.

Rolls off the tongue like *God's On Our Side*, don't it?

Damned Places.

As we say in Latin, the *situs* of malevolent shit. The *venue* of evil happenings. Locations forever existing under a black cloud, like residing in a rooming house run by Jesse Helms or Strom Thurmond. The big slams are like that. Joliet, Dannemora, Attica, Rahway State in Jersey, that hellhole down in Louisiana called Angola, old Folsom—not the new one, the old Folsom—Q, and Ossining. Only people who read about it call it "Sing Sing." Inside, the cons call it Ossining. The Ohio State pen in Columbus. Leavenworth, Kansas. The ones they talk about among themselves when they talk about doing hard time. The Shoe at Pelican Bay State Prison. In there, in those ancient structures mortared with guilt and depravity and no respect for human life and just plain meanness on both sides, cons and screws, in there where the walls and floors have absorbed all the pain and loneliness of a million men and women for decades . . . in there, the stones call out.

Damned places. You can feel it when you walk through the gates and go through the metal detectors and empty your pockets on counters and open your briefcase so that thick fingers can rumple the papers. You feel it. The moaning and thrashing, and men biting holes in their own wrists so they'll bleed to death.

And I felt it worse than anyone else.

I blocked out as much as I could. I tried to hold on to the memory of the scent of orchids in the night. The last thing I wanted was to jaunt into somebody's landscape at random. Go inside and find out what he had done, what had *really* put him here, not just what they'd got him for. And I'm not talking about Spanning; I'm talking about every one of them. Every guy who had kicked to death his girl friend because she brought him Bratwurst instead of spicy Cajun sausage. Every pale, wormy Bible-reciting psycho who had stolen, buttfucked, and sliced up an altar boy in the name of secret voices that "tole him to g'wan *do* it!" Every amoral druggie who'd shot a pensioner for her food stamps. If I let down for a second, if I didn't keep that shield up, I'd be tempted to send out a scintilla and touch one of them. In a moment of human weakness.

So I followed the trusty to the Warden's office, where his secretary checked my papers, and the little plastic cards with my face encased in them, and she kept looking down at the face, and up at my face, and down at my face, and up at the face in front of her, and when she couldn't restrain herself a second longer she said, "We've been expecting you, Mr. Pairis. Uh. Do you *really* work for the President of the United States?"

I smiled at her. "We go bowling together."

She took that highly, and offered to walk me to the conference room where I'd meet Henry Lake Spanning. I thanked her the way a well-mannered gentleman of color thanks a Civil Servant who can make life easier or more difficult, and I followed her along corridors and in and out of guarded steel-riveted doorways, through Administration and the segregation room and the main hall to the brown-paneled, stained walnut, white tile over cement floored, roll-out security windowed, white draperied, drop ceiling with 2″ acoustical Celotex squared conference room, where a Security Officer met us. She bid me fond adieu, not yet fully satisfied that such a one as I had come, that morning, on Air Force One, straight from a 7–10 split with the President of the United States.

It was a big room.

I sat down at the conference table; about twelve feet long and four feet wide; highly polished walnut, maybe oak. Straight back chairs: metal tubing with a light yellow upholstered cushion. Everything quiet, except for the sound of matrimonial rice being dumped on a connubial tin roof. The rain had not slacked off. Out there on the I-65 some luck-lost bastard was being sucked down into red death.

"He'll be here," the Security Officer said.

"That's good," I replied. I had no idea why he'd tell me that, seeing as how it was the reason I was there in the first place. I imagined him to be the kind of guy you dread sitting in front of, at the movies, because he always explains everything to his date. Like a *bracero* laborer with a valid green card interpreting a Woody Allen movie line-by-line to his illegal-alien cousin Humberto, three weeks under the wire from Matamoros. Like one of a pair of Beltone-wearing octogenarians on the loose from a rest home for a wild Saturday afternoon at the mall, plonked down in the third level multiplex, one of them describing whose ass Clint Eastwood is about to kick, and why. All at the top of her voice.

"Seen any good movies lately?" I asked him.

He didn't get a chance to answer, and I didn't jaunt inside to find out, because at that moment the steel door at the far end of the conference room opened, and another Security Officer poked his head in, and called across to Officer Let-Me-State-the-Obvious, "Dead man walking!"

Officer Self-Evident nodded to him, the other head poked back out, the door slammed, and my companion said, "When we bring one down from Death Row, he's gotta walk through the Ad Building and Segregation and the Main Hall. So everything's locked down. Every man's inside. It takes some time, y'know."

I thanked him.

"Is it true you work for the President, yeah?" He asked it so politely, I decided to give him a straight answer; and to hell with all the phony credentials Ally had worked up. "Yeah," I said, "we're on the same *bocce* ball team."

"Izzat so?" he said, fascinated by sports stats.

I was on the verge of explaining that the President was, in actuality, of Italian descent, when I heard the sound of the key turning in the security door, and it opened outward, and in came this messianic apparition in white, being led by a guard who was seven feet in any direction.

Henry Lake Spanning, sans halo, hands and feet shackled, with the chains cold-welded into a wide anodized steel belt, shuffled toward me; and his neoprene soles made no disturbing cacophony on the white tiles.

I watched him come the long way across the room, and he watched me right back. I thought to myself, *Yeah, she told him I can read minds. Well, let's see which method you use to try and keep me out of the landscape.* But I couldn't tell from the outside of him, not just by the way he shuffled and looked, if he had fucked Ally. But I knew it had to've been. Somehow. Even in the big lockup. Even here.

He stopped right across from me, with his hands on the back of the chair, and he didn't say a word, just gave me the nicest smile I'd ever gotten from anyone, even my momma. *Oh, yes,* I thought, *oh my goodness, yes.* Henry Lake Spanning was either the most masterfully charismatic person I'd ever met, or so good at the charm con that he could sell a slashed throat to a stranger.

"You can leave him," I said to the great black behemoth brother.

"Can't do that, sir."

"I'll take full responsibility."

"Sorry, sir; I was told someone had to be right here in the room with you and him, all the time."

I looked at the one who had waited with me. "That mean you, too?"

He shook his head. "Just one of us, I guess."

I frowned. "I need absolute privacy. What would happen if I were this man's attorney of record? Wouldn't you have to leave us alone? Privileged communication, right?"

They looked at each other, this pair of Security Officers, and they looked back at me, and they said nothing. All of a sudden Mr. Plain-as-the-Nose-on-Your-Face had nothing valuable to offer; and the sequoia with biceps "had his orders."

"They tell you who I work for? They tell you who it was sent me here to talk to this man?" Recourse to authority often works. They mumbled yessir yessir a couple of times each, but their faces stayed right on the mark of *sorry, sir, but we're not supposed to leave anybody alone with this man.* It wouldn't have mattered if they'd believed I'd flown in on Jehovah One.

So I said to myself *fuckit* I said to myself, and I slipped into their thoughts, and it didn't take much rearranging to get the phone wires restrung and the underground cables rerouted and the pressure on their bladders something fierce.

"On the other hand . . ." the first one said.

"I suppose we could . . ." the giant said.

And in a matter of maybe a minute and a half one of them was entirely gone, and the great one was standing outside the steel door, his back filling the double-pane chickenwire-imbedded security window. He effectively sealed off the one entrance or exit to or from the conference room; like the three hundred Spartans facing the tens of thousands of Xerxes's army at the Hot Gates.

Henry Lake Spanning stood silently watching me.

"Sit down," I said. "Make yourself comfortable."

He pulled out the chair, came around, and sat down.

"Pull it closer to the table," I said.

He had some difficulty, hands shackled that way, but he grabbed the leading edge of the seat and scraped forward till his stomach was touching the table.

He was a handsome guy, even for a white man. Nice nose, strong cheekbones, eyes the color of that water in your toilet when you toss in a tablet of 2000 Flushes. Very nice looking man. He gave me the creeps.

If Dracula had looked like Shirley Temple, no one would've driven a stake through his heart. If Harry Truman had looked like Freddy Krueger, he would never have beaten Tom Dewey at the polls. Joe Stalin and Saddam Hussein looked like sweet, avuncular friends of the family, really nice looking, kindly guys—who just incidentally happened to slaughter millions of men, women, and children. Abe Lincoln looked like an axe murderer, but he had a heart as big as Guatemala.

Henry Lake Spanning had the sort of face you'd trust immediately if you saw it in a tv commercial. Men would like to go fishing with him, women would like to squeeze his buns.

Grannies would hug him on sight, kids would follow him straight into the mouth of an open oven. If he could play the piccolo, rats would gavotte around his shoes.

What saps we are. Beauty is only skin deep. You can't judge a book by its cover. Cleanliness is next to godliness. Dress for success. What saps we are.

So what did that make my pal, Allison Roche?

And why the hell didn't I just slip into his thoughts and check out the landscape? Why was I stalling?

Because I was scared of him.

This was fifty-six verified, gruesome, disgusting murders sitting forty-eight inches away from me, looking straight at me with blue eyes and soft, gently blond hair. Neither Harry nor Dewey would've had a prayer.

So why was I scared of him? Because; that's why.

This was damned foolishness. I had all the weaponry, he was shackled, and I didn't for a second believe he was what Ally *thought* he was: innocent. Hell, they'd caught him, literally, red-handed. Bloody to the armpits, fer chrissakes. Innocent, my ass! *Okay, Rudy,* I thought, *get in there and take a look around.* But I didn't. I waited for him to say something.

He smiled tentatively, a gentle and nervous little smile, and he said, "Ally asked me to see you. Thank you for coming."

I looked *at* him, but not *into* him.

He seemed upset that he'd inconvenienced me. "But I don't think you can do me any good, not in just three days."

"You scared, Spanning?"

His lips trembled. "Yes I am, Mr. Pairis. I'm about as scared as a man can be." His eyes were moist.

"Probably gives you some insight into how your victims felt, whaddaya think?"

He didn't answer. His eyes were moist.

After a moment just looking at me, he scraped back his chair and stood up. "Thank you for coming, sir. I'm sorry Ally imposed on your time." He turned and started to walk away. I jaunted into his landscape.

Oh my god, I thought. He was innocent.

Never done any of it. None of it. Absolutely no doubt, not a shadow of a doubt. Ally had been right. I saw every bit of that landscape in there, every fold and crease; every bolt hole and rat run; every gully and arroyo; all of his past, back and back and back to his birth in Lewistown, Montana, near Great Falls, thirty-six years ago; every day of his life right up to the minute they arrested him leaning over that disemboweled cleaning woman the real killer had tossed into the dumpster.

I saw every second of his landscape; and I saw him coming out of the Winn-Dixie in Huntsville; pushing a cart filled with grocery bags of food for the weekend. And I saw him wheeling it around the parking lot toward the dumpster area overflowing with broken-down cardboard boxes and fruit crates. And I heard the cry for help from one of those dumpsters; and I saw Henry Lake Spanning stop and look around, not sure he'd heard anything at all. Then I saw him start to go to his car, parked right there at the edge of the lot beside the wall because it was a Friday evening and everyone was stocking up for the weekend, and there weren't any spaces out front; and the cry for help, weaker this time, as pathetic as a crippled kitten; and Henry Lake Spanning stopped cold, and he looked around; and we *both* saw the bloody hand raise itself above the level of the open dumpster's filthy green steel side. And I saw him desert his groceries without a thought to their cost, or that someone might run off with them if he left them unattended, or that he only had eleven dollars left in his checking account, so if those groceries were snagged by someone he wouldn't be eating for the next few days . . . and I watched him rush to the dumpster and look into the crap filling it . . . and I felt his nausea at the sight of that poor old woman, what was left of her . . . and I was with him as he crawled up onto the dumpster and dropped inside to do what he could for that mass of shredded and pulped flesh.

And I cried with him as she gasped, with a bubble of blood that burst in the open ruin of her throat, and she died. But though *I* heard the scream of someone coming around the corner, Spanning did not; and so he was still there, holding the poor mass of stripped skin and black bloody clothing, when the cops screeched into the parking lot. And only *then*, innocent of anything but decency and rare human compassion, did Henry Lake Spanning begin to understand what it must look like to middle-aged *hausfraus*, sneaking around dumpsters to pilfer cardboard boxes, who see what they think is a man murdering an old woman.

I was with him, there in that landscape within his mind, as he ran and ran and dodged and dodged. Until they caught him in Decatur, seven miles from the body of Gunilla Ascher. But they had him, and they had positive identification, from the dumpster in Huntsville; and all the rest of it was circumstantial, gussied up by bedridden, recovering Charlie Whilborg and the staff in Ally's office. It looked good on paper—so good that Ally had brought him down on twenty-nine-*cum*-fifty-six counts of murder in the vilest extreme.

But it was all bullshit.

The killer was still out there.

Henry Lake Spanning, who looked like a nice, decent guy, was exactly that. A nice, decent, goodhearted, but most of all *innocent* guy.

You could fool juries and polygraphs and judges and social workers and psychiatrists and your mommy and your daddy, but you could *not* fool Rudy Pairis, who travels regularly to the place of dark where you can go but not return.

They were going to burn an innocent man in three days.

I had to do something about it.

Not just for Ally, though that was reason enough; but for this man who thought he was doomed, and was frightened, but didn't have to take no shit from a wiseguy like me.

"Mr. Spanning," I called after him.

He didn't stop.

"Please," I said. He stopped shuffling, the chains making their little charm bracelet sounds, but he didn't turn around.

"I believe Ally is right, sir," I said. "I believe they caught the wrong man; and I believe all the time you've served is wrong; and I believe you ought not die."

Then he turned slowly, and stared at me with the look of a dog that has been taunted with a bone. His voice was barely a whisper. "And why is that, Mr. Pairis? Why is it that you believe me when nobody else but Ally and my attorney believed me?"

I didn't say what I was thinking. What I was thinking was that I'd been *in* there, and I *knew* he was innocent. And more than that, I knew that he truly loved my pal Allison Roche.

And there wasn't much I wouldn't do for Ally.

So what I said was: "I know you're innocent, because I know who's guilty."

His lips parted. It wasn't one of those big moves where someone's mouth flops open in astonishment; it was just a parting of the lips. But he was startled; I knew that as I knew the poor sonofabitch had suffered too long already.

He came shuffling back to me, and sat down.

"Don't make fun, Mr. Pairis. Please. I'm what you said, I'm scared. I don't want to die, and I surely don't want to die with the world thinking I did those . . . those things."

"Makin' no fun, captain. I know who ought to burn for all those murders. Not six states, but eleven. Not fifty-six dead, but an even seventy. Three of them little girls in a day nursery, and the woman watching them, too."

He stared at me. There was horror on his face. I know that look real good. I've seen it at least seventy times.

"I know you're innocent, cap'n, because *I'm* the man they want. *I'm* the guy who put your ass in here."

In a moment of human weakness. I saw it all. What I had packed off to live in that place of dark where you can go but not return. The wall-safe in my drawing-room. The four-foot-thick walled crypt encased in concrete and sunk a mile deep into solid granite. The vault whose composite laminate walls of judiciously sloped extremely thick blends of steel and plastic, the equivalent of six hundred to seven hundred mm of homogenous depth protection approached the maximum toughness and hardness of crystaliron, that iron grown with perfect crystal structure and carefully controlled quantities of impurities that in a modern combat tank can shrug off a hollow charge warhead like a spaniel shaking himself dry. The Chinese puzzle box. The hidden chamber. The labyrinth. The maze of the mind where I'd sent all seventy to die, over and over and over, so I wouldn't hear their screams, or see the ropes of bloody tendon, or stare into the pulped sockets where their pleading eyes had been.

When I had walked into that prison, I'd been buttoned up totally. I was safe and secure, I knew nothing, remembered nothing, suspected nothing.

But when I walked into Henry Lake Spanning's landscape, and I could not lie to myself that he was the one, I felt the earth crack. I felt the tremors and the upheavals, and the fissures started at my feet and ran to the horizon; and the lava boiled up and began to flow. And the steel walls melted, and the concrete turned to dust, and the barriers dissolved; and I looked at the face of the monster.

No wonder I had such nausea when Ally had told me about this or that slaughter ostensibly perpetrated by Henry Lake Spanning, the man she was prosecuting on twenty-nine counts of murders I had committed. No wonder I could picture all the details when she would talk to me about the barest description of the murder site. No wonder I fought so hard against coming to Holman.

In there, in his mind, his landscape open to me, I saw the love he had for Allison Roche, for my pal and buddy with whom I had once, just once . . .

Don't try tellin' me that the Power of Love can open the fissures. I don't want to hear that shit. I'm telling *you* that it was a combination, a buncha things that split me open, and possibly maybe one of those things was what I saw between them.

I don't know that much. I'm a quick study, but this was in an instant. A crack of fate. A moment of human weakness. That's what I told myself in the part of me that ventured to the place of dark: that I'd done what I'd done in moments of human weakness.

And it was those moments, not my "gift," and not my blackness, that had made me the loser, the monster, the liar that I am.

In the first moment of realization, I couldn't believe it. Not me, not good old Rudy. Not likeable Rudy Pairis never done no one but hisself wrong his whole life.

In the next second I went wild with anger, furious at the disgusting thing that lived on one side of my split brain. Wanted to tear a hole through my face and yank the killing thing out, wet and putrescent, and squeeze it into pulp.

In the next second I was nauseated, actually wanted to fall down and puke, seeing every moment of what I had done, unshaded, unhidden, naked to this Rudy Pairis who was decent and reasonable and law-abiding, even if such a Rudy was little better than a well-educated fuckup. But not a killer . . . I wanted to puke.

Then, finally, I accepted what I could not deny.

For me, never again, would I slide through the night with the scent of the blossoming Yellow Lady's Slipper. I recognized that perfume now.

It was the odor that rises from a human body cut wide open, like a mouth making a big, dark yawn.

The other Rudy Pairis had come home at last.

They didn't have half a minute's worry. I sat down at a little wooden writing table in an interrogation room in the Jefferson County D.A.'s offices, and I made up a graph with the names and dates and locations. Names of as many of the seventy as I actually knew. (A lot of them had just been on the road, or in a men's toilet, or taking a bath, or lounging in the back row of a movie, or getting some cash from an ATM, or just sitting around doing nothing but waiting for me to come along and open them up, and maybe have a drink off them, or maybe just something to snack on . . . down the road.) Dates were easy, because I've got a good memory for dates. And the places where they'd find the ones they didn't know about, the fourteen with exactly the same m.o. as the other fifty-six, not to mention the old-style rip-and-pull can opener I'd used on that little Catholic bead-counter Gunilla Whatsername, who did Hail Mary this and Sweet Blessed Jesus that all the time I was opening her up, even at the last, when I held up parts of her insides for her to look at, and tried to get her to lick them, but she died first. Not half a minute's worry for the State of Alabama. All in one swell foop they corrected a tragic miscarriage of justice, knobbled a maniac killer, solved fourteen more murders than they'd counted on (in five additional states, which made the police departments of those five additional states extremely pleased with the law enforcement agencies of the Sovereign State of Alabama), and made first spot on the evening news on all three major networks, not to mention CNN, for the better part of a week. Knocked the Middle East right out of the box. Neither Harry Truman nor Tom Dewey would've had a prayer.

Ally went into seclusion, of course. Took off and went somewhere down on the Florida coast, I heard. But after the trial, and the verdict, and Spanning being released, and me going inside, and all like that, well, oo-poppa-dow as they used to say, it was all reordered properly. *Sat cito si sat bene*, in Latin: "It is done quickly enough if it is done well." A favorite saying of Cato. The Elder Cato.

And all I asked, all I begged for, was that Ally and Henry Lake Spanning, who loved each other and deserved each other, and whom I had almost fucked up royally, that the two of them would be there when they jammed my weary black butt into that new electric chair at Holman.

Please come, I begged them.

Don't let me die alone. Not even a shit like me. Don't make me cross over into that place of dark, where you can go, but not return—without the face of a friend. Even a former friend. And as for you, captain, well, hell didn't I save your life so you could enjoy the company of the woman you love? Least you can do. Come on now; be there or be square!

I don't know if Spanning talked her into accepting the invite, or if it was the other way around; but one day about a week prior to the event of cooking up a mess of fried Rudy Pairis, the warden stopped by my commodious accommodations on Death Row and gave me to understand that it would be SRO for the barbeque, which meant Ally my pal, and her boy friend, the former resident of the Row where now I dwelt in durance vile.

The things a guy'll do for love.

Yeah, that was the key. Why would a very smart operator who had gotten away with it, all the way free and clear, why would such a smart operator suddenly pull one of those hokey courtroom "I did it, I did it!" routines, and as good as strap himself into the electric chair?

Once. I only went to bed with her once.

The things a guy'll do for love.

When they brought me into the death chamber from the holding cell where I'd spent the night before and all that day, where I'd had my last meal (which had been a hot roast beef sandwich, double meat, on white toast, with very crisp french fries, and hot brown country gravy poured over the whole thing, apple sauce, and a bowl of Concord grapes), where a representative of the Holy Roman Empire had tried to make amends for destroying most of the gods, beliefs, and cultures of my black forebears, they held me between Security Officers, neither one of whom had been in attendance when I'd visited Henry Lake Spanning at this very same correctional facility slightly more than a year before.

It hadn't been a bad year. Lots of rest; caught up on my reading, finally got around to Proust and Langston Hughes, I'm ashamed to admit, so late in the game; lost some weight; worked out regularly; gave up cheese and dropped my cholesterol count. Ain't nothin' to it, just to do it.

Even took a jaunt or two or ten, every now and awhile. It didn't matter none. I wasn't going anywhere, neither were they. I'd done worse than the worst of them; hadn't I confessed to it? So there wasn't a lot that could ice me, after I'd copped to it and released all seventy of them out of my unconscious, where they'd been rotting in shallow graves for years. No big thang, Cuz.

Brought me in, strapped me in, plugged me in.

I looked through the glass at the witnesses.

There sat Ally and Spanning, front row center. Best seats in the house. All eyes and crying, watching, not believing everything had come to this, trying to figure out when and how and in what way it had all gone down without her knowing anything at all about it. And Henry Lake Spanning sitting close beside her, their hands locked in her lap. True love.

I locked eyes with Spanning.

I jaunted into his landscape.

No, I *didn't.*

I *tried* to, and couldn't squirm through. Thirty years, or less, since I was five or six, I'd been doing it; without hindrance, all alone in the world the only person who could do this listen in on the landscape trick; and for the first time I was stopped. Absolutely no fuckin' entrance. I went wild! I tried running at it full-tilt, and hit something khaki-colored, like beach sand, and only slightly giving, not hard, but resilient. Exactly like being inside a ten-foot-high, fifty-foot-diameter paper bag, like a big shopping bag from a supermarket, that stiff butcher's paper kind of bag, and that color, like being inside a bag that size, running straight at it, thinking you're going to bust through . . . and being thrown back. Not hard, not like bouncing on a trampoline, just shunted aside like the fuzz from a dandelion hitting a glass door. Unimportant. Khaki-colored and not particularly bothered.

I tried hitting it with a bolt of pure blue lightning mental power, like someone out of a Marvel comic, but that wasn't how mixing in other people's minds works. You don't think yourself in with a psychic battering-ram. That's the kind of arrant foolishness you hear spouted by unattractive people on public access cable channels, talking about The Power of Love and The Power of the Mind and the ever-popular toe-tapping Power of a Positive Thought. Bullshit; I don't be home to *that* folly!

I tried picturing myself in there, but that didn't work, either. I tried blanking my mind and drifting across, but it was pointless. And at that moment it occurred to me that I didn't really know *how* I jaunted. I just . . . did it. One moment I was snug in the privacy of my own head, and the next I was over there in someone else's landscape. It was instantaneous, like teleportation, which also is an impossibility, like telepathy.

But now, strapped into the chair, and them getting ready to put the leather mask over my face so the witnesses wouldn't have to see the smoke coming out of my eye-sockets and the little sparks as my nose hairs burned, when it was urgent that I get into the thoughts and landscape of Henry Lake Spanning, I was shut out completely. And right *then*, that moment, I was scared!

Presto, without my even opening up to him, there he was: inside my head.

He had jaunted into *my* landscape.

"You had a nice roast beef sandwich, I see."

His voice was a lot stronger than it had been when I'd come down to see him a year ago. A *lot* stronger inside my mind.

"Yes, Rudy, I'm what you knew probably existed somewhere. Another one. A shrike." He paused. "I see you call it 'jaunting in the landscape.' I just called myself a shrike. A butcherbird. One name's as good as another. Strange, isn't it; all these years; and we never met anyone else? There *must* be others, but I think—now I can't prove this, I have no real data, it's just a wild idea I've had for years and years—I think they don't know they can do it."

He stared at me across the landscape, those wonderful blue eyes of his, the ones Ally had fallen in love with, hardly blinking.

"Why didn't you let me know before this?"

He smiled sadly. "Ah, Rudy. Rudy, Rudy, Rudy; you poor benighted pickaninny.

"Because I needed to suck you in, kid. I needed to put out a bear trap, and let it snap closed on your scrawny leg, and send you over. Here, let me clear the atmosphere in here . . ." And he wiped away all the manipulation he had worked on me, way back a year ago, when he had so easily covered his own true thoughts, his past, his life, the real panorama of what went on inside his landscape—like bypassing a surveillance camera with a looped tape that continues to show a placid scene while the joint is being actively burgled—and when he convinced me not only that he was innocent, but that the real killer was someone who had blocked the hideous slaughters from his conscious mind and had lived an otherwise exemplary life. He wandered around my landscape—and all of this in a second or two, because time has no duration in the landscape, like the hours you can spend in a dream that are just thirty seconds long in the real world, just before you wake up—and he swept away all the false memories and suggestions, the logical structure of sequential events that he had planted that would dovetail with my actual existence, my true memories, altered and warped and rearranged so I would believe that I had done all seventy of those ghastly murders . . . so that I'd believe, in a moment of horrible realization, that I was the demented psychopath who had ranged state to state to state, leaving piles of ripped flesh at every stop. Blocked it all, submerged it all, sublimated it all, me. Good old Rudy Pairis, who never killed anybody. I'd been the patsy he was waiting for.

"There, now, kiddo. See what it's really like?

"You didn't do a thing.

"Pure as the driven snow, nigger. That's the truth. And what a find you were. Never even suspected there was another like me, till Ally came to interview me after Decatur. But there you were, big and black as a Great White Hope, right there in her mind. Isn't she fine, Pairis? Isn't she something to take a knife to? Something to split open like a nice piece of fruit warmed in a summer sunshine field, let all the steam rise off her . . . maybe have a picnic . . ."

He stopped.

"I wanted her right from the first moment I saw her.

"Now, you know, I could've done it sloppy, just been a shrike to Ally, that first time she came to the holding cell to interview me; just jump into her, that was my plan. But what a noise that Spanning in the cell would've made, yelling it wasn't a man, it was a woman, not Spanning, but Deputy D.A. Allison Roche . . . too much noise, too many complications. But I *could* have done it, jumped into her. Or a guard, and then slice her at my leisure, stalk her, find her, let her steam . . .

"You look distressed, Mr. Rudy Pairis. Why's that? Because you're going to die in my place? Because I could have taken you over at any time, and didn't? Because after all this time of your miserable, wasted, lousy life you finally find someone like you, and we don't even have the convenience of a chat? Well, that's sad, that's really sad, kiddo. But you didn't have a chance."

"You're stronger than me, you kept me out," I said.

He chuckled.

"Stronger? Is that all you think it is? Stronger? You still don't get it, do you?" His face, then, grew terrible. "You don't even understand now, right now that I've cleaned it all away and you can *see* what I did to you, do you?

"Do you think I stayed in a jail cell, and went through that trial, all of that, because I couldn't do anything about it? You poor jig slob. I could have jumped like a shrike any time I wanted to. But the first time I met your Ally I saw *you*."

I cringed. "And you waited . . . ? For me, you spent all that time in prison, just to get to me . . . ?"

"At the moment when you couldn't do anything about it, at the moment you couldn't shout 'I've been taken over by someone else, I'm Rudy Pairis here inside this Henry Lake Spanning body, help me, help me!' Why stir up noise when all I had to do was bide my time, wait a bit, wait for Ally, and let Ally go for you."

I felt like a drowning turkey, standing idiotically in the rain, head tilted up, mouth open, water pouring in. "You can . . . leave the mind . . . leave the body . . . go out . . . jaunt, jump permanently . . . ?"

Spanning sniggered like a schoolyard bully.

"You stayed in jail three years just to get *me*?"

He smirked. Smarter than thou.

"Three years? You think that's some big deal to me? You don't think I could have someone like you running around, do you? Someone who can 'jaunt' as I do? The only other shrike I've ever encountered. You think I wouldn't sit in here and wait for you to come to me?"

"But three *years* . . ."

"You're what, Rudy . . . thirty-one, is it? Yes, I can see that. Thirty-one. You've never jumped like a shrike. You've just entered, jaunted, gone into the landscapes, and never understood that it's more than reading minds. You can change domiciles, black boy. You can move out of a house in a bad neighborhood—such as strapped into the electric chair—and take up residence in a brand, spanking, new housing complex of million-and-a-half-buck condos, like Ally."

"But you have to have a place for the other one to go, don't you?" I said it just flat, no tone, no color to it at all. I didn't even think of the place of dark, where you can go . . .

"Who do you think I am, Rudy? Just who the hell do you think I was when I started, when I learned to shrike, how to jaunt, what I'm telling you now about changing residences? You wouldn't know my first address. I go a long way back.

"But I can give you a few of my more famous addresses. Gilles de Rais, France, 1440; Vlad Tepes, Romania, 1462; Elizabeth Bathory, Hungary, 1611; Catherine DeShayes, France, 1680; Jack the Ripper, London, 1888; Henri Désiré Landru, France, 1915; Albert Fish, New York City, 1934; Ed Gein, Plainfield, Wisconsin, 1954; Myra Hindley, Manchester, 1963; Albert DeSalvo, Boston, 1964; Charles Manson, Los Angeles, 1969; John Wayne Gacy, Norwood Park Township, Illinois, 1977.

"Oh, but how I do go on. And on. And on and on and on,

Rudy, my little porch monkey. That's what I do. I go on. And on and on. Shrike will nest where it chooses. If not in your beloved Allison Roche, then in the cheesy fucked-up black boy, Rudy Pairis. But don't you think that's a waste, kiddo? Spending however much time I might have to spend in your socially unacceptable body, when Henry Lake Spanning is such a handsome devil? Why should I have just switched with you when Ally lured you to me, because all it would've done is get you screeching and howling that you weren't Spanning, you were this nigger son who'd had his head stolen . . . and then you might have manipulated some guards or the Warden . . .

"Well, you see what I mean, don't you?

"But now that the mask is securely in place, and now that the electrodes are attached to your head and your left leg, and now that the Warden has his hand on the switch, well, you'd better get ready to do a lot of drooling."

And he turned around to jaunt back out of me, and I closed the perimeter. He tried to jaunt, tried to leap back to his own mind, but I had him in a fist. Just that easy. Materialized a fist, and turned him to face me.

"Fuck you, Jack the Ripper. And fuck you twice, Bluebeard. And on and on and on fuck you Manson and Boston Strangler and any other dipshit warped piece of sick crap you been in your years. You sure got some muddy-shoes credentials there, boy.

"What I care about all those names, Spanky my brother? You really think I don't know those names? I'm an educated fellah, Mistuh Rippuh, Mistuh Mad Bomber. You missed a few. Were you also, did you inhabit, hath thou possessed Winnie Ruth Judd and Charlie Starkweather and Mad Dog Coll and Richard Speck and Sirhan Sirhan and Jeffrey Dahmer? You the boogieman responsible for *every* bad number the human race ever played? You ruin Sodom and Gomorrah, burned the Great Library of Alexandria, orchestrated the Reign of Terror *dans Paree*, set up the Inquisition, stoned and drowned the Salem witches, slaughtered unarmed women and kids at Wounded Knee, bumped off John Kennedy?

"I don't think so.

"I don't even think you got so close as to share a pint with Jack the Ripper. And even if you did, even if you *were* all those maniacs, you were small potatoes, Spanky. The least of us human beings outdoes you, three times a day. How many lynch ropes you pulled tight, M'sieur Landru?

"What colossal egotism you got, makes you blind, makes you think you're the only one, even when you find out there's someone else, you can't get past it. What makes you think I didn't know what you can do? What makes you think I didn't let you do it, and sit here waiting for you like you sat there waiting for me, till this moment when you can't do shit about it?

"You so goddam stuck on yourself, Spankyhead, you never give it the barest that someone else is a faster draw than you.

"Know what your trouble is, Captain? You're old, you're *real* old, maybe hundreds of years who gives a damn old. That don't count for shit, old man. You're old, but you never got smart. You're just mediocre at what you do.

"You moved from address to address. You didn't have to be Son of Sam or Cain slayin' Abel, or whoever the fuck you been . . . you could've been Moses or Galileo or George Washington Carver or Harriet Tubman or Sojourner Truth or Mark Twain or Joe Louis. You could've been Alexander Hamilton and helped found the Manumission Society in New York. You could've discovered radium, carved Mount Rushmore, carried a baby out of a burning building. But you got old real fast, and you never got any smarter. You didn't need to, did you, Spanky? You had it all to yourself, all this 'shrike' shit, just jaunt here and jaunt there, and bite off someone's hand or face like the old, tired, boring, repetitious, no-imagination stupid shit that you are.

"Yeah, you got me good when I came here to see your landscape. You got Ally wired up good. And she suckered me in, probably not even knowing she was doing it . . . you must've looked in her head and found just the right technique to get her to make me come within reach. Good, m'man; you were excellent. But I had a year to torture myself. A year to sit here and think about it. About how many people I'd killed, and how sick it made me, and little by little I found my way through it.

"Because . . . and here's the big difference 'tween us, dummy:

"I unraveled what was going on . . . it took time, but I learned. Understand, asshole? *I* learn! *You* don't.

"There's an old Japanese saying—I got lots of these, Henry m'man—I read a whole lot—and what it says is, 'Do not fall into the error of the artisan who boasts of twenty years experience in his craft while in fact he has had only one year of experience—twenty times.' " Then I grinned back at him.

"Fuck you, sucker," I said, just as the Warden threw the switch and I jaunted out of there and into the landscape and mind of Henry Lake Spanning.

I sat there getting oriented for a second; it was the first time I'd done more than a jaunt . . . this was . . . *shrike*; but then Ally beside me gave a little sob for her old pal, Rudy Pairis, who was baking like a Maine lobster, smoke coming out from under the black cloth that covered my, his, face; and I heard the vestigial scream of what had been Henry Lake Spanning and thousands of other monsters, all of them burning, out there on the far horizon of my new landscape; and I put my arm around her, and drew her close, and put my face into her shoulder and hugged her to me; and I heard the scream go on and on for the longest time, I think it was a long time, and finally it was just wind . . . and then gone . . . and I came up from Ally's shoulder, and I could barely speak.

"Shhh, honey, it's okay," I murmured. "He's gone where he can make right for his mistakes. No pain. Quiet, a real quiet place; and all alone forever. And cool there. And dark."

I was ready to stop failing at everything, and blaming everything. Having fessed up to love, having decided it was time to grow up and be an adult—not just a very quick study who learned fast, extremely fast, a lot faster than anybody could imagine an orphan like me could learn, than *any*body could imagine—I hugged her with the intention that Henry Lake Spanning would love Allison Roche more powerfully, more responsibly, than anyone had ever loved anyone in the history of the world. I was ready to stop failing at everything.

And it would be just a whole lot easier as a white boy with great big blue eyes.

Because—get on this now—all my wasted years didn't have as much to do with blackness or racism or being overqualified or being unlucky or being high-verbal or even the curse of my "gift" of jaunting, as they did with one single truth I learned waiting in there, inside my own landscape, waiting for Spanning to come and gloat:

I have always been one of those miserable guys who *couldn't get out of his own way*.

Which meant I could, at last, stop feeling sorry for that poor nigger, Rudy Pairis. Except, maybe, in a moment of human weakness.

This story, for Bob Bloch, because I promised.

There Are No Snakes in Ireland

Frederick Forsyth

McQueen looked across his desk at the new applicant for a job with some scepticism. He had never employed such a one before. But he was not an unkind man, and if the job-seeker needed the money and was prepared to work, McQueen was not averse to giving him a chance.

"You know it's damn hard work?" he said in his broad Belfast accent.

"Yes, sir," said the applicant.

"It's a quick in-and-out job, ye know. No questions, no pack drill. You'll be working on the lump. Do you know what that means?"

"No, Mr. McQueen."

"Well, it means you'll be paid well but you'll be paid in cash. No red tape. Geddit?"

What he meant was there would be no income tax paid, no National Health contributions deducted at source. He might also have added that there would be no National Insurance cover and that the Health and Safety standards would be completely ignored. Quick profits for all were the order of the day, with a fat slice off the top for himself as the contractor. The job-seeker nodded his head to indicate he had "goddit" though in fact he had not. McQueen looked at him speculatively.

"You say you're a medical student, in your last year at the Royal Victoria?" Another nod. "On the summer vacation?"

Another nod. The applicant was evidently one of those students who needed money over and above his grant to put himself through medical school. McQueen, sitting in his dingy Bangor office running a hole-and-corner business as a demolition contractor with assets consisting of a battered truck and a ton of second-hand sledgehammers, considered himself a self-made man and heartily approved of the Ulster Protestant work ethic. He was not one to put down another such thinker, whatever he looked like.

"All right," he said, "you'd better take lodgings here in Bangor. You'll never get from Belfast and back in time each day. We work from seven in the morning until sundown. It's work by the hour, hard but well paid. Mention one word to the authorities and you'll lose the job like shit off a shovel. OK?"

"Yes, sir. Please, when do I start and where?"

"The truck picks the gang up at the main station yard every morning at six-thirty. Be there Monday morning. The gang foreman is Big Billie Cameron. I'll tell him you'll be there."

"Yes, Mr. McQueen." The applicant turned to go.

"One last thing," said McQueen, pencil poised. "What's your name?"

"Harkishan Ram Lal," said the student. McQueen looked at his pencil, the list of names in front of him and the student.

"We'll call you Ram," he said, and that was the name he wrote down on the list.

The student walked out into the bright July sunshine of Bangor, on the north coast of County Down, Northern Ireland.

By that Saturday evening he had found himself cheap lodgings in a dingy boarding house halfway up Railway View Street, the heart of Bangor's bed-and-breakfast land. At least it was convenient to the main station from which the works truck would depart every morning just after sun-up. From the grimy window of his room he could look straight at the side of the shored embankment that carried the trains from Belfast into the station.

It had taken him several tries to get a room. Most of those houses with a B-and-B notice in the window seemed to be fully booked when he presented himself on the doorstep. But then it was true that a lot of casual labour drifted into the town in the height of summer. True also that Mrs. McGurk was a Catholic and she still had rooms left.

He spent Sunday morning bringing his belongings over from Belfast, most of them medical textbooks. In the afternoon he lay on his bed and thought of the bright hard light on the brown hills of his native Punjab. In one more year he would be a qualified physician, and after another year of intern work he would return home to cope with the sicknesses of his own people. Such was his dream. He calculated he could make enough money this summer to tide himself through to his finals and after that he would have a salary of his own.

On the Monday morning he rose at a quarter to six at the bidding of his alarm clock, washed in cold water and was in the station yard just after six. There was time to spare. He found an early-opening café and took two cups of black tea. It was his only sustenance. The battered truck, driven by one of the demolition gang, was there at a quarter past six and a dozen men assembled near it. Harkishan Ram Lal did not know whether to approach them and introduce himself, or wait at a distance. He waited.

At twenty-five past the hour the foreman arrived in his own car, parked it down a side road and strode up to the truck. He had McQueen's list in his hand. He glanced at the dozen men, recognized them all and nodded. The Indian approached. The foreman glared at him.

"Is youse the darkie McQueen has put on the job?" he demanded.

Ram Lal stopped in his tracks. "Harkishan Ram Lal," he said. "Yes."

There was no need to ask how Big Billie Cameron had earned his name. He stood 6 feet and 3 inches in his stockings but was wearing enormous nail-studded steel-toed boots. Arms like tree trunks hung from huge shoulders and his head was surmounted by a shock of ginger hair. Two small, pale-lashed eyes stared down balefully at the slight and wiry Indian. It was plain he was not best pleased. He spat on the ground.

"Well, get in the fecking truck," he said.

On the journey out to the work site Cameron sat up in the cab which had no partition dividing it from the back of the lorry, where the dozen labourers sat on two wooden benches down the sides. Ram Lal was near the tailboard next to a small, nut-hard man with bright blue eyes, whose name turned out to be Tommy Burns. He seemed friendly.

"Where are youse from?" he asked with genuine curiosity.

"India," said Ram Lal. "The Punjab."

"Well, which?" said Tommy Burns.

Ram Lal smiled. "The Punjab is a part of India," he said.

Burns thought about this for a while. "You Protestant or Catholic?" he asked at length.

"Neither," said Ram Lal patiently. "I am a Hindu."

"You mean you're not a Christian?" asked Burns in amazement.

"No. Mine is the Hindu religion."

"Hey," said Burns to the others, "your man's not a Christian at all." He was not outraged, just curious, like a small child who has come across a new and intriguing toy.

Cameron turned from the cab up front. "Aye," he snarled, "a heathen."

The smile dropped off Ram Lal's face. He stared at the opposite canvas wall of the truck. By now they were well south of Bangor, clattering down the motorway towards Newtownards. After a while Burns began to introduce him to the others. There was a Craig, a Munroe, a Patterson, a Boyd and two Browns. Ram Lal had been long enough in Belfast to recognize the names as being originally Scottish, the sign of the hard Presbyterians who make up the backbone of the Protestant majority of the Six Counties. The men seemed amiable and nodded back at him.

"Have you not got a lunch box, laddie?" asked the elderly man called Patterson.

"No," said Ram Lal, "it was too early to ask my landlady to make one up."

"You'll need lunch," said Burns, "aye, and breakfast. We'll be making tay ourselves on a fire."

"I will make sure to buy a box and bring some food tomorrow," said Ram Lal.

Burns looked at the Indian's rubber-soled soft boots. "Have you not done this kind of work before?" he asked.

Ram Lal shook his head.

"You'll need a pair of heavy boots. To save your feet, you see."

Ram Lal promised he would also buy a pair of heavy ammunition boots from a store if he could find one open late at night. They were through Newtownards and still heading south on the A21 towards the small town of Comber. Craig looked across at him.

"What's your real job?" he asked.

"I'm a medical student at the Royal Victoria in Belfast," said Ram Lal. "I hope to qualify next year."

Tommy Burns was delighted. "That's near to being a real doctor," he said. "Hey, Big Billie, if one of us gets a knock young Ram could take care of it."

Big Billie grunted. "He's not putting a finger on me," he said.

That killed further conversation until they arrived at the work site. The driver had pulled northwest out of Comber and two miles up the Dundonald road he bumped down a track to the right until they came to a stop where the trees ended and saw the building to be demolished.

It was a huge old whiskey distillery, a sheer-sided, long derelict. It had been one of two in these parts that had once turned out good Irish whiskey but had gone out of business years before. It stood beside the River Comber, which had once powered its great waterwheel as it flowed down from Dundonald to Comber and on to empty itself in Strangford Lough. The malt had arrived by horse-drawn cart down the track and the barrels of whiskey had left the same way. The sweet water that had powered the machines had also been used in the vats. But the distillery had stood alone, abandoned and empty for years.

Of course the local children had broken in and found it an ideal place to play. Until one had slipped and broken a leg. Then the county council had surveyed it, declared it a hazard and the owner found himself with a compulsory demolition order.

He, scion of an old family of squires who had known better days, wanted the job done as cheaply as possible. That was where McQueen came in. It could be done faster but more expensively with heavy machinery; Big Billie and his team would do it with sledges and crowbars. McQueen had even lined up a deal to sell the best timbers and the hundreds of tons of mature bricks to a jobbing builder. After all, the wealthy nowadays wanted their new houses to have "style" and that meant looking old. So there was a premium on antique sun-bleached old bricks and genuine ancient timber beams to adorn the new-look-old "manor" houses of the top executives. McQueen would do all right.

"Right lads," said Big Billie as the truck rumbled away back to Bangor. "There it is. We'll start with the roof tiles. You know what to do."

The group of men stood beside their pile of equipment. There were great sledgehammers with 7-pound heads; crowbars 6 feet long and over an inch thick; nailbars a yard long with curved split tips for extracting nails; short-handled, heavy-headed lump hammers and a variety of timber saws. The only concessions to human safety were a number of webbing belts with dogclips and hundreds of feet of rope. Ram Lal looked up at the building and swallowed. It was four storeys high and he hated heights. But scaffolding is expensive.

One of the men unbidden went to the building, prised off a plank door, tore it up like a playing card and started a fire. Soon a billycan of water from the river was boiling away and tea was made. They all had their enamel mugs except Ram Lal. He made a mental note to buy that also. It was going to be thirsty, dusty work. Tommy Burns finished his own mug and offered it, refilled, to Ram Lal.

"Do they have tea in India?" he asked.

Ram Lal took the proffered mug. The tea was ready-mixed, sweet and off-white. He hated it.

They worked through the first morning perched high on the roof. The tiles were not to be salvaged, so they tore them off manually and hurled them to the ground away from the river. There was an instruction not to block the river with falling rubble. So it all had to land on the other side of the building, in the long grass, weeds, broom and gorse which covered the area round the distillery. The men were roped together so that if one lost his grip and began to slither down the roof, the next man would take the strain. As the tiles disappeared, great yawning holes appeared between the rafters. Down below them was the floor of the top storey, the malt store.

At ten they came down the rickety internal stairs for breakfast on the grass, with another billycan of tea. Ram Lal ate no breakfast. At two they broke for lunch. The gang tucked into their piles of thick sandwiches. Ram Lal looked at his hands. They were nicked in several places and bleeding. His muscles ached and he was very hungry. He made another mental note about buying some heavy work gloves.

Tommy Burns held up a sandwich from his own box. "Are you not hungry, Ram?" he asked. "Sure, I have enough here."

"What do you think you're doing?" asked Big Billie from where he sat across the circle round around the fire.

Burns looked defensive. "Just offering the lad a sandwich," he said.

"Let the darkie bring his own fecking sandwiches," said Cameron. "You look after yourself."

The men looked down at their lunch boxes and ate in silence. It was obvious no one argued the toss with Big Billie.

"Thank you, I am not hungry," said Ram Lal to Burns. He walked away and sat by the river where he bathed his burning hands.

By sundown when the truck came to collect them half the tiles on the great roof were gone. One more day and they would start on the rafters, work for saw and nailbar.

Throughout the week the work went on, and the once proud building was stripped of its rafters, planks and beams until it stood hollow and open, its gaping windows like open eyes staring at the prospect of its imminent death. Ram Lal was unaccustomed to the arduousness of this kind of labour. His muscles ached endlessly, his hands were blistered, but he toiled on for the money he needed so badly.

He had acquired a tin lunch box, enamel mug, hard boots and a pair of heavy gloves, which no one else wore. Their hands were hard enough from years of manual work. Throughout the week Big Billie Cameron needled him without let-up, giving him the hardest work and positioning him on the highest points once he had learned Ram Lal hated heights. The Punjabi bit on his anger because he needed the money. The crunch came on the Saturday.

The timbers were gone and they were working on the masonry. The simplest way to bring the edifice down away from the river would have been to plant explosive charges in the corners of the side wall facing the open clearing. But dynamite was out of the question. It would have required special licences in Northern Ireland of all places, and that would have alerted the tax man. McQueen and all his gang would have been required to pay substantial sums in income tax, and McQueen in National Insurance contributions. So they were chipping the walls down in square-yard chunks, standing hazardously on sagging floors as the supporting walls splintered and cracked under the hammers.

During lunch Cameron walked round the building a couple of times and came back to the circle round the fire. He began to describe how they were going to bring down a sizable chunk of one outer wall at third-floor level. He turned to Ram Lal.

"I want you up on the top there," he said. "When it starts to go, kick it outwards."

Ram Lal looked up at the section of wall in question. A great crack ran along the bottom of it.

"That brickwork is going to fall at any moment," he said evenly. "Anyone sitting on top there is going to come down with it."

Cameron stared at him, his face suffusing, his eyes pink with rage where they should have been white. "Don't you tell me my job; you do as you're told, you stupid fecking nigger." He turned and stalked away.

Ram Lal rose to his feet. When his voice came, it was in a hard-edged shout. "*Mister Cameron* . . ."

Cameron turned in amazement. The men sat open-mouthed. Ram Lal walked slowly up to the big ganger.

"Let us get one thing plain," said Ram Lal, and his voice carried clearly to everyone else in the clearing. "I am from the Punjab in northern India. I am also a Kshatria, member of the warrior caste. I may not have enough money to pay for my medical studies, but my ancestors were soldiers and princes, rulers and scholars, two thousand years ago when yours were crawling on all fours dressed in skins. Please do not insult me any further."

Big Billie Cameron stared down at the Indian student. The whites of his eyes had turned a bright red. The other labourers sat in stunned amazement.

"Is that so?" said Cameron quietly. "Is that so, now? Well, things are a bit different now, you black bastard. So what are you going to do about that?"

On the last word he swung his arm, open-palmed, and his hand crashed into the side of Ram Lal's face. The youth was thrown bodily to the ground several feet away. His head sang. He heard Tommy Burns call out, "Stay down, laddie. Big Billie will kill you if you get up."

Ram Lal looked up into the sunlight. The giant stood over him, fists bunched. He realized he had not a chance in combat against the big Ulsterman. Feelings of shame and humiliation flooded over him. His ancestors had ridden, sword and lance in hand, across plains a hundred times bigger than these Six Counties, conquering all before them.

Ram Lal closed his eyes and lay still. After several seconds he heard the big man move away. A low conversation started among the others. He squeezed his eyes tighter shut to hold back the tears of shame. In the blackness he saw the baking plains of the Punjab and men riding over them; proud, fierce men, hook-nosed, bearded, turbaned, black-eyed, the warriors from the land of Five Rivers.

Once, long ago in the world's morning, Iskander of Macedon had ridden over these plains with his hot and hungry eyes; Alexander, the young god, whom they called The Great, who at twenty-five had wept because there were no more worlds to conquer. These riders were the descendants of his captains, and the ancestors of Harkishan Ram Lal.

He was lying in the dust as they rode by, and they looked down at him in passing. As they rode each of them mouthed one single word to him. Vengeance.

Ram Lal picked himself up in silence. It was done, and what still had to be done had to be done. That was the way of his people. He spent the rest of the day working in complete silence. He spoke to no one and no one spoke to him.

That evening in his room he began his preparations as night was about to fall. He cleared away the brush and comb from the battered dressing table and removed also the soiled doily and the mirror from its stand. He took his book of the Hindu religion and from it cut a page-sized portrait of the great goddess Shakti, she of power and justice. This he pinned to the wall above the dressing table to convert it into a shrine.

He had bought a bunch of flowers from a seller in front of the main station, and these had been woven into a garland. To one side of the portrait of the goddess he placed a shallow bowl half-filled with sand, and in the sand stuck a candle which he lit. From his suitcase he took a cloth roll and extracted half a dozen joss sticks. Taking a cheap, narrow-necked vase from the bookshelf, he placed them in it and lit the ends. The sweet, heady odour of the incense began to fill the room. Outside, big thunderheads rolled up from the sea.

When his shrine was ready he stood before it, head bowed, the garland in his fingers, and began to pray for guidance. The first rumble of thunder rolled over Bangor. He used not the modern Punjabi but the ancient Sanskrit, language of prayer. *Devi Shakti . . . Maa . . .* Goddess Shakti . . . great mother . . ."

The thunder crashed again and the first raindrops fell. He plucked the first flower and placed it in front of the portrait of Shakti.

"I have been grievously wronged. I ask vengeance upon the wrongdoer . . ." He plucked the second flower and put it beside the first.

He prayed for an hour while the rain came down. It drummed on the tiles above his head, streamed past the window behind him. He finished praying as the storm subsided. He needed to know what form the retribution should take. He needed the goddess to send him a sign.

When he had finished, the joss sticks had burned themselves out and the room was thick with their scent. The candle guttered low. The flowers all lay on the lacquered surface of the dressing table in front of the portrait. Shakti stared back at him unmoved.

He turned and walked to the window to look out. The rain had stopped but everything beyond the panes dripped water. As he watched, a dribble of rain sprang from the guttering above the window and a trickle ran down the dusty glass, cutting a path through the grime. Because of the dirt it did not run straight but meandered sideways, drawing his eye farther and farther to the corner of the window as he followed its path. When it stopped he was staring at the corner of his room, where his dressing gown hung on a nail.

He noticed that during the storm the dressing-gown cord had slipped and fallen to the floor. It lay coiled upon itself, one knotted end hidden from view, the other lying visible on the carpet. Of the dozen tassels only two were exposed, like a forked tongue. The coiled dressing-gown cord resembled nothing so much as a snake in the corner. Ram Lal understood. The next day he took a train to Belfast to see the Sikh.

Ranjit Singh was also a medical student, but he was more fortunate. His parents were rich and sent him a handsome allowance. He received Ram Lal in his well-furnished room at the hostel.

"I have received word from home," said Ram Lal. "My father is dying."

"I am sorry," said Ranjit Singh, "you have my sympathies."

"He asks to see me. I am his first born. I should return."

"Of course," said Singh. "The first-born son should always be by his father when he dies."

"It is a matter of the air fare," said Ram Lal. "I am working and making good money. But I do not have enough. If you will lend me the balance I will continue working when I return and repay you."

Sikhs are no strangers to moneylending if the interest is right and repayment secure. Ranjit Singh promised to withdraw the money from the bank on Monday morning.

That Sunday evening Ram Lal visited Mr. McQueen at his home at Groomsport. The contractor was in front of his television set with a can of beer at his elbow. It was his favourite way to spend a Sunday evening. But he turned the sound down as Ram Lal was shown in by his wife.

"It is about my father," said Ram Lal. "He is dying."

"Oh, I'm sorry to hear that, laddie," said McQueen.

"I should go to him. The first-born son should be with his father at this time. It is the custom of our people."

McQueen had a son in Canada whom he had not seen for seven years.

"Aye," he said, "that seems right and proper."

"I have borrowed the money for the air fare," said Ram Lal. "If I went tomorrow I could be back by the end of the week. The point is, Mr. McQueen, I need the job more than ever now; to repay the loan and for my studies next term. If I am back by the weekend, will you keep the job open for me?"

"All right," said the contractor. "I can't pay you for the time you're away. Nor keep the job open for a further week. But if you're back by the weekend, you can go back to work. Same terms, mind."

"Thank you," said Ram, "you are very kind."

He retained his room in Railway View Street but spent the night at his hostel in Belfast. On the Monday morning he accompanied Ranjit Singh to the bank where the Sikh withdrew the necessary money and gave it to the Hindu. Ram took a taxi to Aldergrove airport and the shuttle to London where he bought an economy-class ticket on the next flight to India. Twenty-four hours later he touched down in the blistering heat of Bombay.

On the Wednesday he found what he sought in the teeming bazaar at Grant Road Bridge. Mr. Chatterjee's Tropical Fish and Reptile Emporium was almost deserted when the young student, with his textbook on reptiles under his arm, wandered in. He found the old proprietor sitting near the back of his shop in half-darkness, surrounded by his tanks of fish and glass-fronted cases in which his snakes and lizards dozed through the hot day.

Mr. Chatterjee was no stranger to the academic world. He supplied several medical centres with samples for study and dissection, and occasionally filled a lucrative order from abroad. He nodded his white-bearded head knowledgeably as the student explained what he sought.

"Ah yes," said the old Gujerati merchant, "I know the snake. You are in luck. I have one, but a few days arrived from Rajputana."

He led Ram Lal into his private sanctum and the two men stared silently through the glass of the snake's new home.

Echis carinatus, said the textbook, but of course the book had been written by an Englishman, who had used the Latin nomenclature. In English, the saw-scaled viper, smallest and deadliest of all his lethal breed.

Wide distribution, said the textbook, being found from West Africa eastwards and northwards to Iran, and on to India and Pakistan. Very adaptable, able to acclimatize to almost any environment, from the moist bush of western Africa to the cold hills of Iran in winter to the baking hills of India.

Something stirred beneath the leaves in the box.

In size, said the textbook, between 9 and 13 inches long and very slim. Olive brown in colour with a few paler spots, sometimes hardly distinguishable, and a faint undulating darker line down the side of the body. Nocturnal in dry, hot weather, seeking cover during the heat of the day.

The leaves in the box rustled again and a tiny head appeared.

Exceptionally dangerous to handle, said the textbook, causing more deaths than even the more famous cobra, largely because of its size which makes it so easy to touch unwittingly with hand or foot. The author of the book had added a footnote to the effect that the small but lethal snake mentioned by Kipling in his marvellous story "Rikki-Tikki-Tavy" was almost certainly not the krait, which is about 2 feet long, but more probably the saw-scaled viper. The author was obviously pleased to have caught out the great Kipling in a matter of accuracy.

In the box, a little black forked tongue flickered towards the two Indians beyond the glass.

Very alert and irritable, the long-gone English naturalist had concluded his chapter on *Echis carinatus.* Strikes quickly without warning. The fangs are so small they make a virtually unnoticeable puncture, like two tiny thorns. There is no pain, but death is almost inevitable, usually taking between two and four hours, depending on the body-weight of the victim and the level of his physical exertions at the time and afterwards. Cause of death is invariably a brain haemorrhage.

"How much do you want for him?" whispered Ram Lal.

The old Gujerati spread his hands helplessly. "Such a prime specimen," he said regretfully, "and so hard to come by. Five hundred rupees."

Ram Lal clinched the deal at 350 rupees and took the snake away in a jar.

For his journey back to London Ram Lal purchased a box of cigars, which he emptied of their contents and in whose lid he punctured twenty small holes for air. The tiny viper, he knew, would need no food for a week and no water for two or three days. It could breathe on an infinitesimal supply of air, so he wrapped the cigar box, resealed and with the viper inside it among his leaves, in several towels whose thick sponginess would contain enough air even inside a suitcase.

He had arrived with a handgrip, but he bought a cheap fibre suitcase and packed it with clothes from market stalls, the cigar box going in the centre. It was only minutes before he left his hotel for Bombay airport that he closed and locked the case. For the flight back to London he checked the suitcase into the hold of the Boeing airliner. His hand baggage was searched, but it contained nothing of interest.

The Air India jet landed at London Heathrow on Friday morning and Ram Lal joined the long queue of Indians trying to get into Britain. He was able to prove he was a medical student and not an immigrant, and was allowed through quite quickly. He even reached the luggage carousel as the first suitcases were tumbling onto it, and saw his own in the first two dozen. He took it to the toilet, where he extracted the cigar box and put it in his handgrip.

In the Nothing-to-Declare channel he was stopped all the same, but it was his suitcase that was ransacked. The customs officer glanced in his shoulder bag and let him pass. Ram Lal crossed Heathrow by courtesy bus to Number One Building and caught the midday shuttle to Belfast. He was in Bangor by teatime and able at last to examine his import.

He took a sheet of glass from the bedside table and slipped it carefully between the lid of the cigar box and its deadly contents before opening wide. Through the glass he saw the viper going round and round inside. It paused and stared with angry black eyes back at him. He pulled the lid shut, withdrawing the pane of glass quickly as the box top came down.

"Sleep, little friend," he said, "if your breed ever sleep. In the morning you will do Shakti's bidding for her."

Before dark he bought a small screw-top jar of coffee and poured the contents into a china pot in his room. In the morning, using his heavy gloves, he transferred the viper from the box to the jar. The enraged snake bit his glove once, but he did not mind. It would have recovered its venom by midday. For a moment he studied the snake, coiled and cramped inside the glass coffee jar, before giving the top a last, hard twist and placing it in his lunch box. Then he went to catch the works truck.

Big Billie Cameron had a habit of taking off his jacket the moment he arrived at the work site, and hanging it on a convenient nail or twig. During the lunch break, as Ram Lal had observed, the giant foreman never failed to go to his jacket after eating, and from the right-hand pocket extract his pipe and tobacco pouch. The routine did not vary. After a satisfying pipe, he would knock out the dottle, rise and say, "Right, lads, back to work," as he dropped his pipe back into the pocket of his jacket. By the time he turned round everyone had to be on their feet.

Ram Lal's plan was simple but foolproof. During the morning he would slip the snake into the right-hand pocket of the hanging jacket. After his sandwiches the bullying Cameron would rise from the fire, go to his jacket and plunge his hand into the pocket. The snake would do what great Shakti had ordered that he be brought halfway across the world to do. It would be he, the viper, not Ram Lal, who would be the Ulsterman's executioner.

Cameron would withdraw his hand with an oath from the pocket, the viper hanging from his finger, its fangs deep in the flesh. Ram Lal would leap up, tear the snake away, throw it to the ground and stamp upon its head. It would by then be harmless, its venom expended. Finally, with a gesture of disgust he, Ram Lal, would hurl the dead viper far into the River Comber, which would carry all evidence away to the sea. There might be suspicion, but that was all there would ever be.

Shortly after eleven o'clock, on the excuse of fetching a fresh sledgehammer, Harkishan Ram Lal opened his lunch box, took out the coffee jar, unscrewed the lid and shook the contents into the right-hand pocket of the hanging jacket. Within sixty seconds he was back at his work, his act unnoticed.

During lunch he found it hard to eat. The men sat as usual in a circle round the fire; the dry old timber baulks crackled and spat, the billycan bubbled above them. The men joshed and joked as ever, while Big Billie munched his way through the pile of doorstep sandwiches his wife had prepared for him. Ram Lal had made a point of choosing a place in the circle near to the jacket. He forced himself to eat. In his chest his heart was pounding and the tension in him rose steadily.

Finally Big Billie crumpled the paper of his eaten sandwiches, threw it in the fire and belched. He rose with a grunt and walked towards his jacket. Ram Lal turned his head to watch. The other men took no notice. Billie Cameron reached his jacket and plunged his hand into the right-hand pocket. Ram Lal held his breath. Cameron's hand rummaged for several seconds and then withdrew his pipe and pouch. He began to fill the bowl with fresh tobacco. As he did so he caught Ram Lal staring at him.

"What are youse looking at?" he demanded belligerently.

"Nothing," said Ram Lal, and turned to face the fire. But he could not stay still. He rose and stretched, contriving to half turn as he did so. From the corner of his eye he saw Cameron replace the pouch in the pocket and again withdraw his hand with a box of matches in it. The foreman lit his pipe and pulled contentedly. He strolled back to the fire.

Ram Lal resumed his seat and stared at the flames in disbelief. Why, he asked himself, why had great Shakti done this to him? The snake had been her tool, her instrument brought at her command. But she had held it back, refused to use her own implement of retribution. He turned and sneaked another glance at the jacket. Deep down in the lining at the very hem, on the extreme left-hand side, something stirred and was still. Ram Lal closed his eyes in shock. A hole, a tiny hole in the lining, had undone all his planning. He worked the rest of the afternoon in a daze of indecision and worry.

On the truck ride back to Bangor, Big Billie Cameron sat up front as usual, but in view of the heat folded his jacket and put it on his knees. In front of the station Ram Lal saw him throw the still-folded jacket onto the back seat of his car and drive away. Ram Lal caught up with Tommy Burns as the little man waited for his bus.

"Tell me," he asked, "does Mr. Cameron have a family?"

"Sure," said the little labourer innocently, "a wife and two children."

"Does he live far from here?" said Ram Lal. "I mean, he drives a car."

"Not far," said Burns, "up on the Kilcooley estate. Ganaway Gardens, I think. Going visiting are you?"

"No, no," said Ram Lal, "see you Monday."

Back in his room Ram Lal stared at the impassive image of the goddess of justice.

"I did not mean to bring death to his wife and children," he told her. "They have done nothing to me."

The goddess from far away stared back and gave no reply.

Harkishan Ram Lal spent the rest of the weekend in an agony of anxiety. That evening he walked to the Kilcooley housing estate on the ring road and found Ganaway Gardens. It lay just off Owenroe Gardens and opposite Woburn Walk. At the corner of Woburn Walk there was a telephone kiosk, and here he waited for an hour, pretending to make a call, while he watched the short street across the road. He thought he spotted Big Billie Cameron at one of the windows and noted the house.

He saw a teenage girl come out of it and walk away to join some friends. For a moment he was tempted to accost her and tell her what demon slept inside her father's jacket, but he dared not.

Shortly before dusk a woman came out of the house carrying

a shopping basket. He followed her down to the Clandeboye shopping centre, which was open late for those who took their wage packets on a Saturday. The woman he thought to be Mrs. Cameron entered Stewarts supermarket and the Indian student trailed round the shelves behind her, trying to pluck up the courage to approach her and reveal the danger in her house. Again his nerve failed him. He might, after all, have the wrong woman, even be mistaken about the house. In that case they would take him away as a madman.

He slept ill that night, his mind racked by visions of the saw-scaled viper coming out of its hiding place in the jacket lining to slither, silent and deadly, through the sleeping council house.

On the Sunday he again haunted the Kilcooley estate, and firmly identified the house of the Cameron family. He saw Big Billie clearly in the back garden. By mid-afternoon he was attracting attention locally and he knew he must either walk boldly up to the front door and admit what he had done, or depart and leave all in the hands of the goddess. The thought of facing the terrible Cameron with the news of what deadly danger had been brought so close to his children was too much. He walked back to Railway View Street.

On Monday morning the Cameron family rose at a quarter to six, a bright and sunny August morning. By six the four of them were at breakfast in the tiny kitchen at the back of the house, the son, daughter and wife in their dressing gowns, Big Billie dressed for work. His jacket was where it had spent the weekend, in a closet in the hallway.

Just after six his daughter Jenny rose, stuffing a piece of marmaladed toast into her mouth.

"I'm away to wash," she said.

"Before ye go, girl, get my jacket from the press," said her father, working his way through a plate of cereal. The girl reappeared a few seconds later with the jacket, held by the collar. She proffered it to her father. He hardly looked up.

"Hang it behind the door," he said. The girl did as she was bid, but the jacket had no hanging tab and the hook was no rusty nail but a smooth chrome affair. The jacket hung for a moment, then fell to the kitchen floor. Her father looked up as she left the room.

"Jenny," he shouted, "pick the damn thing up."

No one in the Cameron household argued with the head of the family. Jenny came back, picked up the jacket and hung it more firmly. As she did, something thin and dark slipped from its folds and slithered into the corner with a dry rustle across the linoleum. She stared at it in horror.

"Dad, what's that in your jacket?"

Big Billie Cameron paused, a spoonful of cereal halfway to his mouth. Mrs. Cameron turned from the cooker. Fourteen-year-old Bobby ceased buttering a piece of toast and stared. The small creature lay curled in the corner by the row of cabinets, tight-bunched, defensive, glaring back at the world, tiny tongue flickering fast.

"Lord save us, it's a snake," said Mrs. Cameron.

"Don't be a bloody fool, woman. Don't you know there are no snakes in Ireland? Everyone knows that," said her husband. He put down the spoon. "What is it, Bobby?"

Though a tyrant inside and outside his house, Big Billie had a grudging respect for the knowledge of his young son, who was good at school and was being taught many strange things. The boy stared at the snake through his owlish glasses.

"It must be a slowworm, Dad," he said. "They had some at school last term for the biology class. Brought them in for dissection. From across the water."

"It doesn't look like a worm to me," said his father.

"It isn't really a worm," said Bobby. "It's a lizard with no legs."

"Then why do they call it a worm?" asked his truculent father.

"I don't know," said Bobby.

"Then what the hell are you going to school for?"

"Will it bite?" asked Mrs. Cameron fearfully.

"Not at all," said Bobby. "It's harmless."

"Kill it," said Cameron senior, "and throw it in the dustbin."

His son rose from the table and removed one of his slippers, which he held like a flyswat in one hand. He was advancing, bare-ankled towards the corner, when his father changed his mind. Big Billie looked up from his plate with a gleeful smile.

"Hold on a minute, just hold on there, Bobby," he said, "I have an idea. Woman, get me a jar."

"What kind of a jar?" asked Mrs. Cameron.

"How should I know what kind of a jar? A jar with a lid on it."

Mrs. Cameron sighed, skirted the snake and opened a cupboard. She examined her store of jars.

"There's a jamjar, with dried peas in it," she said.

"Put the peas somewhere else and give me the jar," commanded Cameron. She passed him the jar.

"What are you going to do, Dad?" asked Bobby.

"There's a darkie we have at work. A heathen man. He comes from a land with a lot of snakes in it. I have in mind to have some fun with him. A wee joke, like. Pass me that oven glove, Jenny."

"You'll not need a glove," said Bobby. "He can't bite you."

"I'm not touching the dirty thing," said Cameron.

"He's not dirty," said Bobby. "They're very clean creatures."

"You're a fool, boy, for all your school learning. Does the Good Book not say: 'On thy belly shalt thou go, and dust shalt thou eat . . .'? Aye, and more than dust, no doubt. I'll not touch him with me hand."

Jenny passed her father the oven glove. Open jamjar in his left hand, right hand protected by the glove, Big Billie Cameron stood over the viper. Slowly his right hand descended. When it dropped, it was fast; but the small snake was faster. Its tiny fangs went harmlessly into the padding of the glove at the centre of the palm. Cameron did not notice, for the act was masked from his view by his own hands. In a trice the snake was inside the jamjar and the lid was on. Through the glass they watched it wriggle furiously.

"I hate them, harmless or not," said Mrs. Cameron. "I'll thank you to get it out of the house."

"I'll be doing that right now," said her husband, "for I'm late as it is."

He slipped the jamjar into his shoulder bag, already containing his lunch box, stuffed his pipe and pouch into the right-hand pocket of his jacket and took both out to the car. He arrived at the station yard five minutes late and was surprised to find the Indian student staring at him fixedly.

"I suppose he wouldn't have the second sight," thought Big Billie as they trundled south to Newtownards and Comber.

By mid-morning all the gang had been let into Big Billie's secret joke on pain of a thumping if they let on to "the darkie." There was no chance of that; assured that the slowworm was perfectly harmless, they too thought it a good leg-pull. Only Ram Lal worked on in ignorance, consumed by his private thoughts and worries.

At the lunch break he should have suspected something. The tension was palpable. The men sat in a circle around the fire as usual, but the conversation was stilted and had he not been so preoccupied he would have noticed the half-concealed grins and the looks darted in his direction. He did not notice. He placed his own lunch box between his knees and opened it. Coiled between the sandwiches and the apple, head back to strike, was the viper.

The Indian's scream echoed across the clearing, just ahead of the roar of laughter from the labourers. Simultaneously with the scream, the lunch box flew high in the air as he threw it away from himself with all his strength. All the contents of the box flew in a score of directions, landing in the long grass, the broom and gorse all around them.

Ram Lal was on his feet, shouting. The gangers rolled helplessly in their mirth, Big Billie most of all. He had not had such a laugh in months.

"It's a snake," screamed Ram Lal, "a poisonous snake. Get out of here, all of you. It's deadly."

The laughter redoubled; the men could not contain themselves. The reaction of the joke's victim surpassed all their expectations.

"Please, believe me. It's a snake, a deadly snake."

Big Billie's face was suffused. He wiped tears from his eyes, seated across the clearing from Ram Lal, who was standing looking wildly round.

"You ignorant darkie," he gasped, "don't you know? There are no snakes in Ireland. Understand? There aren't any."

His sides ached with laughing and he leaned back in the grass, his hands behind him to support him. He failed to notice the two pricks, like tiny thorns, that went into the vein on the inside of the right wrist.

The joke was over and the hungry men tucked into their lunches. Harkishan Ram Lal reluctantly took his seat, constantly glancing round him, a mug of steaming tea held ready, eating only with his left hand, staying clear of the long grass. After lunch they returned to work. The old distillery was almost down, the mountains of rubble and savable timbers lying dusty under the August sun.

At half past three Big Billie Cameron stood up from his work, rested on his pick and passed a hand across his forehead. He licked at a slight swelling on the inside of his wrist, then started work again. Five minutes later he straightened up again.

"I'm not feeling so good," he told Patterson, who was next to him. "I'm going to take a spell in the shade."

He sat under a tree for a while and then held his head in his hands. At a quarter past four, still clutching his splitting head, he gave one convulsion and toppled sideways. It was several minutes before Tommy Burns noticed him. He walked across and called to Patterson.

"Big Billie's sick," he called. "He won't answer me."

The gang broke and came over to the tree in whose shade the foreman lay. His sightless eyes were staring at the grass a few inches from his face. Patterson bent over him. He had been long enough in the labouring business to have seen a few dead ones.

"Ram," he said, "you have medical training. What do you think?"

Ram Lal did not need to make an examination, but he did. When he straightened up he said nothing, but Patterson understood.

"Stay here all of you," he said, taking command. "I'm going to phone an ambulance and call McQueen." He set off down the track to the main road.

The ambulance got there first, half an hour later. It reversed down the track and two men heaved Cameron onto a stretcher. They took him away to Newtownards General Hospital, which has the nearest casualty unit, and there the foreman was logged in as DOA—dead on arrival. An extremely worried McQueen arrived thirty minutes after that.

Because of the unknown circumstance of the death an autopsy had to be performed and it was, by the North Down area pathologist, in the Newtownards municipal mortuary to which the body had been transferred. That was on the Tuesday. By that evening the pathologist's report was on its way to the office of the coroner for North Down, in Belfast.

The report said nothing extraordinary. The deceased had been a man of forty-one years, big-built and immensely strong. There were upon the body various minor cuts and abrasions, mainly on the hands and wrists, quite consistent with the job of navvy, and none of these were in any way associated with the cause of death. The latter, beyond a doubt, had been a massive brain haemorrhage, itself probably caused by extreme exertion in conditions of great heat.

Possessed of this report, the coroner would normally not hold an inquest, being able to issue a certificate of death by natural causes to the registrar at Bangor. But there was something Harkishan Ram Lal did not know.

Big Billie Cameron had been a leading member of the Bangor council of the outlawed Ulster Volunteer Force, the hard-line Protestant paramilitary organization. The computer at Lurgan, into which all deaths in the province of Ulster, however innocent, are programmed, threw this out and someone in Lurgan picked up the phone to call the Royal Ulster Constabulary at Castlereagh.

Someone there called the coroner's office in Belfast, and a formal inquest was ordered. In Ulster death must not only be accidental; it must be seen to be accidental. For certain people, at least. The inquest was in the Town Hall at Bangor on the Wednesday. It meant a lot of trouble for McQueen, for the Inland Revenue attended. So did two quiet men of extreme Loyalist persuasion from the UVF council. They sat at the back. Most of the dead man's workmates sat near the front, a few feet from Mrs. Cameron.

Only Patterson was called to give evidence. He related the events of the Monday, prompted by the coroner, and as there was no dispute none of the other labourers was called, not even Ram Lal. The coroner read the pathologist's report aloud and it was clear enough. When he had finished, he summed up before giving his verdict.

"The pathologist's report is quite unequivocal. We have heard from Mr. Patterson of the events of that lunch break, of the perhaps rather foolish prank played by the deceased upon the Indian student. It would seem that Mr. Cameron was so amused that he laughed himself almost to the verge of apoplexy. The subsequent heavy labour with pick and shovel in the blazing sun did the rest, provoking the rupture of a large blood vessel in the brain or, as the pathologist puts it in more medical language, a cerebral haemorrhage. This court extends its sympathy to the widow and her children, and finds that Mr. William Cameron died of accidental causes."

Outside on the lawns that spread before Bangor Town Hall McQueen talked to his navvies.

"I'll stand fair by you, lads," he said. "The job's still on, but I can't afford not to deduct tax and all the rest, not with the Revenue breathing down my neck. The funeral's tomorrow, you can take the day off. Those who want to go on can report on Friday."

Harkishan Ram Lal did not attend the funeral. While it was in progress at the Bangor cemetery he took a taxi back to Comber and asked the driver to wait on the road while he walked down the track. The driver was a Bangor man and had heard about the death of Cameron.

"Going to pay your respects on the spot, are you?" he asked.

"In a way," said Ram Lal.

"That the manner of your people?" asked the driver.

"You could say so," said Ram Lal.

"Aye, well, I'll not say it's any better or worse than our way, by the graveside," said the driver, and prepared to read his paper while he waited.

Harkishan Ram Lal walked down the track to the clearing and stood where the camp fire had been. He looked around at the long grass, the broom and the gorse in its sandy soil.

"Visha serp," he called out to the hidden viper. "O venomous snake, can you hear me? You have done what I brought you so far from the hills of Rajputana to achieve. But you were supposed to die. I should have killed you myself, had it all gone as I planned, and thrown your foul carcass in the river.

"Are you listening, deadly one? Then hear this. You may live a little longer but then you will die, as all things die. And you will die alone, without a female with which to mate, because there are no snakes in Ireland."

The saw-scaled viper did not hear him, or if it did, gave no hint of understanding. Deep in its hole in the warm sand beneath him, it was busy, totally absorbed in doing what nature commanded it must do.

At the base of a snake's tail are two overlapping platescales which obscure the cloaca. The viper's tail was erect, the body throbbed in ancient rhythm. The plates were parted, and from the cloaca, one by one, each an inch long in its transparent sac, each as deadly at birth as its parent, she was bringing her dozen babies into the world.

SCRIMSHAW

Brian Garfield

SHE SUGGESTED LIQUID undulation: a lei-draped girl in a grass skirt under a windblown palm tree, her hands and hips expressive of the flow of the hula. Behind her, beyond the surf, a whaling ship was poised to approach the shore, its square-rigged sails bold against a polished white sky.

The scene was depicted meticulously upon ivory: a white fragment of tusk the size of a dollar bill. The etched detail was exquisite: the scrimshaw engraving was carved of thousands of thread-like lines and the artist's knife hadn't slipped once.

The price tag may have been designed to persuade tourists of the seriousness of the art form: it was in four figures. But Brenda was unimpressed. She put the piece back on the display cabinet and left the shop.

The hot Lahaina sun beat against her face and she went across Front Street to the Sea Wall, thrust her hands into the pockets of her dress and brooded upon the anchorage.

Boats were moored around the harbor—catamarans, glass-bottom tourist boats, marlin fishermen, pleasure sailboats, outrigger canoes, yachts. Playthings. It's the wrong place for me, she thought.

Beyond the wide channel the islands of Lanai and Kahoolawe made lovely horizons under their umbrellas of delicate cloud, but Brenda had lost her eye for that sort of thing; she noticed the stagnant heat, the shabbiness of the town, and the offensiveness of the tourists who trudged from shop to shop in their silly hats, their sunburnt flab, their hapless T-shirts emblazoned with local graffiti: "Here Today, Gone to Maui."

A leggy young girl went by, drawing Brenda's brief attention: one of those taut tan sunbleached creatures of the surfboards—gorgeous and luscious and vacuous. Filled with youth and hedonism, equipped with all the optional accessories of pleasure. Brenda watched gloomily, her eyes following the girl as far as the end of the Sea Wall, where the girl turned to cross the street. Brenda then noticed two men in conversation there.

One of them was the wino who always seemed to be there: a stringy unshaven tattered character who spent the days huddling in the shade sucking from a bottle in a brown bag and begging coins from tourists. At night he seemed to prowl the alleys behind the seafood restaurants, living off scraps like a stray dog: she had seen him once, from the window of her flyspecked room, scrounging in the can behind the hotel's kitchen; and then two nights ago near a garbage bin she had taken a short cut home after a dissatisfying lonely dinner and she'd nearly tripped over him.

The man talking with the wino seemed familiar and yet she could not place the man. He had the lean bearded look of one who had gone native; but not really, for he was set apart by his fastidiousness. He wore sandals, yet his feet seemed clean, the toenails glimmering; he wore a sandy beard but it was neatly trimmed and his hair was expensively cut, not at all shaggy; he wore a blue denim short-sleeved shirt, fashionably faded but it had sleeve pockets and epaulets and had come from a designer shop; and his white sailor's trousers fit perfectly.

I know him, Brenda thought, but she couldn't summon the energy to stir from her spot when the bearded man and the wino walked away into the town. Vaguely and without real interest she wondered idly what those two could possibly have to talk about together.

She found shade on the harborfront. Inertia held her there for hours while she recounted the litany of her misfortunes. Finally hunger bestirred her and she slouched back to her miserable little third-class hotel.

The next day, half drunk in the afternoon and wilting in the heat, Brenda noticed vaguely that the wino was no longer in his usual place. In fact, she hadn't seen the wino at all, not last night and not today.

The headache was painful and she boarded the jitney bus to go up-island a few miles. She got off near the Kapalua headland and trudged down to the public beach. It was cooler here because the northwest end of the island was open to the fresh trade winds; she settled under a palm tree, pulled off her ragged sneakers, and dug her toes into the cool sand. The toes weren't very clean. She was going too long between baths these days. The bathroom in the hotel was at the end of the corridor and she went there as infrequently as possible because she couldn't be sure who she might encounter and anyhow, the tub was filthy and there was no shower.

Across the channel loomed the craggy mountains of Molokai, infamous island, leper colony, its dark volcanic mass shadowed by perpetual sinister rain clouds, and Brenda lost herself in gruesome speculations about exile, isolation, loneliness, and wretched despair, none of which seemed at all foreign to her.

The sun moved and took the shade with it and she moved round to the other side of the palm tree, tucking the fabric of the cheap dress under her when she sat down. The dress was about gone—frayed, faded, the material ready to disintegrate. She only had two others left. Then it would be jeans and the boatneck. It didn't matter, really. There was no one to dress up for.

It wasn't that she was altogether ugly; she wasn't ugly; she wasn't even plain, really; she had studied photographs of herself over the years and she had gazed in the mirror and tried to understand, but it had eluded her. All right, perhaps she was too bony, her shoulders too big, flat in front, not enough flesh on her—but there were men who liked their women bony; that didn't explain it. She had the proper features in the proper places and, after all, Modigliani hadn't found that sort of face abominable to behold, had he?

But ever since puberty there'd been something about her gangly gracelessness that had isolated her. Invitations to go out had been infrequent. At parties no one ever initiated conversations with her. No one, in any case, until Briggs had appeared in her life.

. . . She noticed the man again: the well-dressed one with the neatly trimmed beard. A droopy brown Hawaiian youth was picking up litter on the beach and depositing it in a burlap sack he dragged along; the bearded man ambled beside the youth, talking to him. The Hawaiian said something; the bearded man nodded with evident disappointment and turned to leave the beach. His path brought him close by Brenda's palm tree and Brenda sat up abruptly. "Eric?"

The bearded man squinted into the shade, trying to recognize her. Brenda removed her sunglasses. She said, "Eric? Eric Morelius?"

"Brenda?" The man came closer and she contrived a wan smile. "Brenda Briggs? What the devil are you doing here? You look like a beachcomber gone to seed."

Over a drink in Kimo's she tried to put on a front. "Well, I thought I'd come out here on a sabbatical and, you know, loaf around the islands, recharge my batteries, take stock."

She saw that Eric wasn't buying it. She tried to smile. "And what about you?"

"Well, I live here, you know. Came out to Hawaii nine years ago on vacation and never went back." Eric had an easy relaxed attitude of confident assurance. "Come off it, duckie, you look like hell. What's happened to you?"

She contrived a shrug of indifference. "The world fell down around my ankles. Happens to most everybody sometimes, I suppose. It doesn't matter."

"Just like that? It must have been something terrible. You had more promise than anyone in the department."

"Well, we were kids then, weren't we. We were all promising young scholars. But what happens after you've broken all the promises?"

"Good Lord. The last I saw of you, you and Briggs were off to revitalize the University of what, New Mexico?"

"Arizona." She tipped her head back with the glass to her mouth; ice clicked against her teeth. "And after that a state college in Minnesota. And then a dinky jerkwater diploma mill in California. The world," she said in a quiet voice, "has little further need of second-rate Greek and Roman literature scholars—or for any sort of non-tenured Ph.D.'s in the humanities. I spent last year waiting on tables in Modesto."

"Duckie," Eric said, "there's one thing you haven't mentioned. Where's Briggs?"

She hesitated. Then—what did it matter?—she told him: "He left me. Four years ago. Divorced me and married a buxom life-of-the-party girl fifteen years younger than me. She was writing advertising copy for defective radial tires or carcinogenic deodorants or something like that. We had a kid, you know. Cute little guy, we named him Geoff, with a G—you know how Briggs used to love reading Chaucer. In the original. In retrospect, you know, Briggs was a prig and a snob."

"Where's the kid, then?"

"I managed to get custody and then six months ago he went to visit his father for the weekend and all three of them, Briggs and the copy-writer and my kid Geoff well, there was a six-car pileup on the Santa Monica Freeway and I had to pay for the funerals and it wiped me out."

Eric brought another pair of drinks and there was a properly responsive sympathy in his eyes and it had been so long since she'd talked about it that she covered her face with the table napkin and sobbed. "God help me, Eric. Briggs was the only man who ever gave me a second look."

* * *

He walked her along the Sea Wall. "You'll get over it, duckie. Takes time."

"Sure," she said listlessly. "I know."

"Sure, it can be tough. Especially when you haven't got anybody. You don't have any family left, do you?"

"No. Only child. My parents died young. Why not? The old man was on the assembly line in Dearborn. We're all on the assembly line in Dearborn. What have we got to aim for? A condominium in some ant-hill and a bag full of golf clubs? Let's change the subject, all right? What about you, then? You look prosperous enough. Did you drop out or were you pushed too?"

"Dropped out. Saw the light and made it to the end of the tunnel. I'm a free man, duckie."

"What do you do?"

"I'm a scrimshander."

"A what?"

"A bone-ivory artist. I do scrimshaw engravings. You've probably seen my work in the shop windows around town."

Eric's studio, high under the eaves in the vintage whaler's house that looked more New Englandish than tropical, revealed its owner's compulsion for orderly neatness.

She had never liked him much. He and Briggs had got along all right, but she'd always found Eric an unpleasant sort. It wasn't that he was boorish; hardly anything like that. But she thought him pretentious and totally insincere. He'd always had that air of arrogant self-assurance. And the polish was all on the surface; he had the right manners but once you got to know him a little you realized he had no real understanding of courtesy or compassion. Those qualities were meaningless to people like Eric. She'd always thought him self-absorbed and egotistical to the point of solipsism; she'd felt he had cultivated Briggs's friendship simply because Eric felt Briggs could help him advance in the department.

Eric had been good at toadying up to anyone who could help him learn the arts of politics and ambition. Eric had always been very actorish: he wasn't real—everything was a role, a part, a performance: everything Eric did was done with his audience in mind. If you couldn't be any help to him he could, without a second thought, cut you dead.

He wasn't really handsome. He had a small round head and ordinary features. But he'd always kept himself trim and he'd always been a natty dresser. And the beard sharpened his face, made it longer, added polish to his appearance. Back on the mainland, she remembered, he'd tended to favor three-piece suits.

Eric's studio was spartan, dominated by a scrubbed-clean workbench under the dormer window's north light. An array of carving tools filled a wooden rack, each tool seated in its proper niche, and there were four tidy wooden bins containing pieces of white bone of graduated sizes. Antique inkwells and jars were arranged beside a tray of paintbrushes and other slender implements. In three glass display cases, each overhung by a museum light, lay examples of Eric's art. One piece, especially striking, was a large ivory cribbage board in the shape of a Polynesian outrigger canoe with intricate black-and-white scenes engraved upon its faceted surfaces.

"That's a sort of frieze," Eric explained. "If you follow those little scenes around the board, they illustrate the whole mythology of the Polynesian emigration that led to the original settlement of Hawaii a thousand years ago. I'm negotiating to sell it to the museum over in Honolulu."

"It must be pretty lucrative, this stuff."

"It can be. Do you know anything about scrimshaw?"

"No," she said, and she didn't particularly care to; but Eric had paid for the bottle and was pouring a drink for her, and she was desperate for company—anyone's, even Eric's—and so she stayed and pretended interest.

"It's a genuine American folk art. It was originated in the early 1800s by the Yankee whalers who came out to the Pacific with endless time on their hands on shipboard. They got into the habit of scrimshanding to pass the time. The early stuff was crude, of course, but pretty quickly some of them started doing quite sophisticated workmanship. They used sail needles to carve the fine lines of the engraving and then they'd trace India ink or lampblack into the carvings for contrast. About the only materials they had were whalebone and whales' teeth, so that's what they carved at first.

"The art became very popular for a while, about a century ago, and there was a period when scrimshanding became a profession in its own right. That was when they ran short of whalebone and teeth and started illustrating elephant ivory and other white bone materials. Then it all went out of fashion. But it's been coming back into favor the past few years. We've got several scrimshanders here now. The main problem today, of course, is the scarcity of ivory."

At intervals Brenda sipped his whiskey and vocalized sounds indicative of her attentiveness to his monologue. Mainly she was thinking morosely of the pointlessness of it all. Was Eric going to ask her to stay the night? If he did, would she accept? In either case, did it matter?

Watching her with bemused eyes, Eric went on, "The Endangered Species laws have made it impossible for us to obtain whalebone or elephant ivory in any quantities anymore. It's a real problem."

"You seem to have a fair supply in those bins there."

"Well, some of us have been buying mastodon ivory and other fossilized bones from the Eskimos—they dig for it in the tundra up in Alaska. But that stuff's in short supply too, and the price has gone through the ceiling."

Eric took her glass and filled it from the bottle, extracting ice cubes from the half-size fridge under the workbench. She rolled the cold glass against her forehead and returned to the wicker chair, balancing herself with care. Eric smiled with the appearance of sympathy and pushed a little box across the bench. It was the size of a matchbox. The lid fit snugly. Etched into its ivory surface was a drawing of a humpback whale.

"Like it?"

"It's lovely." She tried to summon enthusiasm in her voice.

"It's nearly the real thing," he said. "Not real ivory, of course, but real bone at least. We've been experimenting with chemical processes to bleach and harden it."

She studied the tiny box and suddenly looked away. Something about it had put her in mind of little Geoff's casket.

"The bones of most animals are too rough and porous," Eric was saying. "They tend to decompose, of course, being organic. But we've had some success with chemical hardening agents. Still, there aren't many types of bone that are suitable. Of course, there are some people who're willing to make do with vegetable ivory or hard plastics, but those really aren't acceptable if you care about the artistry of the thing. The phony stuff has no grain, and anybody with a good eye can always tell."

She was thinking she really had to pull herself together. You couldn't get by indefinitely on self-pity and the liquid largess of old acquaintances, met by chance, whom you didn't even like. She'd reached a point-of-no-return: the end of this week her room rent would be due again and she had no money to cover it; the time to make up her mind was now, right now, because either she got a job or she'd end up like that whiskered wino begging for pennies and eating out of refuse bins.

Eric went on prattling about his silly hobby or whatever it was: something about the larger bones of primates—thigh bone, collarbone. "Young enough to be in good health of course—bone grows uselessly brittle as we get older . . ." But she wasn't really listening; she stood beside the workbench looking out through the dormer window at the dozens of boats in the anchorage, wondering if she could face walking into one of the tourist dives and begging for a job waiting on tables.

The drink had made her unsteady. She returned to the chair, resolving to explore the town first thing in the morning in search of employment. She *had* to snap out of it. It was time to come back to life and perhaps these beautiful islands were the place to do it: the proper setting for the resurrection of a jaded soul.

Eric's voice paused interrogatively and it made her look up. "What? Sorry."

"These two here," Eric said. She looked down at the two etched pendants. He said, "Can you tell the difference?"

"They look pretty much the same to me."

"There, see that? That one, on the left, that's a piece of whale's tooth. This other one's ordinary bone, chemically hardened and bleached to the consistency and color of true ivory. It's got the proper grain, everything."

"Fine." She set the glass down and endeavored to smile pleasantly. "That's fine, Eric. Thank you so much for the drinks. I'd better go now—" She aimed herself woozily toward the door.

"No need to rush off, is there? Here, have one more and then we'll get a bite to eat. There's a terrific little place back on the inland side of town."

"Thanks, really, but—"

"I won't take no for an answer, duckie. How often do we see each other, after all? Come on—look, I'm sorry, I've been boring you to tears with all this talk about scrimshaw and dead bones, and we haven't said a word yet about the really important things."

"What important things?"

"Well, what are we going to do about you, duckie? You seem to have a crucial problem with your life right now and I think, if you let me, maybe I can help sort it out. Sometimes all it takes is the counsel of a sympathetic old friend, you know."

By then the drink had been poured and she saw no plausible reason to refuse it. She settled back in the cane chair. Eric's smile was avuncular. "What are friends for, after all? Relax a while, duckie. You know, when I first came out here I felt a lot the way you're feeling. I guess in a way I was lucky not to've been as good a scholar as you and Briggs were. I got through the Ph.D. program by the skin of my teeth but it wasn't enough. I applied for teaching jobs all over the country, you know. Not one nibble."

Then the quick smile flashed behind the neat beard. "I ran

away, you see—as far as I could get without a passport. These islands are full of losers like you and me, you know. Scratch any charter-boat skipper in that marina and you'll find a bankrupt or a failed writer who couldn't get his epic novel published."

Then he lifted his glass in a gesture of toast. "But it's possible to find an antidote for our failure, you see. Sometimes it may take a certain ruthlessness, of course—a willingness to suspend the stupid values we were brought up on. So-called civilized principles are the enemies of any true individualist—you have to learn that or you're doomed to be a loser for all time. The kings and robber barons we've honored throughout history—none of them was the kind to let himself be pushed around by the imbecilic bureaucratic whims of college deans or tenure systems.

"Establishments and institutions and laws are designed by winners to keep losers in their place, that's all. You're only free when you learn there's no reason to play the game by their rules. Hell, duckie, the fun of life only comes when you discover how to make your own rules and laugh at the fools around you. Look—consider your own situation. Is there any single living soul right now who truly gives a damn whether you, Brenda Briggs, are alive or dead?"

Put that starkly it made her gape. Eric leaned forward, brandishing his glass as if it were a searchlight aimed at her face. "Well?"

"No. Nobody," she murmured reluctantly.

"There you are, then." He seemed to relax; he leaned back. "There's not a soul you need to please or impress or support, right? If you went right up Front Street here and walked into the Bank of Hawaii and robbed the place of a fortune and got killed making your escape, you'd be hurting no one but yourself. Am I right, duckie?"

"I suppose so."

"Then why not give it a try?"

"Give what a try?"

"Robbing a bank. Kidnapping a rich infant. Hijacking a yacht. Stealing a million in diamonds. Whatever you feel like, duckie—whatever appeals to you. Why not? What have you got to lose?"

She twisted her mouth into an uneven smile. "You remind me of the sophomoric sophistry we used to spout when we were undergraduates. Existentialism and nihilism galore." She put her glass down. "Well, I guess not, Eric. I don't think I'll start robbing banks just yet."

"And why not?"

"Maybe I'm just not gaited that way."

"Morality? Is that it? What's morality ever done for *you?*"

She steadied herself with a hand against the workbench, set her feet with care, and turned toward the door. "It's a drink too late for morbid philosophical dialectics. Thanks for the booze, though. I'll see you . . ."

"You'd better sit down, duckie. You're a little unsteady there."

"No, I—"

"Sit down." The words came out in a harsher voice. "The door's locked anyway, duckie—you're not going anywhere."

She scowled, befuddled. "What?"

He showed her the key; then he put it away in his pocket. She looked blankly at the door, the keyhole, and—again—his face. It had gone hard; the polite mask was gone.

"I wish you'd taken the bait," he said. "Around here all they ever talk about is sunsets and surfing and the size of the marlin some fool caught. At least you've got a bigger vocabulary than that. I really wish you'd jumped at it, duckie. It would have made things easier. But you didn't, so that's that."

"What on earth are you talking about?"

She stumbled to the door then—and heard Eric's quiet laughter when she tried the knob.

She put her back to the door. Her head swam. "I don't understand . . ."

"It's the ivory, duckie. The best material is fresh human bone. The consistency, the hardness—it takes a fine polish if it's young and healthy enough . . ."

She stared at him and the understanding seeped into her slowly and she said, "That's where the wino went."

"Well, I have to pick and choose, don't I? I mean, I can't very well use people whose absence would be noticed."

She flattened herself against the door. She was beginning to pass out; she tried to fight it but she couldn't; in the distance, fading, she heard Eric say, "You'll make fine bones, duckie. Absolutely first-rate scrimshaw."

Prisoners

Ed Gorman

I AM IN MY sister's small room with its posters of Madonna and Tiffany. Sis is fourteen. Already tall, already pretty. Dressed in jeans and a blue t-shirt. Boys call and come over constantly. She wants nothing to do with boys.

Her back is to me. She will not turn around. I sit on the edge of her bed, touching my hand to her shoulder. She smells warm, of sleep. I say, "Sis listen to me."

She says nothing. She almost always says nothing.

"He wants to see you Sis."

Nothing.

"When he called last weekend—you were all he talked about. He even started crying when you wouldn't come to the phone Sis. He really did."

Nothing.

"Please, Sis. Please put on some good clothes and get ready 'cause we've got to leave in ten minutes. We've got to get there on time and you know it." I lean over so I can see her face.

She tucks her face into her pillow.

She doesn't want me to see that she is crying.

"Now you go and get ready, Sis. You go and get ready, all right?"

"I don't know who she thinks she is," Ma says when I go downstairs. "Too good to go and see her own father."

As she talks Ma is packing a big brown grocery sack. Into it go a cornucopia of goodies—three cartons of Lucky Strike filters, three packages of Hershey bars, two bottles of Ban roll-on deodorant, three Louis L'Amour paperbacks as well as all the stuff that's in there already.

Ma looks up at me. I've seen pictures of her when she was a young woman. She was a beauty. But that was before she started putting on weight and her hair started thinning and she stopped caring about how she dressed and all. "She going to go with us?"

"She says not."

"Just who does she think she is?"

"Calm down Ma. If she doesn't want to go, we'll just go ahead without her."

"What do we tell your Dad?"

"Tell him she's got the flu."

"The way she had the flu the last six times?"

"She's gone a few times."

"Yeah twice out of the whole year he's been there."

"Well."

"How do you think he feels? He gets all excited thinking he's going to see her and then she doesn't show up. How do you think he feels? She's his own flesh and blood."

I sigh. Ma's none too healthy and getting worked up this way doesn't do her any good. "I better go and call Riley."

"That's it. Go call Riley. Leave me here alone to worry about what we're going to tell your Dad."

"You know how Riley is. He appreciates a call."

"You don't care about me no more than your selfish sister does."

I go out to the living room where the phone sits on the end table I picked up at Goodwill last Christmastime. A lot of people don't like to shop at Goodwill, embarassed about going in there and all. The only thing I don't like is the smell. All those old clothes hanging. Sometimes I wonder if you opened up a grave if it wouldn't smell like Goodwill.

I call K-Mart, which is where I work as a manager trainee while I'm finishing off my retail degree at the junior college. My girlfriend Karen works at K-Mart, too. "Riley?"

"Hey, Tom."

"How're things going in my department?" A couple months ago Riley, who is the assistant manager over the whole store, put me in charge of the automotive department.

"Good, great."

"Good. I was worried." Karen always says she's proud 'cause I worry so much about my job. Karen says it proves I'm responsible. Karen says one of the reasons she loves me so much is 'cause I'm responsible. I guess I'd rather have her love me for my blue eyes or something but of course I don't say anything because Karen can get crabby about strange things sometimes.

"You go and see your old man today, huh?" Riley says.

"Yeah."

"Hell of a way to spend your day off."

"It's not so bad. You get used to it."

"Any word on when he gets out?"

"Be a year or so yet. Being his second time in and all."

"You're a hell of a kid, Tom, I ever tell you that before?"

"Yeah you did Riley and I appreciate it." Riley is a year older than me but sometimes he likes to pretend he's my uncle or something. But he means well and, like I told him, I appreciate it. Like when Dad's name was in the paper for the burglary and everything. The people at K-Mart all saw it and started treating me funny. But not Tom. He'd walk up and down the aisles with me and even put his arm on my shoulder like we were the best buddies in the whole world or something. In the coffee room this fat woman made a crack about it and Tom got mad and said "Why don't you shut your fucking fat mouth Shirley?" Nobody said anything more about my Dad after that. Of course poor Sis had it a lot worse than me at Catholic school. She had it real bad. Some of those kids really got vicious. A lot of nights I'd lay awake thinking of all the things I wanted to do to those kids. I'd do it with my hands too, wouldn't even use weapons.

"Well say hi to your mom."

"Thanks Riley. I'll be sure to."

"She's a hell of a nice lady." Riley and his girl came over one night when Ma'd had about three beers and was in a really good mood. They got along really well. He had her laughing at his jokes all night. Riley knows a lot of jokes. A lot of them.

"I sure hope we make our goal today."

"You just relax Tom and forget about the store. OK?"

"I'll try."

"Don't try Tom. Do it." He laughs, being my uncle again. "That's an order."

In the kitchen, done with packing her paper bag, Ma says, "I shouldn't have said that."

"Said what?" I say.

"About you being like your sister."

"Aw Ma. I didn't take that seriously."

"We couldn't've afforded to stay in this house if you hadn't been promoted to assistant manager. Not many boys would turn over their whole paychecks to their Ma." She doesn't mention her sister who is married to a banker who is what bankers aren't supposed to be, generous. I help but he helps a lot.

She starts crying.

I take her to me, hold her. Ma needs to cry a lot. Like she fills up with tears and will drown if she can't get rid of them. When I hold her I always think of the pictures of her as a young woman, of all the terrible things that have cost her her beauty.

When she's settled down some I say, "I'll go talk to Sis."

But just as I say that I hear the old boards of the house creak and there in the doorway, dressed in a white blouse and a blue skirt and blue hose and the blue flats I bought her for her last birthday, is Sis.

Ma sees her too and starts crying all over again. "Oh God hon thanks so much for changing your mind."

Then Ma puts her arms out wide and she goes over to Sis and

throws her arms around her and gets her locked inside this big hug.

I can see Sis' blue eyes staring at me over Ma's shoulder.

In the soft fog of the April morning I see watercolor brown cows on the curve of the green hills and red barns faint in the rain. I used to want to be a farmer till I took a two week job summer of junior year where I cleaned out dairy barns and it took me weeks to get the odor of wet hay and cowshit and hot pissy milk from my nostrils and then I didn't want to be a farmer ever again.

"You all right hon?" Ma asks Sis.

But Sis doesn't answer. Just stares out the window at the watercolor brown cows.

"Ungrateful little brat" Ma says under her breath.

If Sis hears this she doesn't let on. She just stares out the window.

"Hon slow down" Ma says to me. "This road'z got a lot of curves in it."

And so it does.

Twenty-three curves—I've counted them many times—and you're on top of a hill looking down into a valley where the prison lies.

Curious, I once went to the library and read up on the prison. According to the historical society it's the oldest prison still standing in the Midwest, built of limestone dragged by prisoners from a nearby quarry. In 1948 the west wing had a fire that killed 18 blacks (they were segregated in those days) and in 1957 there was a riot that got a guard castrated with a busted pop bottle and two inmates shot dead in the back by other guards who were never brought to trial.

From the two-lane asphalt road that winds into the prison you see the steep limestone walls and the towers where uniformed guards toting riot guns look down at you as you sweep west to park in the visitors' parking lot.

* * *

As we walk through the rain to the prison, hurrying as the fat drops splatter on our heads, Ma says "I forgot. Don't say anything about your cousin Bessie."

"Oh. Right."

"Stuff about cancer always makes your Dad depressed. You know it runs in his family a lot."

She glances over her shoulder at Sis shambling along. Sis had not worn a coat. The rain doesn't seem to bother her. She is staring out at something still as if her face was nothing more than a mask which hides her real self. "You hear me?" Ma asks Sis.

If Sis hears she doesn't say anything.

"How're you doing this morning Jimmy?" Ma asks the fat guard who lets us into the waiting room.

His stomach wriggles beneath his threadbare uniform shirt like something troubled struggling to be born.

He grunts something none of us can understand. He obviously doesn't believe in being nice to Ma no matter how nice Ma is to him. Would break prison decorum apparently the sonofabitch. But if you think he's cold to us—and most people in the prison are—you should see how they are to the families of queers or with men who did things with children.

The cold is in my bones already. Except for July and August prison is always cold to me. The bars are cold. The walls are cold. When you go into the bathroom and run the water your fingers tingle. The prisoners are always sneezing and coughing. Ma always brings Dad lots of Contac and Listerine even though I told her about this article that said Listerine isn't anything except a mouthwash.

In the waiting room—which is nothing more than the yellow-painted room with battered old wooden chairs—a turnkey named Stan comes in and leads you right up to the visiting room, the only problem being that separating you from the visiting room is a set of bars. Stan turns the key that raises these bars and then you get inside and he lowers the bars behind you. For a minute or so you're locked in between two walls and two sets of bars. You get a sense of what it's like to be in a cell. The first couple times this happened I got scared. My chest started heaving and I couldn't catch my breath, sort of like the nightmares I have sometimes.

Stan then raises the second set of bars and you're one room away from the visiting room or VR as the prisoners call it. In prison you always lower the first set of bars before you raise the next one. That way nobody escapes.

In this second room, not much bigger than a closet with a stand-up clumsy metal detector near the door leading to the VR, Stan asks Ma and Sis for their purses and me for my wallet. He asks if any of us have got any open packs of cigarettes and if so to hand them over. Prisoners and visitors alike can carry only full packs of cigarettes into the VR. Open packs are easy to hide stuff in.

You pass through the metal detector and straight into the VR room.

The first thing you notice is how all the furniture is in color coded sets—loungers and vinyl molded chairs makes up a set—orange green blue or red. Like that. This is so Mona the guard in here can tell you where to sit just by saying a color such as "Blue" which means you go sit in the blue set. Mona makes Stan look like a real friendly guy. She's fat with hair cut man short and a voice man deep. She wears her holster and gun with real obvious pleasure. One time Ma didn't understand what color she said and Mona's hand dropped to her service revolver like she was going to whip it out or something. Mona doesn't like to repeat herself. Mona is the one the black prisoner knocked unconscious a year ago. The black guy is married to this white girl which right away you can imagine Mona not liking at all so she's looking for any excuse to hassle him so the black guy one time gets down on his hands and knees to play with his little baby and Mona comes over and says you can only play with kids in the Toy Room (TR) and he says can't you make an exception and Mona sly like bumps him hard on the shoulder and he just flashes the way prisoners sometimes do and jumps up from the floor and not caring that she's a woman or not just drops her with a right hand and the way the story is told now anyway by prisoners and their families, everybody in TR instead of rushing to help her break out into applause just like it's a movie or something. Standing ovation. The black guy was in the hole for six months but was quoted afterward as saying it was worth it.

Most of the time it's not like that at all. Nothing exciting I mean. Most of the time it's just depressing.

Mostly it's women here to see husbands. They usually bring their kids so there's a lot of noise. Crying laughing chasing around. You can tell if there's trouble with a parole—the guy not getting out when he's supposed to—because that's when the arguments always start, the wife having built her hopes up and then the husband saying there's nothing he can do I'm sorry honey nothing I can do and sometimes the woman will really start crying or arguing, I even saw a woman slap her husband once, the worst being of course when some little kid starts crying and says "Daddy I want you to come home!" That's usually when the prisoner himself starts crying.

As for touching or fondling, there's none of it. You can kiss your husband for thirty seconds and most guards will hassle you even before your time's up if you try it open mouth or anything. Mona in particular is a real bitch about something like this. Apparently Mona doesn't like the idea of men and women kissing.

Another story you hear a lot up here is how this one prisoner cut a hole in his pocket so he could stand by the Coke machine and have his wife put her hand down his pocket and jack him off while they just appeared to be innocently standing there, though that may be one of those stories the prisoners just like to tell.

The people who really have it worst are those who are in the hole or some other kind of solitary. On the west wall there's this long screen for them. They have to sit behind the screen the whole time. They can't touch their kids or anything. All they can do is look.

I can hear Ma's breath take up sharp when they bring Dad in.

He's still a handsome man—thin, dark curly hair with no gray, and more solid than ever since he works out in the prison weight room all the time. He always walks jaunty as if to say that wearing a gray uniform and living in an interlocking set of cages has not yet broken him. But you can see in his blue eyes that they broke him a long long time ago.

"Hiya everybody" he says trying to sound real happy.

Ma throws her arms around him and they hold each other. Sis and I sit down on the two chairs. I look at Sis. She stares at the floor.

Dad comes over then and says "'You two sure look great."

"So do you" I say. "You must be still lifting those weights."

"Bench pressed two-twenty-five this week."

"Man" I say and look at Sis again. I nudge her with my elbow. She won't look up.

Dad stares at her. You can see how sad he is about her not looking up. Soft he says "It's all right."

Ma and Dad sit down then and we go through the usual stuff, how things are going at home and at my job and in junior college, and how things are going in prison. When he first got here, they put Dad in with this colored guy—he was Jamaican—but then they found out he had AIDS so they moved Dad out right away. Now the guy he's with is this guy who was in Viet Nam and got one side of his face burned. Dad says once you get used to looking at him he's a nice guy with two kids of his own and not queer in any way or into drugs at all. In prison the drugs get pretty bad.

We talk a half hour before Dad looks at Sis again. "So how's my little girl."

She still won't look up.

"Ellen" Ma says "you talk to your Dad and right now."

Sis raises her head. She looks right at Dad but doesn't seem to see him at all. Ellen can do that. It's real spooky.

Dad puts his hand out and touches her.

Sis jerks her hand away. It's the most animated I've seen her in weeks.

"You give your Dad a hug and you give him a hug right now" Ma says to Sis.

Sis, still staring at Dad, shakes her head.

"It's all right" Dad says. "It's all right. She just doesn't like to come up here and I don't blame her at all. This isn't a nice place to visit at all." He smiles. "Believe me I wouldn't be here if they didn't make me."

Ma asks "Any word on your parole?"

"My lawyer says two years away. Maybe three, 'cause it's a second offense and all." Dad sighs and takes Ma's hand. "I know it's hard for you to believe hon—I mean practically every guy in here says the same thing—but I didn't break into that store that night. I really didn't. I was just walkin' along the river."

"I do believe you hon" Ma says "and so does Tom and so does Sis. Right kids?"

I nod. Sis has gone back to staring at the floor.

"'cause I served time before for breaking and entering the cops just automatically assumed it was me." Dad says. He shakes his head. The sadness is back in his eyes. "I don't have no idea how my billfold got on the floor of that place." He sounds miserable and now he doesn't look jaunty or young. He looks old and gray.

He looks back at Sis. "You still gettin' straight A's hon?"

She looks up at him. But doesn't nod or anything.

"She sure is" Ma says. "Sister Rosemary says Ellen is the best student she's got. Imagine that."

Dad starts to reach out to Sis again but then takes his hand back.

Over in the red section this couple start arguing. The woman is crying and this little girl maybe six is holding real tight to her

Dad who looks like he's going to start crying too. That bitch Mona has put on her mirror sunglasses again so you can't tell what she's thinking but you can see from the angle of her face that she's watching the three of them in the red section. Probably enjoying herself.

"Your lawyer sure it'll be two years?" Ma says.

"Or three."

"I sure do miss you hon" Ma says.

"I sure do miss you too hon."

"Don't know what I'd do without Tom to lean on." She makes a point of not mentioning Sis who she's obviously still mad at because Sis won't speak to Dad.

"He's sure a fine young man" Dad says. "Wish I woulda been that responsible when I was his age. Wouldn't be in here today if I'da been."

Sis gets up and leaves the room. Says nothing. Doesn't even look at anybody exactly. Just leaves. Mona directs her to the ladies room.

"I'm sorry hon she treats you this way" Ma says. "She thinks she's too good to come see her Dad in prison."

"It's all right" Dad says looking sad again. He watches Sis leave the visiting room.

"I'm gonna have a good talk with her when we leave here hon" Ma says.

"Oh don't be too hard on her. Tough for a proud girl her age to come up here."

"Not too hard for Tom."

"Tom's different. Tom's mature. Tom's responsible. When Ellen gets Tom's age I'm sure she'll be mature and responsible too."

Half hour goes back before Sis comes. Almost time to leave. She walks over and sits down.

"You give your Dad a hug now." Ma says.

Sis looks at Dad. She stands up then and goes over and puts her arms out. Dad stands up grinning and takes her to him and hugs her tighter than I've ever seen him hug anybody. It's funny because right then and there he starts crying. Just holding Sis so tight. Crying.

"I love you hon" Dad says to her. "I love you hon and I'm sorry for all the mistakes I've made and I'll never make them again I promise you."

Ma starts crying too.

Sis says nothing.

When Dad lets her go I look at her eyes. They're the same as they were before. She's staring right at him but she doesn't seem to see him somehow.

Mona picks up the microphone that blasts through the speakers hung from the ceiling. She doesn't need a speaker in a room this size but she obviously likes how loud it is and how it hurts your ears.

"Visiting hours are over. You've got fifteen seconds to say good-bye and then the inmates have to start filing over to the door."

"I miss you so much hon" Ma says and throws her arms around Dad.

He hugs Ma but over his shoulder he's looking at Sis. She is standing up. She has her head down again.

Dad looks so sad so sad.

"I'd like to know just who the hell you think you are treatin' your own father that way" Ma says on the way back to town.

The rain and the fog are real bad now so I have to concentrate on my driving. On the opposite side of the road cars appear quickly in the fog and then vanish. It's almost unreal.

The wipers are slapping loud and everything smells damp, the rubber of the car and the vinyl seat covers and the ashtray from Ma's menthol cigarettes. Damp.

"You hear me young lady?" Ma says.

Sis is in the back seat again alone. Staring out the window. At the fog I guess.

"Come on Ma, she hugged him" I say.

"Yeah when I practically had to twist her arm to do it." Ma shakes her head. "Her own flesh and blood."

Sometimes I want to get mad and really let it out but I know it would just hurt Ma to remind her what Dad was doing to Ellen those years after he came out of prison the first time. I know for a fact he was doing it because I walked in on them one day little eleven-year-old Ellen there on the bed underneath my naked dad, staring off as he grunted and moved around inside her, staring off just the way she does now.

Staring off.

Ma knew about it all along of course but she wouldn't do anything about it. Wouldn't admit it probably not even to herself. In psychology, which I took last year at the junior college, that's called denial. I even brought it up a couple times but she just said I had a filthy mind and don't ever say nothing like that again.

Which is why I broke into that store that night and left Dad's billfold behind. Because I knew they'd arrest him and then he couldn't force Ellen into the bed anymore. Not that I blame Dad entirely. Prison makes you crazy no doubt about it and he was in there four years the first time. But even so I love Sis too much.

"Own flesh and blood" Ma says again lighting up one of her menthols and shaking her head.

I look into the rearview mirror at Sis's eyes. "Wish I could make you smile" I say to her. "Wish I could make you smile."

But she just stares out the window.

Sis hasn't smiled for a long time of course.

Not for a long time.

McIntyre's Donald

Joseph Hansen

AROUND MIDNIGHT, the sound of rain woke him, lashing the window glass, sluicing from the eaves. Wind bent the trees and made them creak. It interfered with his listening. For sounds from Margaret. He was going to lose her. It was only a matter of time—days, a week or two at most. So he slept lightly, though to lie awake in the dark was pointless. He could do nothing for her. Even the hospital, with all its glittering equipment, couldn't stop the inevitable. They plainly had given up when last Sunday the staff let her have her way and come home. She wanted to die at home.

She'd been through surgery twice, and chemotherapy, and feeble, fretful combat with the cheerful, no-nonsense experts sent around to help her tone up her muscles, get her to walking again, feeding herself, all that. Feeding herself? She scarcely ate anymore, a spoonful of soup, a sip of juice. To make him think she was trying. But the pain was worsening, and she wanted to die. She had not said so for fear of hurting him, careful as always of his feelings. But he knew.

He reached out, switched on the lamp, and with an old man's heavy slowness threw off the bedclothes, swung his feet to the floor, sat on the edge of the bed, sighing, putting on his glasses. He took his teeth from the bedside water tumbler, fitted them into his mouth. Ridiculous, like everything about growing old. He pushed his swollen feet into slippers, stood, took his bathrobe off the bedpost, flapped into it, and crossed the hall to look in at her.

There was a night-light. She was sleeping, breathing stertorously. That was the effect of the medication. So . . . all was as well as it would ever be. He started to turn away, heard the drip of water, and turned back. He flicked the light switch. Rain was leaking through the ceiling. Not on the bed. Not yet. But he must stop it. He got a flashlight from a kitchen drawer, struggled into the stiff old raincoat that hung by the back door for emergencies, found a pail of patching tar and a putty knife in a wooden locker on the rear deck, and went down the steps.

An aluminum ladder lay beside the carport. He dragged it to the lowest segment of the roof, stood it up, settled its legs firmly, stuffed flashlight and putty knife into coat pockets, and, tar pail in hand, began to climb, squinting up into the dark, the rain in his face making his glasses useless.

He was too old for this. Stiff. Rheumatic. Every step was a struggle. He would have done better with both hands free, but not much better. It was slow going. His heart pounded with urgency, but he knew better than to try to hurry. At his age, when you tried to hurry you only made mistakes. And he mustn't fail. What would become of Margaret then?

His head came above the roofline. He was getting there. He drew a deep breath and took another step. Right leg. Left leg—the one that sometimes gave out on him without warning. The roof was at chest level. Another step. Now he could crawl onto the roof. He set the pail there. He brought his left leg up and pushed with the right, because it was the strongest.

But nothing happened. He'd grown too heavy, hadn't he? He'd have to climb higher on the ladder. And step out onto the roof. Grunting, he climbed higher on the ladder. How cold rain-wet metal felt to his hands! Now, then, he had to calculate how to get off the ladder onto the roof. To step off sounded fine when he said it to himself. But how to manage it? This side?

That side? There was a pine branch to duck under. He leaned, put out one leg, thrust with the other, dropped onto the roof on hands and knees.

To get to his feet was a struggle, but he managed it. Picking up the tar pail, he climbed to the place where he knew the leak originated—a join in the roof that had given the same trouble before. He shone the flashlight on the place, knelt, pried open the pail, and smeared on the tar with the putty knife. He took out the flashlight again to inspect his work, added more tar, resealed the pail, and one small, cautious step at a time, made his way back down the wet slope to the ladder. He set the tar pail at the roof's edge, gripped again the cold metal of the ladder, and put out a leg, groping with his foot for a rung. He found the rung all right, but his leg wouldn't hold him. And he fell.

He was in his bed. It was still night, still raining. He should have been soaking, but he was dry, and in dry pajamas, and the bedclothes lay over him neatly. He switched on the lamp. His teeth leaned in the water glass. His bifocals lay folded beside the glass. What the hell had happened? He'd fallen off the roof. Crazy old fool. He tested fingers, arms, legs. All seemed in working order. His head ached. He touched his skull. Tender at the back. Painful. But how had he got here? He started to struggle up. He was bruised, all right, bruised all over. With a groan he lay back down.

And the door opened. A young man in a black leather jacket looked in, then stepped inside, a strapping young man with a round face, thick dark eyebrows, and blue eyes. For a split second McIntyre thought he ought to know him. The young man said, "You're awake. Good. I was afraid you might be in a coma. I thought about calling an ambulance, but I couldn't find any broken bones. There could be internal injuries, though. You tell me."

"Just bruises." McIntyre peered. "I climbed up to patch the roof. It was leaking. Did I do it?"

A nod. "You did it. What's wrong?"

McIntyre was struggling to get up. "Across the hall. I want to see if the dripping's stopped. My wife—"

"I checked," the young man said. "It's stopped."

"Is she all right?"

"She's sleeping."

McIntyre felt lost. "Who are you? Where did you come from? It's the middle of the night."

"I was—just getting home," the young man said. "I heard you fall."

"I appreciate it," McIntyre said.

"Can I bring you anything? Aspirin? Hot milk?"

"No, thank you."

"You want me to phone Dr. Hesseltine?"

"I'm all right," McIntyre said. "You know me—a tough old bird."

The young man was watching him steadily. As if he expected something. Not like money. Not that. Something else. Did he want to be recognized? *You know me.* Now, why had McIntyre said that? To a stranger. Only he wasn't a stranger, was he? Inside McIntyre a beautiful light went on, and "Donald," he said, before he could stop himself.

"Yes?" The young man cocked his head, half smiling, half frowning.

"I'm sorry." McIntyre groped out for his glasses, put them on. His face grew hot with embarrassment. He felt preposterous. "I mistook you for someone else."

"I guess not," the young man said. "I'm Donald."

McIntyre shut his eyes. It was his head, wasn't it? He had struck it when he fell, and he was hallucinating. He squeezed his eyelids tight and breathed in and out deeply for a count of ten and opened his eyes again, and the young man was gone. He laughed shakily to himself. *Donald.* What had made him say that? Donald was not real. He was McIntyre's private dream. His imaginary son. He had no son. He had three daughters. Used to have. Now they lived in other corners of the country. They wrote, and sometimes phoned, but rarely visited. They had husbands, and children in high school, even in college. They were busy with their own lives. He had no son. He had lived his entire long life surrounded by women, as a boy with his widowed mother and her sister and his own three sisters, then as a man with Margaret and the three girls. He had never had a son.

But the old saying was not true—you *could* miss what you never had. He'd yearned for a son, and whimsically brought a son to life. In his mind, his daydreams. Whenever it pleased him, whenever he felt the need, alone at his insurance agency, when business was slow, or since retiring, walking on the beach, say, exploring the tide rocks for shellfish, chopping out poison oak from under the pines around the house, waiting long hours at the hospital. My son Donald. A tear-away runner and climber of trees, an artful looper of scuffed basketballs through rusty hoops, a hotdog rider of spiderbikes, a surfer in long, sun-faded trunks, a glum student slouched over homework at the kitchen table, can of soda in one hand, slice of pizza in the other, a boy. Sometimes younger, sometimes older. Donald, my son.

Smiling, McIntyre slept.

He skipped his early-morning walk today. He washed and fed Margaret. He changed the bed linens, while, wrapped in a blanket against the damp and chill, she huddled in a chair by the window, where she could look out. Ordinarily at these times, she was silent. In pain. This morning she spoke. "That's the second sheriff's car that's passed," she said. "I think they're coming from Gertrude Schumwald's." But that was all. Her eyes closed. Her head drooped. His bruises made it painful to lift her—out of the bed, into the bed. He groaned, but not aloud. Thrusting needles into her pathetically wasted flesh always made him flinch inside, but he smiled and spoke gently, doing it. She murmured, smiled for him, feebly squeezed his hand, and slept again.

Now he sat in the kitchen with coffee and the newspaper, and Henry Winston knocked on the back door and stepped inside. They'd been neighbors for years. Henry was retired, too. Used to own a drugstore in Morro Bay. Sold it to a chain outfit. It had lost all its character now. He hung up a Giants baseball cap and a windbreaker jacket. "You all right? Got a shopping list for me? Have to drive into San Luis today. Means a market with a lot more variety. Craving anything exotic?" He pulled out a chair and sat at the table. "How's Margaret?"

"No change." With a wince, McIntyre rose to get him a mug of coffee. When he set it down, he laid the list beside it. "Keeping her out of pain's about all I hope for."

"I see the ladder's up." Henry poked the list into his shirt pocket, and emptied a packet of sweetener into his coffee. "Roof leaking again, was it?"

"I patched it," McIntyre said.

"It needs to be replaced." Henry reached across for McIntyre's spoon, and rattled it in his coffee.

"Can't afford it." Henry had left the door ajar. McIntyre got up and closed it. "Hospitals, doctors."

"You've got insurance—you were in the business."

McIntyre snorted. "We'd be on the beach without it. Doesn't mean I've got thousands lying around for a new roof."

Henry shrugged. "Long as you can still climb up there."

McIntyre opened his mouth to tell Henry about his fall and what had happened afterward, but he didn't. In all his life, he had told no one about Donald. Not even Margaret. Especially not Margaret. She might have construed his daydream as a reproach to her for failing to give him a son. Were he to confide about Donald now, Henry would think he was out of his mind. Which, of course, at least last night, he had been. From concussion. But to explain away the many visitations of Donald in the past wouldn't be so easy. He could think of no excuse for those himself. "May I?" Henry picked up the newspaper and, squinting, turned over the pages noisily.

"What are you looking for?"

"Gertrude Schumwald had a break-in last night." Henry laid the paper down. "Guess it happened too late to get in here. They print this early so they can truck it up here from L.A."

A widow, Gertrude Schumwald lived in a two-story place up

at the corner, surrounded by shaggy old pepper trees. Most of the trees in Settlers Cove were high-reaching spindly pines, shallow-rooted, likely to blow down in storms off the sea, but fast-growing, so the place remained a community in deep woods.

"A break-in?" McIntyre said. These had become common lately. Settlers Cove had once been free of crime. Now street people drove up from Los Angeles or down from San Francisco to mug elderly walkers of dogs in the woodsy lanes, to hold up the souvenir shops in Madrone, across the highway, to invade houses and take televisions, microwaves, jewelry—whatever they could sell to buy drugs.

"Gertrude heard a noise," Henry said, "got Ernie's old revolver out of the dresser drawer, walked to the stair head in her nightgown in the dark, and shot it off."

McIntyre laughed. "That's our Gertie."

Henry grinned. "He dropped the silverware chest, dived out the window, and ran like hell."

"On the other hand," McIntyre said, "it could have got her killed. Impulsive, foolhardy. She always was that way. Did she get a look at him?"

"A glimpse. There's the corner streetlight, you know, but it's dim, and the rain made it dimmer. He was young, that's all." Henry took a swallow of coffee, remembered, shook his head. "That's not all. He left footprints in the mud. Big fella—heavy, too, the way they sank in."

"Black, of course?" McIntyre said regretfully.

"Not this time. Deputies asked Gertrude more than once, but she stuck to her story—he was white."

McIntyre woke to heavy footsteps on the front deck. A stranger, then. Only strangers came to this house that way, up the long path and wooden stairs from the trail below. Friends came by the side trail to the back door. He lay on the couch, an afghan over him, the book he'd been reading splayed open on his big belly. His glasses? He pawed around for them, found them, laid the book aside, threw off the afghan, sat up. Pains jabbed at his lower back, his joints. His head still throbbed. He struggled to his feet. Someone knocked on the door. A firm, loud knocking.

"Coming," he said hoarsely and hobbled to open the door. The day was beautiful though chilly. The sky was washed a flawless blue. Splintered sunlight fell through the pines. The man who'd knocked wore neat khaki. He was a sheriff's deputy. He pushed back his hat. "Mr. McIntyre?"

"Yes. It's Lieutenant Gerard, isn't it?"

Gerard sketched a smile, and nodded. "How are you?"

"That's quite a question to ask an old man. I could keep you here for hours listening to a catalogue of my aches and pains. What's on your mind, deputy?"

"Mrs. Schumwald was robbed last night," Gerard said. "Around midnight."

"So Henry Winston told me."

"We're busy after the storm, so I'm on my own asking neighbors if they saw or heard anything. Mrs. Schumwald scared him off with a handgun. She says he hit the ground running. He didn't run past here, by any chance, did he?"

"If you mean down the road, I wouldn't have seen him. I was out back." He pointed with a thumb over his shoulder. "I doubt if I'd have heard him, either. Storm was making too much noise. My roof started leaking. I climbed up and put tar on the leak. Then I proceeded to fall off."

Gerard frowned concern. "Oh, no. Are you all right?"

McIntyre touched his skull, wincing. "Slight concussion—I think that's the worst of it. Wasn't much of a fall. It's a low roof back there. No bones broken."

"I can run you to the hospital. You should have X-rays. Best to be sure about these things."

"Thanks, I'm all right," McIntyre said.

"Well, you take it easy, now." Gerard went off across the damp deck that was strewn with pine needles and twigs the storm had brought down. "Sorry to bother you."

McIntyre said, "No bother," and closed the door.

"Aren't you going to tell him about me?" Donald said. There he was, big as life. He'd laid new logs on the fire and was poking up a blaze. He looked over his shoulder at McIntyre. What was his expression exactly? Those thick, dark eyebrows were raised. Was he smiling? The blue eyes seemed to twinkle, but McIntyre couldn't say whether they were mocking him or not.

"What are you doing here?" he said.

"You were asleep." The poker clanked against the fire basket. "I thought I'd better sit with Mother just in case. I read to her awhile. But I don't think she heard me."

"She's not your mother," McIntyre said sharply.

Donald straightened, set the poker back in place, and read his watch. "She'll need her medication in ten minutes." He left the room. "Don't forget." His voice came from the kitchen. A moment later, the back door closed.

McIntyre had never before in his life spoken a cross word to Donald. He felt a stab of remorse, and hurried to the kitchen. He snatched open the door. "Donald?" He stepped out onto the rear deck. "Please, I'm sorry." But Donald was gone. No one was in sight. Only a mule deer, a few yards off up the slope among the pines. It raised its antlered head, ears alert and twitching, looked at him for a second with large brown eyes, then bounded away, crashing through the undergrowth.

McIntyre stood on the deck, frowning to himself, wondering if the deer were real. Donald was certainly not real. Donald was a part of his mind—a maverick part, broken loose. Telling him it would soon be time for Margaret's injection. No stranger would know that. He, McIntyre, knew it, and had put the reminder to himself into Donald's mouth. *Aren't you going to tell him about me?* McIntyre had wondered for a moment there if he oughtn't to tell Gerard about Donald, and had tossed away the notion. And Donald had caught it. *Mother.* McIntyre shut the kitchen door. In Margaret's room, the book lay face down on the chair arm. *Pride and Prejudice.* He picked it up, peered at the page, but couldn't remember whether this was the place where he'd last left off reading to her himself or not.

Margaret spoke softly. She was very white against the pillows. He knew why: the morphine was wearing off.

"Something wrong?" she asked him.

"No, no. I fell asleep. Meant to come in and read to you. Would you—like me to read to you?"

She shook her head and turned it to see the small white bedside clock. "It's time for my injection."

"Of course." He laid the book down.

He was sweeping the front deck when the sound of a car in the driveway out back made him lift his head. A big, tough engine and, a moment later, the slam of a heavy door. A Cherokee. He knew those sounds, and wondered what had brought Belle Hesseltine. He leaned the broom by the door and went inside. By the time he reached the kitchen, Belle had let herself in.

A gaunt, upright old woman, in blue jeans, mackinaw, cowboy boots, she'd come to Settlers Cove years ago to retire, and had been busier doctoring here than she'd been in all her life before, or so she claimed. The fact seemed to be, she had no idea how to retire. Doctoring was what she'd always lived for. A love and compassion for people that she tried to hide behind a gruff manner wouldn't let her stop helping them. She hung up her Stetson. Her medical kit was in her hand.

"Sit down, Raymond. Sheriff Gerard is worried about you. He rang me to say you had a bad fall last night." She pulled out a chair at the table. "Concussion, he said, and you wouldn't let him take you to the hospital. Come on, sit down. Let me look at your head."

"What's wrong with my head," McIntyre said, "is inside. Nothing you can see. Forgetting names. Losing things."

"That's just old age." She pushed him down on the chair, set the kit on the table among the breakfast dishes he hadn't yet cleared away—he hadn't felt up to it earlier. She bent him forward, parted the hair at the back of his skull, gently touched the place he'd banged in his fall. She straightened him, removed his glasses, laid them with a click on the tabletop. She tilted up his chin, bent, and looked hard and closely into his eyes.

"How's your vision?" she asked. "Seeing double?"

He almost said he was seeing what wasn't there, but he bit that back. "No. Vision's about as good as usual—which isn't saying much."

"You've had these ten years." She handed him back the glasses. "Time you got fitted with new ones."

"Can you talk to Margaret a few minutes?" McIntyre put the glasses on. "You're one of her favorites. Not many people come anymore."

"A good many that would if they could," Belle said wryly, "are dead and gone."

"I know." McIntyre rose with a sigh. "But I can't say it to her anymore." He gathered up the dishes from the table and set them in the sink. "It sticks in my throat."

"I almost didn't make it myself." Belle took up her kit. "Big blacktailed buck cut across the road right in front of me. I didn't hit him. I braked, but the road's wet and slippery. I damn near piled up in the ditch."

"I saw him around noon," McIntyre said. "Out back here in the trees. Must be ten years since we had deer in Settlers Cove. Over across the highway, yes, but with all the building here—"

"There's been bears reported," Belle said, and headed for the hallway. "Haven't been bears on the central coast in a century. I wonder if our four-footed friends are trying to tell us something."

McIntyre laughed briefly, and began to run hot water into the sink. He poured detergent into the stream of the water. Fumbled for the dish mop. Began to wash the breakfast dishes. He rinsed each plate, mug, glass, under the running hot water and set it in a rubber-coated wire rack on the counter. He moved slowly, and winced at the ache of his bruises. He must have groaned aloud. He did that sometimes in his weariness these days, more often than he should, because there was no one to hear. But at this moment there was. Belle had not left the kitchen. She'd stood watching him, and now she touched his arm.

"Raymond, where are those girls of yours? Why aren't they here, looking after their mother? You're not up to it. Seventy-six years old. All on your own."

"I manage," McIntyre said stiffly.

"Have you written them? Have you telephoned?"

"They've got husbands, children, jobs to look after. And they're none of them nurses. What could they do that I can't do? Besides"—annoyingly, tears came to his eyes, his voice wobbled, and he turned away—"it won't be much longer." He pulled a paper towel off the rack, dried his eyes, blew his nose. "For them to come all this way . . ."

"It's their mother who's dying, for God's sake," Belle said. "Aren't you even going to give them a chance to show they love their mother?"

McIntyre shook his head. "Emotional blackmail? That's not our style, Belle—not Margaret's, not mine."

Belle snorted again. "Raymond, what ails you is pride. You don't want anyone able to say you failed in your duty. You'll carry all the weight yourself if it kills you."

"Margaret will be waiting for you," McIntyre said. "She knows the sound of your car."

Belle sighed, studied him a moment, then with a grim shake of her head went off down the hall. By the time the dishes were dried and put away, the effort had drained him. He sat down heavily at the table to catch his breath. The table felt sticky. He looked at it—splotches, smears. And then at the floor, the counters, the stove. Everything was dingy, soiled, neglected. No wonder Belle felt he wasn't up to the task he'd assigned himself.

Well, it wasn't true. He'd been lazy, self-indulgent. Thrusting out his jaw, he pushed to his feet and shuffled out to get the plastic bucket, mop, sponges, scrub brush, soap, bleach. He'd make the place shine. He was coming in with his hands full when Belle entered the kitchen from the hall, carrying her kit. She studied him and his janitor's gear sardonically for a moment, and said, "I'd call a cleaning service, Raymond. Don't do this."

"Cleaning service, hell," he said. "Waste of good money. Nothing to mopping up a kitchen."

"Youth and strength," she said. "Raymond, no one keeps those forever." She took down her hat from the rack. "Growing old is nothing to be ashamed of." She went out into the sunlight of the deck and turned back. "One thing. Keep a written record when it comes to the morphine, will you? If I hadn't stopped by, Margaret would have been in a bad way. You were down to the last three cc's."

He scowled. "No. Really? I was sure I had—"

"I replenished the supply from my kit," Belle said.

"Thank you," he said, bewildered. He seemed to see in his memory's eye three of the now all-too-familiar clear, bulbous vials lined up on the medicine chest shelf. But his memory's eyesight, it seemed, was no more to be trusted now than was his actual vision, blurred, mistaking what he thought he saw for what he saw. "I'll try to keep better track," he mumbled, and poured soap powder and bleach into the dusty bucket and ran hot water into it. The mop, which had hung in the locker on the deck, was dusty, and a spider ran out of it just as he was about to plunge it into the water. He stood watching the spider scurry under the cabinet doors beneath the sink. And Belle Hesseltine was back. She stepped inside and held something up in her thin fingers. It glinted in the sunlight.

"I think you ought to look at this," she said.

McIntyre leaned the mop against the counter and went to do as she asked. It was a silver spoon. Muddy, but until it had fallen into the mud, polished to a fine gleam. Sterling. Heavy. An ornate, old-fashioned pattern. He rinsed it under the tap, dried it, and stood turning it over in his fingers, examining it. He frowned.

"Where did you find it?"

"Lying at the foot of your ladder out here. Doesn't belong to you. Not with the initial S."

"Gertrude Schumwald?" McIntyre said.

Belle said, "I'm told she had a burglary last night."

"Well, how did it get here?" McIntyre asked.

But he knew, and the knowledge made him sick.

He blinked awake. The light outside was slanting from the west and turning ruddy. He had called the sheriff's substation in Madrone as soon as Belle Hesseltine had left. To report the spoon. He was too bruised to walk over to Schumwald's. Anyway, it was the correct thing to give the evidence to a law officer. But Gerard wasn't in. McIntyre left his name, then went back to the kitchen. He began mopping the floor, but grew tired before he'd finished, winded, achy, his heart pounding, and the back of his skull throbbing again. Henry Winston arrived with white plastic sacks from the supermarket in San Luis, and when McIntyre had written Henry a check, and put the groceries away, he went and lay down on the couch. And fell asleep. Now he wheezed to his feet and went to tackle the kitchen once more.

But he was too late. It gleamed in the red sunlight, every surface spotless, floor, stove, refrigerator shiny, cabinets as free of hand smears as if new. Donald stood on the top of the little aluminum step stool, wiping down the last of the cupboards. He grinned at the gaping McIntyre.

"Pass muster?" he asked.

McIntyre said stupidly, "What are you doing here?"

"I live here," Donald said cheerfully, "don't I?" He climbed down the ladder, took the sponge to the sink, and rinsed it under the tap. "Haven't I always lived here?"

Far more quickly than usual these days, McIntyre's head cleared. Maybe anger cleared it. "Never," he said. The spoon was in the pocket of his shirt. He flung it on the table. "You're a thief. You robbed Mrs. Schumwald up at the corner last night. You were running away when you stumbled on me out here." He jerked his head to indicate the place of his fall. "You stopped to help me, and that dropped out of your pocket."

"I'll put these things away," Donald said, and began gathering up the cleaning stuff.

"I can do it, thanks," McIntyre said. "You've done enough."

"Youth and strength," Donald said with a smile, and went out with the mop, wrung dry and white, the bucket loaded with sponges, bleach, soap box, scrub brush.

McIntyre cried, "No, wait." He mustn't leave. He must be here when the sheriff came. McIntyre looked frantically down the hall, as if Gerard might have materialized in the front room. He took a step—he'd phone him again quickly. He stopped and shook his head in disgust. What good would that do? "Donald, wait." He hobbled across the kitchen and out onto the deck. But the locker doors were shut, and Donald was gone. "Donald?" he shouted. Into emptiness. There was only the wind in the pines, and from far off down the hill the crash of surf among the rocks.

Gerard touched his hat. "Sorry to have taken so long. Like I said before, the storm got us a lot of auto accidents, downed trees and power lines, runaway horses. Busy day. What's this about Mrs. Schumwald's spoon?"

"Yes. Come in. Sit down. Get you anything?"

Gerard stepped inside, took off his hat. "Thank you, that's all right. I'll head home soon for supper."

"This is the spoon." McIntyre gave it to him. "Belle Hesseltine found it this noon, out in back. At the foot of the ladder I put up last night to fix a leak in the roof. Around midnight."

"It's certainly clean," Gerard said.

"It was covered with mud. I washed it."

"Damn." Gerard rubbed a hand down over his face and blew out air. "That's no way to treat evidence, Mr. McIntyre. It could have had the thief's fingerprints on it."

McIntyre felt his face grow red. "Of course. You're right. I'm sorry."

"Belle shouldn't have picked it up in the first place." Gerard put the spoon into his pocket. "I must have told her twenty times to leave evidence alone." He sighed and looked past McIntyre, searching the sunset room with his eyes. "All right if I change my mind? I think I could use a drink."

"Good," McIntyre said. "Sit down. I'll fetch us some bourbon." He went to the kitchen, feeling strangely elated. It was a long time since he'd sat and had a drink with a man. Henry Winston never touched the stuff. And McIntyre didn't believe in drinking alone. He dropped ice cubes into glasses, poured generously from his dusty bottle of Old Grand-Dad, and carried the drinks back to the living room almost with a spring in his step.

"Thank you," Gerard said. "All right if I smoke?"

"Go right ahead," McIntyre said. "Belle won't let me use them anymore, but I still enjoy the smell."

Gerard lit up, tasted his drink, smiled appreciatively, and lifted the glass to McIntyre. "That's good whiskey." McIntyre nodded, smiled, tasted his own drink. It hit him like a blow in the chest. Another pleasure gone off limits? What was there to recommend old age? Nothing he could think of. Gerard said, "The spoon says he ran past out in back there, but you didn't see him, didn't hear him?"

"I did. I didn't understand you, earlier."

Gerard narrowed his eyes. "Didn't understand?"

"You said the thief ran down the road. The man I saw didn't. And I had no reason to think he was a thief. I fell off the roof, knocked myself cold. Next thing I knew I was safe and dry in my own bed. A young man was here. Said he'd heard me fall. Plainly he'd carried me in out of the rain, cleaned me up, put me to bed. If I hadn't regained consciousness, he was going to call the doctor."

Gerard stared. "A young man? What sort?"

McIntyre shifted in his chair. "White, six feet, late twenties, dark hair, blue eyes, hefty. Maybe he'd had some medical experience. He seemed to know I hadn't broken anything, that all that was wrong with me was a concussion."

Gerard said, "You should have told me this right off."

"I didn't connect him with the robbery," McIntyre said, shading the truth, wanting to believe in Donald, the Donald he'd created in his daydreams. There was no way his Donald could turn out to be a housebreaker. McIntyre refused to believe that. "After all, he was a good Samaritan. You don't think of someone like that as a criminal."

Gerard grunted and took another swallow of Old Grand-Dad. "You're sure you didn't come into the house on your own, get cleaned up, get into bed, without remembering it. A bad bump on the head can give people blackouts."

"You mean I imagined Donald?"

Gerard blinked. "Donald?"

"That's what he calls himself." This was like a dream. McIntyre heard himself say next, "He's been back twice today. Once, to read to my wife when I fell asleep. A second time, to clean up the kitchen for me—not an hour ago."

Gerard listened with a poker face. "Is that so?"

"Come look." McIntyre led him to the kitchen, switched on the light. "See how it shines? Well, I can tell you, it wasn't that way. It was very grubby. My wife's ill, you see, dying, and looking after her is about all I've got strength for." He grimaced. "Years do that to you."

"Looks nice." Gerard regarded the glistening surfaces thoughtfully. "And you say Donald did this for you?"

"I hate to think he was the one that stole Gertrude Schumwald's silverware," McIntyre said.

"You sure you didn't clean up the kitchen yourself?"

"Do you think I've lost my mind?" McIntyre said.

"I think you had a blow on the head." Gerard had brought along his drink and cigarette. He sat down at the table. "What did this Donald tell you about himself?"

McIntyre almost said, *He didn't have to tell me anything, I know everything about him. I invented him. Long ago. When I wanted a son for company, a son I could spend time with away from women, at ball games, hiking, sailing.* He didn't let himself say these things. Gerard was already half persuaded Raymond McIntyre was a loony. "He didn't tell me anything. Just asked how he could help."

"Why do you suppose he kept coming back?"

"He won't come back again. The second time, I knew about the spoon. I showed it to him, called him a thief."

Gerard frowned. "Risky. He could have hurt you."

"If he was that kind," McIntyre said, "why didn't he rob me? I'm old and slow. I don't keep a gun, like Gertrude Schumwald. My wife's helpless. He could have plundered this house—instead all he did was help me."

"Right." Gerard finished off his whiskey, put out his cigarette, rose. "Describe him again, will you?"

McIntyre obliged and added the black leather jacket.

"I'm going to send somebody here to take fingerprints." Gerard went to pick up his hat. As he started down the steps into the trees, McIntyre remembered how quickly Donald had vanished this noon, and called to the deputy:

"Have you seen that blacktailed buck?"

"We've had reports," Gerard said. "Fish and Game will catch him, truck him back up in the canyons. Unless some trigger-happy householder around here shoots him first."

There were only two of them, but they seemed to fill the house. A towheaded, simple-looking kid named Vern and a slender dark young woman whose badge said she was T. Hodges. She had slightly buck teeth, and beautiful brown eyes. They wore the same tan uniforms as Gerard, the same hats, and they were everywhere with their dusting powder, brushes, cellotape, blank white cards, ballpoint pens. They went over the kitchen inch by inch, the locker on the rear deck, mop, bucket, soap-powder box.

While they took his own fingerprints at the kitchen table, they asked him to recall for them just where Donald had been in the house, and so they checked the fireplace poker, too, didn't they? And quietly, courteously, the copy of *Pride and Prejudice*, and the chair beside sleeping Margaret's bed where Donald would have sat to read to her. They checked the bathroom, in case Donald had turned the taps there when he'd cleaned the mud off McIntyre after his fall.

They took photographs. They brought in a vacuum cleaner to run over all the places Donald had stepped and climbed and stood. They softly carried the chair out of Margaret's room and vacuumed that, and softly carried it back. When the door of their county car slammed below on the road and they drove off, the house seemed empty and lonely. McIntyre suddenly missed the girls. His daughters. Karen, the youngest, in particular—T. Hodges had reminded him of Karen. He closed the front door slowly, thoughtfully, and started toward the telephone. But Margaret called out to him, and he went to do what he could for her instead.

They were up in Sills Canyon, away back in the mountains. The trail they'd followed had finally just petered out. Driving in twisty ruts, McIntyre had grown doubtful, but Donald had kept urging him on. He was fifteen, now, and sure of himself. He knew this place. No, he wasn't mixed up. This was the way. And now they stood side by side at a pool shaded by old oaks draped with moss, a cool, hidden place, quiet except for the buzz of insects, the soft babble of Sills Creek as it washed down over boulders into the pool.

"Didn't I tell you?" Donald said. "A real trout pool."

"If you say so," McIntyre said.

"Give me the key," Donald said. "I'll get the rods."

He scrambled up the rocky, brushy slope. McIntyre gazed into the pool. And saw at its far side the clear, motionless, reflection of a mule deer, a buck, with antlers.

"Donald, come see," he called.

But right away the buck took fright and bounced off.

It was a cemetery, an old one, crowded with mossy headstones, statuary, even an occasional tomb. Where? He didn't know. He'd never been here. Out there was the ocean, slate-gray today, under a cold, gray sky. Gulls circled overhead, crying their creaking cries. A canvas awning on shiny poles sheltered a double row of metal folding chairs that faced a grave into which a casket had been lowered, a heap of hothouse flowers on its lid. The girls, their husbands, and five of their offspring whom McIntyre hardly recognized sat on the folding chairs, hands in their laps. They were dressed up, all of them. So was he, in a suit he hadn't worn in a long time. It was too tight. The white shirt he'd taken from a very old laundry wrapping strained its buttons over his belly. A bald clergyman, a folded umbrella hanging from his arm, read from a book so worn some of its leaves were loose. In the King James English McIntyre had requested. Margaret loved that language, and when she still had her vitality used to rail against the modernizing of the *Book of Common Prayer.* At "dust to dust," McIntyre stooped stiffly, picked up a handful of earth, dropped it onto the flowers below, and straightened, to find Donald beside him. He, too, was dressed up. He smiled, and said, "Don't worry. You won't be alone. I'll always be here." McIntyre awoke and, heart pounding, stumbled purblind and toothless across the hall. Margaret was there, drugged asleep, but there. He almost wept with relief.

When he came back from his sunrise walk, Donald was at the stove. His black leather jacket hung by the door. He'd tied on McIntyre's apron over a plaid shirt and jeans. The kitchen smelled of perking coffee and frying bacon.

McIntyre stopped in the doorway. Disbelieving. Angry. Afraid. "What are you doing here?"

"Cooking your breakfast." Donald nodded toward the hall. "By the time you're finished with Mother, it will all be ready."

"The sheriff is after you," McIntyre said.

"She's been calling for you. Wait, here's her cereal."

Carrying the warm bowl of Cream of Wheat along the hall, McIntyre paused and put a hand on the telephone, but Margaret called out again, sounding panicky, and he went to her. He went through the gentle rituals. There was no need to change the sheets this morning, thank God, and that shortened the time a little. But impossibly he'd got mixed up about the morphine again. He couldn't imagine how or why, but there was only one vial in the medicine chest. His hand trembled as he gave Margaret the injection. He broke into a cold sweat as he hurried back to the kitchen with the cereal Margaret had barely touched, however much he'd coaxed her. Henry Winston looked at him from his place at the table.

"Where's Donald?" McIntyre set the bowl in the sink.

"You're white as a sheet," Henry said. "What's wrong?"

"How long ago did he leave?" McIntyre cried.

Alarmed, Henry stood up and pulled out a chair. "You'd better sit down. Nobody left. Nobody was here."

McIntyre looked wildly at the stove. A saucepan, two skillets. And through the oven's glass pane, he saw inside eggs, bacon, and toast on a plate. A mug of coffee steamed in front of Henry. One stood at McIntyre's place as well. He yanked open the door, stepped out on the deck. "Donald!"

Henry called. "What the hell's the matter with you?"

"You sure you didn't see a young man?"

"I told you—there was no one to see."

"He was cooking breakfast"—McIntyre came inside again and closed the door—"when I got back from my walk." He took the warm plate from the oven. "See here? And where do you think your coffee came from?"

Henry tilted his head. "The pot—like every morning."

"No," McIntyre said. "I mean, yes, but Donald made it." He banged the plate down on the table. "Donald made my breakfast while I looked after Margaret."

Henry eyed him, worried, rubbing his white beard stubble. It was a privilege of retirement that a man didn't have to shave every morning of his life. Sometimes Henry indulged it for days running. "Donald?" he said.

"The one who rescued me when I fell off the roof," McIntyre said crossly. "The one who cleaned up this kitchen yesterday. I guess you didn't notice how it shines?"

"Fell off the roof? When was that? Look at you. You're shaking. Sit down here now, and eat."

McIntyre turned away. "I have to phone the sheriff."

"Will you make sense? The sheriff? What for?"

"It was Donald who stole Gertude Schumwald's silver."

"Well, give Belle Hesseltine a call, while you're at it," Henry said. "Trying to do everything alone here, cook, housekeeper, nurse—the strain is affecting your mind. Raymond, nobody was in this kitchen. You made the coffee and cooked like always. You just forgot."

"Matter of fact," McIntyre said. "I'll call Belle first. You eat that breakfast. I'm not hungry." And he went to the phone and punched out the familiar number. Belle answered from her car. McIntyre could hear the engine. He asked, "About the morphine. You told me you'd replenished Margaret's supply. Are you sure?"

"I set them on the usual shelf in your bathroom cabinet. What's the matter?"

"How many?" McIntyre asked.

"Three," she said.

"There's only one this morning," McIntyre said.

"Call the sheriff," she said. "Don't waste any time."

"You call him," McIntyre said. "He'll believe you. He thinks that bump on the head scrambled my brains."

Gerard came to the back door this time. Henry was still present. McIntyre had hinted to him to leave, but his old neighbor was plainly worried about him and didn't think he ought to be alone. Left alone, McIntyre imagined things. Gerard sat with a mug of coffee at the kitchen table now and smoked a cigarette and listened without comment or even facial expression while McIntyre recited his story again. He followed McIntyre to the bathroom to look at the lone vial of morphine on the shelf there.

"So now we know why he keeps coming back," he said, and closed the mirrored cabinet door.

"Now we know," McIntyre said bleakly. "To get his hands on drugs."

"Urban scum." Henry had tagged along and stood in the hall. "They're all the same."

"Not exactly." Gerard left the bathroom. McIntyre and Henry followed him back to the kitchen. "His fingerprints tell us he used to be an orderly at the hospital in San Luis. He stole from the supplies there. They fired him without pressing charges." Gerard poured himself more coffee and sat down again at the table. "Everybody liked him and felt sorry for him." He lit a cigarette and made a face. "They ought to have had him arrested and charged, tried and locked up. He's been all over the area thieving to feed his habit." The deputy looked glumly at McIntyre. "You were the best break he ran into yet. No middle man."

McIntyre said, "The hospital. That's how he knew about Margaret's medication. That's where I'd seen him, isn't it? And he'd seen me. Funny thing—when I came to, after I fell off the roof, I thought I knew him. But not from where."

"Don't suppose he was wearing an orderly's outfit," Henry said, "was he? Clothes change a man."

"I thought he was—" McIntyre began, and stopped.

Gerard cocked an eyebrow. "Yes?"

"Nobody," McIntyre said, and added lamely, "someone I—used to know. As a—as a boy."

"He grew up in Seattle," Gerard said. "Alan Donald Abbott. Wanted to be a doctor. Flunked out."

"They say everybody has a look-alike," Henry said. "Someplace in the world. An identical twin."

"Is there any chance you'll catch him?" McIntyre asked.

"Unless he leaves the neighborhood," Gerard said. "Yes. When desperation drives people, they trip up." He snubbed out his cigarette and got to his feet. "Thanks for calling me. Appreciate your help." He opened the door, started out, and turned back. "I'm posting officers to watch this house, Mr. McIntyre.

Abbott seems to regard it as home." Putting on his hat, he moved off across the deck. "All the same, I'd lock up at night, if I were you."

Supper and the hour after supper were the best times. He read to her by lamplight, or they watched television. Then she was tired. (He sensed often these days that she was tired well before she said so, and concealed it from him, aware of how he cherished their time together, and of how little time was left them in this life.) He set aside her extra pillows, gave her morphine, drew up the bedclothes, and she smiled and pressed his hand, and slept.

He tiptoed out, and went to lock the doors. Not possible. The lock on the front door was corroded in place, the spring lock on the kitchen door was clotted with coats of old enamel. How long had it been since they'd locked this house? Had they ever done so? He doubted it. There'd been no dangers to lock out in Settlers Cove. Not then.

He put on a jacket, took the flashlight, and went out. Across the front deck, down the steps to the trail. A patrol car sat there in the dark. It was dimly lit inside. Plainly, Gerard had meant Donald to see he'd posted guards to watch the house. Probably there was another car up the side trail. Vern, the towheaded boy, sat in this car. He blinked in the flashlight's beam.

"Mr. McIntyre?" He sat up quickly and squinted out. "Anything wrong?" He reached to open the car door.

"No, no," McIntyre said. "I just came out to tell you, my door locks don't work. Lieutenant Gerard asked me to lock up, but I can't. Haven't turned those locks in years."

"That right?" Vern said. "Well, it's okay. Don't worry. We'll keep an eye on things."

"I don't think he'll come back, anyway," McIntyre said.

"Best to be on the safe side," Vern said.

McIntyre looked into the darkness of the pines. "Is there another car?"

"Up at the rear," Vern said. "Lundquist."

McIntyre started off. "I'd better tell him."

"Save yourself a walk," Vern said. "I'll tell him on the walkie-talkie."

Now came the time of day he liked least of all, when he sat alone in the kitchen, waiting for his mind's weariness to catch up to the weariness of his body. He tried to concentrate on a book, or on *Newsweek* or *Natural History*, classical music from the college station faint from a small radio on the counter. He used to make himself cocoa to help summon sleep. But lately someone—had it been Gertrude Schumwald?—had told him chicken was the best of all nature's soporifics. So he'd had Henry Winston fetch him cans of chicken broth and, when he didn't forget, he heated up and drank chicken broth. He guessed it helped. He didn't dare sleep deeply, anyway—he had to keep an ear out for Margaret.

Now he was sipping at the soup, leafing over an article about Kodiak bears, looking at the pictures, when noises on the rear deck made him raise his head. There, at the window, stood the mule deer buck, peering in curiously, eyes wide, big ears poised. McIntyre was too startled to move, and he and the beautiful animal simply stared at each other for what seemed a long time.

Then there was a bang. Someone had fired a rifle. The deer shied. Its hoofs clattered away across the deck. McIntyre stumbled to his feet, flung himself toward the door, pulled it open. Darkness. He fumbled for the switch beside the door, and light fell across the deck. Splashes of blood. A trail of bloodstains. Someone came at a run into the light. A stocky deputy he hadn't seen before. He had drawn his pistol.

"Did you shoot?" he said.

"No. Someone out here." McIntyre's heart knocked in his chest. He couldn't get his breath. He caught the deck rail and leaned on it heavily. "Shot the blacktailed buck. Did you see the blacktailed buck?"

"No," Lundquist said. "Are you sure?"

"He was here, on the deck," McIntyre said, "looking in the window. What was the harm in that?"

"Don't look at me," Lundquist said. "I didn't do it."

Vern called out of the night, "What's going on?"

"Some son of a bitch shot that mule deer," Lundquist shouted. Someone, or maybe the deer, was crashing among the trees above the house. Whitefaced Vern appeared panting in the kitchen doorway. He carried a rifle. Lundquist said, "Come on. Let's get the bastard."

And the two of them charged up into the woods. McIntyre listened to them tramping around in the dark. He caught glimpses of their flashlight beams. Then he realized that now was the time for Donald to appear. No one was guarding the house. He went back indoors, took the half-empty vial from the bathroom shelf and dropped it into his pocket, got the poker from beside the fireplace, and went to sit by Margaret. He knew he wasn't worth much as a guardian. But he was the only one left.

Vern found him there, nodding in the chair. He cleared his throat. "'Scuse me, Mr. McIntyre."

McIntyre looked up. "Did you catch him?"

"No. No sign of the deer, either." His smooth young face showed grief and anger. "But from the way he bled on your deck, I'd say he won't make it."

"You going to stay on guard now?" McIntyre was filled with a heavy sadness. He pushed up out of the chair. "If so, I'll go to bed. The young thrive on excitement." He managed a wan smile for Vern. "It wears old people out."

"We'll keep watching," Vern said.

He woke in the dark, and knew it was no use their being out there. Donald was in the room. He could hear him breathing. Panting, rather, and whimpering. He reached out and switched on the lamp. It shone on the glass with his teeth leaning in it, and glanced brightly off the lenses of his spectacles. He put these on, and turned. Donald sat on the floor, slumped back against the closet door. His right hand was over his heart. As if to salute the flag in a sixth-grade classroom. But the hand was bloody. Blood had run down the black jacket. He was staring at McIntyre and trying to speak. McIntyre couldn't hear the words. He argued his heavy old bulk out of bed, and bent over Donald.

"I'm here," he said. "How did this happen?"

"Drugstore. In Morro Bay." The words came gasping. Donald caught McIntyre's sleeve. "Water?"

McIntyre brought water from the bathroom, knelt stiffly, and held the glass to Donald's mouth. But he was too weak to take more than a sip. He turned away his head.

"What were you doing at the drugstore?" McIntyre asked. "No, don't try to answer." He set the glass down. "I know."

"You know." Donald closed his eyes and nodded. "You always knew. Everything about me." He opened his eyes again and pleaded with his eyes. "I can't help it. You know that, too, don't you? I can't help it."

"There are police cars outside." McIntyre struggled to his feet. "They'll call an ambulance."

Donald whispered, "I didn't know that drugstore had a security guard, or I'd never have broken in." Blood leaked out of his mouth. "I'm dying. I don't want to die."

McIntyre looked down at him. "You told me I'd never be alone," he said bitterly. "At the funeral. You promised. You'd always be with me."

Donald didn't answer. His chin rested on his chest.

McIntyre went to find Vern. Vern called on the radio for Lieutenant Gerard and for an ambulance, then ran up the steps two at a time. When slow old McIntyre came in, the young officer was kneeling on the floor beside Donald. He climbed to his feet, shaking his head grimly.

"It's over. He didn't make it."

"He tried to rob a drugstore in Morro Bay."

"I know. They radioed us. He was wounded. I figured they'd catch him. I didn't want to wake you up over it." He tilted his head. "Why did he come back here, Mr. McIntyre? It's a long way, the shape he was in."

McIntyre shrugged numbly. "He'd helped me. I guess he thought I'd help him."

"We'll get him out of your way," Vern said, "just as soon as we can."

"Thank you."

McIntyre went to look at Margaret.

The Most Dangerous Man Alive

Edward D. Hoch

ABBY TENYON WAS having a nightmare.

She was struggling against the softness of the sheets, fighting to come awake, while a masked man was beating her about the face with a huge padded fist. She could feel the blows, feel the jarring pain as they landed, and she tried to cry out. She wondered what had happened to Ron who had always rescued her in the past.

Then a final blow landed and she stopped caring, drifting back into the sleep that was deeper than sleep, the land that was almost beyond recall. She remembered wondering if she was dying, if this was what that final mystery was all about.

Presently she came awake, aware without opening her eyes that it was daylight. She stirred in the bed and felt a great throbbing pain centered about her face and head. She touched her cheek, winced, and immediately withdrew her hand. She tried to open her left eye and found that she couldn't.

What was wrong with her?

Opening her right eye with difficulty she could make out her husband still asleep in the other bed. "Ron," she called out. "Ron!"

He stirred but didn't wake up. The digital clock between the beds showed 8:14. He'd never slept this late since the campaign began.

"Ron!" she called louder, trying to move, trying to reach him across the gulf between the beds. Something was terribly wrong with her.

He came awake slowly, his eyes opening and then widening as he saw her. He sat up suddenly in the bed. "My God, Abby! Your face!"

"I . . . I've been hurt, Ron. Something hurt me terribly."

"Abby!" He was out of the bed, holding her.

"I dreamed a man was beating me."

Ron Tenyon reached for the telephone.

Ordinarily the case would have been handled by one of Captain Leopold's staff—Fletcher, perhaps, or more likely Connie Trent. But Ron Tenyon was three days away from the special election for Congress, and that added an important aspect to whatever misadventure had befallen his wife Abby.

Leopold arrived at the hotel room shortly after nine o'clock, having been summoned a half hour earlier by a call from Connie, who'd taken the original report. He found the house physician just finishing his ministrations to Ron Tenyon's wife, who nestled like an ill child in one of the wide twin beds of the room.

"Whatever happened to her has been very upsetting," the doctor said as he headed for the door. "I've given her a tranquilizer. She'll be relaxed and she may doze off."

"What was it, doctor?" Leopold asked.

"She's been beaten about the face. She has two black eyes and some bruises and swelling. But nothing that won't go away in a few weeks' time." He spoke in a calm, low voice as if he'd seen it all before.

"Did she say who did it?"

Ron Tenyon interrupted with the answer. "A masked man with a big padded fist. She thought it was a dream."

"She didn't cry out? You heard nothing?"

"Not a thing," Tenyon admitted. "And I don't usually sleep that heavily."

Leopold nodded to the doctor, indicating he had no further need of him at the moment. Then he sat down on the bed opposite Mrs. Tenyon. The room was large and tastefully furnished, with a view overlooking the river. It was the city's best hotel, the sort a man like Tenyon would choose for his campaign stop. Leopold knew little about him, except what the papers had printed. He was a thirty-nine-year-old financial expert who'd parlayed a successful business career and an attractive wife into a try at the United States Congress in a special election called because of the incumbent's death.

But right now Abby Tenyon wasn't looking very attractive. She sat propped up in bed, swaddled in blankets, her battered face only just beginning to show the swelling and discoloration that the bruises had caused. "Can you tell me what happened?" Leopold asked.

"N—no, I'm afraid I can't." She had to speak out of the side of her mouth, and it added to her bizarre, trampled-upon look.

"She thought it was a dream," her husband explained. "A nightmare. She wasn't fully conscious."

"Not even while you were being beaten?" Leopold found that difficult to understand.

"I think we were both drugged," Ron Tenyon said. "I didn't hear a thing, and I slept later than usual this morning. After last night's speech we came back here and ordered room service. I think the food was drugged."

Leopold made some notes. "Was anything stolen from the room?"

"No."

"Was Mrs. Tenyon sexually molested?"

"No."

"You're claiming that the two of you were drugged simply to allow your wife to be beaten up like this?"

"That appears to be the case."

"Do you have any enemies who might have done such a thing?"

"In politics everyone makes enemies. But I can't think of anyone perverse enough to attack me through Abby."

"And you, Mrs. Tenyon?"

She shook her head. "I don't know. I don't know anything. This whole thing is a nightmare." The swelling had almost closed both her eyes, and she searched in her purse for some dark glasses to cover them.

"This is the last weekend before the special election," Tenyon pointed out. "Abby was scheduled to make several public appearances with me. Do you think the beating could be linked to that in some manner?"

"I don't know," Leopold said. "Mrs. Tenyon, suppose you tell me everything you can about this dream of the man beating you."

He listened as she spoke, making notes, nodding from time to time. "The huge padded fist would have been a boxing glove. They wanted to mark you but not seriously injure you."

"But why?"

"And why go to the trouble of drugging us and sneaking into our hotel room?" Tenyon wondered. "They could have assaulted her on the street a lot easier."

Leopold considered that. "They may have chosen this method because no one would believe it."

"What do you mean?"

"Weren't you aware of the house physician's blasé attitude? It was nothing new or strange to him. He viewed it as a simple wife-beating."

"You mean—"

"A large segment of the public is going to think you beat your wife, Mr. Tenyon, and that the two of you made up this story of a masked intruder and drugged food because the election is so close."

Ron Tenyon began to pace the floor, his indignation growing. "My opponent would never do a thing like that. Crystal is an honorable man."

"It wouldn't have to be Crystal. Some of his supporters could be acting without his knowledge."

"Then at all costs we must keep this story out of the papers."

"That may be difficult."

"We'll say she has the flu."

But even as he spoke the phone between the beds rang. He answered it and spoke quickly with growing indignation. When he finally hung up his face was tense. "That was my campaign manager. The reporters are already onto it. They've been calling him for the story."

"Someone tipped them off," Leopold suggested.

"It seems so," Tenyon agreed. "The man who beat her up."

"Or perhaps a hotel employee. Maybe even the doctor."

"Well, there's no keeping it secret now."

And there wasn't. It was front-page news on Sunday morning.

Two days later Ron Tenyon lost the special Congressional election by about 1100 votes.

On the morning after the election Leopold called Lieutenant Fletcher into his office. "Get us a couple cups of coffee from the machine," he suggested. "I want to talk."

"About that Tenyon thing, Captain?"

"Yeah, I guess so."

"He lost the election."

Leopold nodded. "Eleven hundred votes. If five hundred and fifty or so people changed their minds he would have won."

"You think the bad publicity influenced the election?"

"Yes, I do. And since when is it bad publicity when a man's wife gets beaten up in a hotel room? Why is the press and public so quick to disbelieve his story, and his wife's story?"

"The room was locked, Captain. The idea of somebody drugging them both and getting past those locks, and then not even stealing anything, is just too far-fetched."

"Of course it's far-fetched! The person who did it deliberately made it seem far-fetched so the public would think Tenyon was a wife beater."

"You think George Crystal was involved?" Fletcher asked, stirring some sugar into his coffee.

"He seems decent enough. But there were other interests at work. It was well known that Tenyon opposed casino gambling in the state while Crystal supports it. The gambling interests are working hard to pass that bill, and they wanted Tenyon defeated. Of course, a Congressman doesn't vote directly on state measures, but his influence carries a lot of weight. That's especially true of Tenyon, who'd promised to stump the state in opposition to the casino bill if he was elected to Congress."

"So the casino people hired someone to do the job? They could get a hit man from organized crime easily enough."

"Yes," Leopold agreed, sipping his coffee. "But this whole thing is a bit too subtle for organized crime. They'd be more likely to run Tenyon's car off the road and make a sure thing of it. The idea of drugging them both, breaking into the hotel room, and beating his wife, then leaking the story to the papers, is an almost baroque scheme. Mobsters don't think in those terms."

"Are you giving me the case, Captain?" Fletcher asked.

"Nose around and see what you can find out."

"Any suggestions?" He knew Leopold always had suggestions.

"The hotel. If they were drugged, it was in the food that room service delivered. And if the room was entered in the night it had to be by someone who had a key and knew how to get past the night bolt. Run a check on any ex-convicts who might be employed there."

"I'll get right on it," Fletcher said.

Sometimes in an investigation the police get lucky. Fletcher got lucky on the Tenyon case. By the end of the week he'd discovered that a man named Carl Forsyth, employed in the hotel kitchen, had a record of two convictions—for breaking and entering and simple assault.

Then Fletcher got lucky a second time. As he approached Forsyth in the hallway of his apartment building on a cool May evening, identifying himself as a police officer, the burly man reacted instinctively. He drew a small automatic pistol from an inside pocket and pointed it at Fletcher's chest, squeezing the trigger as Fletcher went for his own weapon. The pistol jammed, and Fletcher smashed the barrel of his revolver down on the man's gun hand before he could try again.

Later, in the interrogation room at headquarters, Leopold faced the man. "You're a two-time loser, Carl. Assault with a deadly weapon, attempted murder, resisting arrest—any way you look at it, you're going back to prison for a good long stay."

"I thought he was a mugger," Forsyth insisted. He held up his bandaged hand. "Hell, I try to defend myself and I get a broken hand!"

"Who paid you to drug the Tenyons' food and beat her up?"

"I don't know what you're talking about!"

"Come on, Carl. You work in the kitchen. Someone tampered with their food and we think it was you. After they were drugged you picked the lock, or used a passkey. Once inside the room you put on a mask and a boxing glove and punched Abby Tenyon about the face. Then you or someone else phoned the papers, trying to make it look as if Tenyon beat his wife and the story she gave was a coverup."

"You know a lot, don't you?"

"Who hired you, Carl? All we want is the name."

"I'm not saying a word till my lawyer gets here."

And so they waited.

Carl Forsyth's lawyer proved to be Samuel Judge. He was well known in local legal circles, and every time his name was mentioned as a possibility for a judgeship the newsmen had a field day speculating about "Judge Judge." But so far he'd been passed over by the governor—possibly because of his eagerness to defend even the most disreputable criminals, or possibly because he so often got them off. His specialty was plea bargaining, that oddity of the modern legal system, and he was not a welcome figure around headquarters. Too many of the men felt the way Leopold did—that weeks of work in building a case should not be bargained away so easily by the District Attorney's office.

But Samuel Judge it was, and he emerged from a meeting with his client to confront a testy Captain Leopold. "When are you going to release him, Captain? You don't have a case."

"Don't I?" Leopold stormed. "He fired a pistol point-blank at Fletcher!"

"The pistol didn't fire," the lawyer replied quietly.

"It would have!"

"That's a matter of conjecture. My client drew a pistol when he was suddenly accosted in a hallway. He immediately surrendered it when Fletcher identified himself."

"Cut out the bull! The gun's not licensed and Forsyth is on parole. That alone is enough to put him back behind bars."

The lawyer thought about it, weighing the possibilities. "What do you want?" he asked at last.

"You plea bargain with the District Attorney's office, not with me."

"Look, your man Fletcher is the one pressing the gun charge."

"The attempted murder charge," Leopold corrected.

"You're onto this Tenyon thing, aren't you?"

"We want him for that. And we want the name of the person who hired him."

Samuel Judge shook his head. "Impossible. My client is too frightened to talk. That's why he drew on Fletcher so fast. He's been afraid of being silenced ever since the Tenyon thing."

"That's his problem."

"He could never testify in court. All the witness-protection programs in the world wouldn't protect him."

"Suppose," Leopold said, speaking slowly, "he didn't have to testify. Suppose he just wrote the name on a piece of paper and we took it from there. It would all be off the record."

Judge considered that. He stood up and began to pace. "I don't think he'd go for that. What would he get in return?"

"Fletcher might forget what happened in that hallway."

"And the Tenyon thing?"

Leopold shook his head. "No, he'd have to be charged with that."

"No deal."

"Why not ask him? The gun charge is more serious. That could put him away for life, with his record."

Judge shrugged and went back to speak with his client. Leopold had gone through this sort of thing before and he knew it would be a long session. It was.

Two hours later Samuel Judge took a folded piece of paper from his vest pocket and slid it across the table to Leopold. "That's all you get," he said. "I didn't even look at it myself. If you bring it into court I'll deny my client ever wrote it."

Leopold unfolded the paper and read the name that was neatly written on it.

Jules Dermain, with a New York City address.

"All right," Leopold turned to Fletcher. "Is this deal agreeable with you?"

"Sure. What the hell, the gun didn't fire."

"Good. Book Forsyth for the Tenyon thing and we'll forget the other." He turned back to the lawyer. "You'll plead him guilty to our charges?"

"I'll plead him guilty to something. That's for me to work out with the D.A."

"Still the plea bargainer! You amaze me, Judge."

"Just looking after my client's interests. Whose interests do you look after, Captain?"

"The victim's."

It took Leopold and Fletcher the better part of two weeks to assemble a file on Mr. Jules Dermain of New York City. When they'd completed their task, Leopold looked over the typewritten sheets and wondered just what it was they had.

Jules Dermain was 63 years old, a native of France who'd come to America after World War II and achieved a somewhat surprising success as a creator and manufacturer of games and puzzles. One of them, *Melrose*, had captured the public fancy in the mid-1960s and made Dermain a millionaire. As far as could be determined the man had no link with organized crime, and he certainly didn't need the money.

Had Forsyth lied to them?

That was what Leopold intended to find out.

New York was familiar territory to him. He'd spent his first years as a police officer and detective there, before returning home. He knew Manhattan especially well, and the little East Side neighborhoods like Gramercy Park brought back fond memories of younger days. Stuyvesant Park was one of these, a few blocks south of Gramercy. It was surrounded by brownstone townhouses dating back to the mid-19th century, and it was in one of these that Jules Dermain resided.

Dermain saw Leopold in an upstairs office lined with books and samples of the games he'd manufactured. There were a dozen different versions of *Melrose* alone, including foreign language and Braille editions and even a magnetized game to play while traveling. Dermain was slender and white-haired, with the appearance of a professor. A tiny smile played about his lips as he spoke, but his eyes seemed always alert and serious.

"What can I do for you, Captain Leopold? As I understand it, you're not connected with the New York Police Department?"

"That's correct. I spent some years in New York, but at present I'm up in Connecticut. I'm head of our Violent Crimes Squad, and I'm down here investigating a recent crime." Briefly he outlined the circumstances of Abby Tenyon's mysterious beating, omitting the fact that Carl Forsyth was in custody and had supplied Jules Dermain's name.

The Frenchman listened to all this with the slight smile still on his lips, as if awaiting the punch line of a lengthy shaggy-dog story. When Leopold finished he asked, "But how could this possibly concern me? I have never heard of Mr. Ron Tenyon or his wife Abby."

"You must understand that I'm here unofficially, Mr. Dermain. But your name has been mentioned in the course of the investigation. I felt a personal interview with you might be the best way to clear the air."

"So? My name has been mentioned. By whom, may I ask?"

"I'm not at liberty to say."

Dermain leaned back in his chair, unconcerned. "Oh, I suppose it was that fool who was hired to do the job."

Leopold sat as if stunned by an ax. He would have been less startled if the Frenchman had drawn a pistol from his desk drawer and started shooting. "You're admitting it?"

"Why not? You're here unofficially, out of your jurisdiction. You have not advised me of my rights or given me a chance to call a lawyer. Nothing I tell you could be used against me."

Leopold began to think it had been a mistake to visit this man. But now that he was here he had to make the best of it. "You admit you hired Carl Forsyth to drug Abby Tenyon and her husband, enter their hotel room and beat her up?"

"Of course! You wouldn't be here if you didn't know that much already. You must realize that I offer a service, Captain Leopold. Just as you are employed to solve crimes, I am sometimes employed to invent them: We are two sides of the same coin—the puzzle maker and the puzzle solver. As a matter of fact I take some pleasure in meeting you like this. Just as an author sometimes enjoys meeting his readers, I enjoy meeting one of those who is called upon to solve my little plots. You are the first, I must tell you, who has ever come this far."

"Who hired you to construct this particular puzzle?"

He shrugged. "The casino interests in your state. Their names are unimportant. I was presented with a challenge—to be certain that Ron Tenyon lost the election. Anything short of murder was allowed. Of course I considered the usual blind items planted in the newspapers, but the voting public becomes more sophisticated each year. The little game I devised was designed for indirection. The press would report the facts, and I would leave it to the public to draw a conclusion. I learned their schedule in advance and found that there was a man available who was employed at one of the hotels. In the kitchen, no less! And he was also an expert on locks.

"The pieces almost came together by themselves. He drugged their food, obtained a passkey, tampered with the night bolt in advance, and entered while they slept. Tenyon's wife was beaten enough to mark her face, but not to do permanent injury. I assumed, correctly I think, that a certain number of people reading that story on the weekend before the special election would be skeptical enough to believe the man beat his wife. It was a close election. I didn't need to change many minds."

Leopold had sat in the company of thieves and murderers on many occasions, but nothing had prepared him for this. The man across the desk was bragging of his crime, spreading the details for Leopold's admiration. "I'm speechless at your audacity," he admitted. "We'll see what you have to say in court when Carl Forsyth testifies against you."

The amused smile remained. "Oh, he wouldn't do that."

"Why not?"

"I have a certain reputation in underworld circles. Even in prison Mr. Forsyth would not feel entirely safe. The reputation is unearned, of course."

"Of course."

"Still, the plotting of a perfect murder is even more of a challenge than a game like the Tenyon affair. Many years ago, when I first came to this country, I was offered an assignment which might amuse you. There was a certain wealthy man, hunted by many nations, who took refuge in Ireland, buying a large country manor house and surrounding it with an exasperating maze made of brick walls overgrown with dense hedges." As he spoke he took down a maze game from the bookshelf behind him and opened it on the desk. "The incident inspired me to create this puzzle."

"You were hired to kill the man?" Leopold asked.

"I was hired to remove him, by one means or another. The house had been reinforced to make it virtually bombproof, you see, and the maze itself was guarded with electric-eye beams to warn if anyone entered it. He kept a staff of armed servants to guard against siege, and he never left the place except to walk the grounds each day safely inside the maze. A service road at the back of the house was kept sealed by iron gates. How, Captain Leopold, would you have gone about killing such a man?"

"I solve murder cases, I don't plan them."

"Still, as an exercise in tactics you might consider this one."

"Land a helicopter inside the grounds."

"There was no room for one, since the maze came up almost to the walls of the house."

"Bribe a servant."

"They were loyal to him unto death. They had served together during the war."

"Shoot him from a plane while he's out for his daily walk."

"He quickly retreated at the sound of approaching aircraft. And the house, as I have said, was quite resistant to most bombs."

"Poison his food supply before it reaches the house."

"The servants would eat it first, as tasters did for kings of old."

Leopold walked to the window and looked out at the park across the street. Seeing the children playing there, watching them run along the paths to the center fountain, brought him back to the reality of the world. He had not come here to play games with Jules Dermain, and this book-lined study with its boxed puzzles was a long way from the hotel room where Abby Tenyon had suffered her torment.

"Tell me," he said at last. "Tell me your secret of the maze."

"Ah, you are giving up so easily?"

"Tell me this one, so I might be better prepared to outwit you on the next."

"Spoken like a true puzzle fan! You delight me, Captain Leopold! The Irish matter is simply told. I happened to read that snakes can be trained to negotiate mazes. I photographed this maze from the air and built a duplicate out of boards. I trained three deadly black mambas to travel through the maze and strike at the first person they saw. The mamba was chosen because it is both fast and deadly. Of course the serpents could slither in beneath the electric-eye alarms, and since there are no snakes in Ireland as a rule, the victim had prepared no defense against such an attack. They were loosed at the hour of his daily walk. They sought him out within the maze and he died ten minutes later."

Leopold thought about that. "I don't believe a word of it," he said finally. "If I did, I'd consider you the most dangerous man alive."

Jules Dermain laughed heartily, shaking his small body. "You shouldn't believe it—of course not! Any more than you should believe I employed that man to beat Mrs. Tenyon! They're all games, played out in my mind. Go away now, Captain Leopold. It has been a pleasant hour, but I have other business."

Leopold nodded. There was nothing more for him here. But at the door he paused to ask, "How would someone go about killing *you*, Mr. Dermain?"

Another laugh. There was a television set at one side of the room, and Dermain stood against it as he answered. "You're not the first to ask that question, Captain. Of course I guard against it. My telephone and this office are constantly checked for listening devices. And I'm careful where I go. Still, it could be done. This video tape recorder on my television can be set to turn on up to a week in advance. If the tape cartridge contained a bomb instead of tape, it could destroy this entire building."

"Ever use that idea somewhere else?"

"Perhaps."

"We'll talk again," Leopold said.

"Come any time. I will tell you of an elderly corporate executive whose salary was such a drain on the company that we hastened his departure from this earth. And a United States Senator whose assassination was not quite what it seemed."

All the way back home Leopold was uneasy. The day had been a waste of time. Even if Dermain had conspired with Forsyth in the Tenyon affair, surely the rest of it was a myth. The man was a puzzle maker, not a master criminal who plotted assassinations halfway around the world. He'd spun a good yarn for Leopold and that was all.

But the memory of Jules Dermain still made him uneasy, and he wondered what he would do if he discovered it was all true.

As casually as possible he asked Connie Trent to run a check with the Dublin police. Had there ever been a case of murder by snakebite in Ireland, especially involving a man on a large country estate during the postwar years?

"There aren't supposed to be any snakes in Ireland," Connie protested. "St. Patrick drove them out."

"It was more likely due to the Ice Age and the fact that Ireland is surrounded by water. I'm sure you won't find anything, but check on it anyway."

"Is this connected with the Tenyon case?" She knew he'd gone to New York about that.

"In a way, yes."

He plunged into the other cases that called for his attention and he'd managed to put Jules Dermain almost out of his mind when Connie reported back two days later. "Here's that report from the Dublin police, Captain. You asked me to check with them."

"They didn't have anything, right?"

"On the contrary. A German named Von Buff, suspected of being a former Nazi, was killed by black mamba snakes at his country estate in Cork in 1958. No one ever explained how the snakes got there. The house was surrounded by a maze of hedges."

"Yes, I know," Leopold said, feeling suddenly light-headed. It couldn't be, but it was.

"The guards killed the snakes."

"I'm sure they did."

"Are you all right, Captain?"

"Fine. I'm fine."

When he was alone Leopold thought about a course of action. He considered phoning the New York police, but he really didn't know what he could tell them. Jules Dermain had committed no crime in New York that Leopold was aware of—unless perhaps it was conspiracy.

In the end he did nothing.

It was about a week later when Ron Tenyon came to see him. He sat in the uncomfortable wooden chair opposite Leopold's desk and said, "I want to know about the investigation into Abby's beating."

"You know what there is to know. The grand jury has indicted Carl Forsyth and we have every reason to believe he'll plead guilty. His lawyer, Samuel Judge, has been plea bargaining with the D.A.'s office."

"So what will he get? Two years? Three?"

"It's a third offense. He could go away for a long time."

"And what about the man who hired him?"

"He was hired by pro-casino money out to defeat you. But I guess that's no surprise."

"It's a surprise to hear it like that. Do you have their names?"

Leopold pondered how much to tell him. "I have the name of one man, but nothing we can use in court."

"Why not?"

"Because the man is clever. He might be the most clever criminal I've ever encountered."

"A master criminal like Professor Moriarty?" Tenyon smiled as he said it. Leopold had not seen him smile since the attack on his wife.

"Something like that," Leopold replied in all seriousness. "We don't like to admit they exist, because they rarely get caught. Today's master criminal isn't usually concerned with planning bank heists or mob killings. He's far more interested in pulling off a commodities swindle or falsifying the ownership of a tanker full of crude oil. The man I speak of is especially dangerous because he puts his talent at the disposal of anyone who can pay his price. The men who wanted to defeat you could pay."

"Losing the election was one thing. What they did to Abby was something else. I can never forgive that."

"How is she?"

"Her face is pretty well healed, but that's only part of it. Even our friends look at us a bit oddly now. Every time Abby gets a bruise someone will remember the stories that went around, and they'll forget that Forsyth was arrested for beating her."

Leopold was silent for a time. Then he reached a decision and said, "After what you've been through I guess I owe you some information." He told Tenyon about Jules Dermain. "That's the sort of man we're up against. I checked the Irish story and it's true."

Ron Tenyon thought about that, his face lined with concern. "As long as you can't touch him, he's free to do this sort of thing again, to continue plotting the maiming and killing."

"Oh, yes," Leopold admitted. "But what can we do about it?"

"Do? We can stop him!"

"How? By killing him ourselves?"

Tenyon's face was very serious. "Why not?"

Never in his life had Leopold seriously considered killing a person, except in the line of duty and then always in self-defense. There was a brief scandal once when he'd been accused of killing his former wife, but even in the depths of it, knowing how much the woman had hated him, he never entertained the idea that he could have taken her life. The law was an important institution to him, and he was sworn to uphold it. Even a man like Jules Dermain must be protected.

"I want to meet Dermain," Ron Tenyon told him the following day. "I've thought it all out and I want to meet him."

"Do you now? So you can pull out a little pistol and avenge your wife?"

"If it's the only way to stop a man like that."

"You're not meeting him. It would accomplish nothing."

"If you won't go with me, I'll go alone."

"That's out of the question. I'm sorry I told you as much as I did."

"I have to confront him," Tenyon said. "If I don't do it, Abby will."

"You told her about it?"

He nodded. "Last night. With me it's the fact that he had her beaten. With Abby it's what he did to me and to my chances in the election. She wants revenge for that, and I can't say I blame her. If the police are helpless I have to do something myself."

Leopold could see the man was serious. "I can't stand by while you do violence to him. I can't even condone a punch in the nose, though I might look the other way."

"Arrange a meeting. Tell him I have to see him."

"Do I have your promise there'll be no violence?"

Ron Tenyon hesitated, running a damp hand through his thinning hair.

"All right, if that's what it takes. You have my promise."

"What are you going to say to him?"

"Even if Dermain planned it, I want the men who paid him to do it. They may be unimportant names, but I want those names. I'm prepared to pay for them."

"I'll see what I can do," Leopold promised.

He telephoned Jules Dermain later that afternoon. The Frenchman was friendly but guarded on the phone. There was no talk of mambas in Ireland or beatings in hotel rooms—not when he could assume his conversation was being recorded. "What can I do for you today, Captain?" he asked after some preliminary remarks about the weather.

"Ron Tenyon wants to meet you. He asked me to arrange it."

"Oh? I don't really see that any good could be served by such a meeting."

"He has a business proposition to offer you."

A dry chuckle came over the line. "Really, now, you can't expect me to agree to such a thing."

"If you're concerned about recording devices, the meeting could be held outdoors," Leopold suggested. "That fountain in the park across the street could effectively muffle conversation."

"What's your interest in all this?" the Frenchman asked.

It was a good question, and one that Leopold couldn't answer with complete satisfaction. "Maybe I'm trying to prevent a murder," he replied.

There was another laugh. "I trust you, Captain. If you accompany Tenyon I'll meet the two of you tomorrow noon, at the fountain across from my house."

Leopold met Tenyon at the railroad station shortly before nine o'clock. The express into New York took 90 minutes, and they wanted to be on time. "I told Abby about it," Tenyon said. "She wanted to come along."

"It's better to keep her away. I don't know what we'll be getting into."

"I promise to behave myself," Tenyon said.

"But I wonder about Jules Dermain. He didn't make any promises."

They talked little during the train trip to New York, though Tenyon did speak of his future plans a bit. "George Crystal is a lightweight. Two years of him and the public will be ready for a change. I just might run again."

"You're sounding more optimistic than you did the other day."

"I've had time to think."

"Do you really believe George Crystal is the name Dermain will give you?"

Tenyon's head came up. "Did I say that?"

"You didn't have to. Crystal is the man to beat and you're going to New York today to start your campaign. It's not even two years—he'll have to run again in the next regular election, in eighteen months. But tell me—what changed you? When this thing first happened to you and Abby it was the casino interests behind it—not George Crystal."

"He profited from it. He can take some of the blame for it."

"There's enough blame to spread around," Leopold agreed. "Just make sure he deserves the part he gets."

When the train finally arrived at Grand Central, it was a bright May morning with the temperature well into the sixties. "It's not too far," Leopold said. "Want to walk?"

"Why not?"

They were still early when they reached Stuyvesant Park.

Leopold pointed out Jules Dermain's house and considered presenting himself at the door. But if the Frenchman was nervous about their visit that would only increase his suspicions. Better to wait for his arrival at the fountain.

There were a few children at play, watched over by mothers or nursemaids, and an illegally unleashed dog made the rounds of the litter barrels situated at each of the two park entrances. "Looking down on this from Dermain's second-floor office, it seems a little like one of his game boards," Leopold observed. "An entrance on the east and west sides, the fountain in the middle. I could almost imagine wooden chessmen moving along the paths."

"He probably sits in there and plots his assassinations on it."

"I'd like to—"

Leopold stopped speaking. Though it was only twenty to twelve, the door of Dermain's brownstone had opened and he was emerging.

"Is that him?"

"That's him," Leopold confirmed.

Jules Dermain paused at his door to unlock the mailbox and extract a single slim envelope. He seemed puzzled by it but placed it in his inside pocket unopened. Then he came down the steps and crossed the street to the park. His brownstone was in midblock, facing south; so he had to walk around to one or the other park entrance. He hesitated an instant before choosing the one on the east side. "Shall we go meet him?" Tenyon suggested.

"No. I told him we'd speak by the fountain, so the sound of the water would help protect him against listening devices."

They watched Dermain strolling along the edge of the park toward the entrance. He did not look at them, and anyone watching would have thought he was only out for a casual walk.

He'd almost reached the entrance when Leopold gripped Tenyon's arm. "Isn't that your wife over there?"

"My God—Abby!"

It was indeed Abby Tenyon. She'd materialized from somewhere, striding purposefully across the grass to intercept the path the Frenchman would be taking once he entered the park. Leopold could see her right hand go into her purse just as Tenyon shouted, "*Abby! Don't!*"

Leopold waited no longer. He sprang forward, trying to get to her in time. She'd reached the path and was standing in the center of it, facing the open gate where Jules Dermain was just entering. Her purse had dropped to the ground and she held a small automatic pistol firmly in both hands, pointing it at arm's length directly at Dermain.

The Frenchman saw the pistol too, as he started into the park. Then everything seemed frozen in Leopold's vision as he tried to reach her.

Behind him Tenyon was shouting. Ahead, Abby Tenyon took aim.

Then Leopold hit her, lunging into her back just as the pistol went off. He saw its flash aimed at the sky and knew he'd reached her in time.

Knew, and yet froze again watching Jules Dermain as he vanished in a flash of fire.

Leopold hit the ground on top of Abby as a clap of thunder shook the park, echoing off the brownstones around the park. Then there was smoke and flying bits of wood and metal and flesh.

Finally, after a moment that lasted an eternity, Leopold lifted himself to his knees and stared toward the gate.

The litter barrel had exploded as Jules Dermain passed by. Where he and it had stood there was now only a hole in the earth.

The New York police blocked off the area as they searched for clues and the scattered remains of Jules Dermain's body. Even though he'd seen it happen, Leopold couldn't avoid the suspicion that the whole thing was some final trick of the puzzle master. Perhaps he'd been so frank in his meeting with Leopold because he planned exactly this sort of grand exit—a double to die in his place while he flew off to the easy life in South America.

New York City's bomb squad was represented by a calm, laconic man named Sergeant Phillips who went about his job with an assurance that brought admiration from a fellow professional like Leopold. "You say the lady fired the gun at the same time the bomb went off?" he asked.

"That's right. See any connection?"

Phillips was stooping over the twisted remains of the metal litter barrel. He seemed to be sniffing the air near the ground. "Plastic explosives in the barrel. Could have been set off by a sound-activated device but that's pretty doubtful. Too dangerous—a backfire might do it. Besides, if she was out there with the gun anyway, she could just as easily have shot him."

Leopold suggested the other possibilities to the man. "It might have been a double."

"We've got the fingers on one hand. We can check it soon enough."

"Any chance it could be suicide?"

The bomb squad man shrugged. "Hell of a way to kill yourself, but we've seen it happen."

"He had admitted some criminal activities to me during a prior meeting. He might have feared arrest."

Sergeant Phillips grunted. He was working a portion of scorched clothing from the remains of the dead man. Finally he abandoned the gruesome task and stood up to survey the scene. "Couldn't have been set off by a trip-wire," he decided. "Too many kids playing in the area. Probably a radio signal, which means the killer had to be nearby."

Leopold's thoughts went back again to Ron Tenyon and his wife. He could see them across the street, being questioned by detectives. Leopold himself had undergone questioning too, but they'd accepted his credentials and allowed him to remain on the scene. "Wait a minute," he said suddenly. "There's something wrong here. Dermain's house is across the street, in mid-block. When he started over here to meet us, he had a choice of either entrance. How could the killer possibly know which one he'd use?"

Phillips shrugged again. "Habit."

"No, I saw Dermain hesitate before coming the way he did. Would a killer this clever risk spoiling his plot because his victim turned right instead of left?"

The sergeant was suddenly interested. "You're saying—?"

"I'm saying let's take a look at the trash barrel at the west entrance."

Leopold reached it first and gingerly removed a crumpled newspaper and assorted litter. Underneath, resting in the bottom of the barrel, was a large package wrapped in plain brown paper. "Good hunch," Phillips said. "That's it."

The bomb experts carefully transported it to a truck with a covered-wagon look, made of woven steel cables that had the appearance of wicker from a distance. Later, when the package had been opened and the detonator removed from the mound of plastic explosives inside, Phillips came back to Leopold holding it in his hand.

"What do you make of it, Sergeant?"

"Radio-activated, as I suspected, but very short range." He turned the metal part over in his hand.

"A hundred feet?"

"No, no—more like ten feet."

"But the killer couldn't have been that close!" Leopold protested. "Even Abby Tenyon wasn't that close!"

One of Phillips's men came up to them. "We found it, Sergeant," he said, holding out a little plastic evidence bag containing a round metal disc about the size of a dime.

"Good." Phillips took the bag and showed it to Leopold. "The latest thing in electronic detonating devices. One of these was used in a recent Middle East assassination. It was attached magnetically to the victim's car fender, and when the car passed a second vehicle loaded with plastic explosives both of them were blown up."

"Where did you find it?" Leopold asked the man.

"Breast pocket of the victim's coat, inside a badly scorched envelope."

"Of course! The letter!" Leopold remembered Dermain's puzzlement at the letter in the mailbox. "Can you read any of it?"

"Seems to be an order for games."

"From a fictitious address, no doubt."

Sergeant Phillips nodded. "Have the lab work on it."

"That's why Dermain seemed puzzled—because he wasn't expecting a mail delivery at that time. No doubt the postman had been there earlier. But the bomber couldn't risk the uncertainties of the mail service. The letter must have been put in the box by the killer himself, who knew Dermain would see it and remove it as he left the house to meet me in the park."

"A clever man to anticipate Dermain's movements like that."

Leopold nodded. "A puzzle master—as good as Jules Dermain himself."

"Are we back to the suicide theory?"

"No, no. If Dermain had committed suicide we wouldn't have found explosives in that second barrel. He'd have known which way to walk."

It was later in the day, after the fingerprints had finally confirmed Dermain's death, that Leopold found a chance to speak with Abby Tenyon on the train back to Connecticut. "Why did you try to kill Jules Dermain this morning, Abby? Your face is healed now. Your husband is talking of running in the next election. What could you hope to accomplish? Was revenge that important to you?"

"Revenge? No, not revenge." She was staring out the window. "I had to do it for Ron. I had to kill that man before Ron did it and ruined his life forever."

"A self-sacrificing motive for murder! A noble intent, though I can hardly approve of it. In any event, someone else did the job for you."

She took a deep breath and said, "God, I hope so," and in that instant Leopold knew she suspected her husband of the murder.

The killing of Jules Dermain was a three-day wonder in the New York press before it was supplanted by a brutal subway slaying. Since the investigation was not the responsibility of Captain Leopold he lost track of it within a week. Of more local concern was the indictment of Carl Forsyth by the county grand jury on charges of felonious assault. The arraignment was held at ten o'clock on the first Monday morning in June, and Leopold was there with Lieutenant Fletcher. They sat in the back of the courtroom watching while Forsyth stood next to his lawyer, Samuel Judge, and pleaded guilty to the charge. The judge ordered sentencing for June 24th and court was adjourned.

"That was fast," Fletcher said.

Leopold, whose mind had wandered during the court session, was surprised it was over. "What happened?"

"He pleaded guilty. Were you taking a little nap, Captain?"

"No, I was thinking of the most amazing thing."

"What was that?"

"Remember how this all began, Fletcher? Remember that day you arrested Forsyth and he tried to take a shot at you?"

"How could I forget?"

"You knocked the gun from his hand and broke a bone doing it."

"Sure. It was all bandaged up while we were questioning him."

Leopold was on his feet. "There might be a few people in this world who are ambidextrous, but most of us are either right- or left-handed, aren't we?"

Fletcher looked puzzled. "Is this some sort of quiz show, Captain?"

But Leopold was hurrying on, speaking quickly as he moved down the row of seats to the aisle. "It's one of the oddities of our modern civilization, Fletcher, that a person generally uses the same hand to fire a gun and hold a pencil. If you broke Forsyth's gun hand you also broke his writing hand."

"So?"

"So he couldn't have written Jules Dermain's name and address so neatly on that piece of paper Samuel Judge gave me."

He'd reached the aisle now, just in time to intercept the portly lawyer.

"Well, Captain Leopold! Good to see you again!"

"Good to see you too, Mr. Judge. I think the New York police might be even more pleased to see you—and to arrest you for the murder of Jules Dermain."

Samuel Judge stood quietly while Leopold informed him of his rights. Then he walked between Leopold and Fletcher along the covered passageway that connected the county courthouse with police headquarters.

"He's not saying a word," Fletcher said when he came back from booking the lawyer.

"He's a smart attorney. If the people we pick up on the streets ever learn to keep their mouths shut we'll be in big trouble."

"You really think he arranged that bombing?"

"I know it, Fletcher. Look at it this way. The bomber had to possess an important piece of information—the fact that Dermain had agreed to meet us at the fountain at noon on the day in question. Otherwise the twin bombs in the trash baskets and the ideally timed letter in the mailbox would make no sense. Agreed?"

"Agreed."

"The only ones who knew of that meeting were myself and Ron Tenyon—who unfortunately also told his wife about it. Three people. You and Connie knew about the meeting, but not the details of time and place. I could certainly eliminate myself, and I could also eliminate Abby Tenyon. There was no need for the scene with the gun if she'd already arranged to kill him. Ron Tenyon was another matter, but I quickly eliminated him. He might have slipped down to the city the previous night to plant those bombs, but the letter had to have been left in the mailbox that morning—shortly before our arrival."

"Why's that?"

"If the letter was there at, say, nine o'clock, Dermain might have found it earlier and brought it inside. Once opened, it was no good. He certainly wouldn't carry the miniature radio transmitter with him to the park, even if he thought it was only a metal disc. No, we must assume a clever and thoughtful murderer. Thus we must assume the letter was left in the box late that morning. And Ron Tenyon was never out of my sight."

"So who does that leave?"

"No one. I asked myself next if Dermain's phone could have been tapped, but here again the answer was no. He told me on the day of our meeting that his phone and office were constantly checked against listening devices."

"Then the thing's impossible!"

"No, it isn't. One possibility remains—that Jules Dermain himself informed his killer of the time and place of the meeting."

"Why would he do that?"

"It would be the most natural thing in the world, if the killer was the person who engaged Dermain's services originally—the nameless casino interests who were behind this whole thing. And that brings us back up here. The note that gave me Dermain's name and address was written here—not by Carl Forsyth, as I've shown, but by the person who was alone with Forsyth at the time. His lawyer, Samuel Judge. It was Judge who wrote the note, and I suspect it was Judge who hired Forsyth in the first place. Who'd have a better knowledge of ex-convicts working in local hotels—a puzzle maker in Manhattan or a criminal lawyer here in town?"

"Then what did Dermain have to do with the scheme?"

"Judge came to him for the idea, but it was Judge who hired Forsyth to carry it out. When we arrested Forsyth, he must have been close to breaking and implicating Judge. We had to be given a name, any name, so he gave us Jules Dermain. He figured Dermain was beyond reach and beyond arrest. He didn't realize the Frenchman was at a stage of life where he'd begin to brag about past triumphs to the first person who'd listen. When he phoned Judge to say I was coming down again, this time with Ron Tenyon, and that Tenyon had a deal for him, Judge decided Jules Dermain had to die. And he put his mind to it as cleverly as Dermain might have. Who knows—maybe one day when they were together Dermain looked out the window and suggested to Judge the very method of his own murder. He did something of the sort with me regarding a bomb attached to a videotape machine."

"Judge did it himself?"

"Or else found another ex-convict willing to carry out his plan. Start checking local people with records for bombings. Meanwhile I'm going to talk with Forsyth. He hasn't been sentenced yet and now that we know about Judge he might be willing to talk in return for a lighter jail term. We want to hit Samuel Judge with enough evidence so he'll be crying to the New York District Attorney for plea bargaining."

In the end they had more than they needed, including Dermain's carefully coded records of payments made to him by Samuel Judge and others. And Leopold, remembering his sole meeting with the little Frenchman, could feel in a special way that he'd solved the puzzle master's final challenge.

Nine Sons

Wendy Hornsby

I SAW JANOS Bonachek's name in the paper this morning. There was a nice article about his twenty-five years on the federal bench, his plans for retirement. The Boy Wonder, they called him, but the accompanying photograph showed him to be nearly bald, a wispy white fringe over his ears the only remains of his once remarkable head of yellow hair.

For just a moment, I was tempted to write him, or call him, to put to rest forever questions I had about the death that was both a link and a wedge between us. In the end I didn't. What was the point after all these years? Perhaps Janos's long and fine career in the law was sufficient atonement, for us all, for events that happened so long ago.

It occurred on an otherwise ordinary day. It was April, but spring was still only a tease. If anything stood out among the endless acres of black mud and gray slush, it was two bright dabs of color: first the blue crocus pushing through a patch of dirty snow, then the bright yellow head of Janos Bonachek as he ran along the line of horizon toward his parents' farm after school. Small marvels maybe, the spring crocus and young Janos, but in that frozen place, and during those hard times, surely they were miracles.

The year was 1934, the depths of the Great Depression.

Times were bad, but in the small farm town where I had been posted by the school board, hardship was an old acquaintance.

I had arrived the previous September, fresh from teachers' college, with a new red scarf in my bag and the last piece of my birthday cake. At twenty, I wasn't much older than my high-school-age pupils.

Janos was ten when the term began, and exactly the height of ripe wheat. His hair was so nearly the same gold as the bearded grain that he could run through the uncut fields and be no more noticeable than the ripples made by a prairie breeze. The wheat had to be mown before Janos could be seen at all.

On the northern plains, the season for growing is short, a quick breath of summer between the spring thaw and the first frost of fall. Below the surface of the soil, and within the people who forced a living from it, there seemed to be a layer that never had time to warm all the way through. I believe to this day that if the winter hadn't been so long, the chilling of the soul so complete, we would not have been forced to bury Janos Bonachek's baby sister.

Janos came from a large family, nine sons. Only one of them, Janos, was released from chores to attend school. Even then, he brought work with him in the form of his younger brother, Boya. Little Boya was then four or five. He wasn't as brilliant as Janos, but he tried hard. Tutored and cajoled by Janos, Boya managed to skip to the second-grade reader that year.

Around Halloween, that first year, Janos was passed up to me by the elementary teacher. She said she had nothing more to teach him. I don't know that I was any better prepared than she was, except that the high school textbooks were on the shelves in my room. I did my best.

Janos was a challenge. He absorbed everything I had to offer and demanded more, pushing me in his quiet yet insistent way to explain or to find out. He was eager for everything. Except geography. There he was a doubter. Having lived his entire life on a flat expanse of prairie, Janos would not believe the earth was a sphere, or that there were bodies of water vaster than the wheatfields that stretched past his horizon. The existence of mountains, deserts, and oceans, he had to take on faith, like the heavenly world the nuns taught me about in catechism.

Janos was an oddball to his classmates, certainly. I can still see that shiny head bent close to his books, the brow of his pinched little face furrowed as he took in a new set of universal truths from the world beyond the Central Grain Exchange. The other students deferred to him, respected him, though they never played with him. He spent recesses and lunch periods sitting on the school's front stoop, waiting for me to ring the big brass bell and let him back inside. I wonder how that affected him as a judge, this boy who never learned how to play.

Janos shivered when he was cold, but he seemed otherwise oblivious to external discomfort or appearances. Both he and Boya came to school barefoot until there was snow on the ground. Then they showed up in mismatched boots sizes too big, yet no one called attention to them, which I found singular. Janos's coat, even in blizzards, was an old gray blanket that I'm sure he slept under at night. His straight yellow hair stuck out in chunks as if it had been scythed like the wheat. He never acknowledged that he was in any way different from his well-scrubbed classmates.

While this oblivion to discomfort gave Janos an air of stoic dignity, it did impose some hardship on me. When the blizzards came and I knew school should be closed, I went out anyway because I knew Janos would be there, with Boya. If I didn't come to unlock the classroom, I was sure they would freeze waiting.

Getting there was itself a challenge. I boarded in town with the doctor and his wife, my dear friend Martha. When the snow blew in blinding swirls and the road was impassable to any automobile, I would persuade the doctor to harness his team of plow horses to his cutter and drive me out. The doctor made only token protest after the first trip: the boys had been at the school for some time before we arrived, huddled together on the stoop like drifted snow.

Those were the best days, alone, the two boys and I. I would bring books from Martha's shelves, books not always on the school board approved list. We would read together, and talk about the world on the far side of the prairie and how one day we would see it for ourselves. As the snow drifts piled up to the sills outside, we would try to imagine the sultry heat of the tropics, the pitch and roll of the oceans, men in pale suits in electric-lit parlors discussing being and nothingness while they sipped hundred-year-old sherry.

We had many days together. That year the first snow came on All Saints Day and continued regularly until Good Friday. I would have despaired during the ceaseless cold if it weren't for Janos and the lessons I received at home on the evenings of those blizzardy days.

Invariably, on winter nights when the road was impassable and sensible people were at home before the fire, someone would call for the doctor's services. He would harness the cutter, and go. Martha, of course, couldn't sleep until she heard the cutter return. We would keep each other entertained, sometimes until after the sun came up.

Martha had gone to Smith or Vassar. I'm not sure which because Eastern girls' schools were so far from my experience that the names meant nothing to me then. She was my guide to the world I had only seen in magazines and slick-paged catalogues, where people were polished to a smooth and shiny perfection, where long underwear, if indeed any was worn, never showed below their hems. These people were oddly whole, no scars, no body parts lost to farm machinery. In their faces I saw a peace of mind I was sure left them open to the world of ideas. I longed for them, and was sure Martha did as well.

Martha took life in our small community with grace, though I knew she missed the company of other educated women. I had to suffice.

Just as I spent my days preparing Janos, Martha spent her evenings teaching me the social graces I would need if I were ever to make my escape. Perhaps I was not as quick a pupil as Janos, but I was as eager.

Lessons began in the attic where Martha kept her trunks. Packed in white tissue was the elegant trousseau she had brought with her from the East, gowns of wine-colored taffeta moire and green velvet and a pink silk so fine I feared touching it with my calloused hands.

I had never actually seen a live woman in an evening gown, though I knew Martha's gowns surpassed the mail-order gowns that a woman might order for an Eastern Star ritual, if she had money for ready-made.

Martha and I would put on the gowns and drink coffee with brandy and read to each other from Proust, or take turns at the piano. I might struggle through a Strauss waltz or the Fat Lady Polka. She played flawless Dvorak and Debussy. This was my finishing school, long nights in Martha's front parlor, waiting for the cutter to bring the doctor home, praying the cutter hadn't overturned, hoping the neighbor he had gone to tend was all right.

When he did return, his hands so cold he needed help out of his layers of clothes, Martha's standard greeting was, "Delivering Mrs. Bonachek?" This was a big joke to us, because, of course, Mrs. Bonachek delivered herself. No one knew how many pregnancies she had had beyond her nine living sons. Poor people, they were rich in sons.

That's what I kept coming back to that early spring afternoon as I walked away from the Bonachek farm. I had seen Janos running across the fields after school. If he hadn't been hurrying home to help his mother, then where had he gone? And where were his brothers?

It lay on my mind.

As I said, the day in question had been perfectly ordinary. I had stayed after my students to sweep the classroom, so it was nearly four before I started for home. As always, I walked the single-lane road toward town, passing the Bonachek farm about halfway. Though underfoot the black earth was frozen hard as tarmac, I was looking for signs of spring, counting the weeks until the end of the school term.

My feet were cold inside my new Sears and Roebuck boots and I was mentally drafting a blistering letter to the company. The catalogue copy had promised me boots that would withstand the coldest weather, so, as an act of faith in Sears, I had invested a good chunk of my slim savings for the luxury of warm feet. Perhaps the copywriter in a Chicago office could not imagine ground as cold as this road.

I watched for Janos's mother as I approached her farm. For three days running, I had seen Mrs. Bonachek working in the fields as I walked to school in the morning, and as I walked back to town in the dusky afternoon. There was no way to avoid her. The distance between the school and the Bonachek farm was uninterrupted by hill or wall or stand of trees.

Mrs. Bonachek would rarely glance up as I passed. Unlike the other parents, she never greeted me, never asked how her boys were doing in school, never suggested I let them out earlier for farm chores. She knew little English, but neither did many of the other parents, or my own.

She was an enigma. Formless, colorless, Mrs. Bonachek seemed no more than a piece of the landscape as she spread seed grain onto the plowed ground from a big pouch in her apron. Wearing felt boots, she walked slowly along the straight furrows, her thin arm moving in a sweep as regular as any motor-powered machine.

Hers was an odd display of initiative, I thought. No one else was out in the fields yet. It seemed to me she risked losing her seed to mildew or to a last spring freeze by planting so early. Something else bothered me more. While I was a dairyman's daughter and knew little about growing wheat, I knew what was expected of farm children. There were six in my family, my five brothers and myself. My mother never went to the barns alone when there was a child at hand. Mrs. Bonachek had nine sons. Why, I wondered, was she working in the fields all alone?

On the afternoon of the fourth day, as had become my habit, I began looking for Mrs. Bonachek as soon as I locked the schoolhouse door. When I couldn't find her, I felt a pang of guilty relief that I wouldn't have to see her that afternoon, call out a greeting that I knew she wouldn't return.

So I walked more boldly, dressing down Sears in language I could never put on paper, enjoying the anarchy of my phrases even as I counted the blue crocus along the road.

Just as I came abreast of the row of stones that served to define the beginning of the Bonachek driveway, I saw her. She sat on the ground between the road and the small house, head bowed, arms folded across her chest. Her faded calico apron, its big seed pocket looking flat and empty, was spread on the ground beside her. She could have been sleeping, she was so still. I thought she might be sick, and would have gone to her, but she turned her head toward me, saw me, and shifted around until her back was toward me.

I didn't stop. The road curved and after a while I couldn't see her without turning right around. I did look back once and saw Mrs. Bonachek upright again. She had left her apron on the ground, a faded red bundle at the end of a furrow. She gathered up the skirt of her dress, filled it with seed grain, and continued her work. So primitive, I thought. How was it possible she had spawned the bright light that was Janos?

I found Martha in an extravagant mood when I reached home. The weather was frigid, but she, too, had seen the crocus. She announced that we would hold a tea to welcome spring. We would put on the tea frocks from her trunk and invite in some ladies from town. It would be a lark, she said, a coming out. I could invite anyone I wanted.

I still had Mrs. Bonachek on my mind. I couldn't help picturing her rising from her squat in the muddy fields to come sit on Martha's brocade sofa, so I said I would invite her first. The idea made us laugh until I had hiccups. I said the woman had no daughters and probably needed some lively female company.

Martha went to the piano and banged out something suitable for a melodrama. I got a pan of hot water and soaked my cold feet while we talked about spring and the prospect of being warm again, truly warm, in all parts at once. I wondered what magazine ladies did at teas.

We were still planning little sandwiches and petit fours and onions cut into daisies when the doctor came in for supper. There were snowflakes on his beard and I saw snow falling outside, a lacy white curtain over the evening sky. When Martha looked away from the door, I saw tears in her eyes.

"You're late," Martha said to the doctor, managing a smile. "Out delivering Mrs. Bonachek?"

"No such luck." The doctor seemed grim. "I wish that just once the woman would call me in time. She delivered herself again. The baby died, low body temperature I suspect. A little girl. A pretty, perfect little girl."

I was stunned but I managed to blurt, "But she was working in the fields just this afternoon."

Martha and the doctor exchanged a glance that reminded me how much I still had to learn. Then the doctor launched into a speech about some people not having sense enough to take to their beds and what sort of life could a baby born into such circumstances expect, anyway?

"The poor dear," Martha said when he had run down. "She finally has a little girl to keep her company and it dies." She grabbed me by the arm. "We must go offer our consolation."

We put on our boots and coats and waited for the doctor to get his ancient Ford back out of the shed. It made a terrible racket, about which Martha complained gently, but there wasn't enough snow for the cutter. We were both disappointed—the cutter gave an occasion a certain weight.

"Say your piece then leave," the doctor warned as we rattled over the rutted road. "These are private people. They may not understand your intentions."

He didn't understand that Martha and I were suffering a bit of guilt from the fun we had had at poor Mrs. Bonachek's expense. And we were bored. Barn sour, my mother would say.

Tired of being cooped up all winter and in desperate need of some diversion.

We stormed the Bonachek's tiny clapboard house, our offers of consolation translated by a grim-faced Janos. Martha was effusive. A baby girl should have a proper send-off, she said. There needed to be both a coffin and a dress. When was the funeral?

Mrs. Bonachek looked from me to Martha, a glaze over her mud-colored eyes. Janos shrugged his skinny shoulders. There was no money for funerals, he said. When a baby died, you called in the doctor for a death certificate, then the county came for the remains. That was all.

Martha patted Mrs. Bonachek's scaly hands. Not to worry. We would take care of everything. And we did. Put off from our spring tea by the sudden change in the weather, we diverted our considerable social energy to the memorial services.

I found a nice wooden box of adequate size in the doctor's storeroom and painted it white. Martha went up to the attic and brought down her beautiful pink silk gown and an old feather pillow. She didn't even wince as she ran her sewing shears up the delicate hand-turned seams. I wept. She hugged me and talked about God's will being done and Mrs. Bonachek's peasant strength. I was thinking about the spoiled dress.

We worked half the night. We padded the inside of the box with feathers and lined it with pink silk. We made a tiny dress and bonnet to match. The doctor had talked the county into letting us have a plot in the cemetery. It was such a little bit of ground, they couldn't refuse.

We contacted the parish priest, but he didn't want to perform the services. The county cemetery wasn't consecrated and he didn't know the Bonacheks. We only hoped it wasn't a rabbi that was needed because there wasn't one for miles. Martha reasoned that heaven was heaven and the Methodist preacher would have to do, since he was willing.

By the following afternoon everything was ready. The snow

had turned to slush but our spirits weren't dampened. We set off, wearing prim navy-blue because Martha said it was more appropriate for a child's funeral than somber black.

When the doctor drove us up to the small house, the entire Bonachek family, scrubbed and brushed, turned out to greet us.

Janos smiled for the first time I could remember. He fingered a frayed necktie that hung below his twine belt. He looked very awkward, but I knew he felt elegant. Everyone, even Boya, wore some sort of shoes. It was a gala, if solemn event.

Mr. Bonachek, a scrawny, pale-faced man, relieved us of the makeshift coffin and led us into the single bedroom. The baby, wrapped in a scrap of calico, lay on the dresser. I unfolded the little silk dress on the bed while Martha shooed Mr. Bonachek out of the room.

"We should wash her," Martha said. A catch in her voice showed that her courage was failing. She began to unwrap the tiny creature. It was then I recognized the calico—Mrs. Bonachek's faded apron.

I thought of the nine sons lined up in the next room and Mrs. Bonachek sitting in the field with her apron spread on the cold ground beside her. Mrs. Bonachek who was rich in sons.

I needed to know how many babies, how many girls, had died before this little one wrapped in the apron. Janos would tell me, Janos who had been so matter-of-fact about the routine business of death. I hadn't the courage at that moment to ask him.

Martha was working hard to maintain her composure. She had the baby dressed and gently laid her in the coffin. The baby was beautiful, her porcelain face framed in soft pink silk. I couldn't bear to see her in the box, like a shop-window doll.

I wanted to talk with Martha about the nagging suspicion that was taking shape in my mind. I hesitated too long.

Janos appeared at the door and I didn't want him to hear what I had to say. Actually, his face was so thin and expectant that it suddenly occurred to me that we hadn't brought any food for a proper wake.

"Janos," Martha whispered. "Tell your mother she may come in now."

Janos led his mother only as far as the threshold when she stopped stubbornly. I went to her, put my arm around her and impelled her to come closer to the coffin. When she resisted, I pushed. I was desperate to see some normal emotion from her. If she had none, what hope was there for Janos?

Finally, she shuddered and reached out a hand to touch the baby's cheek. She said something in her native language. I could understand neither the words nor the tone. It could have been a prayer, it could have been a curse.

When I let her go, she turned and looked at me. For the barest instant there was a flicker in her eyes that showed neither fear nor guilt about what I might have seen the afternoon before. I was disquieted because, for the length of that small glimmer, she was beautiful. I saw who she might have become at another time, in a different place. When the tears at last came to my eyes, they were for her and not for the baby.

Janos and Boya carried the coffin out to the bare front room and set it on the table. The preacher arrived and he gave his best two-dollar service even though there would be no payment. He spoke to the little group, the Bonacheks, Martha, the doctor and I, as if we were a full congregation. I don't remember what he said. I wasn't listening. I traced the pattern of the cheap, worn linoleum floor with my eyes and silently damned the poverty of the place and the cold that seeped in under the door.

We were a small, depressed-looking procession, walking down the muddy road to the county cemetery at the edge of town, singing along to hymns only the preacher seemed to know. At the gravesite, the preacher prayed for the sinless soul and consigned her to the earth. It didn't seem to bother him that his principal mourners didn't understand a word he said.

Somehow, the doctor dissuaded Martha from inviting all of the Bonacheks home for supper—she, too, had belatedly thought about food.

As we walked back from the cemetery, I managed to separate the doctor from the group. I told him what was on my mind, what I had seen in the fields the day before. She had left her bundled apron at the end of a furrow and gone back to her work. I could not keep that guilty knowledge to myself.

The doctor wasn't as shocked as I expected him to be. But he was a man of worldly experience and I was merely a dairyman's daughter—the oldest child, the only girl in a family of five boys.

As the afternoon progressed, the air grew colder, threatening more snow. To this day, whenever I am very cold, I think of that afternoon. Janos, of course, fills that memory.

I think the little ceremony by strangers was a sort of coming out for him. He was suddenly not only a man of the community, but of the world beyond the road that ran between his farm and the schoolhouse, out where mountains and oceans were a possibility. It had been a revelation.

Janos called out to me and I stopped to wait for him, watching him run. He seemed incredibly small, outlined against the flat horizon. He was golden, and oddly ebullient.

Pale sunlight glinted off his bright head as he struggled through the slush on the road. Mud flew off his big boots in thick gobs and I thought his skinny legs would break with the weight of it. He seemed not to notice—mud was simply a part of the season's change, a harbinger of warmer days.

When he caught up, Janos was panting and red in the face. He looked like a wise little old man for whom life held no secrets. As always, he held himself with a stiff dignity that I imagine suited him quite well when he was draped in his judge's robes.

Too breathless to speak, he placed in my hand a fresh blue crocus he had plucked from the slush.

"Very pretty," I said, moved by his gesture. I looked into his smiling face and found courage. "What was the prayer your mother said for the baby?"

He shrugged and struggled for breath. Then he reached out and touched the delicate flower that was already turning brown from the warmth of my hand.

"No prayer," he said. "It's what she says. 'Know peace. Your sisters in heaven wait to embrace you.' "

I put my hand on his shoulder and looked up at the heavy, gathering clouds. "If it's snowing tomorrow," I said, "which books shall I bring?"

Challenge the Widow-Maker

Clark Howard

THEY BURIED OLD Terangi in a small country cemetery several miles below the crater of Kaneakala volcano. It was a simple funeral. Most of Terangi's neighbors made the drive up-mountain from Lahaina Town to attend, and a few of his fellow merchants who had small stores near Terangi's surfboard shop on the waterfront also attended. Because there were no other family members, Terangi's widow, Marama, was escorted to the services by George Hill, her late husband's sole employee, who was like a son to them. George had been with Terangi when the massive heart attack struck. They had been sanding separate ends of a new competition board Terangi was making for one of the Maui surfers to use in the next big North Shore finals on Oahu.

When the services were over and the other mourners had left, Marama leaned her head against George's arm. "Life will seem very strange without him, Keoki," she said, using the Polynesian form of George.

"Yes, it will," George replied, just as quietly. "I hate to think what my life would have been like if it hadn't been for him. And you."

"You have been a great comfort to us, Keoki," she assured him. "You'll stay on and run the shop, won't you?"

"Yes." George shrugged. "I wouldn't know how to do anything else. All I've ever been was a soldier, a convict, and a surfboard maker."

"And a son," Marama reminded him, squeezing his arm. "You've been a son to two lonely people."

As they walked away from Terangi's grave, George noticed that not all the mourners had gone. A solitary figure stood well back at the edge of the cemetery, watching. Wearing a flowered Hawaiian shirt, his hands shoved into his pants pockets, he was a once-husky islander who had gone to fat. In one corner of his mouth was an ever-present toothpick. His name was Charley Kula. He was George Hill's parole officer from Oahu.

George drove Marama back down-mountain in Terangi's old Plymouth, which he supposed would now become his because Marama had never learned to drive. George had a lot on his mind at the moment. He was wondering how life was going to be without Terangi's wise counseling. He was wondering whether he could run the surfboard shop by himself. And he was wondering what was on Charley Kula's mind. In the rearview mirror he could see Kula following them down-mountain in the white state-owned pool car he used when he was on Maui. Kula was, in George's opinion, exactly what old Terangi had called him in private for years: a *haahaa na mea kino me ka hanu ola*. Literally translated, it meant a low creature, unworthy of a name.

George had been under Charley Kula's thumb for five years, living with the constant threat of being returned to Oahu Prison on the whim of an unfavorable monthly report. For five years George had loaned Kula money—twenty dollars here, twenty dollars there—money that was never paid back; or given him free surfboards for his supervisor's kids; or fixed him up with one of the *wahines* from the Cloud Nine Massage Parlor, at George's expense; or bought his dinner, his lunch, his breakfast, his haircuts, his shoeshines. When Kula came over from Oahu once a month, George always paid for one thing or another.

"Never mind," Terangi had always counseled him, "keep your

hu'ihu'i [your cool]. Don't let a robber like him upset you. Be happy. Take one of the boards and go surf for an hour."

For five years George had worked off his anger out on the waves. For five years he had kept his *hu'ihu'i.* But he had not been happy about it.

When George and Marama got back to Lahaina Town, to the little frame house on Lani Street where Terangi and Marama had lived for forty years, the ladies of the neighborhood were there with dishes of food and doses of comfort, so George only stayed a little while before telling Marama he was going to the shop for a couple of hours.

Then he left to go see what Charley Kula wanted.

Kula was in the bar of the old Missionary Inn, sipping a gin-and-tonic around his toothpick, shooting the breeze with the bartender. When George came in, he moved to a back table, taking his drink with him.

"Aloha, Georgie," he said with a smile. George sat down and a bored cocktail waitress in a sarong came over to take his order.

"Just a Coke," George said.

"I'll have another gin-and-tonic," Kula added. Then to George, he said, "Listen, have something stronger if you want it. I know how much you liked the old man."

George shook his head. "Just a Coke," he repeated. He remembered Terangi's words from the very first day of his parole: *Never let him get anything on you. Never break the rules, even if he tells you it's okay.* Parolees weren't allowed to drink alcoholic beverages.

"I guess the old lady wants you to stay on and run the shop, huh?" Kula asked when the waitress left.

"Yes."

"There's no other family, is there? They all died in that car wreck, didn't they?"

"Yes. I mean no, there's no other family."

"Well, that leaves you pretty well fixed, I guess. I mean, the shop will be all yours someday, won't it?"

"I suppose."

"Lucky day for you when old Terangi helped you make parole and gave you a job in his shop."

"Yes. Lucky day."

The waitress brought their drinks and George paid for them. Kula sat back and patted his ample belly with both hands. "You know, what happened to old Terangi makes a man realize just how short life is. A man's a fool if he don't make the most of the time he's got left. Take me, for instance. Next month's my birthday. I'll be fifty-five. That makes me eligible for early retirement. Know what I'd like to do? Buy a little corn farm in Kansas."

George looked at him incredulously and Kula chuckled. "Yeah, I know that's funny. Probably half the people in Kansas would like to come here to retire, and I want to go back there." He leaned forward on his elbows. "But I'm sick of the islands. I'd like to get up in the mornings and know I can hop in my car and drive more than thirty miles without running into the ocean. I want to live someplace where they have seasons, not the same boring perfect weather all the time."

"But why a corn farm?" George asked.

"I like to grow things," Kula said, taking the toothpick out of his mouth for the first time. "I've got a little garden at home right now. Tomatoes, radishes, carrots. But you need a field for corn—all I've got is the patio of my bachelor apartment. I get this realty catalogue every month. It's got a section on rural properties, with photographs, in color. I'll tell you something: a field of growing corn is a real pretty sight." Kula sat back again, taking a sip of his drink. "Only thing is, it takes a hefty down payment to buy a decent-sized farm in Kansas."

George sat back, too, and drank some of his Coke. "What's on your mind, Mr. Kula?"

The parole officer smiled. "Know what I like about you, Georgie? You cooperate. You always cooperate." The smile faded and the voice lowered. "I've got a parolee over on Oahu named Nicky Dade. Did five for burglary. Young guy, mid-twenties, real hip—he's a surfer, like you. The kid's old man was a locksmith. Nicky can pick damn near any lock there is."

George nodded. "So?"

"So there's a wholesale-costume-jewelry merchant on Oahu that gets a shipment of pearls from Hong Kong the first of every month. They're supposed to be fake, but they're not, they're *real*—the kind divers bring up from the ocean. Nobody knows they're real, of course—everybody assumes they're fake because the business is set up as a costume-jewelry company. It's a perfect cover. The guy doesn't have to pay a big insurance premium, doesn't have to have fancy security at his offices. I mean, who's going to steal a few hundred bucks' worth of fake pearls, right?" Kula sat forward again and his voice became even lower. "This guy brings in between a half and three-quarters of a million dollars' worth every month and nobody's the wiser. I only found out about it by accident, from this guy I know who works for the air-courier service that brings the stuff from Hong Kong."

"What's the point?" George asked.

"The point is that my boy Nicky can pick the locks to this guy's offices *and* his safe."

"Sounds like your boy Nicky's heading for trouble."

"Not at all," Kula said emphatically. "It's a walk-in, walk-out job, sixty minutes from start to finish. It's all set to go on the first of the month. All I have to do is find my boy Nicky a partner. A helper. Nothing heavy—a bag holder, lookout man, that sort of thing. Very easy work."

"Why don't you do it yourself if it's so easy?" George asked flatly.

"Me?" Kula said. There seemed to be genuine surprise in his expression. "Hell, Georgie, I couldn't do a thing like that. I'm no thief."

"Neither am I," George reminded him. "I did time for manslaughter, remember?"

Kula's eyes narrowed a fraction. "Like I said, Georgie, I like you because I figure you always cooperate. But maybe I'm wrong. Maybe I've been wrong writing good parole reports on you all these years."

Sighing quietly, George looked away for a moment. There was hurt in his eyes, and helplessness. Presently he looked back and said, "No, Mr. Kula, you aren't wrong. What do you want me to do?"

Charley Kula smiled.

Two days later, the girl came into his shop. She had what islanders called "mixed-up blood," and it was obvious from her appearance: the brown hair of the Portuguese, the blue eyes of the *keokeos* (whites), the flat lips of the Tahitians, the wide nostrils of the Filipinos, and the long body of the Spaniards. She was almost pretty.

"Hi. You Georgie?" she asked.

"I'm George," he replied.

"I'm Mileka. Nicky's friend. He wants to see you."

"I'm right here," George said. He went on waxing the competition board he was working on.

"Not here," Mileka said. "Nicky doesn't talk business in rooms, only on beaches. He got sent to prison because of a microphone in a motel room." She jerked her head toward the ocean. "He's out surfing."

George thought about it for a moment, then put the board aside and reached under the counter for a printed sign that read: BACK IN TEN MINUTES. Terangi had used a felt-tip marker to cross out IN TEN MINUTES and in its place had hand-lettered SOON.

"Let's go," George said, putting the sign in the door.

He and the girl walked down Front Street a couple of blocks, then cut over to where the beach began. Neither of them tried to make conversation. George was pushing thirty-six and the girl couldn't have been more than twenty, so each assumed they had nothing to say to the other. When they reached the sand, both took off their sandals and left them on the curb with a dozen other pairs. Then they walked along the beach, up away from the water, until they came to a couple of towels with a beach bag on them.

"Nicky's out there." The girl pointed to a figure lying flat on a surfboard on the water fifty yards out, waiting for a swell. As George looked seaward, Mileka dropped her shorts onto one of the towels and pulled her polo shirt over her head. When George looked back, she was stretched out on the towel in a yellow French-cut bikini that made her tanned body look like warm caramel. Sun bunny, George thought derisively.

He waited for five minutes until the figure on the board caught a soft wave and stood up to surf back onto the beach. As the surfer walked toward him, George saw that he was a typical young white islander: blond, golden-tanned, supple, muscular, handsome, confident. Like I used to be, George thought before he could help himself.

"Hi, I'm Nicky Dade," the young man said, not offering to shake hands.

"George Hill," said George.

"I thought we ought to meet once before the job," Nicky said easily. "I guess Kula told you it's a real piece of cake. All you'll really have to do is what I tell you to. I thought we ought to have a look at each other, but Kula says you're okay so that's good enough for me."

"He told me you were okay, too," George countered. He didn't like being talked to as if he were a flunky.

"Of course I'm okay," Nicky retorted, annoyed. "It's my job, man. I'm the one that's doing it. Of course I'm okay."

"Of course."

Nicky stuck his surfboard upright in the sand. It was, George observed, one of the most expensive factory-made boards.

"Kula tells me you surf," Nicky said, seeming to get over his pique as quickly as it came.

"Yes."

"A little old for it, aren't you?"

"I do it anyway," George told him. He noticed that Mileka was leaning up on her elbows, looking curiously at him.

"Maybe we can go out together sometime," Nicky suggested, bobbing his head at the water. "Early in the morning, before you open your shop."

"I don't surf in the harbor," George said. He didn't even try to keep the disdain out of his voice.

"That right?" Nicky said, with a trace of amusement. "Where do you surf?"

"Kaanapali," said George.

Nicky frowned slightly. "*You* surf Kaanapali?"

"I surf Kaanapali."

"At your age?"

"At my age." George could feel himself blush. He wished the girl wasn't there. Or at least that she wasn't looking at him. He forced himself to smile. "The waves aren't big at Kaanapali, but they're tricky. Harbor surfing's too tame for me. Look, I've got to get back to my shop. You can find me there whenever you want me."

He knew their eyes followed him all the way off the beach.

At noon the next day, Marama, as usual, brought George his lunch, as she had always done for Terangi and him. "Couple of nice *opakapaka* sandwiches today," she said. George went into the bathroom at the back of the shop and washed his hands. When he came back out, Marama had his lunch set out on the desk behind the counter. As he started to eat, Mileka came in. Marama got up to leave. "I've got marketing to do, Keoki. Don't be late for supper."

After Marama left, Mileka raised her eyebrows inquiringly. "Keoki?"

"Polynesian for George," he said. "You've got Poly blood—don't you know the dialect?"

"If I spoke the language of every kind of blood *I've* got in me, man, I'd be—what do you call it?—multi-lingual. I'm not real big on being a native girl. What's that you're eating?"

"*Opakapaka*. Pink snapper. Want some?"

"No, thanks. I'm strictly a hamburger-and-fries person.

Listen, the reason I'm here is that Nicky wants to surf Kaanapali with you. He wants to know if tomorrow morning's okay."

"I'm too busy," George said. "I'm all alone in the shop now and I'm getting behind in the work." He saw that she had pursed her lips and was nodding knowingly.

"Nicky said you were probably all talk. I'll tell him you can't make it."

As she started to leave, George said, "Wait a minute. Tell him I'll be at Black Rock at daybreak."

"I'll tell him," she said, a little smugly. Walking out, she looked back over her shoulder. " 'Bye, *Keoki.*"

At sunrise, George was sitting on the beach at the foot of Black Rock, a dark outcropping of lava rock that stood eighty feet high and jutted into the sea like a driven fist, dividing the long, beautiful beach into two lengths. Legend had it that Pele, the ancient fire goddess, had built the rock as a throne for herself. Terangi and Marama believed the story, so George believed it, too. As he sat on the sand, a thick beach towel around his shoulders for warmth, his surfboard resting familiarly between his legs, he wasn't afraid of the shadows of the rock that seemed to shift and adjust as if they had life, or of the eerie noises the wind made as it dervished its way through the throne's crags and crevices.

The sun rose at the edge of Lanai, ten miles away on the horizon, and in an instant sent warm yellow light across the dark water, changing its surface from black to an azure blue that perfectly matched the lightening sky above it. George heard a whistle and turned to see Nicky Dade and Mileka walking down the beach toward him. He rose and was pulling his sweatshirt off over his head as they came up.

"Hello, Keoki," Mileka said pertly. George ignored her.

"These waves look kind of soft to me," Nicky said.

"Like I told you, they're not big but they're tricky." George looked at him. "You a wave counter?"

"What do you mean?"

"On this side of the island, every ninth wave is a good one. So we wait here on the beach for a good one to break, then we start out, counting the incoming waves as we go. When the ninth one is about to come in, we get up and go with it. Clear?"

"Yeah, sure," Nicky said. "Where'd you learn all that?"

"Here and there."

As they waited, Nicky studied George's board. It was a handmade, tapered, hollow board ten feet long and eighteen inches wide, with a skeg, or stabilizing fin, near its back. Etched in a curve across the upper front were the words CHALLENGE THE WIDOW-MAKER.

"What's that mean?" Mileka asked, seeing the inscription.

"The widow-maker is what the old merchant seamen used to call the ocean. The man who helped me make this board said every time a person goes out to ride the water on a piece of wood, that person is challenging the widow-maker. He wanted me to remember that, so he put it on the board." At that moment a good wave broke in the surf and George turned to Nicky. "Ready?"

"Ready, man."

"Let's go."

They walked into the water until they were chest-deep, then belly-flopped onto their boards and began paddling seaward. A low wave rolled in and they pushed easily through it. "That's number one!" George shouted. They kept paddling. Twenty yards, thirty. Another wave rolled in: "Number two!" Fifty yards, sixty. A third wave, perceptibly higher. "Three!"

They paddled in as straight a line as the sea would allow, their bodies flat on the narrow boards, their hands moving rapidly, their faces raised to the mass of water confronting them. In that juxtaposition, their relationship to the ocean was perilous and unpredictable, but at the same time almost carnal. Behind them, the safety of land grew farther and farther away. Ahead of them, the waves grew higher and began rolling and twisting as, far beneath the surface, the water encountered deep reefs and sandbars.

"Number six!"

One hundred eighty yards, one ninety.

Arm, shoulder, and neck muscles began to burn as if raw rope had been pulled across them.

"Seven!"

Two hundred ten yards. Two twenty.

The throat and groin began to react now, tightening, tensing, tickling oddly.

"Eight—!"

Two hundred and fifty yards away from the land, a six-foot wall of water rolled toward them.

"Number nine coming up!" George shouted. He leaped upright and with his feet turned the board so that it was diagonally facing the beach in the path of the wave. In his peripheral vision, he saw Nicky do the same thing. Then both of them were being lifted and carried like feathers on the wind as the swell of ocean rolled, shifted to the right, and rolled some more, taking them back where they belonged. Knees bent, bodies arched, arms akimbo, hearts pounding, faces glowing with the thrill of it, they rode the ocean. It was exhilarating.

When their boards hit sand, they leaped off and grabbed them up, then stood panting and smiling. They had come as close as any mortal ever comes to walking on water.

"Man, I see what you mean about tricky!" Nicky exclaimed as they walked back to where Mileka waited. "But I did all right, didn't I!" It was a boast more than a question.

"You did okay," George allowed. "Good thing the wave wasn't any higher."

"What do you mean?"

"I'm not sure you could have handled a higher swell."

"Oh, yeah? Could you have?"

"Sure, I handle them all the time," George replied confidently. He noticed that Mileka was taking in every word.

"Oh, yeah? Where at?" Nicky demanded.

"Kahana," George said. "The other side of Black Rock."

"Okay, let's surf there tomorrow," Nicky said.

"Look, I've got a business to run."

"You chicken?" Nicky taunted. "Afraid I'll show you up?"

George didn't have to look at Mileka to know she was again appraising him. What the hell do you care? he asked himself. She's just another sun bunny—Lahaina Town was crawling with them. Nevertheless, he said, "Okay. Kahana tomorrow at sunrise."

As George walked away, he heard Nicky ask, "Did I look better than him out there?"

And he heard Mileka reply, "You both looked about the same to me."

George couldn't help smiling.

That night George met Nicky and Charley Kula at a small cafe in Wailea. Mileka was with Nicky, but he sent her to play the pinball machines while the men talked.

"You two getting acquainted?" Kula asked, shifting a toothpick from one side of his mouth to the other.

"Yeah, we're surfing buddies now," Nicky said. Something in his tone told George that Nicky didn't like the fat parole officer any more than he did.

"What do you think of my boy Nicky?" Kula asked George.

"Great guy," George replied blandly.

"I knew you two'd get on." Kula leaned forward. "Speaking of business, I checked on the pearl shipment. It'll be in right on schedule Friday afternoon." He looked at Nicky. "You ready to go to work Friday night?"

"I'm ready," Nicky assured him.

"Good. Now, remember, you have to be in and out of the building before eleven o'clock—that's when the night watchman comes on duty. I'll be at my house all evening, so I'll be able to provide an alibi for either of you on the outside chance you need one—I'll say you were with me all evening, helping me in my garden. After the job, you bring the pearls directly to me, Nicky. I'll hang onto them until it's safe to approach a fence to buy the stuff."

"How long before we get any bread out of this?" Nicky wanted to know.

"You'll get your cut as soon as I make the sale. A month, probably. Georgie, I'll take care of you out of my share."

I can hardly wait, George thought. Just then a waiter brought their dinner and Nicky waved to Mileka to come join them. "I ordered you a steak and fries," he told her when she came over.

"Okay." She glanced at the plate that was set in front of George. Everyone had steak and fries except him. "What's that?" she asked.

"*Ahi,*" he said. When she frowned, he translated, "Yellowfin. It's a tuna."

"You ought to try steak sometime, Keoki," she said.

"Keoki?" Nicky asked, raising his eyebrows.

"That's his Polynesian name."

"Cute," Nicky said drily.

George felt himself turn red again. Silently he called Mileka a little bitch.

The next morning, George was waiting on Kahana beach when Nicky and Mileka got there.

"Hello, Keoki," Mileka teased at once.

"Hello, Mildred," he replied.

Nicky's mouth dropped open. "Mildred?"

"That's what Mileka means in English," George told him. He looked innocently at Mileka, who was glaring at him. "I asked my foster mother last night."

Nicky looked at her incredulously. "I don't believe it. Mildred?" After a moment, he laughed. "That's funny. Mildred!"

"Oh, shut up!" she snapped. "I thought you came here to surf."

Nicky was still laughing as he and George walked down to the water's edge. George looked over his shoulder at Mileka and smiled. She made an obscene gesture at him.

After a good wave broke, George and Nicky put their boards

in the water and began paddling out, counting waves as they went. "Remember," George reminded him, "these aren't as tricky as the ones at Kaanapali, they don't twist as much, but they're higher. You'll need a tighter crouch to keep your balance."

"I know how to surf, man," Nicky said.

Okay, big shot, let's see, George thought. He began to paddle a little faster, to get farther out before the ninth wave swelled. Nicky increased his own paddling to keep up. By the time eight waves had rolled under them, they were nearly three hundred yards from shore. When number nine began to rise up in front of them, George yelled, "Looks like a ten-footer!"

Both of them stood and planted their feet firmly against the boards. Their arms extended like gulls spreading their wings. With the lift of the water, they turned, and as they felt themselves being lifted lightly with the swell they had a brief glimpse of Mileka, far away on the beach, standing with her hands on her hips, looking out at them.

Then they made the oblique shift to ride diagonally and she passed from their line of sight as they faced Kahana far to the right of where she stood. It *was* a ten-footer and it lifted them high and sped them along on its sheet of water as if it were frozen and they were city kids sliding on an icy sidewalk.

They rode in until the big wave broke, then maneuvered their boards into calmer water and coasted until it was shallow enough to jump off.

"Great! That was great!" Nicky exclaimed as they waded in. "Man, it can't get any better than that!"

"Sure it can," George said.

"Huh? What do you mean?"

"At Kapalua," George told him. "Farther up the coast. There the waves are high *and* tricky."

"Let's go there, then," Nicky said at once. "Tomorrow."

George shrugged. "Why not?"

Mileka didn't say goodbye to George when she and Nicky left, but as they were walking away George heard Nicky ask, "How did I look out there?"

"You looked good," Mileka said. Then, after a moment she added, "But he looked better . . ."

Early that afternoon, Mileka came into the surfboard shop. Marama had already been there and George was eating his lunch.

"Fish again?" she asked. "What is it this time?"

"*Ono,*" he said. "The fishermen call it 'wahoo.' It's a grey game fish."

"Do you eat fish all the time?"

"Yes. My foster father said if a man ate fish every day he'd become a better swimmer and surfer because he'd feel more at home in the ocean."

"Come on, you don't really believe that, do you?"

"Yes, I do." Her tone irritated him. "What are you doing here, anyway? Another message from Nicky?"

"No. Nicky's taking a nap." Now it was she who blushed slightly. "Look, I came to say I'm sorry. About the name business, teasing you like I was doing. I didn't realize how you felt until you did the same thing to me. Then I realized how dumb it was. Sometimes I can be really stupid."

George grunted softly. "Can't we all."

"Anyway, I'm sorry."

"Forget it," he said. He pushed his plate toward her. "Want half a wahoo sandwich?" She hesitated. "Go on, try it, you might like it."

"Okay." Mileka sat and joined him for lunch. Presently she asked, "So how'd you get Poly foster parents? Did they adopt you?"

"Kind of." George turned to gaze out the window, across Front Street at the harbor.

"Maybe I shouldn't have asked," she said when he didn't elaborate.

George shrugged. "It's no secret, really. Thirteen years ago I was in the Army, stationed at Fort Shafter over on Oahu. I loved the Army—I was going to be a thirty-year man. To me it was the perfect life: soldier all week, drink beer, surf, and get laid every weekend. Except that one weekend it didn't quite work out that way. Four of us were coming back from surfing the north shore and we'd had a little too much to drink. We were cruising along the Nimitz Highway in a convertible one of the guys owned, when he lost control of the car, crossed the center line, and crashed head-on into an oncoming car.

"A Hawaiian couple and their two children were killed. My three buddies were killed, too. Seven dead—and I survived. I guess they wanted to make an example out of me as a warning to other servicemen stationed on the island, so they indicted me for manslaughter. I hadn't been driving—but I couldn't prove it. The prosecution couldn't prove that I *had*, but there was enough doubt for the jury to convict me. I got fifteen years. I did eight and then Terangi and Marama helped me get out. They offered to provide me with a job and a place to live, and talked to the parole board. The parole board was very impressed by their interest—because the woman killed in the other car had been their daughter. I guess the board figured that if Terangi and Marama could forgive me, so could they. So five years ago I got out and came here to Maui. Terangi and Marama treated me like a son from the first day."

"They sound like wonderful people," Mileka said quietly.

"The best," George said.

Mileka studied him for a moment, then asked, "You don't like being in on this job Nicky's doing, do you?"

He shook his head. "I'm in it because of Kula. I don't want to go back to prison."

"Neither does Nicky." She took one of his hands and held it for a moment. "It'll be okay, Keoki," she said, and this time she spoke his Polynesian name naturally, without teasing. "Things will work out all right."

Yes, they would, George thought, nodding slightly.

Because he would *make* them work out all right.

Off Kapalua beach the next morning, George and Nicky paddled out a hundred yards, let a six-foot wave roll under them, and *then* began to count waves as they pushed farther out to sea.

By the time they had counted eight waves, they were four hundred yards from the beach and facing a twelve-foot swell that was twisting forty degrees to their right. Getting upright on their boards, they turned almost fully around instead of diagonally, braced, crouched, sucked in air, and stopped breathing as the water lifted them like so much driftwood and seemed to hold them aloft for a split instant before rolling under them and rushing them back toward the beach. As their journey began, they breathed again, moving as if in flight, seemingly weightless, soaring along smoothly in defiance of magnetic gravity, marine physics, and mortal fear. For as long as they rode the crest of the wave, they were greater than other men.

When it was over, they waded back onto the beach and dropped to the sand, their chests heaving as the tension of the ride slowly gave way to the calm and safety of land.

"Man," said Nicky, "I never got a charge out of surfing like I get when I surf with you. There's something about the way you know the ocean—it's almost spooky." He propped up on one elbow and glanced at Mileka, who lay sunning farther up the beach. "Look, tonight's the job. When it's over, I figured we'd go our separate ways. But I been thinking. After the payoff, why don't we take a trip together? A surfing trip. We could head down to Peru for the season there, then move on to eastern Australia—hell, we could just follow the waves wherever they were breaking."

George sat up and hugged his knees. "What about her?" he asked, bobbing his chin at Mileka.

"I'll dump her," Nicky said without hesitation. "She's just a sun bunny—there'll be plenty like her wherever we go. Look, my share of tonight's job, and whatever Kula gives you for helping me, ought to last us a year, maybe a year and a half. And when it's gone, we'll find a way to get more. It's the chance of a lifetime, Georgie. What do you say, man?"

George seemed to ponder the proposition for a long moment, but presently he nodded and smiled at Nicky Dade. "Count me in."

"Far out!" Nicky all but cheered. Glancing toward Mileka again, he quickly lowered his voice. "Our little secret, right?"

George winked at him. "Right."

That evening, George flew to Oahu on the six o'clock Aloha flight. Nicky, who had gone over at noon, met him outside the airport in a rental car. When Nicky saw the look on George's face, he asked at once, "What's wrong, man?"

"We've got a problem," George said tensely. He handed Nicky the pink carbon of an airline ticket-confirmation from a Maui travel agency. It was a one-way ticket on the next morning's Continental flight to San Francisco in the name of Charles Kula. Looking at it, Nicky frowned.

"I don't understand."

"A friend of mine works in the travel agency," George said. "He knows Kula's my parole officer. This afternoon he mentioned to me that Kula was flying to the mainland tomorrow. I had my friend get me a copy of the ticket-confirmation, just to be sure." Nicky was now staring incredulously at George. "He's crossing us, man," George concluded simply. "It's a one-way ticket. He's taking the pearls and skipping."

Nicky's eyes scanned the confirmation again. "The dirty bastard," he whispered.

"We'll have to call off the job," George said.

"No!" Nicky snapped. "We're not calling off nothing! I'm not giving up my surfing trip because of this bastard. Besides, this job is too cushy to call off. We'll just do to him what he was going to do to us: take the pearls and skip."

"No good," George vetoed. "He'd find a way to finger us without involving himself. He's the law, remember, and we're ex-cons. We'd better call it off."

"No! We're going to pull this job, man, just like we planned!" Nicky was staring out the windshield as if transfixed. "After we pull it, I'll figure out how to handle Mr. Charles Kula."

* * *

Nicky pulled away from the airport and drove into Honolulu. He parked on a side street off busy Kalakaua Avenue, where the costume-jewelry firm's office building was located. He and George walked around the area for an hour as Nicky briefed him. "Kalakaua's a big tourist street now: lots of shops, places to eat, lots of bars. There's usually people on the street until midnight or later. That's our building over there—"

George looked at a rather ordinary five-story structure that rose above a large drugstore. On one side of the drugstore was the entrance to an underground garage. Stretching beyond it was a string of souvenir shops: T-shirts, seashells, monkey-pod carvings, muu-muus. Shoppers were everywhere.

Just before nine o'clock, Nicky said, "Okay, let's go."

They returned to the car and Nicky drove directly to the building and into the underground garage. It was only about one-third full, most of the building's employees having left for the day. Nicky parked as close as he could to a door marked: ELECTRICAL ROOM–AUTHORIZED PERSONNEL ONLY. Opening the trunk of the car, he said, "Stay here. Bend over the trunk like you're looking for something. If anybody comes, drop the tire iron on the floor."

He walked away, pulling on a pair of gloves. George saw him take something from his pocket and briefly do something with the lock of the electrical-room door. The door opened almost at once and Nicky disappeared inside. Waiting at the trunk, George began to sweat.

In less than five minutes, Nicky was back. "Okay, the alarm's crossed," he said. He took a briefcase from the trunk. "Come on."

They rode the elevator from the garage up to three. No one got on with them and they encountered no one in the hall. "I can't believe there's a fortune in pearls just lying around this place," George said in a tense whisper.

"I told you, it's a cushy job," Nicky whispered back. "Now you see why I wouldn't call it off?" They reached a door with lettering on a frosted-glass pane that read PACIFIC-ORIENT COSTUME JEWELRY CO., LTD. "Watch the elevator indicator," Nicky instructed. "If the light comes on, nudge me and we'll both walk away from the door. Same thing if anyone comes out of another office." He immediately went to work on the door's lock.

The elevator light did not come on, and within a minute Nicky had the door open and was pulling George inside. Nicky had him wait just inside the door to listen for any sound from the hallway. He himself disappeared into one of the inner offices. George began to sweat again. At one point while he was standing there, he heard the sound of footsteps going by in the hall, and for a fleeting moment he thought he was going to be sick. He could challenge the widow-maker atop a rolling wave twice his height, but standing in a dark office at night was something else entirely.

Nicky seemed to take forever in the other room. Several times George heard vague metallic sounds and soft, muted tapping, but aside from that there was only silence. In the light from a nearby outside window, George could see a water cooler. It was sorely tempting as he felt his mouth go drier and drier, but he didn't want to leave his place at the door—somehow being next to the door seemed safer.

After what seemed like half the night, Nicky was suddenly back at his side. "Check the hall."

George opened the door a crack, using a handkerchief around the doorknob. The hall was clear. They left quickly, walking briskly back down to the elevator. Waiting there, Nicky grinned and shook the briefcase once. It sounded as if it was full of dried peas.

Back in the car, Nicky handed the briefcase to George. "I'm gonna drop you at a taxi stand. Go back out to the airport and wait for me around the Aloha ticket counter."

"Where are you going?"

"To see Kula." Nicky smiled coldly. "I want to be the one to tell him that his trip to San Francisco tomorrow has been canceled."

"You sure you know what you're doing?" George asked.

"I know exactly what I'm doing, man."

At the Royal Hawaiian taxi queue, Nicky pulled over and left the engine running. For just an instant, he seemed to hesitate. George knew at once what he was thinking.

"Don't worry," he said easily. "I'll be at the airport when you get there." He patted the briefcase. "And so will this."

Nicky nodded and drove off.

George had to wait in the airport four hours. Then he and Nicky had to wait another two hours for the first early-morning commuter flight back to Maui. The sun was just breaking on the ocean horizon as the twin-engine Otter set down on the airstrip at Kahului.

Both men had been silent during the flight. The night's events lay heavily between them. When Nicky had arrived back at the Honolulu airport, George had immediately asked, "What happened?"

"It's all settled with Kula," Nicky had replied tightly.

"What happened?" George asked again. Nicky glanced around. They were sitting alone in a corner of the passenger terminal.

"I bashed his double-crossing head in with a tire iron," Nicky told him coldly. "Then I put him in the trunk and drove out to Kaneana. You know where that is?"

George nodded. "It's out the Farrington Highway. Out where the underwater caves are."

"Right. I dumped him off the cliff right above the caves."

George swallowed. "Sharks feed in those caves."

"All the time," Nicky had confirmed in a whisper.

Now they were walking out of the Kahului airport toward the parking lot where George had left the old Plymouth that used to belong to Terangi. Nicky, carrying the briefcase, put it on his lap when he got in the car. As George started the engine, he said almost to himself, "Man, I've got an edge on. I need to unwind. After I drop you, I'm hitting the waves."

"I'll go with you," Nicky said. "We'll just stop by and pick up my board."

George shook his head. "Not today, I need a real challenge. I'm going out to Mokolea Point."

"Where's that?"

"It's out past where the highway ends. Out past Lipoa, where the lighthouse is."

"What's out there?"

"Pipelines," George said. "You ever surf a pipeline?"

Nicky shook his head. Pipelines were the twelve-to-eighteen-foot waves that rolled all the way over to form a moving channel of water through which a person could surf—if they were good enough. Fearless enough. Crazy enough.

"I'm going with you," Nicky said.

"You're not good enough to do a pipeline." George kept his tone clinical.

"Up yours," Nicky said. "I'm as good as you are. I'm going."

"Suit yourself," George told him.

They stopped at a little motel in Kahaina Town where Nicky and Mileka had been living. Nicky slipped in and got his board without waking her. Then George headed out Honoapiilani Highway and followed it past all the beaches they had surfed together—Kaanapali, Kahana, Kapalua—then on past Lipoa, where the lighthouse stood, and on around to where the paved highway ended and a dirt road began.

The road curved and wound around the natural lay of the craggy rock on which it rested, twisting and turning as if teasing the great ocean with its presence. George drove slowly, guiding the car carefully in tracks left by other vehicles. As on the plane, the two men did not talk. But George noticed that Nicky drummed his fingertips soundlessly on the briefcase that he again held on his lap.

Finally they arrived at a high point above the beach with a precarious path leading down to it. Beyond the beach, the ocean seemed angry. Great churning waves roiled up and rushed the shore as if in attack, not merely to erode but to shatter, to break apart this speck of rock that usurped its vastness.

Nicky put the briefcase of pearls under a blanket in the back seat and George locked the car, hiding the keys under a rock. Then the two men changed into their swim trunks and stood with their boards, looking out from the point.

"This is a *uhane lele*," George said quietly. "It's a sacred place where the souls of the dead leap into their ancestral spirit land."

"You don't really believe that bullshit, do you?" Nicky asked derisively.

"Yes, I do," George replied, staring at the sea.

Shaking his head disdainfully, Nicky started down the steep path. Then he turned back, eyes suspicious, and said, "You first." Containing a knowing smile, George led the way down to the beach.

There they waited for the next pipeline to break, then plunged in and started paddling. Even though the sea was turbulent, moving against the tide wasn't difficult—the slender boards pierced the oncoming water with almost no resistance, needling through the waves or dipping over them as if without purpose, yet steadily leaving the land behind. They stayed close together, counting the waves. When the ninth one broke before them, Nicky yelled, "It's not the pipeline!"

"The *ninth* ninth wave is the pipeline!" George yelled back. "We've got a long way to go!" Nicky was looking at him in astonishment. "Want to turn back?" George challenged.

"Not me, man! I'm in all the way!"

They kept paddling. And counting. The second ninth wave broke. The third ninth wave. Periodically they rested, letting several waves go past without paddling through or over them, moving their hands only enough to keep from losing distance, then they began thrusting again. They passed the fourth ninth wave, the fifth, the sixth, and rested some more.

Their upper arms burned, hot with fatigue. Their breath came in bursts.

"How far—out are we?" Nicky asked.

"About—eight hundred yards."

"God!"

"It'll be—a great ride!" George bolstered. "Probably—half a mile!"

The seventh ninth wave broke.

The eighth.

Then it came. The pipeline, rolling up in front of them as if the ocean had been tilted on edge. A sixteen-foot wave that looped back to embrace itself and form a tunnel of spiraling water that skimmed toward landfall with unbridled power.

"Waaaa-hoooo!" George yelled as he rose upright on his board. He caught only a brief glimpse of Nicky, just long enough to see the terror in his face, then the pipeline was upon him and he was in the vortex of it. An embryo in the womb of mother ocean.

George rode the great whirlpool all the way back to the beach. And he was right: it *was* a half-mile ride.

He sat on the bluff with a blanket around his shoulders for an hour, but Nicky never came out of the water. Score one more for the widow-maker, he thought.

He got the briefcase out of the car and opened it. The pearls lay spread inside like white caviar from some giant fish. They came from the ocean, they might as well go back to the ocean, he thought. Scooping up a handful, he flung them from the high bluff out into the water. Then he flung a second handful, a third. At some point, he began to laugh at what he was doing. It was a loud, uncontrollable laugh, growing in volume with each new handful of pearls he threw back to the ocean. He kept throwing and laughing, throwing and laughing. Finally, the pearls were all gone and he put a couple of rocks in the briefcase and threw that off the edge, too, watching it sink into the water.

From the glove compartment, he took the airline ticket he had bought in Charley Kula's name, and tore it into tiny pieces, releasing the bits to the sea breeze. Then he got into Terangi's old Plymouth and drove back toward Lahaina Town to open his shop.

The Last Spin

Evan Hunter

THE BOY SITTING opposite him was his enemy.

The boy sitting opposite him was called Tigo, and he wore a green silk jacket with an orange stripe on each sleeve. The jacket told Dave that Tigo was his enemy. The jacket shrieked "Enemy, enemy!"

"This is a good piece," Tigo said, indicating the gun on the table. "This runs you close to forty-five bucks, you try to buy it in a store."

The gun on the table was a Smith & Wesson .38 Police Special.

It rested exactly in the center of the table, its sawed-off, two-inch barrel abruptly terminating the otherwise lethal grace of the weapon. There was a checked walnut stock on the gun, and the gun was finished in a flat blue. Alongside the gun were three .38 Special cartridges.

Dave looked at the gun disinterestedly. He was nervous and apprehensive, but he kept tight control of his face. He could not show Tigo what he was feeling. Tigo was the enemy, and so he presented a mask to the enemy, cocking one eyebrow and saying, "I seen pieces before. There's nothing special about this one."

"Except what we got to do with it," Tigo said. Tigo was studying him with large brown eyes. The eyes were moist-looking. He was not a bad-looking kid, Tigo, with thick black hair and maybe a nose that was too long, but his mouth and chin were good. You could usually tell a cat by his mouth and his chin. Tigo would not turkey out of this particular rumble. Of that, Dave was sure.

"Why don't we start?" Dave asked. He wet his lips and looked across at Tigo.

"You understand," Tigo said. "I got no bad blood for you."

"I understand."

"This is what the club said. This is how the club said we should settle it. Without a big street diddlebop, you dig? But I want you to know I don't know you from a hole in the wall—except you wear a blue and gold jacket."

"And you wear a green and orange one," Dave said, "and that's enough for me."

"Sure, but what I was trying to say . . ."

"We going to sit and talk all night, or we going to get this thing rolling?" Dave asked.

"What I'm trying to say," Tigo went on, "is that I just happened to be picked for this, you know? Like to settle this thing that's between the two clubs. I mean, you got to admit your boys shouldn't have come in our territory last night."

"I got to admit nothing," Dave said flatly.

"Well, anyway, they shot at the candy store. That wasn't right. There's supposed to be a truce on."

"Okay, okay," Dave said.

"So like—like this is the way we agreed to settle it. I mean, one of us and—and one of you. Fair and square. Without any street boppin', and without any Law trouble."

"Let's get on with it," Dave said.

"I'm trying to say, I never even see you on the street before this. So this ain't nothin' personal with me. Whichever way it turns out, like . . ."

"I never seen you neither," Dave said.

Tigo stared at him for a long time. "That's 'cause you're new around here. Where you from originally?"

"My people come down from the Bronx."

"You got a big family?"

"A sister and two brothers, that's all."

"Yeah, I only got a sister," Tigo shrugged. "Well." He sighed. "So." He sighed again. "Let's make it, huh?"

"I'm waitin'," Dave said.

Tigo picked up the gun, and then he took one of the cartridges from the table top. He broke open the gun, slid the cartridge into the cylinder, and then snapped the gun shut and twirled the cylinder. "Round and round she goes," he said, "and where she stops, nobody knows."

"There's six chambers in the cylinder," Tigo said, "and only one cartridge. That makes the odds five-to-one that the cartridge'll be in firing position when the cylinder stops whirling. You dig?"

"I dig."

"I'll go first," Tigo said.

Dave looked at him suspiciously. "Why?"

"You want to go first?"

"I don't know."

"I'm giving you a break," Tigo grinned. "I may blow my head off first time out."

"Why you giving me a break?" Dave asked.

Tigo shrugged. "What the hell's the difference?" He gave the cylinder a fast twirl.

"The Russians invented this, huh?" Dave asked.

"Yeah."

"I always said they was crazy bastards."

"Yeah, I always . . ." Tigo stopped talking. The cylinder was still now. He took a deep breath, put the barrel of the .38 to his temple, and then squeezed the trigger.

The firing pin clicked on an empty chamber.

"Well, that was easy, wasn't it?" he asked. He shoved the gun across the table. "Your turn, Dave."

Dave reached for the gun. It was cold in the basement room, but he was sweating now. He pulled the gun toward him, then left it on the table while he dried his palms on his trousers. He picked up the gun then and stared at it.

"It's a nifty piece," Tigo said. "I like a good piece."

"Yeah, I do too," Dave said. "You can tell a good piece just by the way it feels in your hand."

Tigo looked surprised. "I mentioned that to one of the guys yesterday, and he thought I was nuts."

"Lots of guys don't know about pieces," Dave said, shrugging.

"I was thinking," Tigo said, "when I get old enough, I'll join the Army, you know? I'd like to work around pieces."

"I thought of that, too. I'd join now, only my old lady won't give me permission. She's got to sign if I join now."

"Yeah, they're all the same," Tigo said, smiling. "Your old lady born here or the island?"

"The island," Dave said.

"Yeah, well, you know they got these old-fashioned ideas."

"I better spin," Dave said.

"Yeah," Tigo agreed.

Dave slapped the cylinder with his left hand. The cylinder whirled, whirled and then stopped. Slowly, Dave put the gun to his head. He wanted to close his eyes, but he didn't dare. Tigo, the enemy, was watching him. He returned Tigo's stare, and then he squeezed the trigger.

His heart skipped a beat, and then over the roar of his blood he heard the empty click. Hastily, he put the gun down on the table.

"Makes you sweat, don't it?" Tigo said.

Dave nodded, saying nothing. He watched Tigo. Tigo was looking at the gun.

"Me now, huh?" he said. He took a deep breath, then picked up the .38.

He shrugged. "Well." He twirled the cylinder, waited for it to stop, and then put the gun to his head.

"Bang!" he said, and then he squeezed the trigger. Again, the firing pin clicked on an empty chamber. Tigo let out his breath and put the gun down.

"I thought I was dead that time," he said.

"I could hear the harps," Dave said.

"This is a good way to lose weight, you know that?" He laughed nervously, and then his laugh became honest when he saw that Dave was laughing with him. "Ain't it the truth? You could lose ten pounds this way."

"My old lady's like a house," Dave said, laughing. "She ought to try this kind of a diet." He laughed at his own humor, pleased when Tigo joined him.

"That's the trouble," Tigo said. "You see a nice deb in the street, you think it's crazy, you know? Then they get to be our people's age, and they turn to fat." He shook his head.

"You got a chick?" Dave asked.

"Yeah, I got one."

"What's her name?"

"Aw, you don't know her."

"Maybe I do," Dave said.

"Her name is Juana." Tigo watched him. "She's about five-two, got these brown eyes. . . ."

"I think I know her," Dave said. He nodded. "Yeah, I think I know her."

"She's nice, ain't she?" Tigo asked. He leaned forward, as if Dave's answer was of great importance to him.

"Yeah, she's nice," Dave said.

"The guys rib me about her. You know, all they're after—well, you know—they don't understand something like Juana."

"I got a chick, too," Dave said.

"Yeah? Hey, maybe sometime we could . . ." Tigo cut himself short. He looked down at the gun, and his sudden enthusiasm seemed to ebb completely. "It's your turn," he said.

"Here goes nothing," Dave said. He twirled the cylinder, sucked in his breath, and then fired.

The empty click was loud in the stillness of the room.

"Man!" Dave said.

"We're pretty lucky, you know?" Tigo said.

"So far."

"We better lower the odds. The boys won't like it if we . . ." He stopped himself again, and then reached for one of the cartridges on the table. He broke open the gun again, and slipped the second cartridge into the cylinder. "Now we got two cartridges in here," he said. "Two cartridges, six chambers. That's four-to-two. Divide it, and you get two-to-one." He paused. "You game?"

"That's—that's what we're here for, ain't it?"

"Sure."

"Okay then."

"Gone," Tigo said, nodding his head. "You got courage, Dave."

"You're the one needs the courage," Dave said gently. "It's your spin."

Tigo lifted the gun. Idly, he began spinning the cylinder.

"You live on the next block, don't you?" Dave asked.

"Yeah." Tigo kept slapping the cylinder. It spun with a gently whirring sound.

"That's how come we never crossed paths, I guess. Also I'm new on the scene."

"Yeah, well you know, you get hooked up with one club, that's the way it is."

"You like the guys on your club?" Dave asked, wondering why he was asking such a stupid question, listening to the whirring of the cylinder at the same time.

"They're okay," Tigo shrugged. "None of them really send me, but that's the club on my block, so what're you gonna do, huh?" His hand left the cylinder. It stopped spinning. He put the gun to his head.

"Wait!" Dave said.

Tigo looked puzzled. "What's the matter?"

"Nothing. I just wanted to say—I mean . . ." Dave frowned. "I don't dig too many of the guys on my club, either."

Tigo nodded. For a moment, their eyes locked. Then Tigo shrugged, and fired.

And then the empty click filled the basement room.

"Phew," Tigo said.

"Man, you can say that again."

Tigo slid the gun across the table.

Dave hesitated an instant. He did not want to pick up the gun. He felt sure that this time the firing pin would strike the percussion cap of one of the cartridges. He was sure that this time he would shoot himself.

"Sometimes I think I'm turkey," he said to Tigo, surprised that his thoughts had found voice.

"I feel that way sometimes, too," Tigo said.

"I never told that to nobody," Dave said. "The guys on my club would laugh at me, I ever told them that."

"Some things you got to keep to yourself. There ain't nobody you can trust in this world."

"There should be somebody you can trust," Dave said. "Hell, you can't tell nothing to your people. They don't understand."

Tigo laughed. "That's an old story. But that's the way things are. What're you gonna do?"

"Yeah. Still, sometimes I think I'm turkey."

"Sure, sure," Tigo said. "It ain't only that, though. Like sometimes—well, don't you wonder what you're doing stomping some guy in the street? Like—you know what I mean? Like—who's the guy to you? What you got to beat him up for? 'Cause he messed with somebody else's girl?" Tigo shook his head. "It gets complicated sometimes."

"Yeah, but . . ." Dave frowned again. "You got to stick with the club. Don't you?"

"Sure, sure—no question." Again, their eyes locked.

"Well, here goes," Dave said. He lifted the gun. "It's just . . ." He shook his head, and then twirled the cylinder. The cylinder spun, and then stopped. He studied the gun, wondering if one of the cartridges would roar from the barrel when he squeezed the trigger.

Then he fired.

Click.

"I didn't think you was going through with it," Tigo said.

"I didn't neither."

"You got heart, Dave," Tigo said. He looked at the gun. He picked it up and broke it open.

"What you doing?" Dave asked.

"Another cartridge," Tigo said. "Six chambers, *three* cartridges. That makes it even money. You game?"

"You?"

"The boys said . . ." Tigo stopped talking. "Yeah, I'm game," he added, his voice curiously low.

"It's your turn, you know."

"I know."

Dave watched as Tigo picked up the gun.

"You ever been rowboating on the lake?"

Tigo looked across the table at him, his eyes wide. "Once," he said. "I went with Juana."

"Is it—is it any kicks?"

"Yeah. Yeah, it's grand kicks. You mean you never been?"

"No," Dave said.

"Hey, you got to try it, man," Tigo said excitedly. "You'll like it. Hey, you try it."

"Yeah, I was thinking maybe this Sunday I'd . . ." He did not complete the sentence.

"My spin," Tigo said wearily. He twirled the cylinder. "Here goes a good man," he said, and he put the revolver to his head and squeezed the trigger.

Click.

Dave smiled nervously. "No rest for the weary," he said. "But Jesus you got heart. I don't know if I can go through with it."

"Sure, you can," Tigo assured him. "Listen, what's there to be afraid of?" He slid the gun across the table.

"We keep this up all night?" Dave asked.

"They said—you know . . ."

"Well, it ain't so bad. I mean, hell, we didn't have this operation, we wouldn'ta got a chance to talk, huh?" He grinned feebly.

"Yeah," Tigo said, his face splitting in a wide grin. "It ain't been so bad, huh?"

"No, it's been—well, you know, these guys on the club, who can talk to them?"

He picked up the gun.

"We could . . ." Tigo started.

"What?"

"We could say—well—like we kept shootin' an' nothing happened, so . . ." Tigo shrugged. "What the hell! We can't do this all night, can we?"

"I don't know."

"Let's make this the last spin. Listen, they don't like it, they can take a flying leap, you know?"

"I don't think they'll like it. We supposed to settle this for the clubs."

"Screw the clubs!" Tigo said vehemently. "Can't we pick our own . . ." The word was hard coming. When it came, he said it softly, and his eyes did not leave Dave's face. ". . . friends?"

"Sure we can," Dave said fervently. "Sure we can! Why not?"

"The last spin," Tigo said. "Come on, the last spin."

"Gone," Dave said. "Hey, you know, I'm *glad* they got this idea. You know that? I'm actually glad!" He twirled the cylinder. "Look, you want to go on the lake this Sunday? I mean, with your girl and mine? We could get two boats. Or even one if you want."

"Yeah, one boat," Tigo said. "Hey, your girl'll like Juana, I mean it. She's a swell chick."

The cylinder stopped. Dave put the gun to his head quickly.

"Here's to Sunday," he said. He grinned at Tigo, and Tigo grinned back, and then Dave fired.

The explosion rocked the small basement room, ripping away half of Dave's head, shattering his face. A small sharp cry escaped Tigo's throat, and a look of incredulous shock knifed his eyes.

Then he put his head on the table and began weeping.

Moment of Power*

P. D. James

* This story has also appeared under the title "A Very Commonplace Murder."

"We close at twelve on Saturday," said the blonde in the Estate Office. "So if you keep the key after then, please drop it back through the letter box. It's the only key we have and there may be other people wanting to view on Monday. Sign here please, sir."

The "sir" was grudging, an afterthought. Her tone was reproving. She didn't really think he would buy the flat, this seedy old man with his air of spurious gentility, with his harsh voice. In her job you soon got a nose for the genuine inquirer. Ernest Gabriel. An odd name, half common, half fancy.

But he took the key politely enough and thanked her for her trouble. No trouble, she thought. God knew there were few enough people interested in that sordid little dump, not at the price they were asking. He could keep the key a week for all she cared.

She was right. Gabriel hadn't come to buy, only to view. It was the first time he had been back since it all happened sixteen years ago. He came neither as a pilgrim nor a penitent. He had returned under some compulsion which he hadn't even bothered to analyze. He had been on his way to visit his only living relative, an elderly aunt, who had recently been admitted to a geriatric ward. He hadn't even realized the bus would pass the flat.

But suddenly they were lurching through Camden Town and the road became familiar, like a photograph springing into focus; and with a *frisson* of surprise he recognized the double-fronted shop and the flat above. There was an Estate Agent's notice in the window. Almost without thinking, he had got off at the next stop, gone back to verify the name, and walked the half mile to the office. It had seemed as natural and inevitable as his daily bus journey to work.

Twenty minutes later he fitted the key into the lock of the front door and passed into the stuffy emptiness of the flat. The grimy walls still held the smell of cooking. There was a spatter of envelopes on the worn linoleum, dirtied and trampled by the feet of previous viewers. The light bulb swung naked in the hall and the door into the sitting room stood open. To his right was the staircase, to his left the kitchen.

Gabriel paused for a moment, then went into the kitchen. From the windows, half curtained with grubby gingham, he looked upward to the great black building at the rear of the flat, eyeless except for the one small square of window high on the fifth floor. It was from this window, sixteen years ago, that he had watched Denis Speller and Eileen Morrisey play out their commonplace little tragedy to its end.

He had no right to be watching them, no right to be in the building at all after six o'clock. That had been the nub of his awful dilemma. It had happened by chance. Mr. Maurice Bootman had instructed him, as the firm's filing clerk, to go through the papers in the late Mr. Bootman's upstairs den in case there were any which should be in the files. They weren't confidential or important papers—those had been dealt with by the family and the firm's solicitors months before. They were just a miscellaneous, yellowing collection of out-of-date memoranda, old accounts, receipts, and fading press clippings which had been bundled together into old Mr. Bootman's desk. He had been a great hoarder of trivia.

But at the back of the left-hand bottom drawer Gabriel had found a key. It was by chance that he tried it in the lock of the corner cupboard. It fitted. And in the cupboard Gabriel found the late Mr. Bootman's small but choice collection of pornography.

He knew that he had to read the books; not just to snatch surreptitious minutes with one ear listening for a footstep on the stairs or the whine of the approaching elevator and fearful always that his absence from his filing room would be noticed. No, he had to read them in privacy and in peace. So he devised his plan.

It wasn't difficult. As a trusted member of the staff he had one of the Yale keys to the side door at which goods were delivered. It was locked on the inside at night by the porter before he went off duty. It wasn't difficult for Gabriel, always among the last to leave, to find the opportunity of shooting back the bolts before leaving with the porter by the main door. He dared risk it only once a week and the day he chose was Friday.

He would hurry home, eat his solitary meal beside the gas fire in his bed-sitting-room, then make his way back to the building and let himself in by the side door. All that was necessary was to make sure he was waiting for the office to open on Monday morning so that, among the first in, he could lock the side door before the porter made his ritual visit to unlock it for the day's deliveries.

These Friday nights became a desperate but shameful joy to Gabriel. Their pattern was always the same. He would sit crouched in old Mr. Bootman's low leather chair in front of the fireplace, his shoulders hunched over the book in his lap, his eyes following the pool of light from his torch as it moved over each page. He never dared to switch on the room light and even on the coldest night he never lit the gas fire. He was fearful that its hiss might mask the sound of approaching feet, that its glow might shine through the thick curtains at the window, or that, somehow, the smell of gas would linger in the room next Monday morning to betray him. He was morbidly afraid of discovery, yet even this fear added to the excitement of his secret pleasure.

It was on the third Friday in January that he first saw them. It was a mild evening but heavy and starless. An early rain had slimed the pavements and bled the scribbled headlines from the newspaper placards. Gabriel wiped his feet carefully before climbing to the fifth floor. The claustrophobic room smelled sour and dusty, the air struck colder than the night outside. He wondered whether he dare open the window and let in some of the sweetness of the rain-cleansed sky.

It was then that he saw the woman. Below him were the back entrances of the two shops, each with a flat above. One flat had boarded windows, but the other looked lived in. It was approached by a flight of iron steps leading to an asphalt yard. He saw the woman in the glow of a street lamp as she paused at the foot of the steps, fumbling in her handbag. Then, as if gaining resolution, she came swiftly up the steps and almost ran across the asphalt to the flat door.

He watched as she pressed herself into the shadow of the doorway, then swiftly turned the key in the lock and slid out of his sight. He had time only to notice that she was wearing a pale mackintosh buttoned high under a mane of fairish hair and that she carried a string bag of what looked like groceries. It seemed an oddly furtive and solitary homecoming.

Gabriel waited. Almost immediately he saw the light go on in the room to the left of the door. Perhaps she was in the kitchen. He could see her faint shadow passing to and fro, bending and then lengthening. He guessed that she was unpacking the groceries. Then the light in the room went out.

For a few moments the flat was in darkness. Then the light in the upstairs window went on, brighter this time so that he could see the woman more plainly. She could not know how plainly. The curtains were drawn but they were thinner. Perhaps the owners, confident that they were not overlooked, had grown careless. Although the woman's silhouette was only a faint blur Gabriel could see that she was carrying a tray. Perhaps she was intending to eat her supper in bed. She was undressing now.

He could see her lifting the garments over her head and twisting down to release stockings and take off her shoes. Suddenly she came very close to the window and he saw the outline of her body plainly. She seemed to be watching and listening. Gabriel found that he was holding his breath. Then she moved away and the light dimmed. He guessed that she had switched off the central bulb and was using the bedside lamp. The room was now lit with a softer, pinkish glow within which the woman moved, insubstantial as a dream.

Gabriel stood with his face pressed against the cold window, still watching. Shortly after eight o'clock the boy arrived. Gabriel always thought of him as "the boy." Even from that distance his youth, his vulnerability, were apparent. He approached the flat with more confidence than the woman but still swiftly, pausing at the top of the steps as if to assess the width of the rain-washed yard.

She must have been waiting for his knock. She let him in at once, the door barely opening. Gabriel knew that she had come naked to let him in. And then there were two shadows in the upstairs room, shadows that met and parted and came together again before they moved, joined, to the bed and out of Gabriel's sight.

The next Friday he watched to see if they would come again. They did, and at the same times, the woman first at twenty minutes past seven, the boy forty minutes later. Again Gabriel stood, rigidly intent at his watching post, as the light in the upstairs window sprang on and then was lowered. The two naked figures, seen dimly behind the curtains, moved to and fro, joined and parted, fused and swayed together in a ritualistic parody of a dance.

This Friday Gabriel waited until they left. The boy came out first, sidling quickly from the half-open door and almost leaping down the steps as if in exultant joy. The woman followed five minutes later, locking the door behind her and darting across the asphalt, her head bent.

After that he watched for them every Friday. They held a fascination for him even greater than Mr. Bootman's books. Their routine hardly varied. Sometimes the boy arrived a little late and Gabriel would see the woman watching motionless for him behind the bedroom curtains. He too would stand with held breath, sharing her agony of impatience, willing the boy to come. Usually the boy carried a bottle under his arm but, one week, it was in a wine basket and he bore it with great care. Perhaps it was an anniversary, a special evening for them. Always the woman had the bag of groceries. Always they ate together in the bedroom.

Friday after Friday Gabriel stood in the darkness, his eyes fixed on that upstairs window, straining to decipher the outlines of their naked bodies, picturing what they were doing to each other.

They had been meeting for seven weeks when it happened. Gabriel was late at the building that night. His usual bus did not run and the first to arrive was full. By the time he reached his watching post there was already a light in the bedroom. He pressed his face to the window, his hot breath smearing the pane. Hastily rubbing it clear with the cuff of his coat he looked again. For a moment he thought that there were two figures in the bedroom. But that must surely be a freak of the light. The boy wasn't due for thirty minutes yet. But the woman, as always, was on time.

Twenty minutes later he went into the washroom on the floor below. He had become much more confident during the last few weeks and now moved about the building, silently and using only his torch for light, but with almost as much assurance as during the day. He spent nearly ten minutes in the washroom. His watch showed that it was just after eight by the time he was back at the window, and, at first, he thought that he had missed the boy. But no, the slight figure was even now running up the steps and across the asphalt to the shelter of the doorway.

Gabriel watched as he knocked and waited for the door to open. But it didn't open. She didn't come. There was a light in the bedroom, but no shadow moved on the curtains. The boy knocked again. Gabriel could just detect the quivering of his knuckles against the door. Again he waited. Then the boy drew back and looked up at the lighted window. Perhaps he was risking a low-pitched call. Gabriel could hear nothing but he could sense the tension in that waiting figure.

Again the boy knocked. Again there was no response. Gabriel watched and suffered with him until, at twenty past eight, the boy finally gave up and turned away. Then Gabriel too stretched his cramped limbs and made his way into the night. The wind was rising and a young moon reeled through the torn clouds. It was getting colder. He wore no coat and missed its comfort. Hunching his shoulders against the bite of the wind he knew that this was the last Friday he would come late to the building. For him, as for that desolate boy, it was the end of a chapter.

He first read about the murder in his morning paper on his way to work the following Monday. He recognized the picture of the flat at once although it looked oddly unfamiliar with the bunch of plain-clothes detectives conferring at the door and the stolid uniformed policeman at the top of the steps.

The story so far was slight. A Mrs. Eileen Morrisey, aged thirty-four, had been found stabbed to death in a flat in Camden Town late on Sunday night. The discovery was made by the tenants, Mr. and Mrs. Kealy, who had returned late on Sunday from a visit to Mr. Kealy's parents. The dead woman, who was the mother of twin daughters aged twelve, was a friend of Mrs. Kealy. Detective Chief-Inspector William Holbrook was in charge of the investigation. It was understood that the dead woman had been sexually assaulted.

Gabriel folded his paper with the same precise care as he did on any ordinary day. Of course, he would have to tell the police what he had seen. He couldn't let an innocent man suffer no matter what the inconvenience to himself. The knowledge of his intention, of his public-spirited devotion to justice, was warmly satisfying. For the rest of the day he crept around his filing cabinets with the secret complacency of a man dedicated to sacrifice.

But somehow his first plan of calling at a police station on his way home from work came to nothing. There was no point in acting hastily. If the boy were arrested he would speak. But it would be ridiculous to prejudice his reputation and endanger his job before he even knew whether the boy was a suspect. The police might never learn of the boy's existence. To speak up now might only focus suspicion on the innocent. A prudent man would wait. Gabriel decided to be prudent.

The boy was arrested three days later. Again Gabriel read about it in his morning paper. There was no picture this time and few details. The news had to compete with a society elopement and a major air crash and did not make the first page. The inch of newsprint stated briefly: "Denis John Speller, a butcher's assistant, aged nineteen, who gave an address at Muswell Hill, was today charged with the murder of Mrs. Eileen Morrisey, the mother of twelve-year-old twins, who was stabbed to death last Friday in a flat in Camden Town."

So the police now knew more precisely the time of death. Perhaps it was time for him to see them. But how could he be sure that this Denis Speller was the young lover he had been watching these past Friday nights? A woman like that—well, she might have had any number of men. No photograph of the accused would be published in any paper until after the trial. But more information would come out at the preliminary hearing. He would wait for that. After all, the accused might not even be committed for trial.

Besides, he had himself to consider. There had been time to think of his own position. If young Speller's life were in danger, then, of course, Gabriel would tell what he had seen. But it would mean the end of his job with Bootman's. Worse, he would never get another. Mr. Maurice Bootman would see to that. He, Gabriel, would be branded as a dirty-minded, sneaking little voyeur, a Peeping Tom who was willing to jeopardize his livelihood for an hour or two with a naughty book and a chance to pry into other people's happiness. Mr. Maurice would be too angry at the publicity to forgive the man who had caused it.

And the rest of the firm would laugh. It would be the best joke in years, funny and pathetic and futile. The pedantic, respectable, censorious Ernest Gabriel found out at last! And they wouldn't even give him credit for speaking up. It simply wouldn't occur to them that he could have kept silent.

If only he could think of a good reason for being in the building that night. But there was none. He could hardly say that he had stayed behind to work late when he had taken such care to leave with the porter. And it wouldn't do to say that he had returned later to catch up with his filing. His filing was always up-to-date as he was fond of pointing out. His very efficiency was against him.

Besides, he was a poor liar. The police wouldn't accept his story without probing. After they had spent so much time on the case they would hardly welcome his tardy revelation of new evidence. He pictured the circle of grim, accusing faces, the official civility barely concealing their dislike and contempt. There was no sense in inviting such an ordeal before he was sure of the facts.

But after the preliminary hearing at which Denis Speller was sent up for trial the same arguments seemed equally valid. By now he knew that Speller was the lover he had seen. There had never really been much room for doubt. By now, too, the outlines of the case for the Crown were apparent. The Prosecution would seek to prove that this was a crime of passion, that the boy, tormented by her threat to leave him, had killed in jealousy or revenge. The accused would deny that he had entered the flat that night, would state again and again that he had knocked and gone away. Only Gabriel could support his story. But it would still be premature to speak.

He decided to attend the trial. In that way he would hear the strength of the Crown's case. If it appeared likely that the verdict would be "Not Guilty" he could remain silent. And if things went badly there was an excitement, a fearful fascination, in the thought of rising to his feet in the silence of that crowded court and speaking out his evidence before all the world. The questioning, the criticism, the notoriety would come later. But he would have had his moment of glory.

He was surprised and a little disappointed by the Court. He had expected a more imposing, more dramatic setting for justice than this modern, clean-smelling businesslike room. Everything was quiet and orderly. There was no crowd at the door jostling for seats. It wasn't even a popular trial.

Sliding into his seat at the back of the Court, Gabriel looked round, at first apprehensively and then with more confidence. But he needn't have worried. There was no one there he knew. It was really a very dull collection of people, hardly worthy, he thought, of the drama that was to be played out before them. Some of them looked as if they might have worked with Speller or lived in the same street. All looked ill-at-ease with the slightly furtive air of people who find themselves in unusual or intimidating surroundings. There was a thin woman in black crying softly into a handkerchief. No one took any notice of her, no one comforted her.

From time to time one of the doors at the back of the Court would open silently and a newcomer would sidle almost furtively into his seat. When this happened the row of faces would turn momentarily to him without interest, without recognition, before turning their eyes again to the slight figure in the dock.

Gabriel stared too. At first he dared to cast only fleeting glances, averting his eyes suddenly as if each glance were a desperate risk. It was unthinkable that the prisoner's eyes should meet his, should somehow know that here was the man who could save him and should signal a desperate appeal. But when he had risked two or three glances he realized that there was nothing to fear. That solitary figure was seeing no one, caring about no one except himself. He was only a bewildered and terrified boy, his eyes turned inward to some private hell. He looked like a trapped animal, beyond hope and beyond fight.

The Judge was rotund, red-faced, his chins sunk into the bands at his neck. He had small hands which he rested on the desk before him except when he was making notes. Then Counsel would stop talking for a moment before continuing more slowly as if anxious not to hurry his Lordship, watching him like a worried father explaining with slow deliberation to a not very bright child.

But Gabriel knew where lay the power. The Judge's chubby hands, folded on the desk like a parody of a child in prayer, held a man's life in their grasp. There was only one person in the Court with more power than that scarlet-sashed figure high under the carved coat-of-arms. And that was he, Gabriel. The realization came to him in a spurt of exultation, at once intoxicating and satisfying. He hugged his knowledge to himself gloatingly. This was a new sensation, terrifyingly sweet.

He looked round at the solemn watching faces and wondered how they would change if he got suddenly to his feet and called out what he knew. He would say it firmly, confidently. They wouldn't be able to frighten him. He would say, "My Lord. The accused is innocent. He did knock and go away. I, Gabriel, saw him."

And then what would happen? It was impossible to guess. Would the Judge stop the trial so that they could all adjourn to his chambers and hear his evidence in private? Or would Gabriel be called now to take his stand in the witness box? One thing was certain, there would be no fuss, no hysteria.

But suppose the Judge merely ordered him out of the Court. Suppose he was too surprised to take in what Gabriel had said. Gabriel could picture him leaning forward irritably, hand to his ear, while the police at the back of the Court came silently forward to drag out the offender. Surely in this calm, aseptic atmosphere where justice itself seemed an academic ritual the voice of truth would be merely a vulgar intrusion. No one would believe him. No one would listen. They had set this elaborate scene to play out their drama to the end. They wouldn't thank him for spoiling it now. The time to speak had passed.

Even if they did believe him he wouldn't get any credit now for coming forward. He would be blamed for leaving it so late, for letting an innocent man get so close to the gallows. If Speller were innocent, of course. And who could tell that? They would say that he might have knocked and gone away, only to return later and gain access to kill. He, Gabriel, hadn't waited at the window to see. So his sacrifice would have been for nothing.

And he could hear those taunting office voices: "Trust old Gabriel to leave it to the last minute. Bloody coward. Read any naughty books lately, Archangel?" He would be sacked from Bootman's without even the consolation of standing well in the public eye.

Oh, he would make the headlines all right. He could imagine them: *Outburst in Old Bailey. Man Upholds Accused's Alibi.* Only it wasn't an alibi. What did it really prove? He would be regarded as a public nuisance, the pathetic little voyeur who was too much of a coward to go to the police earlier. And Denis Speller would still hang.

Once the moment of temptation had passed and he knew with absolute certainty that he wasn't going to speak, Gabriel began almost to enjoy himself. After all, it wasn't every day that one could watch British justice at work. He listened, noted, appreciated. It was a formidable case which the Prosecution unfolded. Gabriel approved of the prosecuting Counsel. With his high forehead, beaked nose, and bony, intelligent face, he looked so much more distinguished than the Judge. This was how a famous lawyer should look. He made his case without passion, almost without interest. But that, Gabriel knew, was how the law worked. It wasn't the duty of prosecuting Counsel to work for a conviction. His job was to state with fairness and accuracy the case for the Crown.

He called his witnesses. Mrs. Brenda Kealy, the wife of the tenant of the flat. A blonde, smartly dressed, common little slut if ever Gabriel saw one. Oh, he knew her type all right. He could guess what his mother would have said about her. Anyone could see what she was interested in. And by the look of her she was getting it regularly too. Dressed up for a wedding. A tart if ever he saw one.

Sniveling into her handkerchief and answering Counsel's questions in a voice so low that the Judge had to ask her to speak up. Yes, she had agreed to lend Eileen the flat on Friday nights. She and her husband went every Friday to visit his parents at Southend. They always left as soon as he shut the shop. No, her husband didn't know of the arrangement. She had given Mrs. Morrisey the spare key without consulting him. There wasn't any other spare key that she knew of. Why had she done it? She was sorry for Eileen. Eileen had pressed her. She didn't think the Morriseys had much of a life together.

Here the Judge interposed gently that the witness should confine herself to answering Counsel's questions. She turned to him, "I was only trying to help Eileen, my Lord."

Then there was the letter. It was passed to the sniveling woman in the box and she confirmed that it had been written to her by Mrs. Morrisey. Slowly it was collected by the Clerk and born majestically across to Counsel, who proceeded to read it aloud.

"Dear Brenda,

We shall be at the flat on Friday after all. I thought I'd better let you know in case you and Ted changed your plans. But it will definitely be for the last time. George is getting suspicious and I must think of the children. I always knew it would have to end. Thank you for being such a pal.

Eileen."

The measured, upper-class voice ceased. Looking across at the jury, Counsel laid the letter slowly down. The Judge bent his head and made another notation. There was a moment of silence in the Court. Then the witness was dismissed.

And so it went on. There was the paper seller at the end of Moulton Street who remembered Speller buying an *Evening Standard* just before eight o'clock. The accused was carrying a bottle under his arm and seemed very cheerful. He had no doubt his customer was the accused.

There was the publican's wife from The Rising Sun at the junction of Moulton Mews and High Street who testified that she served the prisoner with a whiskey shortly before half-past eight. He hadn't stayed long. Just long enough to drink it down. He had seemed very upset. Yes, she was quite sure it was the accused. There was a motley collection of customers to confirm her evidence. Gabriel wondered why the prosecution had bothered to call them until he realized that Speller had denied visiting The Rising Sun, had denied that he had needed a drink.

There was George Edward Morrisey, described as an estate agent's clerk, thin-faced, tight-lipped, standing rigidly in his best blue serge suit. He testified that his marriage had been happy, that he had known nothing, suspected nothing. His wife had told him that she spent Friday evenings learning to make pottery at L.C.C. evening classes. The Court tittered. The Judge frowned.

In reply to Counsel's questions Morrisey said that he had stayed at home to look after the children. They were still a little young to be left alone at night. Yes, he had been at home the night his wife was killed. Her death was a great grief to him. Her liaison with the accused had come as a terrible shock. He spoke the word "liaison" with an angry contempt as if it were bitter on his tongue. Never once did he look at the prisoner.

There was the medical evidence—sordid, specific, but mercifully clinical and brief. The deceased had been raped, then stabbed three times through the jugular vein. There was the evidence of the accused's employer who contributed a vague and imperfectly substantiated story about a missing meat screwer. There was the prisoner's landlady who testified that he had arrived home on the night of the murder in a distressed state and that he had not got up to go to work next morning. Some of the threads were thin. Some, like the evidence of the butcher, obviously bore little weight even in the eyes of the prosecution. But together they were weaving a rope strong enough to hang a man.

The defending Counsel did his best but he had the desperate air of a man who knows that he is foredoomed to lose. He called witnesses to testify that Speller was a gentle kindly boy, a generous friend, a good son and brother. The jury believed them. They also believed that he had killed his mistress. He called the accused. Speller was a poor witness, unconvincing, inarticulate. It would have helped, thought Gabriel, if the boy had shown some sign of pity for the dead woman. But he was too absorbed in his own danger to spare a thought for anyone else. Perfect fear casteth out love, thought Gabriel. The aphorism pleased him.

The Judge summed up with scrupulous impartiality, treating the jury to an exposition on the nature and value of circumstantial evidence and an interpretation of the expression "reasonable doubt." The jury listened with respectful attention. It was impossible to guess what went on behind those twelve pairs of watchful, anonymous eyes. But they weren't out long.

Within forty minutes of the Court rising, they were back, the prisoner reappeared in the dock, the Judge asked the formal question. The foreman gave the expected answer, loud and clear. "Guilty, my Lord." No one seemed surprised.

The Judge explained to the prisoner that he had been found guilty of the horrible and merciless killing of the woman who had loved him. The prisoner, his face taut and ashen, stared wild-eyed at the Judge as if only half hearing. The sentence was pronounced, sounding doubly horrible spoken in those soft judicial tones.

Gabriel looked with interest for the black cap and saw with surprise and some disappointment that it was merely a square of some black material perched incongruously atop the Judge's wig. The jury was thanked. The Judge collected his notes like a businessman clearing his desk at the end of a busy day. The Court rose. The prisoner was taken below. It was over.

The trial caused little comment at the office. No one knew that Gabriel had attended. His day's leave "for personal reasons" was accepted with as little interest as any previous absence. He was too solitary, too unpopular, to be included in office gossip.

In his dusty and ill-lit office, insulated by tiers of filing cabinets, he was the object of vague dislike or, at best, of a pitying tolerance. The filing room had never been a center for cosy office chat. But he did hear the opinion of one member of the firm.

On the day after the trial Mr. Bootman, newspaper in hand, came into the general office while Gabriel was distributing the morning mail. "I see they've disposed of our little local trouble," Mr. Bootman said. "Apparently the fellow is to hang. A good thing too. It seems to have been the usual sordid story of illicit passion and general stupidity. A very commonplace murder."

No one replied. The office staff stood silent, then stirred into life. Perhaps they felt that there was nothing more to be said.

It was shortly after the trial that Gabriel began to dream. The dream, which occurred about three times a week, was always the same. He was struggling across a desert under a blood-red sun, trying to reach a distant fort. He could sometimes see the fort clearly although it never got any closer. There was an inner courtyard crowded with people, a silent black-clad multitude whose faces were all turned toward a central platform. On the platform was a gallows. It was a curiously elegant gallows with two sturdy posts at either side and a delicately curved crosspiece from which the noose dangled.

The people, like the gallows, were not of this age. It was a Victorian crowd, the women in shawls and bonnets, the men in tophats or narrow-brimmed bowlers. He could see his mother there, her thin face peaked under the widow's veil. Suddenly she began to cry, and as she cried, her face changed and became the face of the weeping woman at the trial. Gabriel longed desperately to reach her, to comfort her. But with every step he sank deeper into the sand.

There were people on the platform now. One, he knew, must be the prison Governor, tophatted, frock-coated, bewhiskered and grave. His clothes were those of a Victorian gentleman but his face, under that luxuriant beard, was the face of Mr. Bootman. Beside him stood the Chaplain in gown and bands and, on either side, were two warders, their dark jackets buttoned high to their necks.

Under the noose stood the prisoner. He was wearing breeches and an open-necked shirt and his neck was as white and delicate as a woman's. It might have been that other neck, so slender it looked. The prisoner was gazing across the desert toward Gabriel, not with desperate appeal but with great sadness in his eyes. And, this time, Gabriel knew that he had to save him, had to get there in time.

But the sand dragged at his aching ankles and although he called that he was coming, coming, the wind, like a furnace blast, tore the words from his parched throat. His back, bent almost double, was blistered by the sun. He wasn't wearing a coat. Somehow, irrationally, he was worried that his coat was missing, that something had happened to it that he ought to remember.

As he lurched forward, floundering through the gritty morass, he could see the fort shimmering in the heat haze. Then it began to recede, getting fainter and farther until at last it was only a blur among the distant sandhills. He heard a high despairing scream from the courtyard—then awoke to know that it was his voice and that the damp heat on his brow was sweat, not blood.

In the comparative sanity of the morning he analyzed the dream and realized that the scene was one pictured in a Victorian newssheet which he had once seen in the window of an antiquarian bookshop. As he remembered, it showed the execution of William Corder for the murder of Maria Marten in the red barn. The remembrance comforted him. At least he was still in touch with the tangible and sane world.

But the strain was obviously getting him down. It was time to put his mind to his problem. He had always had a good mind, too good for his job. That, of course, was why the other staff resented him. Now was the time to use it. What exactly was he worrying about? A woman had been murdered. Whose fault had it been? Weren't there a number of people who shared the responsibility?

That blonde tart, for one, who had lent them the flat. The

husband who had been so easily fooled. The boy who had enticed her away from her duty to husband and children. The victim herself—particularly the victim. The wages of sin are death. Well, she had taken her wages now. One man hadn't been enough for her.

Gabriel pictured again that dim shadow against the bedroom curtains, the raised arms as she drew Speller's head down to her breast. Filthy. Disgusting. Dirty. The adjectives smeared his mind. Well, she and her lover had taken their fun. It was right that both of them should pay for it. He, Ernest Gabriel, wasn't concerned. It had only been by the merest chance that he had seen them from that upper window, only by chance that he had seen Speller knock and go away again.

Justice was being served. He had sensed its majesty, the beauty of its essential rightness, at Speller's trial. And he, Gabriel, was a part of it. If he spoke now an adulterer might even go free. His duty was clear. The temptation to speak had gone forever.

It was in this mood that he stood with the small silent crowd outside the prison on the morning of Speller's execution. At the first stroke of eight he, like the other men present, took off his hat. Staring up at the sky high above the prison walls he felt again the warm exultation of his authority and power. It was on his behalf, it was at his, Gabriel's, bidding that the nameless hangman inside was exercising his dreadful craft . . .

But that was sixteen years ago. Four months after the trial the firm, expanding and conscious of the need for a better address, had moved from Camden Town to north London. Gabriel had moved with it. He was one of the few people on the staff who remembered the old building. Clerks came and went so quickly nowadays; there was no sense of loyalty to the job.

When Gabriel retired at the end of the year, only Mr. Bootman and the porter would remain from the old Camden Town days. Sixteen years. Sixteen years of the same job, the same bed-sitting-room, the same half-tolerant dislike on the part of the staff. But he had had his moment of power. He recalled it now, looking round the small sordid sitting room with its peeling wallpaper, its stained boards. It had looked different sixteen years ago.

He remembered where the sofa had stood, the very spot where she had died. He remembered other things—the pounding of his heart as he made his way across the asphalt; the quick knock; the sidling through the half-opened door before she could realize it wasn't her lover; the naked body cowering back into the sitting room; the taut white throat; the thrust with his filing bodkin that was as smooth as puncturing soft rubber. The steel had gone in so easily, so sweetly.

And there was something else which he had done to her. But that was something it was better not to remember. And afterward he had taken the bodkin back to the office, holding it under the tap in the washroom until no spot of blood could have remained. Then he had replaced it in his desk drawer with half a dozen identical others. There had been nothing to distinguish it any more, even to his eyes.

It had all been so easy. The only blood had been a gush on his right cuff as he withdrew the bodkin. And he had burned the coat in the office furnace. He still recalled the blast on his face as he thrust it in and the spilled cinders like sand under his feet.

There had been nothing left to him but the key of the flat. He had seen it on the sitting-room table and had taken it away with him. He drew it now from his pocket and compared it with the key from the Estate Agent, laying them side by side on his outstretched palm. Yes, they were identical. They had had another one cut, but no one had bothered to change the lock.

He stared at the key, trying to recall the excitement of those weeks when he had been both judge and executioner. But he could feel nothing. It was all so long ago. He had been fifty then; now he was sixty-six. It was too old for feeling. And then he recalled the words of Mr. Bootman. It was, after all, a very commonplace murder.

* * *

On Monday morning the girl in the Estate Office, clearing the mail from the letter box, called to the Manager.

"That's funny! The old chap who took the key to the Camden Town flat has returned the wrong one. This hasn't got our label on it. Unless he pulled it off. Cheek! But why would he do that?"

She took the key over to the Manager's desk, dumping his pile of letters in front of him. He glanced at it casually.

"That's the right key, anyway—it's the only one of that type we still have. Probably the label worked loose and fell off. You should put them on more carefully."

"But I did!" Outraged, the girl wailed her protest. The Manager winced.

"Then label it again, put it back on the board, and for God's sake don't fuss, that's a good girl."

She glanced at him again, ready to argue. Then she shrugged. Come to think of it he had always been a bit odd about that Camden Town flat.

"Okay, Mr. Morrisey," she said.

One Hit Wonder

Gabrielle Kraft

You probably don't remember me, but ten years ago I was very big. Matter of fact, in the record business I was what we call a one hit wonder. You know, the kind of guy you see on talk shows doing a medley of his hit? That was me, Ricky Curtis.

Remember "Ooo Baby Oooo"? Remember? "Ooo baby oooo, it's you that I do, it's you I truly do?" That was me, Ricky Curtis, crooning the insistent vocal you couldn't get out of your head, me with the moronic whine you loved to hate. Big? Hell, I was huge. "Ooo Baby Oooo" was a monster hit, triple platinum with a million bullets. That was Ricky Curtis, remember me now?

My God, it was great. You can't imagine how it feels, being on top. And it was so easy! I wrote "Ooo Baby Oooo" in minutes, while I was waiting for my teenage bride to put on her makeup, and the next day I played it for my boss at the recording studio where I had a job sweeping up. He loved it. We recorded it with some girl backup singers the next week, and it was alakazam Ricky.

For one long, brilliantly dappled summer, America knew my name and sang the words to my tune. People hummed me and sang me and whistled me, and my voice drifted out of car radios through the airwaves and into the minds of the world. For three sun-drenched months, I was a king and in my twenty-two-year-old wisdom I thought I would live forever.

Then, unaccountably, it was over. Because I didn't have a follow-up record, I was a one hit wonder and my just-add-water career evaporated like steam from a cup of coffee. I was ripped apart by confusion and I didn't know what to do next. Should I try to write more songs like "Ooo Baby Oooo"? I couldn't. Not because I didn't want to, but because I didn't know how. You see, I'd had visions of myself as a troubadour, a road-show Bob Dylan, a man with a message. A guy with heart. I hadn't envisioned myself as a man with a teenage tune wafting out across the shopping malls of the land, and "Ooo Baby Oooo" was merely a fluke, a twisting mirage in the desert. I was battered by doubt, and so, I did nothing. I froze, paralyzed in the klieg lights of L.A. like a drunk in a cop's high beams.

The upshot of my paralysis was that I lost my slot. My ten-second window of opportunity passed, and like a million other one hit wonders, I fell off the edge of the earth. I was yesterday's news. I couldn't get arrested, couldn't get a job. Not even with the golden oldies shows that go out on the tired road every summer, cleaning up the rock-and-roll dregs in the small towns, playing the little county fairs, not the big ones with Willie and Waylon, but the little ones with the racing pigs. I was an instant dinosaur, a joke, a thing of the past.

It hit me hard, being a has-been who never really was, and I couldn't understand what I'd done wrong. I'd signed over my publishing rights to my manager and dribbled away my money. In my confusion I started to drink too much—luckily I was too broke to afford cocaine. I drifted around L.A., hanging out in the clubs nursing a drink, telling my then-agent that I was "getting my head together," telling my then-wife that prosperity would burst over us like fireworks on the glorious Fourth and I'd have another big hit record any day now. Telling myself that I was a deadbeat washout at twenty-two.

Fade out, fade in. Times change and ten years pass, and Ricky Curtis, the one hit wonder, is now a bartender at Eddie Style's

Club Dingo above the Sunset Strip, shoving drinks across a huge marble bar stained a dark faux-malachite-green, smiling and giving a *c'est la vie* shrug if a well-heeled customer realizes that he's a guy who had a hit record once upon a sad old time.

But inside, I seethed. I smoldered. I didn't know what to do and so I did nothing. You don't know how it feels, to be so close to winning, to have your hand on the lottery ticket as it dissolves into dust, to feel the wheel of the red Ferrari one second before it slams into the wall. To smell success, taste the elixir of fame on your tongue, and then stand foolishly as your future rushes down the gutter in a swirl of brown, greasy water because of your inability to make a decision.

So I worked for Eddie Style. I had no choice. I groveled for tips and tugged my spiky forelock like the rest of the serfs; I smiled and nodded, but in the abyss I called my heart there was only anger. My rage at the crappy hand I'd been dealt grew like a horrible cancer eating me alive, and at night I dreamed of the Spartan boy and the fox.

I'd wake up every morning and think about money. Who had it, how to get it, why I didn't have it. In this town, the deals, the plans, the schemes to make money mutate with each new dawn. But I said nothing. I had nothing to say. I smiled, slid drinks across the bar and watched the wealthy enjoying themselves, waiting for crumbs to fall off the table. In a joint like the Dingo where the rich kids come out to play at night and the record business execs plant their cloven hooves in the trough at will, a few crumbs always fall your way.

Like when Eddie Style offered me a hundred thou to kill his wife.

Edward Woffard Stanhope III, known as Eddie Style to his friends and foes alike, owned the Club Dingo, and he was also a very rich guy. Not from the Dingo, or movie money, not record business money, not drug money, not at all. Eddie Style had something you rarely see if you float around the tattered edges of L.A. nightlife the way I do. Eddie Style had inherited money.

Edward Stanhope III, aka Eddie Style, came from a long line

of thieves, but since they were big thieves, nobody called them thieves; they called them Founding Fathers, or Society, or the Best People. Eddie's granddad, Edward Woffard Stanhope Numero Uno, known as "Steady," was one of the guys who helped loot the Owens Valley of its water, real *Chinatown* stuff. You know Stanhope Boulevard over in West Hollywood? Well, Eddie Style called it Me Street, that's the kind of money we're talking about here.

Trouble was, Eddie Style had bad taste in wives. He was a skinny little guy, and he wasn't very bright in spite of the fact that the accumulated wealth of the Stanhope family weighed heavy on his narrow shoulders. Plus, he liked tall women. They were always blond, willowy, fiscally insatiable and smarter than he was. Chrissie and Lynda, the first two, had siphoned off a hefty chunk of the Stanhope change, and Suzanne, the third blond beauty, had teeth like an alligator. At least, according to Eddie. I didn't know. They'd only been married two years and she didn't come around the Dingo. It was going to take another big slice of the pie to divest himself of Suzanne, and Eddie was getting cagey in his old age. After all, he wouldn't come into any more dough until his mother croaked, and she was only fifty-seven. He had a few siblings and half siblings and such scattered around, so a major outlay of capital on a greedy ex-wife didn't seem prudent.

So, one night after closing, he and I are mopping up the bar—I'm mopping up the bar, he's chasing down mimosas—and he starts complaining about his marital situation, just like he's done a thousand nights before.

"Suzanne's a nice girl," he sighed, "but she's expensive." His voice echoed through the empty room, bouncing off the up-ended chairs on the café tables, the ghostly stage and the rock-and-roll memorabilia encased in Plexiglas.

"You don't say?" In my present line of work, I've learned that noncommittal responses are the best choice, and I switch back and forth between "You don't say" and "No kidding" and "Takes all kinds." Oils the waters of drunken conversation.

"I *do* say. Ricky boy, I've been married three times," he said ruefully, "so I ought to know better by now. You see a girl, you think she's . . ." He narrowed his eyes, looked down the bar to the empty stage at the end of the room and gave an embarrassed shrug. "I dunno . . . the answer to a question you can't quite form in your mind. A hope you can't name."

"Takes all kinds." I nodded and kept on mopping the bar. Like I said, the Dingo was empty, Eddie Style was in a philosophical mood, and I had a rule about keeping my trap shut.

But he wouldn't quit. "You get married and you realize she's just another broad who cares more about getting her legs waxed than she does about you. I can't afford a divorce," he said, pinging the edge of his glass with his forefinger. It was middle C. "I don't have enough money to pay her off."

I felt my brain start to boil. He didn't have enough money! What a laugh! Isn't that the way the song always goes in this town? I love you baby, but not enough. I have money but not enough. To me, Eddie Style was loaded. He owned the Club Dingo, he drove a classic Mercedes with a license plate that read STYLEY, he lived in a house in the Hills, he wore Armani suits for business and Hawaiian shirts when he was in a casual mood. Oh yeah, Eddie Style had it all and Ricky Curtis had nothing.

"See, Ricky boy," he nattered as he took a slug of his fourth mimosa. "Guy like you, no responsibilities, you think life's a ball. Hey, you come to work, you go home, it's all yours. Me, I got the weight of my damn ancestors pushing on me like a rock. I feel crushed by my own history."

"Sisyphus," I said, wringing out the bar towel. After my divorce I'd gone to a few night classes at UCLA in hopes of meeting a girl with brains. Some fat chance. Even in Myths and Legends: A Perspective for Today, all the girls knew "Ooo Baby Oooo."

"Whatever," Eddie sighed. Ping on his glass again. "I can't take much more of this kinda life." He gestured absently at his darkened domain. "If only she'd die . . ." He looked up at me and shot a loud ping through the empty club. His lids peeled back from his eyes like skin from an onion, and he gave me a wise smile. "If only somebody'd give her a shove . . ."

"Hold on," I told him. "Wait a minute, Eddie. . . ."

He didn't say anything else, but it was too late. I could smell dark blood seeping over the layer of expensive crud that permeated the Dingo. He'd planted the idea in my brain, and it was putting out feelers like a science-fiction monster sprouting a thousand eyes.

For three nights I lay in my bed, drinking vodka, staring out the window of my one-bedroom apartment on Ivar, at the boarded-up crack house across the street, and thinking about money. If I had money, I could take a few months off, vacation in Mexico and jump start my life. I had no future as a bartender at the Club Dingo. If I stayed where I was—as I was—I would never change, and I *had* to revitalize my life or I would shrivel and die. If I could get out of L.A., lie on the beach for a month or two, maybe I could start writing songs again, maybe I could have another hit. Maybe *something* would happen to me. Maybe I'd get lucky. The way I saw things, it was her or me.

Three days later Eddie made me the offer. A hundred thou cash, no problems. He'd give me the keys to the house; I could pick the time and place and kill her any way I wanted.

"Look, Ricky boy, you've got a gun, right?" he said.

"A thirty-eight." I shrugged. "L.A.'s a crazy town."

"Great. Just shoot her, OK? Whack her over the head, I don't care. Do it fast so she won't feel anything. Make it look like a robbery, steal some jewelry. She's got it lying all over her dressing table; she won't use the damn safe. Christ, I gave her enough stuff the first year we were married to fill a vault; just take some of it, do what you want. Throw it down the drain, it doesn't matter. I just gotta get rid of her, OK?"

"OK, Eddie," I said. By the time he asked me to kill her, it was easy. I'd thought it all out; I knew he was going to ask me, and I knew I was going to do it. Ultimately, it came down to this. If murder was the only way to finance another chance, I would become a killer. I saw it as a career move.

I told him I'd do it. Eddie gave me a set of keys to his house and planned to be at the Dingo all night on Wednesday, my night off. He said it would be a good time to kill Suzanne, anxiously pointing out that he wasn't trying to tell me my job. It was all up to me.

I drove up to his house in the Hills; I'd been there for the Club Dingo Christmas party, so I was vaguely familiar with the layout. It was a Neutra house from the thirties, a huge white block hanging over the edge of the brown canyon like an albino vulture, and as I parked my dirty Toyota next to the red Rolls that Suzanne drove, I felt strong, like I had a rod of iron inside my heart. Suzanne would die, and I would rise like the phoenix from her ashes. I saw it as an even trade—my new life for her old life.

I opened the front door with Eddie's key and went inside, padding silently on my British Knights. My plan was to look around, then go upstairs to the bedroom and shoot her. Eddie said she watched TV most nights, used it to put her to sleep like I used vodka.

The entry was long, and there was a low, flat stairway leading down to the sunken living room. The drapes were pulled back, and I could see all of Los Angeles spread out through the floor-to-ceiling windows that lined the far wall. The shifting shapes of moving blue water in the pool below were reflected on the glass, and in that suspended moment I knew what it meant to live in a world of smoke and mirrors.

"Who the hell are you?" a woman snapped.

It was Suzanne and she had a gun. Dumb little thing, a tiny silver .25 that looked like it came from Le Chic Shooter, but it was a gun all the same. Eddie never mentioned that she had a gun, and I was angry. I hadn't expected it. I hadn't expected her either.

I'd met her at the Christmas party, so I knew she was gorgeous, but I'd been pretty drunk at the time and I wasn't paying attention. Suzanne Stanhope, nobody called her Suzie Style, was a dream in white. She was as tall as I was, and she had legs that would give a lifer fits.

"Eddie sent me," I said brightly. "He forgot his datebook. Didn't he call you? He said he was gonna . . ." I let my voice trail off and hoped I looked slack-jawed and stupid. I thought it was a damn good improvisation, and my ingratiating grin must have helped, because she lowered the gun.

"You're the bartender, the one who used to be a singer, right?" she asked. "Now I recognize you." She loosened up, but she didn't put down the gun.

This was going to be easy. I'd bust her in the head, steal the jewelry and be a new man by morning. I smiled, amazed that one woman could be so beautiful.

She was wearing a white dress, loose, soft material that clung to her body when she moved, and the worst part was, she wasn't even trying to be beautiful. Here she was, probably lying around in bed watching TV, painting her toenails, and she looked like she was going to the Oscars. Once again I saw the futility of life in L.A. without money.

"Tell Eddie I could have shot you," she said, very mild. "He'll get a kick out of that." She still had the little silver gun in her hand, but she was holding it like a pencil, gesturing with it.

"Sure will, Mrs. Stanhope," I said, grinning like an intelligent ape.

"Oh, cut the crap, will you? Just call me Suzanne." She looked me over, and I got the feeling she'd seen better in the cold case. "You want a drink, bartender? What's your name, anyway?"

"Ricky Curtis."

"Rick, huh?" She frowned and started humming my song. "How does that thing go?" she asked.

I hummed "Ooo Baby Oooo" for her. Her hair was shoulder length, blond, not brassy. Blue eyes with crinkles in the corners like she didn't give a damn what she laughed at. "Ooo baby oooo, it's you that I do, . . ." I hummed.

"So how come you don't sing anymore, Rick?" she asked as she led me down the steps into the sunken living room. I could see the lights of the city twinkling down below and idly wondered if, on a clear day, I'd be able to see my apartment on Ivar or the boarded-up crack house across the street.

"How come nobody asks me?" I said.

She went behind the bar, laughing as she poured herself a drink. Sounded like wind chimes. She put the little gun down on the marble bar, and it made a hollow clink.

"Vodka," I told her.

She poured me a shot in a heavy glass, and I drank it off. I had a strange feeling, and I didn't know why. I knew Eddie Style was rich, but this was unlike anything I'd ever seen before. The sheer weight of the Stanhope money was crushing me into the ground. Heavy gravity. I felt like I was on Mars.

She sipped her drink and looked thoughtfully out the huge windows, past the pale translucent lozenge of the pool toward the city lights below. "It's nice here," she said. "Too bad Eddie doesn't appreciate it. He'd have a better life if he appreciated what he has, instead of running around like a dog. The Dingo is aptly named, don't you think, Rick?"

I wanted another drink. I wanted to be drunk when I killed her, so I wouldn't feel it. I hadn't planned on killing a person, just a . . . a what? Just a blond body? Just a lump in the bed that could be anything? I hadn't counted on looking into her clear blue eyes as the light went out of them. I pushed my glass across the counter, motioning for another drink.

"So why are you here, Rick?" she asked softly. "It was a good story about the datebook but Eddie's too frazzled to keep one. I'm surprised you didn't know that about him. Maybe you two aren't as close as you think."

I didn't know what she meant. Was she kidding me? I couldn't tell. What was going on? I had that old familiar feeling of confusion, and once again, I was in over my head. Did she *know* I was there to kill her? I couldn't let her think that, so I did the next best thing. I confessed to a lesser crime.

"I'm broke," I said shortly, "and Eddie said the house was empty. I was here at the Christmas party and I figured I could bag some silver out of the back of the drawer. Maybe nobody would miss a few forks. It was a dumb idea but it's tap city and Eddie has more than he needs. Of everything," I said, looking directly at her. "You gonna call the cops?"

"Robbery? That's an exciting thought," she said, clinking the ice in her glass as she leaned her head back and popped an ice cube in her mouth. She took it out with her fingers and ran it over her lips. "You value Eddie's things, his lifestyle. Too bad he doesn't."

"In this town it's hard to appreciate what you have," I said slowly, wondering how her lips would feel, how cold they really were. "Everybody always wants what they can't get."

"Don't they," she said meaningfully as she dropped the ice cube back in her glass. "What do *you* want, Rick? Since you brought it up."

"Me? I want money," I said. As the phrase popped out of my mouth I realized how pathetic it sounded. Like a teenager wanting to be a rock star, I wanted money. That's the trouble with L.A. Being a bartender isn't a bad gig, but in L.A., it's just a rest stop on the freeway to fame, a cute career to spice up your résumé.

"That shouldn't be tough for a good-looking guy like you. Not in this town." She refilled our glasses and led me over to a white couch. There were four of them in an intimate square around a free-form marble table. I felt like I was somebody else. I'd only had a couple short ones and I was wondering what she wanted in a man. I wondered if she was lonely.

"Sit down," she said, her white dress splitting open to show me those blond legs. "Let's talk, Rick," she said.

"Sure I married him because he's rich, just like he married me because I'm beautiful," she said, running a finger across my stomach. "But I thought there was more to it than that. He was sweet to me at first. He didn't treat me like some whore who spent her life on her knees. Christ, I'm tired of men who want me because I'm beautiful and then don't want me because I'm smart. Am I smart, Rick?" she asked, pulling the sheet around her body as she got out of bed. "Want anything?"

Mars. I was on Mars. You hang around L.A., you think you know the words to the big tune, but you don't. You think you've seen a lot, know it all, but you don't, and as I lay in his bed caressing his wife, I wondered how it would feel to be Eddie Style. Live in his house, sleep with his wife. If I had a room like this, why would I ever leave it? If I had a wife like that, why would I want to kill her? The sheets were smooth, some kind of expensive cotton the rich like; the carpet was soft—was it silk? The glinting perfume bottles on her dressing table were heavy, geometrically cut glass shapes twinkling with a deep interior light far brighter than the city below. If I unstoppered one of those bottles, what would I smell?

She let the sheet drop to the floor as she lowered herself into the bubbling blue marble tub at the far end of the room. I lay in Eddie's bed and watched her as she stretched her head back and exposed a long white highway of throat pointing to a dark and uncharted continent. I thought about killing her and realized it was too late.

"This is insane," I said.

She laughed. "It's so L.A., isn't it? The bartender and the boss's wife, the gardener and the . . ."

"Yeah, I read *Lady Chatterly*. I'm not a complete illiterate," I told her. "What do you want to do about it?"

"Oh, we could get together afternoons in cheesy motels," she said. "Think you'd like that?"

"Sounds great," I said ironically. "Don't you think you'd find cheesy motels boring after a while? Say, after a week or so?" I got up out of bed, went over to the tub and got in with her. The water warmed me to the bone. "You could come live with me in my one-bedroom. You'd fit in just fine. Course, you'd have to leave this house behind," I said as I slipped my hands underneath her body and lifted her on top of me. "And there wouldn't be much time for shopping since you'd have to get a job slinging fries. Think you'd miss the high life?"

"Probably," she gasped.

"Yeah, I think so too. But we can talk about it later, right?"

"Right," she said, clutching at my back with those beautifully sculpted nails. "Yessss."

Of course, I left without killing Suzanne. Then I went back to the Dingo and yelled at Eddie, which was a laugh since I'd been rolling around with his wife all evening. Funny thing, though. As I stared at Eddie Style, sitting on his usual stool at the long faux-malachite bar, I felt contempt for him. He had everything, Eddie did. Money, cars, a beautiful wife. But he didn't know what he had, and that made him a bigger zero than I was. Even with all that money.

"Why the hell didn't you tell me she had a gun?" I snarled over the blast of the head-banging band onstage. I'd never snarled at him before, and it felt good.

"I forgot," he said, very apologetic as he tugged on his mimosa. "Really, Ricky boy, I didn't think about it. It's just a little gun. . . ."

"Easy for you to say," I grumbled. "Don't worry about it, man. I'll take care of it for you."

But I didn't.

I called Suzanne a few days later, she came over to my apartment and we spent the afternoon amusing ourselves.

"Why don't you fix this place up?" she said. "It doesn't have to look like a slum, Rick."

"Sure it does. It *is* a slum," I told her, stroking the long white expanse of her back. "You think it's *La Bohème*? Some sort of arty dungeon? Look out the window, it's a slum."

"Don't complain, you've got me. And," she said as she got out of bed and went over to her purse, "now you've got a nice watch instead of that cheapo."

You think your life changes in grand, sweeping gestures—the day you have your first hit, the day you get married, the day you get divorced—but it doesn't. Your life changes when you stretch out your hand and take a flat velvet-covered jeweler's box with a gold watch inside that costs two or three thousand dollars. Your life changes when you don't care how you got it.

When you're a kid, you never think the situation will arise. You think you'll be a big star, a hero, a rock legend; you don't think you'll be lying in bed in a crummy Hollywood apartment with another guy's wife and she'll be handing you a little gift. Thanks, honey, you were great.

I took the watch. A week later, I took the five hundred bucks she gave me "for groceries." You see the situation I was in? Here I was, supposed to kill Eddie Style's wife for a hundred thousand dollars, and I was too busy boffing her to get the job done. Me, the guy who was so hungry for cash that his hands vibrated every time he felt the walnut dash on a Mercedes.

I was swept by the same confusion I'd felt after "Ooo Baby Oooo." Once again I was staring out over a precipice into an endless expanse of possibilities, and I didn't know what to do. I was looking at a row of choices lined up like prizes at a carnival, and the barker was offering me any prize I wanted. But which one should I take? The doll? The stuffed monkey? The little toy truck? Reach out and grab it, Ricky boy. How do you make a decision that will determine the course of your life? A thick, oozing paralysis sucked at me like an oil slick.

All I had to do was kill her and I couldn't do it. When she wasn't around I fantasized about taking her out for a drive and tossing her down a dry well out in Palm Desert or giving her a little shove over the cliff as we stared at the sunset over the Pacific. But when she was around, I knew it was impossible. I couldn't kill Suzanne. Her beauty held me like a vise.

Beautiful women don't understand their power; their hold on men is far greater than they comprehend. Women like Suzanne sneer at their beauty; they think it's a happy accident. Mostly they think it's a commodity, sometimes they think it's a gift, but they don't understand what the momentary possession of that beauty does to a man, how it feels to see perfection lying beside you in bed, to stare at flawless grace as it sleeps and you know you can touch it at will.

The flip side of my problem was that a rich guy like Eddie Style didn't understand that possessing a woman like Suzanne made me his equal. Within the four corners that comprise the enclosed world of a bed, a fool like me is equal to generations of Stanhope money.

"So, Ricky boy, when you gonna do that thing?" Eddie asked me late one night, giving me a soft punch on the arm. He's acting like it's a joke, some kind of a scene. Kill my wife, please.

"Don't pressure me, Eddie; you want it done fast, do it yourself." Now that I was a hired gun, I no longer felt the need to kiss the hem of his garment quite so fervently or quite so often. Weird, what power does to you. You start sleeping with a rich guy's wife, you feel like a superhero, an invincible Saturday morning kiddie cartoon. "If you'd told me about the gun, I would have killed her that first night. Now the timing's screwed up."

This was true, and it creased a further wrinkle into my murderous plans. The vacationing couple was back at work at Eddie's big white house in the daytime, so it was no longer possible to slip in and kill Suzanne even if I'd had the guts to do it. Too many people around.

Besides, I was no longer an anonymous cipher, a faceless killer. I was a piece of Suzanne's life, although Eddie didn't know it. Now that she was coming to my apartment for nooners, I knew we'd been seen together. The elderly lady with ten thousand cats who lived across the courtyard and peeked out between her venetian blinds at people coming in and going out, Suzanne's big red Rolls parked on Ivar—there were too many telltale traces of my secret life, traces that would give me away if I *did* kill her.

So there I was, stuck between skinny Eddie Style and his beautiful wife, and it was at this point that a brilliant idea occurred to me. What if I killed Eddie Style? What if I killed the husband and not the wife? Assuming Suzanne approved of the idea, it would have a double-edged effect; it would cement Suzanne to all that Stanhope money and it would cement me to Suzanne. For I had no intention of allowing her to remain untouched by Eddie's death, if I chose to kill him instead of her.

Turnabout.

But would Suzanne take to the idea of killing her husband? Would she see me as a lout, as a sociopathic lunatic, or merely as the opportunistic infection I truly was? Or would she, too, see murder as a career move?

At night I worked at the Dingo, and though I poured drinks, laughed and chatted with the customers, I was changed inside, tempered by my connection to death. Now that I was concentrating on murder, I was no longer a failure, a one hit wonder. I was invaded by the knowledge that I possessed a secret power setting me apart from the faceless ants who surrounded me in the bar. A few weeks ago, I was a shabby, sad wreck tossed up on the shores of Hollywood with the rest of the refuse, the flotsam and jetsam of the entertainment business. Now that I was dreaming about murder, I was on top again, and I had the potential of ultimate power.

A week later I decided to talk to Suzanne about killing Eddie. I had no intention of bringing up the question directly; I was too clever for that. I planned to approach her crabwise, manipulate our pillow talk in the direction of murder. If she picked up the cue, well and good. If not, I'd have to alter my plans where she was concerned.

It was Wednesday, my night off, and Eddie was at the Dingo. I called Suzanne and said I'd be at her house that night. She wasn't too happy that I was coming over, but I let my voice go all silky and told her I felt like a hot bath.

The white Neutra house was lit up by soft floodlights, and as I knocked on the door, it reminded me of the glistening sails of tall ships flooding into a safe harbor bathed in sunshine.

The door opened. It was Eddie Style. "Do you think you should be here, Ricky boy?" he asked, very mildly.

Not a good sign. I had a moment of fear, but I covered it. I was feeling omnipotent, and besides, I had my .38 in my jacket pocket. "You mean we've got to stop meeting like this?" I mocked. Simultaneously, I knew I was in over my head and apprehension started nibbling at my shoes.

He held open the door for me, and I went inside, automatically stepping down into the sunken living room. Suzanne, wearing a white kimono with deep, square sleeves, was sitting on the couch, a drink in her hand. Her nails shone red as an exploding sun and her face was flat, expressionless. All the beauty had drained out of it, and there was only the molded mask of a mannequin staring back at me from behind a thick sheet of expensive plate glass. Who was she?

Confusion swept me, and I was carried off down the river like a dinghy in a flash flood.

"Here we all are," Eddie said. "Drink?"

I nodded yes. "Vodka."

"Ricky boy," he said as he went behind the bar, "I've had you followed and I know you're sleeping with my wife. I'm afraid I can't stand still for that," he said slowly. "When the help gets out of line it makes me look foolish and I simply can't allow it to go unpunished." He reached underneath the bar and pulled out the shiny silver .25 Suzanne pointed at me that first night.

Now the dinghy was caught in a whirlpool. "I'm sorry, Eddie," I said. "These things . . . just happen." I indicated Suzanne. "I'm sorry."

"Ricky boy, I know what you think. I've seen you operate." His voice was cold and he was still holding the gun. "You think because I'm rich you can come along, skim a little cream off the top and I'm so stupid I won't notice. You think you're as good as I am, street-smart Ricky boy, the one hit wonder. Wrong, buddy. Dead wrong. You're not as good as I am and you never will be."

The absurd little gun was firmer in his hand, and I had the cold, cold feeling he was going to shoot me. He'd claim I was a robber, that his faithful minion had betrayed his trust. Who'd dare to call Edward Woffard Stanhope III a liar? With his beautiful wife Suzanne by his side to back up his story, why would anybody try?

I looked at Suzanne. Her face was unmoved. I felt empty and desperate in a way I hadn't felt since I'd started sleeping with her. I'd had a taste of invincibility in her bed, but she was giving me up without a backward glance; I could read the news on the shroud that passed as her face. I felt like a fool. What made me think she'd choose me instead of the unlimited pool of Stanhope money? Once Eddie killed me, she'd have him forever. He'd never be able to divorce her; they'd be locked in the harness until the earth quit spinning and died.

"Eddie, that's not it," I said. I heard the helplessness in my own voice. I sounded tinny, like a playback. "OK, man, it was a mistake to get involved with your wife. I know that. I'm sorry." I was trying to sound contrite, once again the serf tugging his forelock. I walked over to him and shifted my right side, the side with the gun in the pocket, up against the bar so neither of them could see what I was doing. Slowly, I dropped my hand and began to inch my fingers toward the gun.

"Yeah?" he laughed, an eerie sound like wind whining down a tunnel. "Tell me how sorry you are."

Confusion butted heads with omnipotence. This was the time, the moment, my last chance for a comeback, and I gave omnipotence free rein as I kept inching my hand toward the gun in my pocket. "Ever try, Eddie? Ever try and fail? You've never had to work, rich boy. You have it all. The house, the wife, the car. You want to own a nightclub? Buy one. You want your wife killed? Hire it done."

Suzanne gasped out loud. "Killed?" she said slowly. "You wanted me *killed*?" she asked Eddie, her voice thick with distaste.

"He promised me a hundred thou to get rid of you, princess. Ain't that a kick in the head?"

"Rick, you were going to kill me?" she asked. "That first night, you were here to kill me. . . ." Now she was thoughtful, pondering her own murder like a stock portfolio.

Eddie Style said nothing.

My fingers closed on the gun and I turned toward him, slowly. "Think about living without that mass of cash behind you, that blanket of money. Ain't easy, Eddie. But you'll never know 'cause whatever happens, you've always got a fallback position. The rich always do."

It wasn't until I said it that I realized how much I hated him, how much I hated his flaccid face, his thin shoulders that had never seen a goddamn day's work, his weak mind that never had to make a tough decision, his patrician arrogance. I pulled the gun out of my pocket, fired and caught him right between the eyes.

I heard Suzanne shriek as blood sprayed out of the back of Eddie's head, splattering the polished sheen of the mirror on the back bar with a fine mist. His body crashed to the floor, taking a row of heavy highball glasses with it, shattering a few bottles. The smell of blood and gin filled the air. I didn't give a damn.

It was all mine. At last I'd turned myself inside out, and the mildewed scent of failure that had clung to me was gone. I was no longer a grinning monkey at the Club Dingo, but Zeus. A king. I was on top, a winner at last.

"Your turn, love," I said softly. "What's it gonna be? The way I see things," I said, pocketing the gun as I went over and sat down on the couch beside her, "Eddie just struck out and I'm on deck. He's dead, I'm alive and you're rich. Time to choose up sides for the Series."

She shuddered like a stalled Ford. "You killed him. You killed Eddie." Her voice was quiet and she sounded vaguely surprised.

"Yeah. I did. Now, you got two choices. You can do what I tell you to do or you can die."

"I thought you said two choices, Rick. I only heard one," she said carefully. Her voice had changed, and her face was no longer an expressionless mask. "Can I go look?" she asked as she got up and went behind the bar. She stood there for a minute, looking down at her dead husband; then she bent down and touched his cheek. "What do you want me to do?" she asked me as she straightened up.

"First thing I want, I want you to come over here and wrap your prints around my gun," I told her. "That'll keep you in line just in case you get tired of me, some faraway night when we're under the stars on the Mexican Riviera. I'll keep the gun for insurance."

"Don't you trust me?"

"This is L.A. I don't trust anybody who's ever breathed smog. Then I give you a black eye and leave. I won't hurt you, much. You call the cops and say a bad, bad robber broke in and killed hubby. You'll have a rough few months, but I'll take care of the Dingo and we can meet there once in a while. Maybe next year, we'll get married. Think you'd like a June wedding?"

"You're a cold son of a bitch; how come I didn't notice it before?"

"You weren't interested in my mind, Suzanne. Look, baby, now that Eddie's out of the picture we can have it all. Don't you understand, I can't afford to blow this off. I had one hit, I blew it. Usually, one hit is all you get in this town but I got a second chance tonight and I'm taking it. I'm not gonna get another. Ever."

"Why did he want me killed?" she said, looking down at Eddie's bloody body.

"Do you have to know? Money, OK? Isn't it always money? He said you cost too much and he didn't have enough money to pay you off."

"Greedy hog," she said and made an ugly snorting noise. "But that's what they all say, right, Ricky boy?"

I walked over to her, very fast, and slapped her in the face, very hard. "Never call me Ricky boy again, Suzanne," I said, a tight hold on her arm. "Call me honey or sweetie or baby or call me you jerk, but don't ever call me Ricky boy."

She pulled away from me, rubbing the red spot on her cheek where I'd hit her. "Why'd you have to hit me? I wish the hell you hadn't hit me. . . ." Her voice trailed off like a little girl's as she stepped back, leaned against the bar and buried her hands in the deep sleeves of her white kimono. She looked up at me and I saw death in her eyes. My death.

I saw it all and there was nothing I could do. She smiled and seemed to move very, very slowly, though in the back of my mind I knew everything was happening normally, skipping along in real time. The little silver gun slipped into her hand like a fish eager for the baited hook, and I realized she'd picked it up when she'd knelt down next to Eddie's dead body. She aimed it at me and fired. I watched as the gun leapt back in her hand and the bullet jumped straight for my heart.

I felt the slug sink into my body, only a .25, I told myself, a girl's gun, nothing to worry about. But Suzanne's aim was true. I put my hand to my chest and it felt scorched and fiery, like I'd fallen asleep with the hot water bottle on my naked flesh. I took my hand away and looked at it foolishly. Red. I had a red hand. Where the hell did I get a red hand? I was hot and tired and all of a sudden I thought a nap would do me good. Somewhere far away I heard her voice. . . .

"You were right, Rick. In this town, one hit is all you get."

The Reluctant Detective

Michael Z. Lewin

It was a Tuesday. I remember because when the doorbell rang I was reading the weekly basketball column in *The Guardian* newspaper—I try to keep up with some of my old interests from the USA, see. It was about ten o'clock and I thought it might be the man to read the gas meter. Dawn was out, visiting her cousin—she's got as many relatives in this little town as I have none, so to speak. A lot is what I am saying.

At the door was a sallow-faced little man—well, I suppose he was about average height for England, but I am awkwardly tall at six foot eight, so I have a distorted perspective on people. He wore a jacket and tie and even though it wasn't raining just then, he looked unhappy.

I thought, not the gas man but maybe a local government official.

"Are you Mr. Herring?" he asked.

"Yes."

"May I talk to you?"

"What about?" I asked.

He glanced at the sign on the house wall by the door. It's so small you can hardly see it even if you know it's there. The minimum size to fulfill legal requirements, Dawn's half-nephew

George said. George and his wife run a sign business here in town.

The man said, "Are you the Mr. Herring who is a private inquiry agent?"

And I suddenly realized he had come on business. I was stunned. I was shocked. Things had been going so well.

I began to shake though I don't know if he noticed but I said, "Yes, yes, of course. Fredrick Herring. Do come in."

For lack of anywhere better, I led him to our living room.

"I like to keep things informal," I said as I cleared the cat off the couch to make some sitting space for the man. "I think people often find it hard to speak freely in a formal office atmosphere," I said. Which I thought was pretty good, off the cuff.

We sat down.

I didn't know what to say next.

But the man made the running. "My name is Goodrich," he said.

"Hi."

"I don't know whether I should even be here."

"It's not a step to take lightly," I said.

"I'm not," he said. "I'm not."

"Oh."

"I don't know whether you know me?"

"No."

"I am a solicitor with Malley, Holmes and Asquith, but I need someone to conduct an investigation for me on a private matter."

"I see."

"Well, you do that kind of thing, don't you?"

He looked at me. There was something devious in his eyes. And I had another sudden shock—suspicion.

You see, Dawn and I had agreed that if ever anybody tried to hire us, we would say we were too busy to take the case on. But there was something about this guy. The same thing that made me think he might be a council official. I suddenly got this idea that he was from one of the tax offices, that he might be checking up on us.

My initial hot flush of embarrassment that somebody might actually want to hire *me* as a detective was replaced by the cold draught of imminent accusation, prosecution.

"Of course," I said. "Fredrick Herring, private detective, at your service."

2

It all began as a tax fiddle, see. Just about the time I had convinced myself for the tenth and final time that I did not want to spend the rest of my life being a bad lawyer, I inherited this house in England and this bit of an income from my Uncle Ted. So, what more natural than to skip over the ocean for a while, see my house, have a think?

Oh, have I said where I am? It's in this little town called Frome, which they pronounce like it was spelled Froom. It's out in the country and is pretty enough that even some English people come as tourists.

Well, you know how life goes. I was here a while and I damaged my knee and met this girl who was just deciding she didn't want to spend the rest of her life being a bad physiotherapist. And after I had a bit of treatment she moved in with me. What with my having this money coming in regularly, we were having a most sympatico time. Not dropouts. Just taking our time deciding about futures and careers.

The tax fidd . . . tax avoidance structurization didn't come up till I had been here a year or so. In fact, it was Dawn's idea, like so many of the crafty things are. In that sense everything that's happened is down to her. In another sense it's down to the root of all evil.

It's just we began to realize there were things we would like to do but didn't have the money for.

Get a car, for instance. Nothing flash, but some wheels to see some more of the country with. And to take some strain off my knee. Yes, it was wanting a car that set us thinking in the first place.

Or set Dawn thinking, actually. She's like that. Don't know

whether it comes from fighting for survival in a big family, but she's got this kind of mind that finds ways to do things. There's something tricky about it, and I sometimes think that maybe *she* would have made the good lawyer. She says I have physiotherapeutic potential too, but that's something else.

Well, her idea was this. If I set up in business, as a self-employed person I could save money in taxes by claiming a lot of our expenses were for the business. The details were all British tax law stuff, but Dawn worked it out and there was no question, it would pay for the car. And maybe a little bit more as we went along.

The question was what kind of business to supposedly set up in. That was Dawn's idea too. See, in Britain you don't need a licence of any kind. And, I have to admit, we yielded to a certain pleasant absurdity attached to the notion. I mean, a private detective, in Frome!

As well, the chances of anybody coming to us for business were, of course, nil.

We didn't want the business to succeed, or, indeed, for there to be any work at all. What we wanted were the deductions. It was all a tax fiddle. As I've mentioned.

And everything was going great until I found myself in my living room listening to a guy in a jacket and tie unburdening his problems to me.

3

Dawn was not pleased when she returned to the house and found that I had taken a case. She's not a big girl, Dawn, not in the sense of tall, but when she's upset she kind of grows. And shakes. And goes all red in the face.

"We agreed!" she said when I told her. "We agreed!" She was vermillion and wobbling and I feared for the tray of eggs that she had brought back from her cousin who had got it half price from a guy who works parttime at the egg farm on the Marston side of town.

But I explained what had happened and about this devious

look in the guy's eyes, and then she accepted the situation as a fact.

We put the eggs away and had a hug and when she was back to her normal color I told her what this Mr. Goodrich wanted us to do.

"It's about his brother-in-law, a guy named Chipperworth, who is a crook," I said.

"Chipperworth . . ." Dawn said. She was thinking. She's lived in Frome all her life and knows a lot of people.

"He has a company that manufactures beds, up on the industrial development. The brand name is Rest Easy."

"Ah."

"You know it?"

"Rest Easy, yes. My Auntie Vi worked up there a few years ago until she had the twins."

"And this man Goodrich says that Chipperworth set fire to a warehouse next to his factory and collected the insurance for it."

"I read about the fire," Dawn said. "But not that it was on purpose. How does Goodrich know?"

"He says Chipperworth was bragging yesterday that he had just collected a cheque for over three hundred thousand pounds and it was for beds he wasn't going to be able to sell."

Dawn seemed to hear this information with at least a little touch of envy, but she said, "But why doesn't Goodrich go to the police?"

"Because that's not what he's trying to sort out."

"Oh."

"What he's worried about is his sister. That Chipperworth is a crook, and that he's dangerous. He wants his sister to divorce Chipperworth."

Dawn cocked her head.

"But his sister refuses to believe the stuff about the insurance fraud."

"What are *we* supposed to do about that?"

"Nothing. What Goodrich wants us to prove is that Chipperworth has a woman on the side. If we can do that, then the sister will divorce him and will be safe. Goodrich is sure that his sister will get a divorce in the end anyway, but if he precipitates it at least she'll be well off financially. If he waits till Chipperworth's activities catch up with him, then it might ruin the sister too."

"Oh," Dawn said.

"I agreed to try. I felt in the circumstances I had to."

She nodded resignedly. Then she looked at me.

And I looked at her.

We were thinking the same thing.

I said, "What the hell do we do now?"

4

All we knew about private detecting was what we'd seen in the movies. But we talked about it over a cup of tea and decided that we would try to go through the motions, as best we could think of them. The first motion was to find Chipperworth and identify him.

It wasn't hard. Mr. Goodrich had given me a photograph and we took the car and hung around outside Rest Easy Beds toward the end of the work day. We realized that we might be sitting around in the car for quite a while with nothing to do, so we brought the cat and when we got tired of trying to teach it tricks Dawn spent some time telling me about her wild youth.

About five thirty we heard a horn from inside the factory and people began to leave. Rest Easy was not a big company. We counted fifteen before Chipperworth came out. He left about six and got into a new red Mercedes.

"OK," Dawn said. "There he is. What do we do now?"

"Drive along after him, I guess," I said.

Chipperworth went directly to a house on the Prowtings Development. He pulled the car into the driveway. Got out. Went to front door. Was met by a woman, 6:06 P.M.

Then Chipperworth went into the house and closed the door.

That would have wrapped the case up if the house hadn't been his home address and the woman his wife.

Dawn and I sat.

"At least we know the licence number of his car now," I said after ten minutes.

But we were both sinking fast.

After another twenty minutes the cat showed distinct signs of feline restlessness. So did Dawn. She said, "This is no good. What are we going to do, sit out here all night without any food or anything? The cat's hungry. I'm hungry."

After some consideration, we decided to get fish and chips from Pangs, satisfying all palates.

When we got back, Chipperworth's car was gone.

5

Solicitor Goodrich rang up at nine the next morning. He seemed annoyed that I didn't have anything to report.

I explained that in the detective business progress is not always rapid, that we'd had less than a day on the job, that patience was a virtue.

But Goodrich knew that Chipperworth had been out the previous night. He'd called his sister and she told him.

"If you want to do the surveillance yourself," I said, "please say so. Otherwise, leave it to us."

He took a breath, then apologized—rather unconvincingly, I thought—and we hung up.

I told Dawn about the call. Neither of us was happy.

"I'm going to see a couple of my cousins," she said.

I looked puzzled.

"Nigel is a telephone engineer. He's a nut case and would probably enjoy finding a way to tap the Chipperworths' telephone. And Paul works in the photographic section at B & T." Butler and Tanner is the big local printing firm. "He is a camera buff. He'll lend us a camera with a telephoto lens."

I sat silently for a moment. "Look, babe," I said. "We're on the verge of taking this seriously in spite of ourselves."

"I know," she said quietly. She took my hand. "But what can we do? If we don't get it sorted out quickly it's going to mess up our lives for weeks. We can hardly go to London next Friday if we've got a client calling up every day asking for a list of the things we've done on his case."

We take a lot of little trips now we have the car, me and Dawn. This one to London was for a basketball tournament. Sometimes it's concerts. She's crazy for The Police, Dawn. Some perverse appeal about the name, I always think. We also go to plays and look at museums and keep track of what's happening in the world. We may live like wastrels now, but we always planned to amount to something. One day.

"If it goes on for long," she said, "we'll have to do shifts to cover Chipperworth for the whole day. We may have to borrow another car. I ought to be able to use Adele's Mini. You remember Adele?"

"No."

"She's the small one with the big—"

"I remember now," I said.

Biggest feet I'd ever seen.

"I just wish I knew someone who could lend us a two-way radio."

"There's your step-brother Mike," I said, remembering his reputation as a CB hobbyist.

"So there is," she said. Then made a face. "But he already pinches and pokes whenever I get close enough. What he'd want for doing me a favor . . ."

"We'll get along without," I said firmly.

6

In the end it only took a day.

It was the afternoon of my first shift. I was fitted out with a thermos, sandwiches and a radio. Even a specimen bottle—from Dawn's friend Elaine, the nurse—in case time was short and need was great.

As you can tell, when Dawn and I get down to it, we're impressive.

The camera from Paul was one of those instant print jobs. No time waiting for the film to come back from the developers. And, Paul said, "Considering what kind of pictures you may get, a commercial firm might not print them." Does a great leer, does Paul.

He also gave us a foot-long lens for the thing. "It'll put you in their pockets. If they're wearing pockets."

And Cousin Nigel jumped at the chance to plant a tape recorder up a telephone pole outside the Chipperworths' home. He volunteered to tap the company phone too. Well, you don't turn down offers like that.

It's struck me that *all* of Dawn's family are just that little bit shady. I offer it as an observation, not a complaint. It's part of what makes her an unusual girl. She can juggle too. I'm terrifically fond of her.

Anyway, after an hour's lunch at home, Chipperworth did not go back to his office. He drove instead out Bath Road and pulled into the driveway of a detached brick house just beyond the town limits. I parked in front of the cottage next door. I left the car and got the camera aimed and focused just in time to see Chipperworth open the door to the house with a key.

The picture came out a treat.

I stood there in the road looking at it. And wondering what to do next.

But Dawn and I had talked it through. First I made a note of the time, date and location on the back of the photograph. Then I set about trying to find out who lived in the house.

I went to the cottage and rang the bell. And had a little luck.

A tiny old woman with big brown eyes came to the door. I said, "Excuse me. I have a registered letter for the people next door, but nobody answers when I knock on the door."

"That's because Wednesday afternoons Mrs. Elmitt has her fancy man in," the old woman said. "And she wouldn't want to be answering the door then, would she? Some of the things I've seen! And they don't even bother to draw the curtains."

Old women can do pretty good leers too, when they try.

"Come in," she said. "Have a look for yourself."

7

Dawn was chuffed, which means pleased as punch. I was pretty pleased too. The wretched case would soon be over and we could get back to life as usual. I resolved to try to arrange for my income to arrive from America so that it looked more like proceeds of the business. Then we wouldn't have to worry about being inspected by the tax people. Worry is a terrible thing.

But just about the time that Dawn and I were getting ready to be chuffed with each other, Cousin Nigel showed up at the front door.

He punched me on the shoulder as he came in, and gave Dawn a big kiss. A hearty type is Nigel.

"I've got your first tape," he said jovially. "Thought you would want to hear it sooner rather than later, so I put another cassette in the machine and brought this one right over. Got any beer?" He dropped into our most comfortable chair. "Hey Dawnie, how about something to eat? Egg and chips? Hungry work, bugging telephones."

The tape was a revelation.

Right off, the very first phone call, and the man was saying, "Darling. I can't wait until I see you again."

And the woman: "I don't know whether I'll be able to bear not being with you full time for very much longer."

"It will be soon. We'll be together, forever. Someplace nice. Away from your wretched husband."

"I don't know what will become of me if our plan doesn't work."

"It will work. We'll make it work."

"Oh darling, I hope so."

And on and on. There were a lot of slobbering sounds too. I would have been embarrassed if I hadn't been so upset.

"Wow!" Nigel said. "All that kissy-kissy, and before lunch too. They must have it bad."

Dawn said, "Isn't that great! We've got all we need now, Freddie, don't you think?"

But I was not happy, not even close.

Because, unlike my two colleagues, I had recognized one of the voices. The man's. The conversation was not between Mr. Chipperworth and Mrs. Elmitt. The man on the telephone was our client, Mr. Goodrich, and the object of his affection was, presumably, Mrs. Chipperworth. His "sister."

8

We got rid of Nigel without even offering seconds of chips. There was no law that a client had to tell us the truth. But neither of us liked it. Yet what can you do?

What we did first was go the next morning to Dawn's great-uncle Steve, who is a police sergeant. We asked him about the fire in the Rest Easy Beds warehouse.

"Always knew it was arson," great-uncle Steve said. "But we couldn't prove who did it. The owner was the only possible beneficiary, but he had an airtight alibi. He was at a civic function with the mayor and he was in full sight, the whole evening."

"I see," Dawn said.

"I interviewed Chipperworth myself," Great-uncle Steve said, "and he was quite open about being delighted about the fire. Business wasn't very good and he was having trouble moving the stock that was destroyed. Personally, I don't think he *did* have anything to do with it. I've been at this job long enough to get a good sense of people, and that's the way he came across."

"I see," Dawn said.

"But we never got so much as a whiff of any other suspect. Checked current and past employees for someone with a grievance. Sounded out all our informants in town for a word about anybody who had heard anything about it. But we didn't get so much as a whisper. It's very unusual for us not to get some kind of lead if we try that hard. In the end, it was written off to kids.

There are so many of them unemployed these days that we are getting all sorts of vandalism."

"Thanks, Uncle Steve," Dawn said.

"Helps you, does that?" he asked.

"I think so."

Great-uncle Steve gave Dawn a hard squint. "If you know anything about the case, you must tell me. You know that, don't you, Dawn?"

"Yes, Uncle Steve."

He studied her and shook his head. Then he said to me, "Young man, there is a look in her eyes that I don't like. You watch yourself."

He was right, of course. Dawn was cooking something up, and it wasn't chips.

When we got home we sat down over a nice cup of tea. She hadn't said a word for the whole drive.

I couldn't bear it any longer. I said, "All right. What *is* the significance of that funny look?"

"I've decided we're going to get Mrs. Chipperworth that divorce after all."

"We are?"

"It's what we were hired to do, isn't it?"

9

I called Solicitor Goodrich to tell him that we had had success in our investigation and to ask if he wanted our report.

He did. He was with us within twenty minutes.

I explained what I had seen the previous afternoon. I gave him the photographs I had taken of Chipperworth entering Mrs. Elmitt's house with a key and, later, adjusting his tie as he came out. Also one or two pocketless ones in between. I explained that the old woman would be willing to testify to the lurid details of what she had seen through Mrs. Elmitt's undrawn curtains. "But I think she would like a little expense money if she does testify," I said.

"I'm sure that can be arranged," Goodrich said through his smiles.

A little ready cash might help the old woman get some curtains for her own windows.

After Goodrich left I rang Rest Easy Beds.

I explained to Mr. Chipperworth that Dawn and I wanted to speak to him immediately.

"What is it that is so urgent, Mr. Herring?" he asked.

"We want to tell you about your wife's plans to sue you for divorce," I said.

As soon as we arrived we were ushered into Chipperworth's office.

"But Felicity's known about Madeleine for years," he said when I explained what we'd been hired to do. "It's an arrangement we have. Felicity doesn't like *it*, you see. So Madeleine keeps me from making . . . demands."

"Felicity doesn't seem to mind *it* with her lover," Dawn said.

"Her what?" Chipperworth asked, suddenly bug-eyed.

"Why don't you ask about her recent telephone calls," Dawn suggested. "We have to be going now. Ta ta."

After stopping at Nigel's, we went on home.

We didn't have long to wait.

A few minutes after noon the bell rang. Before I could get to it, pounding started on the door. When I opened it I faced a furious Solicitor Goodrich. He swung fists at me.

For the most part being as tall as I am is an inconvenience. But at least I have long arms and could keep him out of reach. When he finished flailing, he started swearing. The language seemed particularly unseemly for a member of the legal profession. I would have been embarrassed for Dawn if I hadn't heard worse from her own family. But they are foulmouthed in a friendly way. Goodrich was vicious.

Also defamatory. He claimed that we had sold information to Mr. Chipperworth.

I was about to deny it when Dawn said, "What if we did?"

"I'll have you jailed for this," Goodrich said. "It's illegal."

"That's fine talk from somebody who set fire to a warehouse," Dawn said.

Suddenly Goodrich was still and attentive. "What?"

"You are the arsonist responsible for the fire at Rest Easy Beds."

"That's ridiculous," Goodrich said. But he wasn't laughing.

"The plan," Dawn said, "was that when Mr. Chipperworth collected his insurance money Mrs. Chipperworth would divorce him, which would entitle her to half of it. Between the insurance cash and her share of the rest of the joint property, you and Mrs. Chipperworth would have a nice little nest egg to run away on."

"Prove it," Goodrich said furiously.

"I suppose you have an alibi for the night of the fire?" Dawn said charmingly.

"Why should I need one?"

"Well, I'm sure when we go to the police . . ."

"Don't do that!" Goodrich burst out.

"Ah," Dawn said. "Now we're getting down to serious business." She batted her eyelashes. "We never actually gave our evidence to Mr. Chipperworth, you know, and as long as Mrs. Chipperworth has denied everything . . ."

"You want money, I suppose," Goodrich said.

"Well, poor Freddie is terribly tall, and a bigger car would be so much easier for him to get in and out of."

"All right," Goodrich said. "A car."

"And there are so many improvements that ought to be made on this house."

"How about just getting to a bottom-line figure."

"I think thirty thousand would come in very handy, don't you, Freddie?"

"Oh, very handy."

"Thirty thousand!" Goodrich said.

"Yes," Dawn said. "See how reasonable we are!"

10

When the trial came along it was plastered all over the local papers. Frome is not so big a town that it gets serious court cases involving local people very often.

Especially cases involving solicitors and arson and windowless curtains. Goodrich pleaded guilty, but the local reporter, Scoop Newton, tracked down Mrs. Elmitt's neighbor and she was photographed pointing to the windows she had been forced to witness indescribable acts through. Well, the descriptions didn't make the papers anyway.

However, Great-uncle Steve was not pleased at first when he heard what we had done.

Heard is the operative word, because we had tape-recorded the entire conversation with Goodrich on equipment borrowed from Cousin Nigel.

But Dawn explained. After all this time, the only way Goodrich's arson could be proved was if he confessed to it. The police couldn't have used the threat of exposing his relationship to Mrs. Chipperworth the way we did because that would have transgressed legal niceties. "So it was up to Freddie and me," Dawn said.

Eventually Great-uncle Steve laughed.

"I warned you about her," he said to me.

But it worked out all right in the end.

Except . . . Scoop Newton tracked down Dawn and me too.

We begged her not to put anything about us in the paper, for business reasons.

But she refused. We were key figures in bringing a dangerous solicitor to justice. It was news. And besides, Dawn has good legs and photographs well.

It's not that we weren't proud of what we—or let's be fair—what Dawn had done.

But it meant that the Fredrick Herring Private Inquiry Agency burst from its quiet and total obscurity into the glare of public attention.

We started getting calls. We started getting visitors. We started getting letters. Find this, look for that, unravel the other.

And in the end it wasn't actually the attention which was the problem.

What upset us at first was that we found we quite liked it. We hadn't expected to be inclined to *work*.

Yet, some of the cases we were offered were pretty interesting. And after giving it our very best vertical and horizontal thought, we finally decided to compromise on principle and take maybe one more. Or two.

Ride the Lightning

John Lutz

A slanted sheet of rain swept like a scythe across Placid Cove Trailer Park. For an instant, an intricate web of lightning illumined the park. The rows of mobile homes loomed square and still and pale against the night, reminding Nudger of tombs with awnings and TV antennas. He held his umbrella at a sharp angle to the wind as he walked, putting a hand in his pocket to pull out a scrap of paper and double-check the address he was trying to find in the maze of trailers. Finally, at the end of Tranquility Lane, he found Number 307 and knocked on its metal door.

"I'm Nudger," he said when the door opened.

For several seconds the woman in the doorway stood staring out at him, rain blowing in beneath the metal awning to spot her cornflower-colored dress and ruffle her straw blond hair. She was tall but very thin, fragile-looking, and appeared at first glance to be about twelve years old. Second glance revealed her to be in her mid-twenties. She had slight crow's feet at the corners of her luminous blue eyes when she winced as a raindrop struck her face, a knowing cast to her oversized, girlish, full-lipped mouth, and slightly buck teeth. Her looks were hers alone. There was no one who could look much like her, no middle ground with her; men would consider her scrawny and homely, or they would see her as uniquely sensuous. Nudger liked coltish girl-women; he catalogued her as attractive.

"Whoeee!" she said at last, as if seeing for the first time beyond Nudger. "Ain't it raining something terrible?"

"It is," Nudger agreed. "And on me."

Her entire thin body gave a quick, nervous kind of jerk as she smiled apologetically. "I'm Holly Ann Adams, Mr. Nudger. And you are getting wet, all right. Come on in."

She moved aside and Nudger stepped up into the trailer. He expected it to be surprisingly spacious; he'd once lived in a trailer and remembered them as such. This one was cramped and confining. The furniture was cheap and its upholstery was threadbare; a portable black and white TV on a tiny table near the Scotch-plaid sofa was blaring shouts of ecstasy emitted by *The Price is Right* contestants. The air was thick with the smell of something greasy that had been fried too long.

Holly Ann cleared a stack of *People* magazines from a vinyl chair and motioned for Nudger to sit down. He folded his umbrella, left it by the door, and sat. Holly Ann started to say something, then jerked her body in that peculiar way of hers, almost a twitch, as if she'd just remembered something not only with her mind but with her blood and muscle, and walked over and switched off the noisy television. In the abrupt silence, the rain seemed to beat on the metal roof with added fury. "Now we can talk," Holly Ann proclaimed, sitting opposite Nudger on the undersized sofa. "You a sure-enough private investigator?"

"I'm that," Nudger said. "Did someone recommend me to you, Miss Adams?"

"Gotcha out of the Yellow Pages. And if you're gonna work for me, it might as well be Holly Ann without the Adams."

"Except on the check," Nudger said.

She grinned a devilish twelve-year-old's grin. "Oh, sure, don't worry none about that. I wrote you out a check already, just gotta fill in the amount. That is, if you agree to take the job. You might not."

"Why not?"

"It has to do with my fiancé, Curtis Colt."

Nudger listened for a few seconds to the rain crashing on the roof. "The Curtis Colt who's going to be executed next week?"

"That's the one. Only he didn't kill that liquor store woman; I know it for a fact. It ain't right he should have to ride the lightning."

"Ride the lightning?"

"That's what convicts call dying in the electric chair, Mr. Nudger. They call that chair lotsa things: Old Sparky . . . The Lord's Frying Pan. But Curtis don't belong sitting in it wired up, and I can prove it."

"It's a little late for that kind of talk," Nudger said. "Or did you testify for Curtis in court?"

"Nope. Couldn't testify. You'll see why. All them lawyers and the judge and jury don't even know about me. Curtis didn't want them to know, so he never told them." She crossed her legs and swung her right calf jauntily. She was smiling as if trying to flirt him into wanting to know more about the job so he could free Curtis Colt by a governor's reprieve at the last minute, as in an old movie.

Nudger looked at her gauntly pretty, country-girl face and said, "Tell me about Curtis Colt, Holly Ann."

"You mean you didn't read about him in the newspapers or see him on the television?"

"I only scan the media for misinformation. Give me the details."

"Well, they say Curtis was inside the liquor store, sticking it up—him and his partner had done three other places that night, all of 'em gas stations, though—when the old man that owned the place came out of a back room and seen his wife there behind the counter with her hands up and Curtis holding the gun on her. So the old man lost his head and ran at Curtis, and Curtis had to shoot him. Then the woman got mad when she seen that and ran at Curtis, and Curtis shot her. She's the one that died. The old man, he'll live, but he can't talk nor think nor even feed himself."

Nudger remembered more about the case now. Curtis Colt had been found guilty of first degree murder, and because of a debate in the legislature over the merits of cyanide gas versus electricity, the state was breaking out the electric chair to make him its first killer executed by electricity in over a quarter of a century. Those of the back-to-basics school considered that progress.

"They're gonna shoot Curtis full of electricity next Saturday, Mr. Nudger," Holly Ann said plaintively. She sounded like a little girl complaining that the grade on her report card wasn't fair.

"I know," Nudger said. "But I don't see how I can help you. Or, more specifically, help Curtis."

"You know what they say thoughts really are, Mr. Nudger?" Holly Ann said, ignoring his professed helplessness. Her wide blue eyes were vague as she searched for words. "Thoughts ain't really nothing but tiny electrical impulses in the brain. I read that somewheres or other. What I can't help wondering is, when they shoot all that electricity into Curtis, what's it gonna be like to his thinking? How long will it seem like to him before he finally dies? Will there be a big burst of crazy thoughts along with the pain? I know it sounds loony, but I can't help laying awake nights thinking about that, and I feel I just gotta do whatever's left to try and help Curtis."

There was a sort of checkout-line tabloid logic in that, Nudger conceded; if thoughts were actually weak electrical impulses, then high-voltage electrical impulses could become exaggerated, horrible thoughts. Anyway, try to disprove it to Holly Ann.

"They never did catch Curtis's buddy, the driver who sped away and left him in that service station, did they?" Nudger asked.

"Nope. Curtis never told who the driver was, neither, no matter how much he was threatened. Curtis is a stubborn man."

Nudger was getting the idea.

"But you know who was driving the car."

"Yep. And he told me him and Curtis was miles away from

that liquor store at the time it was robbed. When he seen the police closing in on Curtis in that gas station where Curtis was buying cigarettes, he hit the accelerator and got out of the parking lot before they could catch him. The police didn't even get the car's license plate number."

Nudger rubbed a hand across his chin, watching Holly Ann swing her leg as if it were a shapely metronome. She was barefoot and wearing no nylon hose. "The jury thought Curtis not only was at the liquor store, but that he shot the old man and woman in cold blood."

"That ain't true, though. Not according to—" she caught herself before uttering the man's name.

"Curtis's friend," Nudger finished.

"That's right. And he ought to know," Holly Ann said righteously, as if that piece of information were the trump card and the argument was over.

"None of this means anything unless the driver comes forward and substantiates that he was with Curtis somewhere other than at the liquor store when it was robbed."

Holly Ann nodded and stopped swinging her leg. "I know. But he won't. He can't. That's where you come in."

"My profession might enjoy a reputation a notch lower than dognapper," Nudger said, "but I don't hire out to do anything illegal."

"What I want you to do is legal," Holly Ann said in a hurt little voice. Nudger looked past her into the dollhouse kitchen and saw an empty gin bottle. He wondered if she might be slightly drunk. "It's the eyewitness accounts that got Curtis convicted," she went on. "And those people are wrong. I want you to figure out some way to convince them it wasn't Curtis they saw that night."

"Four people, two of them customers in the store, picked Curtis out of a police lineup."

"So what? Ain't eyewitnesses often mistaken?"

Nudger had to admit that they were, though he didn't see how they could be in this case. There were, after all, four of them. And yet, Holly Ann was right; it was amazing how people could sometimes be so certain that the wrong man had committed a crime just five feet in front of them.

"I want you to talk to them witnesses," Holly Ann said. "Find out *why* they think Curtis was the killer. Then show them how they might be wrong and get them to change what they said. We got the truth on our side, Mr. Nudger. At least one witness will change his story when he's made to think about it, because Curtis wasn't where they said he was."

"Curtis has exhausted all his appeals," Nudger said. "Even if all the witnesses changed their stories, it wouldn't necessarily mean he'd get a new trial."

"Maybe not, but I betcha they wouldn't kill him. They couldn't stand the publicity if enough witnesses said they was wrong, it was somebody else killed the old woman. Then, just maybe, eventually, he'd get another trial and get out of prison."

Nudger was awed. Here was foolish optimism that transcended even his own. He had to admire Holly Ann.

The leg started pumping again beneath the cornflower-colored dress. When Nudger lowered his gaze to stare at it, Holly Ann said, "So will you help me, Mr. Nudger?"

"Sure. It sounds easy."

"Why should I worry about it anymore?" Randy Gantner asked Nudger, leaning on his shovel. He didn't mind talking to Nudger; it meant a break from his construction job on the new Interstate 170 cloverleaf. "Colt's been found guilty and he's going to the chair, ain't he?"

The afternoon sun was hammering down on Nudger, warming the back of his neck and making his stomach queasy. He thumbed an antacid tablet off the roll he kept in his shirt pocket and popped one of the white disks into his mouth. With his other hand, he was holding up a photograph of Curtis Colt for Gantner to see. It was a snapshot Holly Ann had given him of the wiry, shirtless Colt leaning on a fence post and holding a beer can high in a mock toast: this one's for Death!

"This is a photograph you never saw in court. I just want you to look at it closely and tell me again if you're sure the man you saw in the liquor store was Colt. Even if it makes no difference in whether he's executed, it will help ease the mind of somebody who loves him."

"I'd be a fool to change my story about what happened now that the trial's over," Gantner said logically.

"You'd be a murderer if you really weren't sure."

Gantner sighed, dragged a dirty red handkerchief from his jeans pocket, and wiped his beefy, perspiring face. He peered at the photo, then shrugged. "It's him, Colt, the guy I seen shoot the man and woman when I was standing in the back aisle of the liquor store. If he'd known me and Sanders was back there, he'd have probably zapped us along with them old folks."

"You're positive it's the same man?"

Gantner spat off to the side and frowned; Nudger was becoming a pest, and the foreman was staring. "I said it to the police and the jury, Nudger; that little twerp Colt did the old lady in. Ask me, he deserves what he's gonna get."

"Did you actually see the shots fired?"

"Nope. Me and Sanders was in the back aisle looking for some reasonable-priced bourbon when we heard the shots, then looked around to see Curtis Colt back away, turn, and run out to the car. Looked like a black or dark green old Ford. Colt fired another shot as it drove away."

"Did you see the driver?"

"Sort of. Skinny dude with curly black hair and mustache. That's what I told the cops. That's all I seen. That's all I know."

And that was the end of the conversation. The foreman was walking toward them, glaring. *Thunk!* Gantner's shovel sliced deep into the earth, speeding the day when there'd be another place for traffic to get backed up. Nudger thanked him and advised him not to work too hard in the hot sun.

"You wanna help?" Gantner asked, grinning sweatily.

"I'm already doing some digging of my own," Nudger said, walking away before the foreman arrived.

The other witnesses also stood by their identifications. The fourth and last one Nudger talked with, an elderly woman named Iris Langeneckert, who had been walking her dog near the liquor store and had seen Curtis Colt dash out the door and into the getaway car, said something that Gantner had touched on. When she'd described the getaway car driver, like Gantner she said he was a thin man with curly black hair and a beard or mustache, then she had added, "Like Curtis Colt's hair and mustache."

Nudger looked again at the snapshot Holly Ann had given him. Curtis Colt was about five foot nine, skinny, and mean-looking, with a broad bandito mustache and a mop of curly, greasy black hair. Nudger wondered if it was possible that the getaway car driver had been Curtis Colt himself, and his accomplice had killed the shopkeeper. Even Nudger found that one hard to believe.

He drove to his second-floor office in the near suburb of Maplewood and sat behind his desk in the blast of cold air from the window unit, sipping the complimentary paper cup of iced tea he'd brought up from Danny's Donuts directly below. The sweet smell of the doughnuts was heavier than usual in the office; Nudger had never quite gotten used to it and what it did to his sensitive stomach.

When he was cool enough to think clearly again, he decided he needed more information on the holdup, and on Curtis Colt, from a more objective source than Holly Ann Adams. He phoned Lieutenant Jack Hammersmith at home and was told by Hammersmith's son Jed that Hammersmith had just driven away to go to work on the afternoon shift, so it would be awhile before he got to his office.

Nudger checked his answering machine, proving that hope did indeed spring eternal in a fool's breast. There was a terse message from his former wife Eileen demanding last month's alimony payment; a solemn-voiced young man reading an address where Nudger could send a check to help pay to form a watchdog committee that would stop the utilities from continually raising their rates; and a cheerful man informing Nudger that with the labels from ten packages of a brand name hot dog he could get a Cardinals' ballgame ticket at half price. (That meant eating over eighty hot dogs. Nudger calculated that baseball season would be over by the time he did that.) Everyone seemed to want some of Nudger's money. No one wanted to pay Nudger any money. Except for Holly Ann Adams. Nudger decided he'd better step up his efforts on the Curtis Colt case.

He tilted back his head, downed the last dribble of iced tea, then tried to eat what was left of the crushed ice. But the ice clung stubbornly to the bottom of the cup, taunting him. Nudger's life was like that.

He crumpled up the paper cup and tossed it, ice and all, into the wastebasket. Then he went downstairs where his Volkswagen was parked in the shade behind the building and drove east on Manchester, toward downtown and the Third District Station house.

Police Lieutenant Jack Hammersmith was in his Third District office, sleek, obese, and cool-looking behind his wide metal desk. He was pounds and years away from the handsome cop who'd been Nudger's partner a decade ago in a two-man patrol car. Nudger could still see traces of a dashing quality in the flesh-upholstered Hammersmith, but he wondered if that was only because he'd known Hammersmith ten years ago.

"Sit down, Nudge," Hammersmith invited, his lips smiling but his slate gray, cop's eyes unreadable. If eyes were the windows to the soul, his shades were always down.

Nudger sat in one of the straight-backed chairs in front of Hammersmith's desk. "I need some help," he said.

"Sure," Hammersmith said, "you never come see me just to trade recipes or to sit and rock." Hammersmith was partial to irony; it was a good thing, in his line of work.

"I need to know more about Curtis Colt," Nudger said.

Hammersmith got one of his vile greenish cigars out of his shirt pocket and stared intently at it, as if its paper ring label might reveal some secret of life and death. “Colt, eh? The guy who’s going to ride the lightning?”

“That’s the second time in the past few days I’ve heard that expression. The first time was from Colt’s fiancée. She thinks he’s innocent.”

“Fiancées think along those lines. Is she your client?”

Nudger nodded but didn’t volunteer Holly Ann’s name.

“Gullibility makes the world go round,” Hammersmith said. “I was in charge of the Homicide investigation on that one. There’s not a chance Colt is innocent, Nudge.”

“Four eyewitness I.D.’s is compelling evidence,” Nudger admitted. “What about the getaway car driver? His description is a lot like Colt’s. Maybe he’s the one who did the shooting and Colt was the driver.”

“Colt’s lawyer hit on that. The jury didn’t buy it. Neither do I. The man is guilty, Nudge.”

“You know how inaccurate eyewitness accounts are,” Nudger persisted.

That seemed to get Hammersmith mad. He lit the cigar. The office immediately fogged up.

Nudger made his tone more amicable. “Mind if I look at the file on the Colt case?”

Hammersmith gazed thoughtfully at Nudger through a dense greenish haze. He inhaled, exhaled; the haze became a cloud. “How come this fiancée didn’t turn up at the trial to testify for Colt? She could have at least lied and said he was with her that night.”

“Colt apparently didn’t want her subjected to taking the stand.”

“How noble,” Hammersmith said. “What makes this fiancée think her prince charming is innocent?”

“She knows he was somewhere else when the shopkeepers were shot.”

“But not with her?”

“Nope.”

“Well, that’s refreshing.”

Maybe it was refreshing enough to make up Hammersmith's mind. He picked up the phone and asked for the Colt file. Nudger could barely make out what he was saying around the fat cigar, but apparently everyone at the Third was used to Hammersmith and could interpret cigarese.

The file didn't reveal much that Nudger didn't know. Fifteen minutes after the liquor store shooting, officers from a two-man patrol car, acting on the broadcast description of the gunman, approached Curtis Colt inside a service station where he was buying a pack of cigarettes from a vending machine. A car that had been parked near the end of the dimly lighted lot had sped away as they'd entered the station office. The officers had gotten only a glimpse of a dark green old Ford; they hadn't made out the license plate number but thought it might start with the letter "L."

Colt had surrendered without a struggle, and that night at the Third District Station the four eyewitnesses had picked him out of a lineup. Their description of the getaway car matched that of the car the police had seen speeding from the service station. The loot from the holdup, and several gas station holdups committed earlier that night, wasn't on Colt, but probably it was in the car.

"Colt's innocence just jumps out of the file at you, doesn't it, Nudge?" Hammersmith said. He was grinning a fat grin around the fat cigar.

"What about the murder weapon?"

"Colt was unarmed when we picked him up."

"Seems odd."

"Not really," Hammersmith said. "He was planning to pay for the cigarettes. And maybe the gun was still too hot to touch so he left it in the car. Maybe it's still hot; it got a lot of use for one night."

Closing the file folder and laying it on a corner of Hammersmith's desk, Nudger stood up. "Thanks, Jack. I'll keep you tapped in if I learn anything interesting."

"Don't bother keeping me informed on this one, Nudge. It's over. I don't see how even a fiancée can doubt Colt's guilt."

Nudger shrugged, trying not to breathe too deeply in the smoke-hazed office. "Maybe it's an emotional thing. She thinks that because thought waves are tiny electrical impulses, Colt might experience time warp and all sorts of grotesque thoughts when all that voltage shoots through him. She has bad dreams."

"I'll bet she does," Hammersmith said. "I'll bet Colt has bad dreams, too. Only he deserves his. And maybe she's right."

"About what?"

"About all that voltage distorting thought and time. Who's to say?"

"Not Curtis Colt," Nudger said. "Not after they throw the switch."

"It's a nice theory, though," Hammersmith said. "I'll remember it. It might be a comforting thing to tell the murder victim's family."

"Sometimes," Nudger said, "you think just like a cop who's seen too much."

"Any of it's too much, Nudge," Hammersmith said with surprising sadness. He let more greenish smoke drift from his nostrils and the corners of his mouth; he looked like a stone Buddha seated behind the desk, one in which incense burned.

Nudger coughed and said goodbye.

"Only two eyewitnesses are needed to convict," Nudger said to Holly Ann the next day in her trailer, "and in this case there are four. None of them is at all in doubt about their identification of Curtis Colt as the killer. I have to be honest; it's time you should face the fact that Colt is guilty and that you're wasting your money on my services."

"All them witnesses know what's going to happen to Curtis," Holly Ann said. "They'd never want to live with the notion they might have made a mistake, killed an innocent man, so they've got themselves convinced that they're positive it was Curtis they saw that night."

"Your observation on human psychology is sound," Nudger said, "but I don't think it will help us. The witnesses were just as certain three months ago at the trial. I took the time to read the court manuscript; the jury had no choice but to find Colt guilty, and the evidence hasn't changed."

Holly Ann drew her legs up and clasped her knees to her chest with both arms. Her little-girl posture matched her little-girl faith in her lover's innocence. She believed the white knight must arrive at any moment and snatch Curtis Colt from the electrical jaws of death. She believed hard. Nudger could almost hear his armor clank when he walked.

She wanted him to believe just as hard. "I see you need to be convinced of Curtis's innocence," she said wistfully. There was no doubt he'd forced her into some kind of corner. "If you come here tonight at eight, Mr. Nudger, I'll convince you."

"How?"

"I can't say. You'll understand why tonight."

"Why do we have to wait till tonight?"

"Oh, you'll see."

Nudger looked at the waiflike creature curled in the corner of the sofa. He felt as if they were playing a childhood guessing game while Curtis Colt waited his turn in the electric chair. Nudger had never seen an execution; he'd heard it took longer than most people thought for the condemned to die. His stomach actually twitched.

"Can't we do this now with twenty questions?" he asked.

Holly Ann shook her head. "No, Mr. Nudger."

Nudger sighed and stood up, feeling as if he were about to bump his head on the trailer's low ceiling even though he was barely six feet tall.

"Make sure you're on time tonight, Mr. Nudger," Holly Ann said as he went out the door. "It's important."

At eight on the nose that evening Nudger was sitting at the tiny table in Holly Ann's kitchenette. Across from him was a thin, nervous man in his late twenties or early thirties, dressed in a longsleeved shirt despite the heat, and wearing sunglasses with silver mirror lenses. Holly Ann introduced the man as "Len, but that's not his real name," and said he was Curtis Colt's accomplice and the driver of their getaway car on the night of the murder.

"But me and Curtis was nowhere near the liquor store when them folks got shot," Len said vehemently.

Nudger assumed the sunglasses were so he couldn't effectively identify Len if it came to a showdown in court. Len had lank, dark brown hair that fell to below his shoulders, and when he moved his arm Nudger caught sight of something blue and red on his briefly exposed wrist. A tattoo. Which explained the longsleeved shirt.

"You can understand why Len couldn't come forth and testify for Curtis in court," Holly Ann said.

Nudger said he could understand that. Len would have had to incriminate himself.

"We was way on the other side of town," Len said, "casing another service station, when that liquor store killing went down. Heck, we never held up nothing but service stations. They was our specialty."

Which was true, Nudger had to admit. Colt had done time for armed robbery six years ago after sticking up half a dozen service stations within a week. And all the other holdups he'd been tied to this time around were of service stations. The liquor store was definitely a departure in his M.O., one not noted in court during Curtis Colt's rush to judgment.

"Your hair is in your favor," Nudger said to Len.

"Huh?"

"Your hair didn't grow that long in the three months since the liquor store killing. The witnesses described the getaway car driver as having shorter, curlier hair, like Colt's, and a mustache."

Len shrugged. "I'll be honest with you—it don't help at all. Me and Curtis was kinda the same type. So to confuse any witnesses, in case we got caught, we made each other look even more alike. I'd tuck up my long hair and wear a wig that looked like Curtis's hair. My mustache was real, like Curtis's. I shaved it off a month ago. We did look alike at a glance; sorta like brothers."

Nudger bought that explanation; it wasn't uncommon for a team of holdup men to play tricks to confuse witnesses and the police. Too many lawyers had gotten in the game; the robbers, like the cops, were taking the advice of their attorneys and thinking about a potential trial even before the crime was committed.

"Is there any way, then, to prove you were across town at the time of the murder?" Nudger asked, looking at the two small Nudgers staring back at him from the mirror lenses.

"There's just my word," Len said, rather haughtily.

Nudger didn't bother telling him what that was worth. Why antagonize him?

"I just want you to believe Curtis is innocent," Len said with desperation. "Because he is! And so am I!"

And Nudger understood why Len was here, taking the risk. If Colt was guilty of murder, Len was guilty of being an accessory to the crime. Once Curtis Colt had ridden the lightning, Len would have hanging over him the possibility of an almost certain life sentence, and perhaps even his own ride on the lightning, if he were ever caught. It wasn't necessary to actually squeeze the trigger to be convicted of murder.

"I need for you to try extra hard to prove Curtis is innocent," Len said. His thin lips quivered; he was near tears.

"Are you giving Holly Ann the money to pay me?" Nudger asked.

"Some of it, yeah. From what Curtis and me stole. And I gave Curtis's share to Holly Ann, too. Me and her are fifty-fifty on this."

Dirty money, Nudger thought. Dirty job. Still, if Curtis Colt happened to be innocent, trying against the clock to prove it was a job that needed to be done.

"Okay. I'll stay on the case."

"Thanks," Len said. His narrow hand moved impulsively

across the table and squeezed Nudger's arm in gratitude. Len had the look of an addict; Nudger wondered if the longsleeved shirt was to hide needle tracks as well as the tattoo.

Len stood up. "Stay here with Holly Ann for ten minutes while I make myself scarce. I gotta know I wasn't followed. You understand it ain't that I don't trust you; a man in my position has gotta be sure, is all."

"I understand. Go."

Len gave a spooked smile and went out the door. Nudger heard his running footfalls on the gravel outside the trailer. Nudger was forty-three years old and ten pounds overweight; lean and speedy Len needed a ten-minute head start like Sinatra needed singing lessons.

"Is Len a user?" Nudger asked Holly Ann.

"Sometimes. But my Curtis never touched no dope."

"You know I have to tell the police about this conversation, don't you?"

Holly Ann nodded. "That's why we arranged it this way. They won't be any closer to Len than before."

"They might want to talk to you, Holly Ann."

She shrugged. "It don't matter. I don't know where Len is, nor even his real name nor how to get in touch with him. He'll find out all he needs to know about Curtis by reading the papers."

"You have a deceptively devious mind," Nudger told her, "considering that you look like Barbie Doll's country kid cousin."

Holly Ann smiled, surprised and pleased. "Do you find me attractive, Mr. Nudger?"

"Yes. And painfully young."

For just a moment Nudger almost thought of Curtis Colt as a lucky man. Then he looked at his watch, saw that his ten minutes were about up, and said goodbye. If Barbie had a kid cousin, Ken probably had one somewhere, too. And time was something you couldn't deny. Ask Curtis Colt.

* * *

"It doesn't wash with me," Hammersmith said from behind his desk, puffing angrily on his cigar. Angrily because it did wash a little bit; he didn't like the possibility, however remote, of sending an innocent man to his death. That was every good homicide cop's nightmare. "This Len character is just trying to keep himself in the clear on a murder charge."

"You could read it that way," Nudger admitted.

"It would help if you gave us a better description of Len," Hammersmith said gruffly, as if Nudger were to blame for Curtis Colt's accomplice still walking around free.

"I gave you what I could," Nudger said. "Len didn't give me much to pass on. He's streetwise and scared and knows what's at stake."

Hammersmith nodded, his fit of pique past. But the glint of weary frustration remained in his eyes.

"Are you going to question Holly Ann?" Nudger said.

"Sure, but it won't do any good. She's probably telling the truth. Len would figure we'd talk to her; he wouldn't tell her how to find him."

"You could stake out her trailer."

"Do you think Holly Ann and Len might be lovers?"

"No."

Hammersmith shook his head. "Then they'll probably never see each other again. Watching her trailer would be a waste of manpower."

Nudger knew Hammersmith was right. He stood up to go.

"What are you going to do now?" Hammersmith asked.

"I'll talk to the witnesses again. I'll read the court transcript again. And I'd like to talk with Curtis Colt."

"They don't allow visitors on Death Row, Nudge, only temporary boarders."

"This case is an exception," Nudger said. "Will you try to arrange it?"

Hammersmith chewed thoughtfully on his cigar. Since he'd been the officer in charge of the murder investigation, he'd been the one who'd nailed Curtis Colt. That carried an obligation.

"I'll phone you soon," he said, "let you know."

Nudger thanked Hammersmith and walked down the hall into the clear, breathable air of the booking area.

That day he managed to talk again to all four eyewitnesses. Two of them got mad at Nudger for badgering them. They all stuck to their stories. Nudger reported this to Holly Ann at the Right-Steer Steakhouse, where she worked as a waitress. Several customers that afternoon got tears with their baked potatoes.

Hammersmith phoned Nudger that evening.

"I managed to get permission for you to talk to Colt," he said, "but don't get excited. Colt won't talk to you. He won't talk to anyone, not even a clergyman. He'll change his mind about the clergyman, but not about you."

"Did you tell him I was working for Holly Ann?"

"I had that information conveyed to him. He wasn't impressed. He's one of the stoic ones on Death Row."

Nudger's stomach kicked up, growled something that sounded like a hopeless obscenity. If even Curtis Colt wouldn't cooperate, how could he be helped? Absently Nudger peeled back the aluminum foil on a roll of antacid tablets and slipped two chalky white disks into his mouth. Hammersmith knew about his nervous stomach and must have heard him chomping the tablets. "Take it easy, Nudge. This isn't your fault."

"Then why do I feel like it is?"

"Because you feel too much of everything. That's why you had to quit the department."

"We've got another day before the execution," Nudger said. "I'm going to go through it all again. I'm going to talk to each of those witnesses even if they try to run when they see me coming. Maybe somebody will say something that will let in some light."

"There's no light out there, Nudge. You're wasting your time. Give up on this one and move on."

"Not yet," Nudger said. "There's something elusive here that I can't quite grab."

"And never will," Hammersmith said. "Forget it, Nudge. Live your life and let Curtis Colt lose his."

Hammersmith was right. Nothing Nudger did helped Curtis Colt in the slightest. At eight o'clock Saturday morning, while Nudger was preparing breakfast in his apartment, Colt was put to death in the electric chair. He'd offered no last words before two thousand volts had turned him from something into nothing.

Nudger heard the news of Colt's death on his kitchen radio. He went ahead and ate his eggs, but he skipped the toast.

That afternoon he consoled a numbed and frequently sobbing Holly Ann and apologized for being powerless to stop her true love's execution. She was polite, trying to be brave. She preferred to suffer alone. Her boss at the Right-Steer gave her the rest of the day off, and Nudger drove her home.

Nudger slept a total of four hours during the next two nights. On Monday, he felt compelled to attend Curtis Colt's funeral. There were about a dozen people clustered around the grave, including the state-appointed clergyman and pall-bearers. Nudger stood off to one side during the brief service. Holly Ann, looking like a child playing dressup in black, stood well off to the other side. They didn't exchange words, only glances.

As the coffin was lowered into the earth, Nudger watched Holly Ann walk to where a taxi was waiting by a weathered stone angel. The cab wound its way slowly along the snaking narrow cemetery road to tall iron gates and the busy street. Holly Ann never looked back.

That night Nudger realized what was bothering him, and for the first time since Curtis Colt's death, he slept well.

In the morning he began watching Holly Ann's trailer.

At seven-thirty she emerged, dressed in her yellow waitress uniform, and got into another taxi. Nudger followed in his battered Volkswagen Beetle as the cab drove her the four miles to her job at the Right-Steer Steakhouse. She didn't look around as she paid the driver and walked inside through the molded plastic Old-West-saloon swinging doors.

At six that evening another cab drove her home, making a brief stop at a grocery store.

It went that way for the rest of the week, trailer to work to trailer. Holly Ann had no visitors other than the plain brown paper bag she took home every night.

The temperature got up to around ninety-five and the humidity rose right along with it. It was one of St. Louis's legendary summer heat waves. Sitting melting in the Volkswagen, Nudger wondered if what he was doing was really worthwhile. Curtis Colt was, after all, dead, and had never been his client. Still, there were responsibilities that went beyond the job. Or perhaps they were actually the essence of the job.

The next Monday, after Holly Ann had left for work, Nudger used his Visa card to slip the flimsy lock on her trailer door, and let himself in.

It took him over an hour to find what he was searching for. It had been well hidden, in a cardboard box inside the access panel to the bathroom plumbing. After looking at the box's contents—almost seven hundred dollars in loot from Curtis Colt's brief life of crime, and another object Nudger wasn't surprised to see—Nudger resealed the box and replaced the access panel.

He continued to watch and follow Holly Ann, more confident now.

Two weeks after the funeral, when she left work one evening, she didn't go home.

Instead her taxi turned the opposite way and drove east on Watson Road. Nudger followed the cab along a series of side streets in South St. Louis, then part way down a dead-end alley to a large garage, above the door of which was lettered "Clifford's Auto Body."

Nudger backed out quickly onto the street, then parked the Volkswagen near the mouth of the alley. A few minutes later the cab drove by without a passenger. Within ten minutes, Holly

Ann drove past in a shiny red Ford. Its license plate number began with an L.

When Nudger reached Placid Cove Trailer Park, he saw the Ford nosed in next to Holly Ann's trailer.

On the way to the trailer door, he paused and scratched the Ford's hood with a key. Even in the lowering evening light he could see that beneath the new red paint the car's color was dark green.

Holly Ann answered the door right away when he knocked. She tried a smile when she saw it was him, but she couldn't quite manage her facial muscles, as if they'd become rigid and uncoordinated. She appeared ten years older. The little-girl look had deserted her; now she was an emaciated, grief-eroded woman, a country Barbie doll whose features some evil child had lined with dark crayon. The shaded crescents beneath her eyes completely took away their innocence. She was holding a glass that had once been a jelly jar. In it were two fingers of a clear liquid. Behind her on the table was a crumpled brown paper bag and a half-empty bottle of gin.

"I figured it out," Nudger told her.

Now she did smile, but it was fleeting, a sickly bluish shadow crossing her taut features. "You're like a dog with a rag, Mr. Nudger. You surely don't know when to let go." She stepped back and he followed her into the trailer. It was warm in there; something was wrong with the air conditioner. "Hot as hell, ain't it," Holly Ann commented. Nudger thought that was apropos.

He sat down across from her at the tiny Formica table, just as he and Len had sat facing each other two weeks ago. She offered him a drink. He declined. She downed the contents of the jelly jar glass and poured herself another, clumsily striking the neck of the bottle on the glass. It made a sharp, flinty sound, as if sparks might fly.

"Now, what's this you've got figured out, Mr. Nudger?" She didn't want to, but she had to hear it. Had to share it.

"It's almost four miles to the Right-Steer Steakhouse," Nudger told her. "The waitresses there make little more than minimum wage, so cab fare to and from work has to eat a big hole in your salary. But then you seem to go everywhere by cab."

"My car's been in the shop."

"I figured it might be, after I found the money and the wig."

She bowed her head slightly and took a sip of gin. "Wig?"

"In the cardboard box inside the bathroom wall."

"You been snooping, Mr. Nudger." There was more resignation than outrage in her voice.

"You're sort of skinny, but not a short girl," Nudger went on. "With a dark curly wig and a fake mustache, sitting in a car, you'd resemble Curtis Colt enough to fool a dozen eyewitnesses who just caught a glimpse of you. It was a smart precaution for the two of you to take."

Holly Ann looked astounded.

"Are you saying I was driving the getaway car at the liquor store holdup?"

"Maybe. Then maybe you hired someone to play Len and convince me he was Colt's accomplice and that they were far away from the murder scene when the trigger was pulled. After I found the wig, I talked to some of your neighbors, who told me that until recently you'd driven a green Ford sedan."

Holly Ann ran her tongue along the edges of her protruding teeth.

"So Curtis and Len used my car for their holdups."

"I doubt if Len ever met Curtis. He's somebody you paid in stolen money or drugs to sit there where you're sitting now and lie to me."

"If I was driving that getaway car, Mr. Nudger, and *knew* Curtis was guilty, why would I have hired a private investigator to try to find a hole in the eyewitnesses' stories?"

"That's what bothered me at first," Nudger said, "until I realized you weren't interested in clearing Curtis. What you were really worried about was Curtis Colt talking in prison. You didn't want those witnesses' stories changed, you wanted them verified. And you wanted the police to learn about not-his-right-name Len."

Holly Ann raised her head to look directly at him with eyes that begged and dreaded. She asked simply, "Why would I want that?"

"Because you were Curtis Colt's accomplice in all of his robberies. And when you hit the liquor store, he stayed in the car to drive. You fired the shot that killed the old woman. He was the one who fired the wild shot from the speeding car. Colt kept quiet about it because he loved you. He never talked, not to the police, not to his lawyer, not even to a priest. Now that he's dead you can trust him forever, but I have a feeling you could have anyway. He loved you more than you loved him, and you'll have to live knowing he didn't deserve to die."

She looked down into her glass as if for answers and didn't say anything for a long time. Nudger felt a bead of perspiration trickle crazily down the back of his neck. Then she said, "I didn't want to shoot that old man, but he didn't leave me no choice. Then the old woman came at me." She looked up at Nudger and smiled ever so slightly. It was a smile Nudger hadn't seen on her before, one he didn't like. "God help me, Mr. Nudger, I can't quit thinking about shooting that old woman."

"You murdered her," Nudger said, "and you murdered Curtis Colt by keeping silent and letting him die for you."

"You can't prove nothing," Holly Ann said, still with her ancient-eyed, eerie smile that had nothing to do with amusement.

"You're right," Nudger told her, "I can't. But I don't think legally proving it is necessary, Holly Ann. You said it: thoughts are actually tiny electrical impulses in the brain. Curtis Colt rode the lightning all at once. With you, it will take years, but the destination is the same. I think you'll come to agree that his way was easier."

She sat very still. She didn't answer. Wasn't going to.

Nudger stood up and wiped his damp forehead with the back

of his hand. He felt sticky, dirty, confined by the low ceiling and near walls of the tiny, stifling trailer. He had to get out of there to escape the sensation of being trapped.

He didn't say goodbye to Holly Ann when he walked out. She didn't say goodbye to him. The last sound Nudger heard as he left the trailer was the clink of the bottle on the glass.

Do with Me What You Will

Joyce Carol Oates

THEN WHAT?"

"I got very . . . I got very excited and. . . ."

"Did she look at you?"

"Yeah. And it made me want to. . . . It made me want to go after her, you know, like grab hold of her. . . . Because she was thinking the same thing. She was afraid of me and she was thinking. . . ."

"She kept looking back at you?"

"Oh, yes, she did. Yes. Back over her shoulder. I got so excited that I just followed her. I mean I must of followed her, I don't even remember my legs going. . . . It was just her, looking back over her shoulder at me, like checking on me, and me following her, just her and me and nobody else on the street. I never saw nobody else. I just saw her ahead of me, but I didn't even see her face, I was too excited."

"When did she start to run?"

"Oh, my, I don't know, I . . . I guess it was by . . . uh . . . that drugstore there, what is it, some drugstore that. . . . Well, it was closed, of course, because of the late hour. Uh . . . some name you see all the time. . . ."

"Cunningham's."

"Oh, yes, yes. Cunningham's. But I don't know if I really saw that, Mr. Morrissey, so clear as that . . . any place at all . . . like I know the neighborhood upward and downward, but I wasn't watching too close at the time. Because I had my eye on her, you know, to see she couldn't get away. She was like a fox would be, going fast all of a sudden, and damn scared. That makes them clever, when they're scared."

"Then she started to run? Where was this?"

"The other side of the drugstore . . . across a street . . . I don't know the names, but they got them written down, the police. They could tell you."

"I don't want any information from them, I want it from you. The intersection there is St. Ann and Ryan Boulevard. Is that where she started running?"

"If that's what they said. . . ."

"That's what she said. She told them. When she started to run, did you run?"

"Yeah."

"Right away?"

"Yeah, right away."

"Did you start running before she did?"

"No. I don't know."

"But only after she started running. . . ?"

"I think so."

"Did you? After she started running, but not before?"

"Yeah."

"Were there any cars waiting for the light to change at that intersection?"

"I don't know . . . I was in a frenzy. . . . You know how you get, when things happen fast, and you can't pay attention. . . . I . . . I saw her running and I thought to myself, *You ain't going to get away!* I was almost ready to laugh or to scream out, it was so. . . . It was so high-strung a few minutes for me. . . ."

"Did she run across the street, or out into the street?"

"She . . . uh . . . she started screaming. . . . That was when she started screaming. But it didn't scare me off. She ran out into the middle of the street . . . yeah, I can remember that now . . . out into the middle, where it was very wide. . . . I remember some cars waiting for the light to change, now. But I didn't pay much attention to them then."

"Then what happened?"

"Well, uh, she got out there and something like, like her shoe was broke, the heel was snapped . . . and she was yelling at this guy in a car, that waited for the light to change but then couldn't get away because she was in front of the car. And . . . uh . . . that was a . . . a Pontiac Tempest, a nice green car. . . . And it was a man and a woman, both white. She was yelling for them to let her in. But when she ran around to the side of the car, and grabbed the door handle, well, it was locked, of course, and she couldn't get it open and I was just waiting by the curb to see how it would go . . . and the guy, he just pressed down that accelerator and got the hell out of there. Man, he shot off like a rocket. I had to laugh. And she looked over her shoulder at me where I was waiting, you know, and. . . ."

"Yes, then what?"

"Well, then. Then I, uh, I got her. There wasn't anything to it, she was pretty tired by then, and. . . . I just grabbed her and dragged her back somewhere, you know, the way they said . . . she told them all the things that happened. . . . I can't remember it too clear myself, because I was crazylike, like laughing because I was so high, you know. I wasn't scared, either. I felt like a general or somebody in a movie, where things go right, like I came to the edge of a country or a whole continent, you know, and naturally I wouldn't want the movie to end just yet. . . ."

"But you don't remember everything that happened?"

"I don't know. Maybe. But no, I guess not, I mean. . . . You know how you get in a frenzy. . . ."

"You signed a confession."

"Yeah, I s'pose so. I mean, I wanted to cooperate a little. I figured they had me anyway, and anyway I was still so high, I couldn't come in for a landing. I wasn't scared or anything and felt very good. So I signed it."

"Did they tell you you had the right to call an attorney?"

"Yeah, maybe."

"You had the right to counsel. . . ? Did the police tell you that?"

"*Right to counsel*. . . . Yeah, I heard something like that. I don't know. Maybe I was a little scared. My mouth was bleeding down my neck."

"From being struck?"

"Before they got the handcuffs on me. I was trying to get away. So somebody got me in the face."

"Did it hurt?"

"No, naw. I didn't feel it. I started getting wet, then one of the policemen, in the car, he wiped me off with a rag, because it was getting on him. I don't know if it hurt or not. Later on it hurt. The tooth was loose and I fooled around with it, wiggling it, in jail, and took it out myself; so I wouldn't swallow it or something at night. My whole face swoll up afterward. . . ."

"So you waived your right to counsel?"

"I don't know. I guess so. If they said that, then I did."

"Why did you waive your right to counsel?"

"I don't know."

"Were you pressured into it?"

"What? I don't know. I . . . uh . . . I was mixed up and a little high. . . ."

"Did you say, maybe, that you didn't have any money for a lawyer?"

"Uh . . . yeah. In fact, I did say that, yeah. I did."

"You did?"

"I think so."

"You did say that."

"I think I said it. . . ."

"You told them you couldn't afford a lawyer."

"Yeah."

"And did they say you had the right to counsel anyway? Did they say that if you were indigent, counsel would be provided for you?"

"Indigent. . . ?"

"Yes, indigent. If you didn't have money for a lawyer, you'd be given one anyway. Didn't they explain that to you?"

"What was that. . . ? *In*. . . ?"

"Indigent. They didn't explain that to you, did they?"

"About what?"

"If you were indigent, counsel would be provided for you."

"Indigent. . . ."

"Indigent. Did they use that word? Do you remember it?"

"Well, uh. . . . Lots of words got used. . . . I. . . ."

"Did they use the word *indigent*? Did they explain your situation to you?"

"What situation. . . ? I was kind of mixed up and excited and. . . ."

"And they had been banging you around, right? Your tooth was knocked out . . . your face was cut . . . your face swelled up. . . . So you signed a confession, right? After Mrs. Donner made her accusation, you agreed with her, you signed a confession for the police, in order to cooperate with them and not be beaten any more. I think that was a very natural thing to do under the circumstances. Do you know which one of the police hit you?"

"Oh, they all did, they was all scrambling around after me. . . . Damn lucky I didn't get shot. I was fearless, I didn't know shit how close I came to getting killed. Jesus. Never come in for a landing till the next day, I was so high. Pulled the tooth out by the roots and never felt it. But later on it hurt like hell. . . . I couldn't remember much."

"Were you examined by a doctor?"

"No."

"A dentist?"

"Hell, no."

"Let's see your mouth. . . . What about those missing teeth on the side there? What happened to them?"

"Them, they been gone a long time."

"It looks raw there."

"Yeah, well, I don't know. . . . It looks what?"

"It looks sore."

"Well, it might be sore, I don't know. My gums is sore sometimes. They bleed sometimes by themselves."

"What happened to your mouth?"

"I got kicked there. Two, three years back."

"Your mother told me you'd had some trouble back in your neighborhood, off and on, and I see you were arrested for some incidents, but what about some trouble with a girl. . . ? Did you ever get into trouble with a girl?"

"What girl?"

"Your mother says it was a girl in the neighborhood."

"Yeah."

"Yeah what?"

"Yeah, it was a girl, a girl. She never made no trouble for me. Her father was out after me, but he got in trouble himself. So I don't know, I mean, it passed on by. She was. . . . She didn't want no trouble, it was her old man tried to make a fuss. What's my mother been telling you, that old news? That's damn old news; that's last year's news."

"You weren't arrested for rape, were you?"

"No. I tole you, it was only her father; then he had to leave town."

"Before this you've been arrested twice, right? And put on probation twice? And no jail sentence."

"That's a way of looking at it."

"How do you look at it?"

"I hung around a long time waiting to get out . . . waiting for the trial. . . . You know, the trial or the hearing or whatever it was. Then the judge let me go anyway."

"You waited in jail, you mean."

"Sure I waited in jail."

"Why couldn't you get bond?"

"My momma said the hell with me."

"According to the record, you were arrested for theft twice. You pleaded guilty. What about the assault charges?"

"From roughing somebody up? Well, uh, that stuff got put aside. There was a deal made."

"So you got off on probation twice."

"Yeah, that worked out OK."

"You were arrested for the first time when you were nineteen years old, right?"

"If that's what it says."

"That isn't bad. Nineteen years old . . . that's a pretty advanced age for a first offense. . . . And no jail sentence, just probation. Now, tell me, is all this accurate: Your father served a five-year sentence for armed robbery, right?—then he left Detroit? Your mother has been on ADC from 1959 until the present, right? You have four brothers and two sisters, two children are still living at home with your mother, and your sister has a baby herself?—and you don't live at home, but nearby somewhere? And you give her money when you can?"

"Yeah."

"It says here you're unemployed. Were you ever employed?"

"Sure I been employed."

"It isn't down here. What kind of job did you have?"

"How come it ain't down there?"

"I don't know. What kind of job did you have?"

"Look, you write it in yourself, Mr. Morrissey, because I sure was employed. . . . I call that an insult. I was kind of a delivery boy off and on, I could get references to back me up."

"This is just a photostat copy of your file from Welfare; I can't write anything in. . . . Where did you work?"

"Some store that's closed up now."

"Whose was it?"

"I disremember the exact name."

"You're unemployed at the present time, at the age of twenty-three?"

"Well, I can't help that. I. . . . Mr. Morrissey, you going to make a deal for me?"

"I won't have to make a deal."

"Huh? Well, that woman is awful mad at me. She's out to get me."

"Don't worry about her."

"In the police station she was half-crazy, she was screaming so. . . . Her clothes was all ripped. I don't remember none of that. The front of her was all blood. Jesus, I don't know, I must of gone crazy or something. . . . When they brought me in, she was already there, waiting, and she took one look at me and started screaming. That was the end."

"She might reconsider, she might think all this over carefully. Don't worry about her. Let me worry about her. In fact, you have no necessary reason to believe that the woman who identified you was the woman you followed and attacked. . . . It might have been another woman. You didn't really see her face. All you know is that she was white, and probably all she knows about her attacker is that he was black. I won't have to make a deal for you. Don't worry about that."

"She's awful mad at me, she ain't going to back down. . . ."

"Let me worry about her. Tell me: How did the police happen to pick you up? Did they have a warrant for your arrest?"

"Hell, no. It was a goddamn asshole accident like a joke. . . . I, uh, I was running away from her, where I left her . . . and . . . and. . . . I just run into the side of the squad car. Like that. Was running like hell and run into the side of the car, where it was parked, without no lights on. So they picked me up like that."

"Because you were running, they picked you up, right?"

"I run into the side of their goddamn fucking car."

"So they got out and arrested you?"

"One of them chased me."

"Did he fire a shot?"

"Sure he fired a shot."

"So you surrendered?"

"I hid somewhere, by a cellar window. But they found me. It was just a goddamn stupid accident. . . . Jesus, I don't know. I must of been flying so high, couldn't see the car where it was parked. They had it parked back from the big street, with the lights out. I saw one of them with a paper cup, some coffee that got spilled down his front, when I banged into the door. He was surprised."

"So they brought you into the station and the woman was brought in also, this Mrs. Donner, and she identified you. Is that it? She took one look at you and seemed to recognize you?"

"Started screaming like hell."

"She identified you absolutely, in spite of her hysterical state?"

"I guess so."

"And you admitted attacking her?"

"I guess so."

"Was that really the correct woman, though? This 'Mrs. Donner' who is accusing you of rape?"

"Huh?"

"Could you have identified her?"

"Me? I don't know. No. I don't know."

"Let's go back to the bar. You said there were three women there, all white women. Did they look alike to you, or what?"

"I don't know."

"Did one of them catch your attention?"

"Maybe. I don't know. One of them . . . she kind of was watching me, I thought. They was all horsing around."

"It was very crowded in the bar? And this woman, this particular woman, looked at you. Did she smile at you?"

"They was all laughing, you know, and if they looked around the place, why, it would seem they was smiling. . . . I don't know which one it was. I'm all mixed up on that."

"Would you say that this woman, let's call her 'Mrs. Donner' temporarily, this woman was behaving in a way that was provocative? She was looking at you or toward you, and at other men?"

"There was a lot of guys in there, black guys, and some white guys, too. I liked the tone of that place. There was a good feeling there. I wasn't drunk, but. . . ."

"Yes, you were drunk."

"Naw, I was high on my own power, I only had a few drinks."

"You were drunk; that happens to be a fact. That's an important fact. Don't forget it."

"I was drunk. . . ?"

"Yes. You were drunk. And a white woman did smile at you, in a bar on Gratiot; let's say it was this 'Mrs. Donner' who is charging you with rape. Do you know anything about her? No. I'll tell you: She's married, separated from her husband, the husband's whereabouts are unknown, she's been on and off welfare since 1964, she worked for a while at Leonard's Downtown, the department store, and was discharged because she evidently took some merchandise home with her . . . and she's been unemployed since September of last year, but without any visible means of support; no welfare. So she won't be able to account for her means of support since September, if that should come up in court."

"Uh. . . . You going to make a deal with them, then?"

"I don't have to make a deal. I told you to let me worry about her. She has to testify against you, and she has to convince a jury that she didn't deserve to be followed by you, that she didn't entice you, she didn't smile at you. She has to convince a jury that she didn't deserve whatever happened to her. . . . She did smile at you?"

"Well, uh, you know how it was . . . a lot of guys crowding around, shifting around. . . . I don't know which one of the women for sure looked at me, there was three of them, maybe they all did . . . or maybe just one . . . or. . . . It was confused. Some guys was buying them drinks and I couldn't get too close, I didn't know anybody there. I liked the tone of the place, but I was on the outside, you know? I was having my own party in my head. Then I saw this one woman get mad and put on her coat—"

"A light-colored coat? An imitation-fur coat?"

"Jesus, how do I know? Saw her put her arm in a sleeve. . . ."

"And she walked out? Alone?"

"Yeah. So I . . . I got very jumpy. . . . I thought I would follow her, you know, just see what happens. . . ."

"But you didn't follow her with the intention of committing rape."

"I. . . ."

"You wanted to talk to her, maybe? She'd smiled at you and you wanted to talk to her?"

"I don't know if. . . ."

"This white woman, whose name you didn't know, had smiled at you. She then left the bar—that is, Carson's Tavern—at about midnight, completely alone, unescorted, and she walked out along the street. Is this true?"

"Yes."

"When did she notice that you were following her?"

"Right away."

"Then what happened?"

"She started walking faster."

"Did she pause or give any sign to you? You mentioned that she kept looking over her shoulder at you—"

"Yeah."

"Then she started to run?"

"Yeah."

"She tried to get someone to stop, to let her in his car, but he wouldn't. He drove away. She was drunk, wasn't she, and screaming at him?"

"She was screaming. . . ."

"She was drunk, too. That happens to be a fact. You were both drunk, those are facts. This 'Mrs. Donner' who is accusing you of rape was drunk at the time. So. . . . The driver in the Pontiac drove away and you approached her. Was it the same woman who had smiled at you in the tavern?"

"I think . . . uh. . . . I don't know. . . ."

"She was the woman from the tavern?"

"That got mad and put her coat on? Sure. She walked out. . . ."

"Did all three women more or less behave in the same manner? They were very loud, they'd been drinking, you really couldn't distinguish between them. . . ?"

"I don't know."

"When you caught up to the woman, what did she say to you?"

"Say? Nothing. No words."

"She was screaming?"

"Oh, yeah."

"What did you say to her?"

"Nothing."

"Could you identify her?"

"I . . . uh. . . . That's where I get mixed up."

"Why?"

"I don't remember no face to her."

"Why not?"

"Must not of looked at it."

"Back in the bar, you didn't look either?"

"Well, yes . . . but I. . . . It's all a smear, like. Like a blur."

"This 'Mrs. Donner' says you threatened to kill her. Is that true?"

"If she says so. . . ."

"No, hell. Don't worry about what she says. What do *you* say?"

"I don't remember."

"*Lay still or I'll kill you.* Did you say that?"

"Is that what they have down?"

"Did you say it? *Lay still or I'll kill you?*"

"That don't sound like me."

"You didn't say anything to her, did you?"

"When? When we was fighting?"

"At any time."

"I don't remember."

"In the confusion of struggling, it isn't likely you said anything to her, is it?—anything so distinct as that? Or maybe it was another man, another black man, who attacked this 'Mrs. Donner' and she's confusing him with you. . . ?"

"Uh. . . ."

"Did you intend to kill her?"

"No."

"What did you have in mind, when you followed her out of the tavern?"

"Oh, you know . . . I was kind of high-strung. . . ."

"She had smiled at you, so you thought she might be friendly? A pretty white woman like that, only twenty-nine years old, with her hair fixed up and a fancy imitation-fur coat, who had smiled at you, a stranger, in a bar . . . ? You thought she might be friendly, wasn't that it?"

"Friendly? Jesus! I never expected no friendship, that's for sure."

"Well, put yourself back in that situation. Don't be so sure. If a white woman smiled at you, and you followed her out onto the street, it would be logical you might expect her to be friendly toward you. Keep your mind clear. You don't have to believe what other people tell you about yourself; you don't have to believe that you assaulted that woman just because she says you did. Things aren't so simple. Did you expect her to fight you off?"

"Don't know."

"If she hadn't fought you, there wouldn't be any crime committed, would there? She resisted you, she provoked you into a frenzy. . . . But don't think about that. I'll think about that angle. I'm the one who's going to question Mrs. Donner, and then we'll see who's guilty of what. . . . But one important thing: Why didn't you tell the police that you really didn't recognize the woman, yourself?"

"Huh? Jesus, they'd of been mad as hell—"

"Yes, they would have been mad, they might have beaten you some more. You were terrified of a further beating. So, of course, you didn't protest, you didn't say anything. Because she's a white woman and you're black. Isn't that the real reason?"

"I don't know."

"There weren't any black men in the station. You were the only black man there. So you thought it would be the safest, most prudent thing to confess to everything, because this white woman and the white police had you, they had you, and you considered yourself fair game. And already you'd been beaten, your mouth was bleeding, and you didn't know you had the right to an attorney, to any help at all. You were completely isolated. They could do anything to you they wanted. . . . Your instincts told you to go along with them, to cooperate. Nobody can blame you for that: that's how you survived. Does any of this sound familiar to you?"

"Some kind of way, yes. . . . Yes, I think so."

"And the police demonstrated their antagonism toward you, their automatic assumption of your guilt, even though the woman who accused you of rape was a probable prostitute, a woman of very doubtful reputation who led you on, who enticed you out into the street . . . and then evidently changed her mind, or became frightened when she saw how excited you were. Is that it? Why do you think she identified you so quickly, why was she so certain?"

"Must of seen my face."

"How did she see your face, if you didn't see hers?"

"I saw hers but didn't take it in, you know, I kind of blacked out . . . she was fighting me off and that drove me wild . . . it was good luck she stopped, or . . . or something else might of happened. . . . You know how frenzied you get. There was a streetlight there, and I thought to myself, *She ain't going to forget me.*"

"Why not?"

"Gave her a good look at my face. My face is important to me."

Incident in a Neighborhood Tavern

Bill Pronzini

When the holdup went down I was sitting at the near end of the Foghorn Tavern's scarred mahogany bar talking to the owner, Matt Candiotti.

It was a little before seven of a midweek evening, lull-time in working-class neighborhood saloons like this one. Blue-collar locals would jam the place from four until about six-thirty, when the last of them headed home for dinner; the hard-core drinkers wouldn't begin filtering back in until about seven-thirty or eight. Right now there were only two customers, and the juke-box and computer hockey games were quiet. The TV over the back bar was on but with the sound turned down to a tolerable level. One of the customers, a porky guy in his fifties, drinking Anchor Steam out of the bottle, was watching the last of the NBC national news. The other customer, an equally porky and middle-aged female barfly, half in the bag on red wine, was trying to convince him to pay attention to her instead of Tom Brokaw.

I had a draft beer in front of me, but that wasn't the reason I was there. I'd come to ask Candiotti, as I had asked two dozen other merchants here in the Outer Mission, if he could offer any leads on the rash of burglaries that were plaguing small businesses in the neighborhood. The police hadn't come up with anything positive after six weeks, so a couple of the victims had gotten up a fund and hired me to see what I could find out. They'd picked me because I had been born and raised in the Outer Mission, I still had friends and shirttail relatives living here and I understood the neighborhood a good deal better than any other private detective in San Francisco.

But so far I wasn't having any more luck than the SFPD. None of the merchants I'd spoken with today had given me any new ideas, and Candiotti was proving to be no exception. He stood slicing limes into wedges as we talked. They might have been onions the way his long, mournful face was screwed up, like a man trying to hold back tears. His gray-stubbled jowls wobbled every time he shook his head. He reminded me of a tired old hound, friendly and sad, as if life had dealt him a few kicks but not quite enough to rob him of his good nature.

"Wish I could help," he said. "But hell, I don't hear nothin. Must be pros from Hunters Point or the Fillmore, hah?"

Hunters Point and the Fillmore were black sections of the city which was a pretty good indicator of where his head was at. I said, "Some of the others figure it for local talent."

"Out of this neighborhood, you mean?"

I nodded, drank some of my draft.

"Nah, I doubt it," he said. "Guys that organized, they don't shit where they eat. Too smart, you know?"

"Maybe. Any break-ins or attempted break-ins here?"

"Not so far. I got bars on all the windows, double dead-bolt locks on the storeroom door off the alley. Besides, what's for them to steal besides a few cases of whiskey?"

"You don't keep cash on the premises overnight?"

"Fifty bucks in the till," Candiotti said, "that's all; that's my limit. Everything else goes out of here when I close up, down to the night deposit at the B of A on Mission. My mama didn't raise no airheads." He scraped the lime wedges off his board, into a plastic container, and racked the serrated knife he'd been using. "One thing I did hear," he said. "I heard some of the loot turned up down in San Jose. You know about that?"

"Not much of a lead there. Secondhand dealer named Pitman had a few pieces of stereo equipment stolen from the factory outlet store on Geneva. Said he bought it from a guy at the San Jose flea market, somebody he didn't know, never saw before."

"Yeah, sure," Candiotti said wryly. "What do the cops think?"

"That Pitman bought it off a fence."

"Makes sense. So maybe the boosters are from San Jose, hah?"

"Could be," I said, and that was when the kid walked in.

He brought bad air in with him; I sensed it right away and so did Candiotti. We both glanced at the door when it opened, the way you do, but we didn't look away again once we saw him. He was in his early twenties, dark-skinned, dressed in chinos, a cotton windbreaker, sharp-toed shoes polished to a high gloss. But it was his eyes that put the chill on my neck, the sudden clutch of tension down low in my belly. They were bright, jumpy, on the wild side, and in the dim light of the Foghorn's interior, the pupils were so small they seemed nonexistent. He had one hand in his jacket pocket and I knew it was clamped around a gun even before he took it out and showed it to us.

He came up to the bar a few feet on my left, the gun jabbing the air in front of him. He couldn't hold it steady; it kept jerking up and down, from side to side, as if it had a kind of spasmodic life of its own. Behind me, at the other end of the bar, I heard Anchor Steam suck in his breath, the barfly make a sound like a stifled moan. I eased back a little on the stool, watching the gun and the kid's eyes flick from Candiotti to me to the two customers and back around again. Candiotti didn't move at all, just stood there staring with his hound's face screwed up in that holding-back-tears way.

"All right all right," the kid said. His voice was high pitched, excited, and there was drool at one corner of his mouth. You couldn't get much more stoned than he was and still function. Coke, crack, speed—maybe a combination. The gun that kept flicking this way and that was a goddamn Saturday Night Special. "Listen good, man, everybody listen good I don't want to kill none of you, man, but I will if I got to, you believe it?"

None of us said anything. None of us moved.

The kid had a folded-up paper sack in one pocket; he dragged it out with his free hand, dropped it, broke quickly at the middle to pick it up without lowering his gaze. When he straightened again there was sweat on his forehead, more drool coming out of his mouth. He threw the sack on the bar.

"Put the money in there Mr. Cyclone Man," he said to Candiotti. "All the money in the register but not the coins; I don't want the fuckin' coins, you hear me?"

Candiotti nodded; reached out slowly, caught up the sack, turned toward the back bar with his shoulders hunched up against his neck. When he punched No Sale on the register, the ringing thump of the cash drawer sliding open seemed overloud in the electric hush. For a few seconds the kid watched him scoop bills into the paper sack; then his eyes and the gun skittered my way again. I had looked into the muzzle of a handgun before and it was the same feeling each time: dull fear, helplessness, a kind of naked vulnerability.

"Your wallet on the bar, man, all your cash." The gun barrel and the wild eyes flicked away again, down the length of the plank, before I could move to comply. "You down there, dude, you and fat mama put your money on the bar. All of it, hurry up."

Each of us did as we were told. While I was getting my wallet out I managed to slide my right foot off the stool, onto the brass rail, and to get my right hand pressed tight against the beveled edge of the bar. If I had to make any sudden moves, I would need the leverage.

Candiotti finished loading the sack, turned from the register. There was a grayish cast to his face now—the wet gray color of fear. The kid said to him, "Pick up their money, put it in the sack with the rest. Come on come on come on!"

Candiotti went to the far end of the plank, scooped up the wallets belonging to Anchor Steam and the woman; then he came back my way, added my wallet to the contents of the paper sack, put the sack down carefully in front of the kid.

"Okay," the kid said, "okay all right." He glanced over his

shoulder at the street door, as if he'd heard something there; but it stayed closed. He jerked his head around again. In his sweaty agitation the Saturday Night Special almost slipped free of his fingers; he fumbled a tighter grip on it, and when it didn't go off I let the breath I had been holding come out thin and slow between my teeth. The muscles in my shoulders and back were drawn so tight I was afraid they might cramp.

The kid reached out for the sack, dragged it in against his body. But he made no move to leave with it. Instead he said, "Now we go get the big pile, man."

Candiotti opened his mouth, closed it again. His eyes were almost as big and starey as the kid's.

"Come on Mr. Cyclone Man, the safe, the safe in your office. We goin' back there *now*."

"No money in that safe," Candiotti said in a thin, scratchy voice. "Nothing valuable."

"Oh man I'll kill you man I'll blow your fuckin' head off! I ain't playin' no games I want that money!"

He took two steps forward, jabbing with the gun up close to Candiotti's gray face. Candiotti backed off a step, brought his hands up, took a tremulous breath.

"All right," he said, "but I got to get the key to the office. It's in the register."

"Hurry up hurry up!"

Candiotti turned back to the register, rang it open, rummaged inside with his left hand. But with his right hand, shielded from the kid by his body, he eased up the top on a large wooden cigar box adjacent. The hand disappeared inside; came out again with metal in it, glinting in the back bar lights. I saw it and I wanted to yell at him, but it wouldn't have done any good, would only have warned the kid . . . and he was already turning with it, bringing it up with both hands now—the damn gun of his own he'd had hidden inside the cigar box. There was no time for me to do anything but shove away from the bar and sideways off the stool just as Candiotti opened fire.

The state he was in, the kid didn't realize what was happening until it was too late for him to react; he never even got a shot off. Candiotti's first slug knocked him halfway around, and one of the three others that followed it opened up his face like a piece of ripe fruit smacked by a hammer. He was dead before his body, driven backward, slammed into the cigarette machine near the door, slid down it to the floor.

The half-drunk woman was yelling in broken shrieks, as if she couldn't get enough air for a sustained scream. When I came up out of my crouch I saw that Anchor Steam had hold of her, clinging to her as much for support as in an effort to calm her down. Candiotti stood flat-footed, his arms down at his sides, the gun out of sight below the bar, staring at the bloody remains of the kid as if he couldn't believe what he was seeing, couldn't believe what he'd done.

Some of the tension in me eased as I went to the door, found the lock on its security gate, fastened it before anybody could come in off the street. The Saturday Night Special was still clutched in the kid's hand; I bent, pulled it free with my thumb and forefinger, broke the cylinder. It was loaded, all right—five cartridges. I dropped it into my jacket pocket, thought about checking the kid's clothing for identification, didn't do it. It wasn't any of my business, now, who he'd been. And I did not want to touch him or any part of him. There was a queasiness in my stomach, a fluttery weakness behind my knees—the same delayed reaction I always had to violence and death—and touching him would only make it worse.

To keep from looking at the red ruin of the kid's face, I pivoted back to the bar. Candiotti hadn't moved. Anchor Steam had gotten the woman to stop screeching and had coaxed her over to one of the handful of tables near the jukebox; now she was sobbing, "I've got to go home, I'm gonna be sick if I don't go home." But she didn't make any move to get up and neither did Anchor Steam.

I walked over near Candiotti, pushed hard words at him in an undertone. "That was a damn fool thing to do. You could have got us all killed."

"I know," he said. "I know."

"Why'd you do it?"

"I thought . . . hell, you saw the way he was waving that piece of his . . ."

"Yeah," I said. "Call the police. Nine-eleven."

"Nine-eleven. Okay."

"Put that gun of yours down first. On the bar."

He did that. There was a phone on the back bar; he went away to it in shaky strides. While he was talking to the Emergency operator I picked up his weapon, saw that it was a .32 Charter Arms revolver. I held it in my hand until Candiotti finished with the call, set it down again as he came back to where I stood.

"They'll have somebody here in five minutes," he said.

I said, "You know that kid?"

"Christ, no."

"Ever see him before? Here or anywhere else?"

"No."

"So how did he know about your safe?"

Candiotti blinked at me. "What?"

"The safe in your office. Street kid like that . . . how'd he know about it?"

"How should I know? What difference does it make?"

"He seemed to think you keep big money in that safe."

"Well, I don't. There's nothing in it."

"That's right, you told me you don't keep more than fifty bucks on the premises overnight. In the till."

"Yeah."

"Then why have you got a safe, if it's empty?"

Candiotti's eyes narrowed. "I used to keep my receipts in it, all right? Before all these burglaries started. Then I figured I'd be smarter to take the money to the bank every night."

"Sure, that explains it," I said. "Still, a kid like that, looking for a big score to feed his habit, he wasn't just after what was in the till and our wallets. No, it was as if he'd gotten wind of a heavy stash—a grand or more."

Nothing from Candiotti.

I watched him for a time. Then I said, "Big risk you took, using that .32 of yours. How come you didn't make your play the first time you went to the register? How come you waited until the kid mentioned your office safe?"

"I didn't like the way he was acting, like he might start shooting any second. I figured it was our only chance. Listen, what're you getting at, hah?"

"Another funny thing," I said, "is the way he called you 'Mr. Cyclone Man.' Now why would a hopped-up kid use a term like that to a bar owner he didn't know?"

"How the hell should I know?"

"Cyclone," I said. "What's a cyclone but a big destructive wind? Only one other thing I can think of."

"Yeah? What's that?"

"A fence. A cyclone fence."

Candiotti made a fidgety movement. Some of the wet gray pallor was beginning to spread across his cheeks again, like a fungus.

I said, "And a fence is somebody who receives and distributes stolen goods. A Mr. Fence Man. But then you know that, don't you, Candiotti? We were talking about that kind of fence before the kid came in . . . how Pitman, down in San Jose, bought some hot stereo equipment off of one. That fence could just as easily be operating here in San Francisco, though. Right here in this neighborhood, in fact. Hell, suppose the stuff taken in all those burglaries never left the neighborhood. Suppose it was brought to a place nearby and stored until it could be trucked out to other cities—a tavern storeroom, for instance. Might even be some of it is *still* in that storeroom. And the money he got for the rest he'd keep locked up in his safe, right? Who'd figure it? Except maybe a poor junkie who picked up a whisper on the street somewhere—"

Candiotti made a sudden grab for the .32, caught it up, backed up a step with it leveled at my chest. "You smart son of a bitch," he said. "I ought to kill you too."

"In front of witnesses? With the police due any minute?"

He glanced over at the two customers. The woman was still sobbing, lost in a bleak outpouring of self-pity; but Anchor Steam was staring our way, and from the expression on his face he'd heard every word of my exchange with Candiotti.

"There's still enough time for me to get clear," Candiotti said grimly. He was talking to himself, not to me. Sweat had plastered his lank hair to his forehead; the revolver was not quite steady in his hand. "Lock you up in my office, you and those two back there . . ."

"I don't think so," I said.

"Goddamn you, you think I won't use this gun again?"

"I *know* you won't use it. I emptied out the last two cartridges while you were on the phone."

I took the two shells out of my left-hand jacket pocket and held them up where he could see them. At the same time I got the kid's Saturday Night Special out of the other pocket, held it loosely pointed in his direction. "You want to put your piece down now, Candiotti? You're not going anywhere, not for a long time."

He put it down—dropped it clattering onto the bartop. And as he did his sad hound's face screwed up again, only this time he didn't even try to keep the wetness from leaking out of his eyes. He was leaning against the bar, crying like the woman, submerged in his own outpouring of self-pity, when the cops showed up a little while later.

The New Girl Friend

Ruth Rendell

'YOU KNOW WHAT we did last time?' he said.

She had waited for this for weeks. 'Yes?'

'I wondered if you'd like to do it again.'

She longed to but she didn't want to sound too keen. 'Why not?'

'How about Friday afternoon, then? I've got the day off and Angie always goes to her sister's on Friday.'

'Not *always*, David.' She giggled.

He also laughed a little. 'She will this week. Do you think we could use your car? Angie'll take ours.'

'Of course. I'll come for you about two, shall I?'

'I'll open the garage doors and you can drive straight in. Oh, and Chris, could you fix it to get back a bit later? I'd love it if we could have the whole evening together.'

'I'll try,' she said, and then, 'I'm sure I can fix it. I'll tell Graham I'm going out with my new girl friend.'

He said goodbye and that he would see her on Friday. Christine put the receiver back. She had almost given up expecting a call from him. But there must have been a grain of hope still, for she had never left the receiver off the way she used to.

The last time she had done that was on a Thursday three weeks before, the day she had gone round to Angie's and found

David there alone. Christine had got into the habit of taking the phone off the hook during the middle part of the day to avoid getting calls for the Midland Bank. Her number and the Midland Bank's differed by only one digit. Most days she took the receiver off at nine-thirty and put it back at three-thirty. On Thursday afternoons she nearly always went round to see Angie and never bothered to phone first.

Christine knew Angie's husband quite well. If she stayed a bit later on Thursdays she saw him when he came home from work. Sometimes she and Graham and Angie and David went out together as a foursome. She knew that David, like Graham, was a salesman or sales executive, as Graham always described himself, and she guessed from her friend's life style that David was rather more successful at it. She had never found him particularly attractive, for, although he was quite tall, he had something of a girlish look and very fair wavy hair.

Graham was a heavily built, very dark man with a swarthy skin. He had to shave twice a day. Christine had started going out with him when she was fifteen and they had got married on her eighteenth birthday. She had never really known any other men at all intimately and now if she ever found herself alone with a man she felt awkward and apprehensive. The truth was that she was afraid a man might make an advance to her and the thought of that frightened her very much. For a long while she carried a penknife in her handbag in case she should need to defend herself. One evening, after they had been out with a colleague of Graham's and had had a few drinks, she told Graham about this fear of hers.

He said she was silly but he seemed rather pleased.

'When you went off to talk to those people and I was left with John I felt like that. I felt terribly nervous. I didn't know how to talk to him.'

Graham roared with laughter. 'You don't mean you thought old John was going to make a pass at you in the middle of a crowded restaurant?'

'I don't know,' Christine said. 'I never know what they'll do.'

'So long as you're not afraid of what I'll do,' said Graham, beginning to kiss her, 'that's all that matters.'

There was no point in telling him now, ten years too late, that she was afraid of what he did and always had been. Of course she had got used to it, she wasn't actually terrified, she was resigned and sometimes even quite cheerful about it. David was the only man she had ever been alone with when it felt all right.

That first time, that Thursday when Angie had gone to her sister's and hadn't been able to get through on the phone and tell Christine not to come, that time it had been fine. And afterwards she had felt happy and carefree, though what had happened with David took on the colouring of a dream next day. It wasn't really believable. Early on he had said:

'Will you tell Angie?'

'Not if you don't want me to.'

'I think it would upset her, Chris. It might even wreck our marriage. You see . . .' He had hesitated. 'You see, that was the first time I—I mean, anyone ever . . .' And he had looked into her eyes. 'Thank God it was you.'

The following Thursday she had gone round to see Angie as usual. In the meantime there had been no word from David. She stayed late in order to see him, beginning to feel a little sick with apprehension, her heart beating hard when he came in.

He looked quite different from how he had when she had found him sitting at the table reading, the radio on. He was wearing a grey flannel suit and a grey striped tie. When Angie went out of the room and for a minute she was alone with him, she felt a flicker of that old wariness that was the forerunner of her fear. He was getting her a drink. She looked up and met his eyes and it was all right again. He gave her a conspiratorial smile, laying a finger on his lips.

'I'll give you a ring,' he had whispered.

She had to wait two more weeks. During that time she went twice to Angie's and twice Angie came to her. She and Graham and Angie and David went out as a foursome and while Graham was fetching drinks and Angie was in the Ladies, David looked at her and smiled and lightly touched her foot with his foot under the table.

'I'll phone you. I haven't forgotten.'

It was a Wednesday when he finally did phone. Next day Christine told Graham she had made a new friend, a girl she had met at work. She would be going out somewhere with this new friend on Friday and she wouldn't be back till eleven. She was desperately afraid he would want the car—it was *his* car or his firm's—but it so happened he would be in the office that day and would go by train. Telling him these lies didn't make her feel guilty. It wasn't as if this were some sordid affair, it was quite different.

When Friday came she dressed with great care. Normally, to go round to Angie's, she would have worn jeans and a tee shirt with a sweater over it. That was what she had on the first time she found herself alone with David. She put on a skirt and blouse and her black velvet jacket. She took the heated rollers out of her hair and brushed it into curls down on her shoulders. There was never much money to spend on clothes. The mortgage on the house took up a third of what Graham earned and half what she earned at her part-time job. But she could run to a pair of sheer black tights to go with the highest heeled shoes she'd got, her black pumps.

The doors of Angie and David's garage were wide open and their car was gone. Christine turned into their driveway, drove into the garage and closed the doors behind her. A door at the back of the garage led into the yard and garden. The kitchen door was unlocked as it had been that Thursday three weeks before and always was on Thursday afternoons. She opened the door and walked in.

'Is that you, Chris?'

The voice sounded very male. She needed to be reassured by the sight of him. She went into the hall as he came down the stairs.

'You look lovely,' he said.

'So do you.'

He was wearing a suit. It was of navy silk with a pattern of pink and white flowers. The skirt was very short, the jacket clinched into his waist with a wide navy patent belt. The long golden hair fell to his shoulders, he was heavily made-up and this time he had painted his fingernails. He looked far more beautiful than he had that first time.

Then, three weeks before, the sound of her entry drowned in loud music from the radio, she had come upon this girl sitting at the table reading *Vogue*. For a moment she had thought it must be David's sister. She had forgotten Angie had said David was an only child. The girl had long fair hair and was wearing a red summer dress with white spots on it, white sandals and around her neck a string of white beads. When Christine saw that it was not a girl but David himself she didn't know what to do.

He stared at her in silence and without moving and then he switched off the radio. Christine said the silliest and least relevant thing.

'What are you doing home at this time?'

That made him smile. 'I'd finished so I took the rest of the day off. I should have locked the back door. Now you're here you may as well sit down.'

She sat down. She couldn't take her eyes off him. He didn't look like a man dressed up as a girl, he looked like a girl and a much prettier one than she or Angie. 'Does Angie know?'

He shook his head.

'But why do you do it?' she burst out and she looked about the room, Angie's small, rather untidy living room, at the radio, the *Vogue* magazine. 'What do you get out of it?' Something came back to her from an article she had read. 'Did your mother dress you as a girl when you were little?'

'I don't know,' he said. 'Maybe. I don't remember. I don't want to *be* a girl. I just want to dress up as one sometimes.'

The first shock of it was past and she began to feel easier with him. It wasn't as if there was anything grotesque about the way he looked. The very last thing he reminded her of was one of those female impersonators. A curious thought came into her head, that it was *nicer*, somehow more civilized, to be a woman and that if only all men were more like women . . . That was silly, of course, it couldn't be.

'And it's enough for you just to dress up and be here on your own?'

He was silent for a moment. Then, 'Since you ask, what I'd really like would be to go out like this and . . .' He paused, looking at her, 'and be seen by lots of people, that's what I'd like. I've never had the nerve for that.'

The bold idea expressed itself without her having to give it a moment's thought. She wanted to do it. She was beginning to tremble with excitement.

'Let's go out then, you and I. Let's go out now. I'll put my car in your garage and you can get into it so the people next door don't see and then we'll go somewhere. Let's do that, David, shall we?'

She wondered afterwards why she had enjoyed it so much. What had it been, after all, as far as anyone else knew but two girls walking on Hampstead Heath? If Angie had suggested that the two of them do it she would have thought it a poor way of spending the afternoon. But with David . . . She hadn't even minded that of the two of them he was infinitely the better dressed, taller, better-looking, more graceful. She didn't mind now as he came down the stairs and stood in front of her.

'Where shall we go?'

'Not the Heath this time,' he said. 'Let's go shopping.'

He bought a blouse in one of the big stores. Christine went into the changing room with him when he tried it on. They walked about in Hyde Park. Later on they had dinner and Christine noted that they were the only two women in the restaurant dining together.

'I'm grateful to you,' David said. He put his hand over hers on the table.

'I enjoy it,' she said. 'It's so—crazy. I really love it. You'd better not do that, had you? There's a man over there giving us a funny look.'

'Women hold hands,' he said.

'Only *those* sort of women. David, we could do this every Friday you don't have to work.'

'Why not?' he said.

There was nothing to feel guilty about. She wasn't harming Angie and she wasn't being disloyal to Graham. All she was doing was going on innocent outings with another girl. Graham wasn't interested in her new friend, he didn't even ask her name. Christine came to long for Fridays, especially for the moment when she let herself into Angie's house and saw David coming down the stairs and for the moment when they stepped out of the car in some public place and the first eyes were turned on him. They went to Holland Park, they went to the zoo, to Kew Gardens. They went to the cinema and a man sitting next to David put his hand on his knee. David loved that, it was a triumph for him, but Christine whispered they must change their seats and they did.

When they parted at the end of an evening he kissed her gently on the lips. He smelled of Alliage or Je Reviens or Opium. During the afternoon they usually went into one of the big stores and sprayed themselves out of the tester bottles.

Angie's mother lived in the north of England. When she had to convalesce after an operation Angie went up there to look after her. She expected to be away two weeks and the second weekend of her absence Graham had to go to Brussels with the sales manager.

'We could go away somewhere for the weekend,' David said.

'Graham's sure to phone,' Christine said.

'One night then. Just for the Saturday night. You can tell him you're going out with your new girl friend and you're going to be late.'

'All right.'

It worried her that she had no nice clothes to wear. David had a small but exquisite wardrobe of suits and dresses, shoes and scarves and beautiful underclothes. He kept them in a cupboard in his office to which only he had a key and he secreted items home and back again in his briefcase. Christine hated the idea of going away for the night in her grey flannel skirt and white silk blouse and that velvet jacket while David wore his Zandra Rhodes dress. In a burst of recklessness she spent all of two weeks' wages on a linen suit.

They went in David's car. He had made the arrangements and Christine had expected they would be going to a motel twenty miles outside London. She hadn't thought it would matter much to David where they went. But he surprised her by his choice of an hotel that was a three-hundred-year-old house on the Suffolk coast.

'If we're going to do it,' he said, 'we may as well do it in style.'

She felt very comfortable with him, very happy. She tried to imagine what it would have felt like going to spend a night in an hotel with a man, a lover. If the person sitting next to her were dressed, not in a black and white printed silk dress and scarlet jacket but in a man's suit with shirt and tie. If the face it gave her so much pleasure to look at were not powdered and rouged and mascara'd but rough and already showing beard growth. She couldn't imagine it. Or, rather, she could only think how in that case she would have jumped out of the car at the first red traffic lights.

They had single rooms next door to each other. The rooms were very small but Christine could see that a double might have been awkward for David who must at some point—though she didn't care to think of this—have to shave and strip down to being what he really was.

He came in and sat on her bed while she unpacked her night-dress and spare pair of shoes.

'This is fun, isn't it?'

She nodded, squinting into the mirror, working on her eyelids with a little brush. David always did his eyes beautifully. She turned round and smiled at him.

'Let's go down and have a drink.'

The dining room, the bar, the lounge were all low-ceilinged timbered rooms with carved wood on the walls David said was called linenfold panelling. There were old maps and pictures of men hunting in gilt frames and copper bowls full of roses. Long windows were thrown open on to a terrace. The sun was still high in the sky and it was very warm. While Christine sat on the terrace in the sunshine David went off to get their drinks. When he came back to their table he had a man with him, a thickset paunchy man of about forty who was carrying a tray with four glasses on it.

'This is Ted,' David said.

'Delighted to meet you,' Ted said. 'I've asked my friend to join us. I hope you don't mind.'

She had to say she didn't. David looked at her and from his look she could tell he had deliberately picked Ted up.

'But why did you?' she said to him afterwards. 'Why did you want to? You told me you didn't really like it when that man put his hand on you in the cinema.'

'That was so physical. This is just a laugh. You don't suppose I'd let them touch me, do you?'

Ted and Peter had the next table to theirs at dinner. Christine was silent and standoffish but David flirted with them. Ted kept leaning across and whispering to him and David giggled and smiled. You could see he was enjoying himself tremendously. Christine knew they would ask her and David to go out with them after dinner and she began to be afraid. Suppose David got carried away by the excitement of it, the 'fun', and went off somewhere with Ted, leaving her and Peter alone together? Peter had a red face and a black moustache and beard and a wart with black hairs growing out of it on his left cheek. She and David were eating steak and the waiter had brought them sharp pointed steak knives. She hadn't used hers. The steak was very tender. When no one was looking she slipped the steak knife into her bag.

Ted and Peter were still drinking coffee and brandies when David got up quite abruptly and said, 'Coming?' to Christine.

'I suppose you've arranged to meet them later?' Christine said as soon as they were out of the dining room.

David looked at her. His scarlet-painted lips parted into a wide smile. He laughed.

'I turned them down.'

'Did you *really*?'

'I could tell you hated the idea. Besides, we want to be alone, don't we? I know I want to be alone with you.'

She nearly shouted his name so that everyone could hear, the relief was so great. She controlled herself but she was trembling. 'Of course I want to be alone with you,' she said.

She put her arm in his. It wasn't uncommon, after all, for girls to walk along with linked arms. Men turned to look at David and one of them whistled. She knew it must be David the whistle was directed at because he looked so beautiful with his long golden hair and high-heeled red sandals. They walked along the sea front, along the little low promenade. It was too warm even at eight-thirty to wear a coat. There were a lot of people about but not crowds for the place was too select to attract crowds. They walked to the end of the pier. They had a drink in the Ship Inn and another in the Fishermen's Arms. A man tried to pick David up in the Fishermen's Arms but this time he was cold and distant.

'I'd like to put my arm round you,' he said as they were walking back, 'but I suppose that wouldn't do, though it is dark.'

'Better not,' said Christine. She said suddenly, 'This has been the best evening of my life.'

He looked at her. 'You really mean that?'

She nodded. 'Absolutely the best.'

They came into the hotel. 'I'm going to get them to send us up a couple of drinks. To my room. Is that OK?'

She sat on the bed. David went into the bathroom. To do his face, she thought, maybe to shave before he let the man with the drinks see him. There was a knock at the door and a waiter came in with a tray on which were two long glasses of something or other with fruit and leaves floating in it, two pink table napkins, two olives on sticks and two peppermint creams wrapped up in green paper.

Christine tasted one of the drinks. She ate an olive. She opened her handbag and took out a mirror and a lipstick and painted her lips. David came out of the bathroom. He had taken off the golden wig and washed his face. He hadn't shaved, there was a pale stubble showing on his chin and cheeks. His legs and feet were bare and he was wearing a very masculine robe made of navy blue towelling. She tried to hide her disappointment.

'You've changed,' she said brightly.

He shrugged. 'There are limits.'

He raised his glass and she raised her glass and he said:

'To us!'

The beginnings of a feeling of panic came over her. Suddenly he was so evidently a man. She edged a little way along the mattress.

'I wish we had the whole weekend.'

She nodded nervously. She was aware her body had started a faint trembling. He had noticed it too. Sometimes before he had noticed how emotion made her tremble.

'Chris,' he said.

She sat passive and afraid.

'I'm not really like a woman, Chris. I just play at that sometimes for fun. You know that, don't you?' The hand that touched her smelt of nail varnish remover. There were hairs on the wrist she had never noticed before. 'I'm falling in love with you,' he said. 'And you feel the same, don't you?'

She couldn't speak. He took her by the shoulders. He brought his mouth up to hers and put his arms round her and began kissing her. His skin felt abrasive and a smell as male as

Graham's came off his body. She shook and shuddered. He pushed her down on the bed and his hands began undressing her, his mouth still on hers and his body heavy on top of her.

She felt behind her, put her hand into the open handbag and pulled out the knife. Because she could feel his heart beating steadily against her right breast she knew where to stab and she stabbed again and again. The bright red heart's blood spurted over her clothes and the bed and the two peppermint creams on the tray.

Mary, Mary, Shut the Door

Benjamin M. Schutz

ENZO SCOLARI MOTORED into my office and motioned me to sit. What the hell, I sat. He pulled around to the side of my desk, laced his fingers in his lap, and sized me up.

"I want to hire you, Mr. Haggerty," he announced.

"To do what, Mr. Scolari?"

"I want you to stop my niece's wedding."

"I see. And why is that?"

"She is making a terrible mistake, and I will not sit by and let her do it."

"Exactly what kind of mistake is she making?"

"She knows nothing about him. They just met. She is infatuated, nothing more. She knows nothing about men. Nothing. The first one to pay any attention to her and she wants to get married."

"You said they just met. How long ago, exactly?" Just a little reality check.

"Two weeks. Can you believe it? Two weeks. And I just found out about it yesterday. She brought him to the house last night. There was a party and she introduced him to everyone and told us she was going to marry him. How can you marry someone you've known for two weeks? That's ridiculous. It's a guarantee of failure and it'll break her heart. I can't let that happen."

"Mr. Scolari, I'm not sure we can help you with this. Your niece may be doing something foolish, but she has a right to do it. I understand your concern for her well-being, but I don't think you need a detective, maybe a priest or a therapist. We don't do premarital background checks. Our investigations are primarily criminal."

"The crime just hasn't happened yet, Mr. Haggerty. My niece may be a foolish girl, but he isn't. He knows exactly what he's doing."

"And what is that?"

"He's taking advantage of her naïveté, her innocence, her fears, her loneliness, so he can get her money. That's a crime, Mr. Haggerty."

And a damn hard one to prove. "What are you afraid of, Mr. Scolari? That he'll kill her for her money? That's quite a leap from an impulsive decision to marry. Do you have any reason to think that this guy is a killer?"

He straightened up and gave that one some thought. Enzo Scolari was wide and thick with shoulders so square and a head so flat he could have been a candelabra. His snow-white eyebrows and mustache hung like awnings for his eyes and lips.

"No. Not for that. But I can tell he doesn't love Gina. Last night I watched him. Every time Gina left his side his eyes went somewhere else. A man in love, his eyes follow his woman everywhere. No, he's following the maid or Gina's best friend. Gina comes back and he smiles like she's the sunrise. And she believes it.

"He spent more time touching the tapestries than he did holding her hand. He went through the house like a creditor, not a guest. No, he doesn't want Gina, he wants her money. You're right, murder is quite a step from that, but there are easier ways to steal. Gina is a shy, quiet woman who has never had to make any decisions for herself. I don't blame her for that. My sister, God rest her soul, was terrified that something awful would happen to Gina and she tried to protect her from everything. It didn't work. My sister was the one who died and it devastated the girl. Now Gina has to live in the world and she doesn't know how. If this guy can talk her into marrying him so quickly, he'll have no trouble talking her into letting him handle her money."

"How much money are we talking about here?"

"Ten million dollars, Mr. Haggerty." Scolari smiled, having made his point. People have murdered or married for lots less.

"How did she get all this money?"

"It's in a trust for her. A trust set up by my father. My sister and I each inherited half of Scolari Enterprises. When she died, her share went to Gina as her only child."

"This trust, who manages it?"

"I do, of course."

Of course. Motive number two just came up for air. "So, where's the problem? If you control the money, this guy can't do anything."

"I control the money as trustee for my sister. I began that when Gina was still a little girl. Now she is of age and can control the money herself if she wants to."

"So you stand to lose the use of ten million dollars. Have I got that right?"

Scolari didn't even bother to debate that one with me. I liked that. I'll take naked self-interest over the delusions of altruism any day.

"If they've just met, how do you know that this guy even knows that your niece has all this money?"

Scolari stared at me, then spat out his bitter reply. "Why else would he have pursued her? She is a mousy little woman, dull and plain. She's afraid of men. She spent her life in those fancy girls' schools where they taught her how to set the table. She huddled with her mother in that house, afraid of everything. Well, now she is alone and I think she's latched onto the first person who will rescue her from that."

"Does she know how you feel?"

He nodded. "Yes, she does. I made it very clear to her last night."

"How did she take it?"

"She told me to mind my own business." Scolari snorted. "She doesn't even know that that's what I'm doing. She said she loved him and she was going to marry him, no matter what."

"Doesn't sound so mousy to me. She ever stand up to you before?"

"No, never. On anything else, I'd applaud it. But getting married shouldn't be the first decision you ever make."

"Anyone else that might talk to her that she'd listen to?"

"No. She's an only child. Her father died when she was two in the same explosion that killed my father and took my legs. Her mother died in an automobile accident a little over a year ago. I am a widower myself and Gina was never close to my sons. They frightened her as a little girl. They were loud and rough. They teased her and made her cry." Scolari shrugged as if boys would be boys. "I did not like that and would stop it whenever I caught them, but she was such a timid child, their cruelty sprouted whenever she was around. There is no other family."

I picked up the pipe from my desk, stuck it in my mouth, and chewed on it. A glorified pacifier. Kept me from chewing up the inside of my mouth, though. Wouldn't be much of a stretch to take this one on. What the hell, work is work.

"Okay, Mr. Scolari, we'll take the case. I want you to understand that we can't and we won't stop her wedding. There are guys who will do that, and I know who they are, but I wouldn't give you their names. We'll do a background check on this guy and see if we can find something that'll change her mind or your mind. Maybe they really love each other. That happens, you know. This may be a crazy start, but I'm not sure that's a handicap. What's the best way to run a race when you don't know where the finish is?" I sure didn't have an answer and Scolari offered none.

"Mr. Haggerty, I am not averse to taking a risk, but not a blind one. If there's information out there that will help me calculate the odds, then I want it. That's what I want you to get for me. I appreciate your open mind, Mr. Haggerty. Perhaps you will change my mind, but I doubt it."

"Okay, Mr. Scolari. I need a description of this guy, his name and anything else you know about him. First thing Monday morning, I'll assign an investigator and we'll get on this."

"That won't do, Mr. Haggerty. You need to start on this immediately, this minute."

"Why is that?"

"Because they flew to St. Mary's this morning to get married."

"Aren't we a little late, then?"

"No. You can't apply for a marriage license on St. Mary's until you've been on the island for two days."

"How long to get the application approved?"

"I called the embassy. They say it takes three days to process the application. I'm looking into delaying that, if possible. Once it's issued they say most people get married that day or the next."

"So we've got what, five or six days? Mr. Scolari, we can't run a complete background check in that period of time. Hell, no one can. There just isn't enough time."

"What if you put everyone you've got on this, round the clock?"

"That gets you a maybe and just barely that. He'd have to have a pimple on his backside the size of Mount Rushmore for us to find it that fast. If this guy's the sneaky, cunning, opportunist that you think he is, then he's hidden that, maybe not perfectly, but deep enough that six days won't turn it up. Besides, I can't put everyone on this, we've got lots of other cases that need attention."

"So hire more staff, give them the other cases, and put everyone else on this. Money is no object, Mr. Haggerty. I want you to use all your resources on this."

My jaw hurt from clamping on the dead pipe. Scolari was old enough to make a foolish mistake. I told him it was a long shot at best. What more could I tell him? When did I become clairvoyant, and know how things would turn out? Suppose we did find something, like three dead ex-wives? Right! Let's not kid ourselves—all the staff for six days—round the clock—that's serious money. What was it Rocky said? When you run a business, money's always necessary but it's never sufficient. Don't confuse the two and what you do at the office won't keep you up at night.

I sorted everything into piles and then decided. "All right, Mr. Scolari, we'll do it. I can't even tell you what it'll cost. We'll bill you at our hourly rates plus all the expenses. I think a reasonable retainer would be thirty thousand dollars."

He didn't even blink. It probably wasn't a week's interest on ten million dollars.

"There's no guarantee that we'll find anything, Mr. Scolari, not under these circumstances. You'll know that you did everything you could, but that's all you'll know for sure."

"That's all you ever know for sure, Mr. Haggerty."

I pulled out a pad to make some notes. "Do you know where they went on St. Mary's?"

"Yes. A resort called the Banana Bay Beach Hotel. I have taken the liberty of registering you there."

"Excuse me." I felt like something under his front wheel.

"The resort is quite remote and perched on the side of a cliff. I have been assured that I would not be able to make my way around. I need you to be my legs, my eyes. If your agents learn anything back here, someone has to be able to get that information to my niece. Someone has to be there. I want that someone to be you, Mr. Haggerty. That's what I'm paying for. Your brains, your eyes, your legs, to be there because I can't."

I stared at Scolari's withered legs and the motorized wheelchair he got around in. More than that he had money, lots of money. And money's the ultimate prosthetic.

"Let's start at the top. What's his name?"

The island of St. Mary's is one of lush green mountains that drop straight into the sea. What little flat land there is, is on the west coast, and that's where almost all the people live. The central highlands and peaks are still wild and pristine.

My plane banked around the southern tip of the island and headed toward one of those flat spots, the international airport. I flipped through the file accumulated in those few hours between Enzo Scolari's visit and my plane's departure. While Kelly, my secretary, made travel arrangements I called everyone into the conference room and handed out jobs. Clancy Hopper was to rearrange caseloads and hire temporary staff to keep the other cases moving. Del Winslow was to start investigating our man Derek Marshall. We had a name, real or otherwise, an address, and phone number. Del would do the house-to-house with the drawing we made from Scolari's description. Larry Burdette would be smilin' and dialin'. Calling every computerized data base we could access to get more information. Every time Marshall's name appeared he'd take the information and hand it to another investigator to verify every fact and then backtrack each one by phone or in person until we could recreate the life of Derek Marshall. Our best chance was with the St. Mary's Department of Licenses. To apply for a marriage license Marshall had to file a copy of his passport, birth certificate, decrees of divorce if previously married, death certificate if widowed, and proof of legal name change, if any. If the records were open to the public, we'd get faxed copies or I'd go to the offices myself and look at them personally. I took one last look at the picture of Gina Dalesandro and then the sketch of Derek Marshall, closed the file, and slipped it into my bag as the runway appeared outside my window.

I climbed out of the plane and into the heat. A dry wind moved the heat around me as I walked into the airport. I showed my passport and had nothing to declare. They were delighted to have me on their island. I stepped out of the airport and the cabmaster introduced me to my driver. I followed him to a battered Toyota, climbed into the front seat, and stowed my bag between my feet. He slammed the door and asked where to.

"Banana Bay Beach Hotel," I said as he turned the engine on and pulled out.

"No problem."

"How much?" We bounced over a sleeping policeman.

"Eighty ecee."

Thirty-five dollars American. "How far is it?"

"Miles or time?"

"Both."

"Fifteen miles. An hour and a half."

I should have gotten out then. If the road to hell is paved at all, then it doesn't pass through St. Mary's. The coast road was a lattice of potholes winding around the sides of the mountains. There were no lanes, no lights, no signs, and no guardrails. The sea was a thousand feet below and we were never more than a few inches from visiting it.

Up and down the hills, there were blue bags on the trees.

"What are those bags?" I asked.

"Bananas. The bags keep the insects away while they ripen."

I scanned the slopes and tried to imagine going out there to put those bags on. Whoever did it, they couldn't possibly be paying him enough. Ninety minutes of bobbing and weaving on those roads like a fighter on the ropes and I was exhausted from defying gravity. I half expected to hear a bell to end the trip as we pulled up to the resort.

I checked in, put my valuables in a safe-deposit box, took my key and information packet, and headed up the hill to my room. Dinner was served in about an hour. Enough time to get oriented, unpack, and shower.

My room overlooked the upstairs bar and dining area and below that the beach, the bay, and the surrounding cliffs. I had a thatched-roof verandah with a hammock and clusters of flamboyant and chenille red-hot cattails close enough to pluck. The bathroom was clean and functional. The bedroom large and sparely furnished. Clearly, this was a place where the attractions were outdoors and rooms were for sleeping in. The mosquito netting over the bed and the coils on the dresser were not good signs. It was the rainy season and Caribbean mosquitoes can get pretty cheeky. In Antigua one caught me in the bathroom and pulled back the shower curtain like he was Norman Bates.

I unpacked quickly and read my information packet. It had a map of the resort, a list of services, operating hours, and tips on how to avoid common problems in the Caribbean such as sunburn, being swept out to sea, and a variety of bites, stings, and inedible fruits. I familiarized myself with the layout and took out the pictures of Gina and Derek. Job one was to find them and then tag along unobtrusively until the home office gave me something to work with.

I showered, changed, and lay down on the bed to wait for dinner. The best time to make an appearance was midway through the meal. Catch the early birds leaving and the stragglers on their way in.

Around 8:30, I sprayed myself with insect repellent, slipped my keys into my pocket, and headed down to dinner. The schedule said that it would be a barbecue on the beach.

At the reception area I stopped and looked over the low wall to the beach below. Scolari was right, he wouldn't be able to get around here. The rooms jutted out from the bluff and were connected by a steep roadway. However, from this point on, the hillside was a precipice. A staircase wound its way down to the beach. One hundred and twenty-six steps, the maid said.

I started down, stopping periodically to check the railing. There were no lights on the trail. Late at night, a little drunk on champagne, a new bride could have a terrible accident. I peered over the side at the concrete roadway below. She wouldn't bounce and she wouldn't survive.

I finished the zigzagging descent and noted that the return trip would be worse.

Kerosene lamps led the way to the beach restaurant and bar. I sat on a stool, ordered a Yellowbird, and turned to look at the dining area. Almost everyone was in couples, the rest were families. All white, mostly Americans, Canadians, British, and German. At least that's what the brochure said.

I sipped my drink and scanned the room. No sign of them. No problem, the night was young even if I wasn't. I had downed a second drink when they came in out of the darkness. Our drawing of Marshall was pretty good. He was slight, pale, with brown hair parted down the middle, round-rimmed tortoise-shell glasses, and a deep dimpled smile he aimed at the woman he gripped by the elbow. He steered her between the tables as if she had a tiller.

They took a table and I looked about to position myself. I wanted to be able to watch Marshall's face and be close enough to overhear them without looking like it. One row over and two up a table was coming free. I took my drink from the bar and ambled over. The busboy cleared the table and I took a long sip from my drink and set it down.

Gina Dalesandro wore a long flower-print dress. Strapless, she had tan lines where her bathing suit had been. She ran a finger over her ear and flipped back her hair. In profile she was thin-lipped, hook-nosed, and high-browed. Her hand held Marshall's, and then, eyes on his, she pulled one to her and kissed it. She moved from one knuckle to the next, and when she was done she took a finger and slowly slid it into her mouth.

"Gina, please, people will look," he whispered.

"Let them," she said, smiling around his finger.

Marshall pulled back and flicked his eyes around. My waitress had arrived and I was ordering when he passed over me. I had the fish chowder, the grilled dolphin with stuffed christophene, and another drink.

Gina picked up Marshall's hand and held it to her cheek and said something soothing because he smiled and blew her a kiss. They ordered and talked in hushed tones punctuated with laughter and smiles. I sat nearby, watching, waiting, her uncle's gargoyle in residence.

When dessert arrived, Gina excused herself and went toward the ladies' room. Marshall watched her go. I read nothing in his face or eyes. When she disappeared into the bathroom, his eyes wandered around the room, but settled on no one. He locked in on her when she reappeared and led her back to the table with his eyes. All in all it proved nothing.

We all enjoyed the banana cake and coffee and after a discreet pause I followed them back toward the rooms. We trudged silently up the stairs, past the bar and the reception desk, and back into darkness. I kept them in view as I went toward my room and saw that they were in Room 7, two levels up and one over from me. When their door clicked closed, I turned around and went back to the activities board outside the bar. I scanned the list of trips for tomorrow to see if they had signed up for any of them. They were down for the morning trip to the local volcano. I signed aboard and went to arrange a wake-up call for the morning.

After a quick shower, I lit the mosquito coils, dialed the lights way down, and crawled under the netting. I pulled the phone and my book inside, propped up the pillows, and called the office. For his money, Scolari should get an answer. He did.

"Franklin Investigations."

"Evening, Del. What do we have on Derek Marshall?"

"Precious little, boss, that's what."

"Well, give it to me."

"Okay, I canvassed his neighborhood. He's the invisible man. Rented apartment. Manager says he's always on time with the rent. Nothing else. I missed the mailman, but I'll catch him tomorrow. See if he can tell me anything. Neighbors know him by sight. That's about it. No wild parties. Haven't seen him with lots of girls. One thought he was seeing this one particular woman but hasn't seen her around in quite a while."

"How long has he been in the apartment?"

"Three years."

"Manager let you look at the rent application?"

"Leo, you know that's confidential. I couldn't even ask for that information."

"We prosper on the carelessness of others, Del. Did you ask?"

"Yes, and he was offended and indignant."

"Tough shit."

"Monday morning we'll go through court records and permits and licenses for the last three years, see if anything shakes out."

"Neighbors tell you anything else?"

"No, like I said, they knew him by sight, period."

"You find his car?"

"Yeah. Now that was a gold mine. Thing had stickers all over it."

"Such as?"

"Bush-Quayle. We'll check him out with Young Republican organizations. Also, Georgetown Law School."

"You run him through our directories?"

"Yeah, nothing. He's either a drone or modest."

"Call Walter O'Neil, tonight. Give him the name, see if he can get a law firm for the guy, maybe even someone who'll talk about him."

"Okay. I'm also going over to the school tomorrow, use the library, look up yearbooks, et cetera. See if we can locate a classmate. Alumni affairs will have to wait until Monday."

"How about NCIC?"

"Clean. No warrants or arrests. He's good or he's tidy."

"Anything else on the car?"

"Yeah, a sticker for something called Ultimate Frisbee. Nobody here knows anything about it. We're trying to track down an association for it, find out where it's played, then we'll interview people."

"Okay. We've still got three, maybe four days. How's the office doing? Are the other cases being covered?"

"Yeah, we spread them around. Clancy hired a couple of freelancers to start next week. Right now, me, Clancy, and Larry are pulling double shifts on this. Monday when the offices are open and the data bases are up, we'll probably put the two new guys on it."

"Good. Any word from the St. Mary's registrar's office?"

"No. Same problem there. Closed for the weekend. Won't know anything until Monday."

"All right. Good work, Del." I gave him my number. "Call here day or night with anything. If you can't get me directly, have me paged. I'll be out tomorrow morning on a field trip with Marshall and Gina, but I should be around the rest of the day."

"All right. Talk to you tomorrow."

I slipped the phone under the netting. Plumped the pillows and opened my book. Living alone had made me a voracious reader, as if all my other appetites had mutated into a hunger for the words that would make me someone else, put me somewhere else, or at least help me to sleep. The more I read, the harder it was to keep my interest. Boredom crept over me like the slow death it was. I was an old jaded john needing ever kinkier tricks just to get it up, or over with. Pretty soon nothing would move me at all. Until then, I was grateful for Michael Malone and the jolts and length of *Time's Witness*.

I woke up to the telephone's insistent ring, crawled out of bed, and thanked the front desk for the call. A chameleon darted out from under the bed and headed out the door. "Nice seeing you," I called out, and hoped he'd had a bountiful evening keeping my room an insect-free zone. I dressed and hurried down to breakfast.

After a glass of soursop, I ordered saltfish and onions with bakes and lots of coffee. Derek and Gina were not in the dining room. Maybe they'd ordered room service, maybe they were sleeping in and wouldn't make it. I ate quickly and kept checking my watch while I had my second cup of coffee. Our driver had arrived and was looking at the activities board. Another couple came up to him and introduced themselves. I wiped my mouth and left to join the group. Derek and Gina came down the hill as I checked in.

Our driver told us that his name was Wellington Bramble and that he was also a registered tour guide with the Department of the Interior. The other couple climbed into the back of the van, then Derek and Gina in the middle row. I hopped in up front, next to Wellington, turned, and introduced myself.

"Hi, my name is Leo Haggerty."

"Hello, I'm Derek Marshall and this is my fiancée, Gina Dalesandro."

"Pleasure to meet you."

Derek and Gina turned and we were all introduced to Tom and Dorothy Needham of Chicago, Illinois.

Wellington stuck his head out the window and spoke to one of the maids. They spoke rapidly in the local patois until the woman slapped him across the forearm and waved a scolding finger at him.

He engaged the gears, pulled away from the reception area, and told us that we would be visiting the tropical rain forests that surround the island's active volcano. All this in perfect English, the language of strangers and for strangers.

Dorothy Needham asked the question on all of our minds. "How long will we be on this road to the volcano?"

Wellington laughed. "Twenty minutes, ma'am, then we go inland to the volcano."

We left the coast road and passed through a gate marked ST. MARY'S ISLAND CONSERVANCY—DEVIL'S CAULDRON VOLCANO AND TROPICAL RAIN FOREST. I was first out and helped the women step down into the muddy path. Wellington lined us up and began to lead us through the jungle, calling out the names of plants and flowers and answering questions.

There were soursop trees, lime trees, nutmeg, guava, bananas, coconuts, cocoa trees, ginger lilies, lobster-claw plants, flamboyant and hibiscus, impression fern, and chenille red-hot cattails. We stopped on the path at a large fern. Wellington turned and pointed to it.

"Here, you touch the plant, right here," he said, pointing at Derek, who eyed him suspiciously. "It won't hurt you."

Derek reached out a finger and touched the fern. Instantly the leaves retracted and curled in on themselves.

"That's Mary, Mary, Shut the Door. As you can see, a delicate and shy plant indeed."

He waved us on and we followed. Gina slipped an arm through Derek's and put her head on his shoulder. She squeezed him once.

"Derek, you know I used to be like that plant. Before you came along. All closed up and frightened if anybody got too close. But not anymore. I am so happy," she said, and squeezed him again.

Other than a mild self-loathing, I was having a good time, too. We came out of the forest and were on the volcano. Wellington turned to face us.

"Ladies and gentlemen, please listen very carefully. We are on top of an active volcano. There is no danger of an eruption, because there is no crust, so there is no pressure buildup. The last eruption was over two hundred years ago. That does not mean that there is no danger here. You must stay on the marked path at all times and be very careful on the sections that have no guardrail. The water in the volcano is well over three hundred degrees Fahrenheit; should you stumble and fall in, you would be burned alive. I do not wish to alarm you unreasonably, but a couple of years ago we did lose a visitor, so please be very careful. Now follow me."

We moved along, single file and well spaced through a setting unlike any other I'd ever encountered. The circular top of the volcano looked like a wound on the earth. The ground steamed and smoked and nothing grew anywhere. Here and there black water leaked out of crusty patches like blood seeping from under a scab. The smell of sulfur was everywhere.

I followed Derek and Gina and watched him stop a couple of times and test the railings before he let her proceed. Caution, Derek? Or a trial run?

We circled the volcano and retraced our path back to the van. As promised, we were back at the hotel twenty minutes later. Gina was flushed with excitement and asked Derek if they could go back again. He thought that was possible, but there weren't any other guided tours this week, so they'd have to rent a car and go themselves. I closed my eyes and imagined her by the side of the road, taking a picture perhaps, and him ushering her through the foliage and on her way to eternity.

We all went in for lunch and ate separately. I followed them back to their room and then down to the beach. They moved to the far end of the beach and sat facing away from everyone else. I went into the bar and worked my way through a pair of long necks.

A couple in the dining room was having a spat, or maybe it was a tiff. Whatever, she called him a *schwein* and really tagged him with an open forehand to the chops. His face lit up redder than a baboon's ass.

She pushed back her chair, swung her long blond hair in an about-face, and stormed off. I watched her go, taking each step like she was grinding out a cigarette under her foot. Made her hips and butt do terrible things.

I pulled my eyes away when I realized I had company. He was leering at me enthusiastically.

I swung around slowly. "Yes?"

It was one of the local hustlers who patrolled the beach, as ubiquitous and resourceful as the coconuts that littered the sand.

"I seen you around, man. Y'all alone. That's not a good thin', man. I was thinkin' maybe you could use some company. Someone to share paradise wit'. Watcha say, man?"

I shook my head. "I don't think so."

He frowned. "I know you ain't that way, man. I seen you watch that blonde with the big ones. What'sa matter? What you afraid of?" He stopped and tried to answer that one for me. "She be clean, man. No problem."

When I didn't say anything, he got pissed. "What is it then? You don't fuck strange, man?"

"Watch my lips, bucko. I'm not interested. Don't make more of it than there is."

He sized me up and decided I wasn't worth the aggravation.

Spinning off his stool, he called me something in patois. I was sure it wasn't "sir."

I found a free lounge under a bohio and kept an eye on Derek and Gina. No sooner had I settled in than Gina got up and headed across the cocoa-colored volcanic sands to the beach bar. She was a little pink around the edges. Probably wouldn't be out too long today. Derek had his back to me, so I swiveled my head to keep her in sight. She sat down and one of the female staff came over and began to run a comb through her hair. Cornrowing. She'd be there for at least an hour. I ordered a drink from a wandering waiter, closed my eyes, and relaxed.

Gina strolled back, her hair in tight little braids, each one tipped with a series of colored beads. She was smiling and kicking up little sprays of water. I watched her take Derek by the hands and pull him up out of his chair. She twirled around and shook her head back and forth, just to watch the braids fly by. They picked up their snorkels and fins and headed for the water. I watched to see which way they'd go. The left side of the bay had numerous warning signs about the strong current including one on the point that said TURN BACK—NEXT STOP PANAMA.

They went right and so did I. Maybe it was a little fear, maybe it was love, but she held on to his hand while they hovered over the reef. I went farther out and then turned back so I could keep them in sight. The reef was one of the richest I'd ever been on and worthy of its reputation as one of the best in the Caribbean.

I kept my position near the couple, moving when they did, just like the school of squid I was above. They were in formation, tentacles tucked in, holding their position by undulating the fins on each lateral axis. When the school moved, they all went at once and kept the same distance from each other. I drifted off the coral to a bed of sea grass. Two creatures were walking through the grass. Gray green, with knobs and lumps everywhere, they had legs and wings! They weren't toxic-waste mutants, just the flying gurnards. I dived down on them and they spread their violet wings and took off.

When I surfaced, Derek and Gina were heading in. I swam downstream from them and came ashore as they did. Gina was holding her side and peeking behind her palm. Derek steadied her and helped get her flippers off.

"I don't know what it was, Derek. It just brushed me and then it felt like a bee sting. It really burns," Gina said.

I wandered by and said, "Looks like a jellyfish sting. When did it happen?"

"Just a second ago." They answered in unison.

"Best thing for that is papaya skins. Has an enzyme that neutralizes the toxin. The beach restaurant has plenty of them. They keep it just for things like this. You better get right over, though. It only works if you apply it right away."

"Thanks. Thanks a lot," Derek said, then turned to help Gina down the beach. "Yes, thank you," she said over his shoulder.

"You're welcome," I said to myself, and went to dry off.

I sat at the bar, waiting for dinner and playing backgammon with myself. Derek and Gina came in and went to the bar to order. Her dress was a swirl of purple, black, and white and matched the color of the beads in her hair. Derek wore lime-green shorts and a white short-sleeved shirt. Drinks in hand, they walked over to me. I stood up, shook hands, and invited them to join me.

"That tip of yours was a lifesaver. We went over to the bar and got some papaya on it right away. I think the pain was gone in maybe five minutes. How did you know about it?" Gina asked.

"I've been stung myself before. Somebody told me about it. Now I tell you. Word of mouth."

"Well, we're very grateful. We're getting married here on the island and I didn't want anything to mess this time up for us," Derek said.

I raised my glass in a toast. "Congratulations to you. This is a lovely place to get married. When is the ceremony?" I asked, sipping my drink.

"Tomorrow," Gina said, running her arm through Derek's. "I'm so excited."

I nearly drowned her in rerouted rum punch but managed to turn away and choke myself instead. I pounded my chest and waved off any assistance.

"Are you okay?" Derek asked.

"Yes, yes, I'm fine," I said as I got myself under control. Tomorrow? How the hell could it be tomorrow? "Sorry. I was trying to talk when I was drinking. Just doesn't work that way."

Derek asked if he could buy me another drink and I let him take my glass to the bar.

"I read the tourist brochure about getting married on the island. How long does it take for them to approve an application? They only said that you have to be on the island for two days before you can submit an application."

Gina leaned forward and touched my knee. "It usually takes two or three days, but Derek found a way to hurry things up. He sent the papers down early to the manager here and he agreed to file them for us as if we were on the island. It'll be ready tomorrow morning and we'll get married right after noon."

"That's wonderful. Where will the ceremony be?" My head was spinning.

"Here at the hotel. Down on the beach. They provide a cake, champagne, photographs, flowers. Would you join us afterward to celebrate?"

"Thank you, that's very kind. I'm not sure that I'll still be here, though. My plane leaves in the afternoon, and you know with that ride back to the airport, I might be gone. If I'm still here, I'd be delighted."

Derek returned with drinks and sat close to Gina and looped an arm around her.

"Honey, I hope you don't mind, but I invited Mr. Haggerty to join us after the ceremony." She smiled anxiously.

"No, that sounds great, love to have you. By the way, it

sounded like you've been to the islands before. This is our first time. Have you ever gone scuba diving?" Derek was all graciousness.

"Yeah, are you thinking of trying it?"

"Maybe, they have a course for beginners tomorrow. We were talking about taking the course and seeing if we liked it," he said.

"I'm a little scared. Is it really dangerous?" Gina asked.

Absolutely lethal. Russian roulette with one empty chamber. Don't do it. Wouldn't recommend it to my worst enemy.

"No, not really. There are dangers if you're careless, and they're pretty serious ones. The sea is not very forgiving of our mistakes. But if you're well trained and maintain some respect for what you're doing, it's not all that dangerous."

"I don't know. Maybe I'll just watch you do it, Derek."

"Come on, honey. You really liked snorkeling. Can you imagine how much fun it would be if you didn't have to worry about coming up for air all the time?" Derek gave Gina a squeeze. "And besides, I love the way you look in that new suit."

I saw others heading to the dining room and began to clean up the tiles from the board.

"Mr. Haggerty, would you—" Gina began.

"I'm sure we'll see Mr. Haggerty again, Gina. Thanks for your help this afternoon," Derek said, and led her to the dining room.

I finished my drink and took myself to dinner. After that, I sat and watched them dance to the shak-shak band. She put her head on his shoulder and molded her body to his. They swayed together in the perfect harmony only lovers and mothers and babies have.

They left that way, her head on his shoulder, a peaceful smile on her lips. I could not drink enough to cut the ache I felt and went to bed when I gave up trying.

Del was in when I called and gave me the brief bad news.

"The mailman was a dead end. I went over to the school library and talked to teachers and students. So far, nobody's had anything useful to tell us. I've got a class list and we're working our way through it. Walt did get a lead on him, though. He's a junior partner in a small law firm, a 'boutique' he called it."

"What kind of law?" Come on, say tax and estate.

"Immigration and naturalization."

"Shit. Anything else?"

"Yeah, he's new there. Still don't know where he came from. We'll try to get some information from the partners first thing in the morning."

"It better be first thing. Our timetable just went out the window. They're getting married tomorrow at noon."

"Jesus Christ, that puts the screws to us. We'll only have a couple of hours to work with."

"Don't remind me. Is that it?"

"For right now. Clancy is hitting bars looking for people that play this 'Ultimate Frisbee' thing. He's got a sketch with him. Hasn't called in yet."

"Well, if he finds anything, call me no matter what time it is. I'll be around all morning tomorrow. If you don't get me direct, have me paged, as an emergency. Right now we don't have shit."

"Hey, boss, we just ran out of time. I'm sure in a couple of days we'd have turned something up."

"Maybe so, Del, but tomorrow around noon somebody's gonna look out over their heads and ask if anybody has anything to say or forever hold your peace. I don't see myself raising my hand and asking for a couple of more days, 'cause we're bound to turn something up."

"We did our best. We just weren't holding very good cards is all."

"Del, we were holding shit." I should have folded when Scolari dealt them.

I hung up and readied my bedroom to repel all boarders. Under the netting, I sat and mulled over my options. I had no reason to stick my nose into Gina's life. No reason at all to think that Derek was anything but the man she'd waited her whole life for. Her happiness was real, though. She was blossoming under his touch. I had seen it. And happiness is a fragile thing. Who was I to cast a shadow on hers? And without any reason. Tomorrow was a special day for her. How would she remember it? How would I?

I woke early from a restless night and called the office. Nothing new. I tried Scolari's number and spoke briefly to him. I told him we were out of time and had nothing of substance. I asked him a couple of questions and he gave me some good news and some bad. There was nothing else to do, so I went down to see the betrothed.

They were in the dining room holding hands and finishing their coffee. I approached and asked if I could join them.

"Good morning, Mr. Haggerty. Lovely day, isn't it?" Gina said, her face aglow.

I settled into the chair and decided to smack them in the face with it. "Before you proceed with your wedding, I have some news for you."

They sat upright and took their hands, still joined, off the table.

"Gina's uncle, Enzo Scolari, wishes me to inform you that he has had his attorneys activate the trustee's discretionary powers over Miss Dalesandro's portion of the estate so that she cannot take possession of the money or use it in any fashion without his consent. He regrets having to take this action, but your insistence on this marriage leaves him no choice."

"You son of a bitch. You've been spying on us for that bastard," Derek shouted, and threw his glass of water at me. I sat there dripping while I counted to ten. Gina had gone pale and was on the verge of tears. Marshall stood up. "Come on, Gina, let's go. I don't want this man anywhere near me." He leaned forward and stabbed a finger at me. "I intend to call your employer, Mr. Scolari, and let him know what a despicable piece of shit I think he is, and that goes double for you." He turned away. "Gina, are you coming?"

"Just a second, honey," she whispered. "I'll be along in just a second." Marshall crashed out of the room, assaulting chairs and tables that got in his way.

"Why did you do this to me? I've waited my whole life for this day. To find someone who loves me and wants to live with me and to celebrate that. We came here to get away from my uncle and his obsessions. You know what hurts the most? You reminded me that my uncle doesn't believe that anyone could love me for myself. It has to be my money. What's so wrong with *me*? Can you tell me that?" She was starting to cry and wiped at her tears with her palms. "Hell of a question to be asking on your wedding day, huh? You do good work, Mr. Haggerty. I hope you're proud of yourself."

I'd rather Marshall had thrown acid in my face than the words she hurled at me. "Think about one thing, Miss Dalesandro. This way you can't lose. If he doesn't marry you now, you've avoided a lot of heartache and maybe worse. If he does, knowing this, then you can relax knowing it's you and not your money. The way I see it, either way you can't lose. But I'm sorry. If there had been any other way, I'd have done it."

"Yes, well, I have to go, Mr. Haggerty." She rose, dropped her napkin on the table, and walked slowly through the room, using every bit of dignity she could muster.

I spent the rest of the morning in the bar waiting for the last act to unfold.

At noon, Gina appeared in a long white dress. She had a bouquet of flowers in her hands and was trying hard to smile. I sipped some anesthetic and looked away. No need to make it any harder now. I wasn't sure whether I wanted Marshall to show up or not.

Derek appeared at her side in khaki slacks and an embroidered white shirt. What will be, will be. They moved slowly down the stairs. I went to my room, packed, and checked out. By three o'clock I was off the island and on my way home.

It was almost a year later when Kelly buzzed me on the intercom to say that a Mr. Derek Marshall was here to see me.

"Show him in."

He hadn't changed a bit. Neither one of us moved to shake hands. When I didn't invite him to sit down, he did anyway.

"What do you want, Marshall?"

"You know, I'll never forget that moment when you told me that Scolari had altered the trust. Right there in public. I was so angry that you'd try to make me look bad like that in front of Gina and everyone else. It really has stayed with me. And here I am, leaving the area. I thought I'd come by and return the favor before I left."

"How's Gina?" I asked with a veneer of nonchalance over trepidation.

"Funny you should ask. I'm a widower, you know. She had a terrible accident about six months ago. We were scuba diving. It was her first time. I'd already had some courses. I guess she misunderstood what I'd told her and she held her breath coming up. Ruptured a lung. She was dead before I could get her to shore."

I almost bit through my pipe stem. "You're a real piece of work, aren't you? Pretty slick, death by misinformation. Got away with it, didn't you?"

"The official verdict was accidental death. Scolari was beside himself, as you can imagine. There I was, sole inheritor of Gina's estate, and according to the terms of the trust her half of the grandfather's money was mine. It was all in Scolari stock, so I made a deal with the old man. He got rid of me and I got paid fifty percent more than the shares were worth."

"You should be careful, Derek, that old man hasn't got long to live. He might decide to take you with him."

"That thought has crossed my mind. So I'm going to take my money and put some space between him and me."

Marshall stood up to leave. "By the way, your bluff wasn't half-bad. It actually threw me there for a second. That's why I tossed the water on you. I had to get away and do some thinking, make sure I hadn't overlooked anything. But I hadn't."

"How did you know it was a bluff?" You cocky little shit.

Marshall pondered that a moment. "It doesn't matter. You'll never be able to prove this. It's not on paper anywhere. While I was in law school I worked one year as an unpaid intern at the law firm handling the estate of old man Scolari, the grandfather. This was when Gina's mother died. I did a turn in lots of different departments. I read the documents when I was Xeroxing them. That's how I knew the setup. Her mother's share went to Gina. Anything happens to her and the estate is transferred according to the terms of Gina's will. An orphan, with no siblings. That made me sole inheritor, even if she died intestate. Scolari couldn't change the trust or its terms. Your little stunt actually convinced Gina of my sincerity. I wasn't in any hurry to get her to write a will and she absolutely refused to do it when Scolari pushed her on it.

"Like I said, for a bluff it wasn't half-bad. Gina believed you, but I think she was the only one who didn't know anything about her money. Well, I've got to be going, got a plane to catch." He smiled at me like he was a dog and I was his favorite tree.

It was hard to resist the impulse to threaten him, but a threat is also a warning and I had no intention of playing fair. I consoled myself with the fact that last time I only had two days to work with. Now I had a lifetime. When I heard the outer door close, I buzzed Kelly on the intercom.

"Yes, Mr. Haggerty?"

"Reopen the file on Derek Marshall."

The Imperial Icehouse

Paul Theroux

OF ALL THE grand buildings on my island, the grandest by far was The Imperial Icehouse—white pillars and a shapely roof topped by ornate lettering on a gilded sign. Unlike the warehouses and the shops on the same street, it had no smell. It was whiter than the church, and though you would not mistake it for a church, the fresh paint and elongated windows—and the gold piping on the scrollwork of the sign—gave it at once a look of holiness and of purpose. I cannot think of human endeavor without that building coming to mind, shimmering in my memory as it did on the island, the heat distorting it like a reflection in water.

The icehouse did more than cater to the comforts of the islanders. It provided ice for the fisherman's catch and the farmer's delicate produce. A famous Victorian novelist visited us in 1859 and remarked on it, describing it as "a drinking shop." It was certainly that, but it was more. It was "well attended," he said. He was merely passing through, a traveler interested in recording our eccentricities. He could not have known that The Imperial Icehouse was our chief claim to civilization. Ice in that climate! It was shipped to the island whole, and preserved. It was our achievement and our boast.

Then one day, decades later, four men came to town for a

wagonload of ice. Three were black and had pretty names; the fourth was a white planter called Mr. Hand. He had made the trip with his Negroes because it was high summer and he wanted cold drinks. His plan was to carry away a ton of ice and store it in his estate up-country. He was a new man on the island and had the strengths and weaknesses peculiar to all new arrivals. He was hardworking and generous; he talked a good deal about progress; he wore his eagerness on his face. He looked stunned and happy and energetic. He did not listen or conceal. On this, the most British of the islands, it was a satisfaction to newcomers to see the Victoria Statue on Victoria Street, and the horses in Hyde Park, and Nelson in Trafalgar Square. Mr. Hand saw no reason that he should not drink here as he had done in England.

He had taken over Martlet's estate, which had been up for sale ever since Martlet's death. That again revealed Mr. Hand as a newcomer, considering what had happened to old Martlet. And the estate was as far from town as it was possible to be on this island: Mr. Hand, a bachelor, must have needed consolation and encouragement.

He had, against all good advice, taken over the Martlet Negroes, and three of these accompanied him on that trip to town for the ice. Mr. Hand closed the deal at the icehouse by having a drink, and he sent a bucket of beer out to his men. They were called John Paul, Macaque, and Jacket. He had another drink, and another, and sent out more beer for those men, who kept in the shade. It was not unlawful for Negro estate workers to drink in the daytime, but it was not the custom, either. Even if he had known, Mr. Hand probably would not have cared.

The Negroes drank, conversing in whispers, shadows in shadow, accepting what they were offered, and waiting to be summoned to load the ice.

They had arrived in the coolness of early morning, but the drinking meant delay: by noon the wagon was still empty, the four horses still tethered to a tree, the Negroes sitting with their backs to the icehouse and their long legs stretched out. Perhaps the racket from inside told them there would be no hurry. In any case, they expected to leave at dusk, for not even the rankest newcomer would risk hauling ice across the island in the mid-afternoon heat.

Just as they had begun to doze, they were called. Mr. Hand stood and swayed on the veranda. He was ready, he yelled. He had to repeat it before his words were understood. Some other men came out of the icehouse and argued with him. Mr. Hand took them over to the wagon and showed them the sheets of canvas he had brought. He urged the men to watch as the Negroes swung the big wagon to the back door, and he supervised the loading, distributing sawdust between the great blocks of ice as if cementing for good the foundation of an imperial building.

For an hour or more the Negroes labored, two men to a cake, and Mr. Hand joked to them about it: Had they known water to be so heavy? An enormous block was winched from the door. John Paul, who was the leader of the three, withdrew an ice pick from his shirt and began to work its stiletto point on that block. There was a shout from Mr. Hand—again, the unexpected voice—and John Paul stood and patiently wiped the ice pick on his arm. When the block was loaded, the wheels were at a slant and the floor of the wagon had squashed the springs to such an extent that the planks rested on the axletrees. Mr. Hand continued to trowel the sawdust and separate the cakes with canvas until at last all the ice was loaded and the four horses hitched.

The news of the loading had reached the men drinking in the icehouse. A noisy crowd gathered on the veranda to watch the tipping wagon creak down Regent Street, Mr. Hand holding the reins, Macaque and Jacket tugging the bridles of the forward horses, John Paul sauntering at the rear. Their progress was slow, and even before they disappeared past the tile kiln at the far end of the street, many of the icehouse men had left the veranda to seek the cool bar.

Past the Wallace estate, Villeneuve's dairy, the milestone at the flour mill; children had followed, but they dropped back because of the heat. Others had watched from doorways, attracted by the size of the load and the rumble and wobble of the wheels in the rutted lanes. Now, no one followed.

There were no more houses. They had begun to climb the first range of hills. In this heat, on the exposed road, the birds were tiny and silent, and the flowers had no aroma. There was only a sawing of locusts and a smell of dust. From time to time, Jacket implored the straining horse he held and looked over at Macaque, who frowned at the higher hills beyond.

The hills loomed; no one saw the hole in the road, only the toppling horses, the one behind Jacket's rearing from a broken trace and, free of one strap, swinging himself and snapping another. Empty, the wagon had seemed secure; but this weight, and the shock of the sudden hole, made it shudder feebly and look as if it might burst. Jacket calmed the horse and quickly roped him. The others steadied the wagon.

Mr. Hand, asleep on his seat, had tumbled to his knees. He woke and swore at the men, then at the horses, and he cursed the broken straps. But he had more straps in the chest he had brought, and he was so absorbed in the repair that he did not leave the road. He mended the traces—spurning the men's help—in the middle of the North Road, squinting in the sunshine.

They were soon on their way. There was a rime of froth on the necks and fetlocks of the horses, and great syrupy strings of yellow saliva dripped from their jaws. The road narrowed as it grew steep; then it opened again. The horses fought for footing and the wheels chimed as they banged against the wagon. The Negroes did not sing as they had on the early morning ride, nor did they speak. Mr. Hand nodded, sat upright, slumped again, and was asleep.

Sensing the wagon slowing, John Paul put his shoulder under the back flap and gave a push. His shoulder was soaked; the wagon had begun to drip, dark pennies in the dust that dried almost as soon as they fell. He placed his forearms on the flap and put his head down and let the wagon carry him.

Passing the spring where they had stopped that morning for a drink, John Paul called out to Mr. Hand and asked if they could rest. No, said Mr. Hand, waking again and spreading his fingers to push at the sunlight. They would go on, he said; they were in a hurry. Now Jacket sang out—a brief, squawking ditty, interrupting the silence of the hot road. He was answered by John Paul, another birdlike cry, and then Macaque's affirming gabble. John Paul took his ice pick and reached beneath the canvas. He chopped a wedge, and sucked it, then shared it with the two other Negroes. Mr. Hand gasped in sleep.

There was a cracking, a splintering of wood like a limb twisting from a tree. John Paul tossed his chunk of ice into the grass by the roadside, and he saw the rear wheel in pieces, a bunch of spindles settling under the wagon.

Glassy-eyed from his nap, Mr. Hand announced to them that he had a spare wheel. He unbolted it from the bottom of the wagon and fitted it to the axle, but from where the others stood idle they could see that the ice had shifted and cracked the sideboards. And yet, when the trip was resumed, the wagon rolled more smoothly, as if the load were lighter than before—the springs had bounce, the wheels were straighter.

More ice was chopped away by John Paul, and this he shared, and while Mr. Hand slept the three Negroes quarreled silently, sniffing and sighing, because John Paul had the ice pick and he would not let any of the others use it.

The road became bumpy again, the ice moved in the wagon. It had been securely roped, but now it was loose; it was a smaller load; its jarring woke Mr. Hand. He worked himself into a temper when he saw the diminished load. He stopped to tighten the canvas around it and screamed at the puddle that collected under the wagon. He would not let the Negroes drink. There will be cold drinks in plenty, he said, when we arrive home. Later, he got down from the seat on a steep grade and went behind and pushed with his shoulder like John Paul, and he said: That's how we do it.

They passed a fragrant valley. Negroes in that valley whispered and laughed and jeered at the Negroes in this procession. Now the ice was melting so quickly that there was a stream of water pouring from the wagon and its cracks. The mockery was loud and several Negroes followed for some distance, yelling about the melting ice and the trail of mud they left through the pretty valley. The wagon wood was dark with moisture, as dark as the Negroes' faces, which were streaming with sweat.

Mr. Hand began to talk—crazy talk about England—and his men laughed at the pitch of his voice, which was a child's complaint. They did not understand his words; he ignored their laughter.

The left trace snapped as the right had done; a spoke worked loose and dropped from a wheel, although the wheel itself remained in position. One horse's shoe clanged as he kicked it into the belly of the wagon. These incidents were commented upon, and now the Negroes talked loudly of the stupidity of the trip, the waste of effort, the wrong time of day, the color of Mr. Hand's cheeks. Mr. Hand sat holding the reins loosely, his head tipped onto his shoulder. His straw hat fell off and the Negroes left it on the road where it fell. John Paul looked back and saw his footprint crushed into the crown.

They had gained the second range of hills, and as they were descending—slowly, so that the wagon would not be shot forward—the late afternoon sun, unshielded by any living tree, struck their faces like metal. The road was strewn with boulders on which the horses did a tired dance, stepping back. There was a curve, another upward grade, and at that bend the horses paused to crop the grass.

There was no sound from Mr. Hand. He was a crouching infant in his seat, in the sun's glare, his mouth open. The horses tore at the grass with their lips. The Negroes crept under the wagon, and there they stayed in the coolness for an hour or more, the cold water dripping on them.

Mr. Hand woke, stamping his feet on the planks. They scrambled to their places.

His anger was exhausted in three shouts. He promised them ice, cold drinks, a share for everyone, and as he spoke the Negroes could see how the ice beneath the sagging canvas was a quarter the size of what it had been. Divided, it would be nothing. They did not respond to Mr. Hand's offer: it was a promise of water, which they had already, as their right, from their own spring.

Mr. Hand tugged the reins and the men helped the horses, dragged the wagon, dragged the ice, dragged this man through the tide of heat. Mr. Hand chattered, repeating his promises, but when he saw the impassive faces of the Negroes he menaced them with whining words. He spoke sharply, like an insect stirred by the sun.

If you don't pull hard, he said to the men, I'll free the horses and hitch you to the wagon—and you'll take us home. He thwacked the canvas with his whip. There was no thud, nothing solid, only a thin, echoless smack, and he clawed open the canvas. Shrunken ice blocks rattled on the planks.

He stopped the wagon and leaped out and faced each man in turn and accused him. The men did nothing; they waited for him to move. And he did. He hit Macaque and called him a thief. Jacket was lazy, he said, and he hit him. John Paul prepared himself for worse. Mr. Hand came close to him and screamed and, as he did, the wagon lurched. The horses had found grass; they pulled the wagon to the roadside.

The sounds of the horses' chewing, the dripping of the wagon in the heat—it was regular, like time leaking away. Mr. Hand raised his whip and rushed at John Paul. And then, in that low sun, Mr. Hand cast three shadows; two helped him aside, and he struggled until a sound came, the sound John Paul had made in town with his ice pick, like ice being chipped, or bone struck, and the hatless man cried out—plea, promise, threat, all at once—and staggered to the wagon and shouted at the water dripping into the dust. The ice was no larger than a man, and bleeding in the same way.

At last it was cool and dark and they were passing the first fences of the farm and turning into the drive. There were lighted huts and lights moving toward them, swinging tamely on nothing in the darkness. Voices near those lanterns cried out—timid questions. The three men answered in triumph from the top of the heavy wagon, which rumbled in the road like a broken catafalque, streaming, still streaming, though all the ice was gone.

Too Many Crooks

Donald E. Westlake

DID YOU HEAR something?" Dortmunder whispered.

"The wind," Kelp said.

Dortmunder twisted around in his seated position and deliberately shone the flashlight in the kneeling Kelp's eyes. "What wind? We're in a tunnel."

"There's underground rivers," Kelp said, squinting, "so maybe there's underground winds. Are you through the wall there?"

"Two more whacks," Dortmunder told him. Relenting, he aimed the flashlight past Kelp back down the empty tunnel, a meandering, messy gullet, most of it less than three feet in diameter, wriggling its way through rocks and rubble and ancient middens, traversing 40 tough feet from the rear of the basement of the out-of-business shoe store to the wall of the bank on the corner. According to the maps Dortmunder had gotten from the water department by claiming to be with the sewer department, and the maps he'd gotten from the sewer department by claiming to be with the water department, just the other side of this wall was the bank's main vault. Two more whacks and this large, irregular square of concrete that Dortmunder and Kelp had been scoring and scratching at for some time now would at last fall away onto the floor inside, and there would be the vault.

Dortmunder gave it a whack.

Dortmunder gave it another whack.

The block of concrete fell onto the floor of the vault. "Oh, thank God," somebody said.

What? Reluctant but unable to stop himself, Dortmunder dropped sledge and flashlight and leaned his head through the hole in the wall and looked around.

It was the vault, all right. And it was full of people.

A man in a suit stuck his hand out and grabbed Dortmunder's and shook it while pulling him through the hole and on into the vault. "Great work, Officer," he said. "The robbers are outside."

Dortmunder had thought he and Kelp were the robbers. "They are?"

A round-faced woman in pants and a Buster Brown collar said, "Five of them. With machine guns."

"Machine guns," Dortmunder said.

A delivery kid wearing a mustache and an apron and carrying a flat cardboard carton containing four coffees, two decafs and a tea said, "We all hostages, mon. I gonna get fired."

"How many of you are there?" the man in the suit asked, looking past Dortmunder at Kelp's nervously smiling face.

"Just the two," Dortmunder said, and watched helplessly as willing hands dragged Kelp through the hole and set him on his feet in the vault. It was really very full of hostages.

"I'm Kearney," the man in the suit said. "I'm the bank manager, and I can't tell you how glad I am to see you."

Which was the first time any bank manager had said *that* to Dortmunder, who said, "Uh-huh, uh-huh," and nodded, and then said, "I'm, uh, Officer Diddums, and this is Officer, uh, Kelly."

Kearney, the bank manager, frowned. "Diddums, did you say?"

Dortmunder was furious with himself. Why did I call myself Diddums? Well, I didn't know I was going to need an alias inside a bank vault, did I? Aloud, he said, "Uh-huh. Diddums. It's Welsh."

"Ah," said Kearney. Then he frowned again and said, "You people aren't even armed."

"Well, no," Dortmunder said. "We're the, uh, the hostage-rescue team; we don't want any shots fired, increase the risk for you, uh, civilians."

"Very shrewd," Kearney agreed.

Kelp, his eyes kind of glassy and his smile kind of fixed, said, "Well, folks, maybe we should leave here now, single file, just make your way in an orderly fashion through—"

"They're coming!" hissed a stylish woman over by the vault door.

Everybody moved. It was amazing; everybody shifted at once. Some people moved to hide the new hole in the wall, some people moved to get farther away from the vault door and some people moved to get behind Dortmunder, who suddenly found himself the nearest person in the vault to that big, round, heavy metal door, which was easing massively and silently open.

It stopped halfway, and three men came in. They wore black ski masks and black leather jackets and black work pants and black shoes. They carried Uzi submachine guns at high port. Their eyes looked cold and hard, and their hands fidgeted on the metal of the guns, and their feet danced nervously, even when they were standing still. They looked as though anything at all might make them overreact.

"Shut up!" one of them yelled, though nobody'd been talking. He glared around at his guests and said, "Gotta have somebody to stand out front, see can the cops be trusted." His eye, as Dortmunder had known it would, lit on Dortmunder. "You," he said.

"Uh-huh," Dortmunder said.

"What's your name?"

Everybody in the vault had already heard him say it, so what choice did he have? "Diddums," Dortmunder said.

The robber glared at Dortmunder through his ski mask. "Diddums?"

"It's Welsh," Dortmunder explained.

"Ah," the robber said, and nodded. He gestured with the Uzi. "Outside, Diddums."

Dortmunder stepped forward, glancing back over his shoulder at all the people looking at him, knowing every goddamn one of them was glad he wasn't him—even Kelp, back there pretending to be four feet tall—and then Dortmunder stepped through the vault door, surrounded by all those nervous maniacs with machine guns, and went with them down a corridor flanked by desks and through a doorway to the main part of the bank, which was a mess.

The time at the moment, as the clock high on the wide wall confirmed, was 5:15 in the afternoon. Everybody who worked at the bank should have gone home by now; that was the theory Dortmunder had been operating from. What must have happened was, just before closing time at three o'clock (Dortmunder and Kelp being already then in the tunnel, working hard, knowing nothing of events on the surface of the planet), these gaudy showboats had come into the bank waving their machine guns around.

And not just waving them, either. Lines of ragged punctures had been drawn across the walls and the Lucite upper panel of the tellers' counter, like connect-the-dot puzzles. Wastebaskets and a potted Ficus had been overturned, but fortunately, there were no bodies lying around; none Dortmunder could see, anyway. The big plate-glass front windows had been shot out, and two more of the black-clad robbers were crouched down, one behind the OUR LOW LOAN RATES poster and the other behind the OUR HIGH IRA RATES poster, staring out at the street, from which came the sound of somebody talking loudly but indistinctly through a bullhorn.

So what must have happened, they'd come in just before three, waving their guns, figuring a quick in and out, and some brown-nose employee looking for advancement triggered the alarm, and now they had a stalemate hostage situation on their hands; and, of course, everybody in the world by now has seen *Dog Day Afternoon* and therefore knows that if the police get the drop on a robber in circumstances such as these circumstances right here, they'll immediately shoot him dead, so now hostage negotiation is trickier than ever. This isn't what I had in mind when I came to the bank, Dortmunder thought.

The boss robber prodded him along with the barrel of his Uzi, saying, "What's your first name, Diddums?"

Please don't say Dan, Dortmunder begged himself. Please, please, somehow, anyhow, manage not to say Dan. His mouth opened. "John," he heard himself say, his brain having turned desperately in this emergency to that last resort, the truth, and he got weak-kneed with relief.

"OK, John, don't faint on me," the robber said. "This is very simple what you got to do here. The cops say they want to talk, just talk, nobody gets hurt. Fine. So you're gonna step out in front of the bank and see do the cops shoot you."

"Ah," Dortmunder said.

"No time like the present, huh, John?" the robber said, and poked him with the Uzi again.

"That kind of hurts," Dortmunder said.

"I apologize," the robber said, hard-eyed. "Out."

One of the other robbers, eyes red with strain inside the black ski mask, leaned close to Dortmunder and yelled, "You wanna shot in the foot first? You wanna *crawl* out there?"

"I'm going," Dortmunder told him. "See? Here I go."

The first robber, the comparatively calm one, said, "You go as far as the sidewalk, that's all. You take one step off the curb, we blow your head off."

"Got it," Dortmunder assured him, and crunched across broken glass to the sagging-open door and looked out. Across the street was parked a line of buses, police cars, police trucks, all in blue and white with red gumdrops on top, and behind them moved a seething mass of armed cops. "Uh," Dortmunder said. Turning back to the comparatively calm robber, he said, "You wouldn't happen to have a white flag or anything like that, would you?"

The robber pressed the point of the Uzi to Dortmunder's side. "Out," he said.

"Right," Dortmunder said. He faced front, put his hands way up in the air and stepped outside.

What a *lot* of attention he got. From behind all those blue-and-whites on the other side of the street, tense faces stared. On the rooftops of the red-brick tenements, in this neighborhood deep in the residential heart of Queens, sharpshooters began to familiarize themselves through their telescopic sights with the contours of Dortmunder's furrowed brow. To left and right, the ends of the block were sealed off with buses parked nose to tail pipe, past which ambulances and jumpy white-coated medics could be seen. Everywhere, rifles and pistols jittered in nervous fingers. Adrenaline ran in the gutters.

"I'm not with *them*!" Dortmunder shouted, edging across the sidewalk, arms upraised, hoping this announcement wouldn't upset the other bunch of armed hysterics behind him. For all he knew, they had a problem with rejection.

However, nothing happened behind him, and what happened out front was that a bullhorn appeared, resting on a police-car roof, and roared at him, *"You a hostage?"*

"I sure am!" yelled Dortmunder.

"What's your name?"

Oh, not again, thought Dortmunder, but there was nothing for it. "Diddums," he said.

"What?"

"Diddums!"

A brief pause: *"Diddums?"*

"It's Welsh!"

"Ah."

There was a little pause while whoever was operating the bullhorn conferred with his compatriots, and then the bullhorn said, *"What's the situation in there?"*

What kind of question was that? "Well, uh," Dortmunder said, and remembered to speak more loudly, and called, "kind of tense, actually."

"Any of the hostages been harmed?"

"Uh-uh. No. Definitely not. This is a . . . this is a . . . nonviolent confrontation." Dortmunder fervently hoped to establish that idea in everybody's mind, particularly if he were going to be out here in the middle much longer.

"Any change in the situation?"

Change? "Well," Dortmunder answered, "I haven't been in there that long, but it seems like—"

"Not that long? What's the matter with you, Diddums? You've been in that bank over two hours now!"

"Oh, yeah!" Forgetting, Dortmunder lowered his arms and stepped forward to the curb. "That's right!" he called. "Two hours! *More* than two hours! Been in there a long time!"

"Step out here away from the bank!"

Dortmunder looked down and saw his toes hanging ten over the edge of the curb. Stepping back at a brisk pace, he called, "I'm not supposed to do that!"

"Listen, Diddums, I've got a lot of tense men and women over here. I'm telling you, step away from the bank!"

"The fellas inside," Dortmunder explained, "they don't want me to step off the curb. They said they'd, uh, well, they just don't want me to do it."

"Psst! Hey, Diddums!"

Dortmunder paid no attention to the voice calling from behind him. He was concentrating too hard on what was happening right now out front. Also, he wasn't that used to the new name yet.

"Diddums!"

"Maybe you better put your hands up again."

"Oh, yeah!" Dortmunder's arms shot up like pistons blowing through an engine block. "There they are!"

"Diddums, goddamn it, do I have to *shoot* you to get you to pay attention?"

Arms dropping, Dortmunder spun around. "Sorry! I wasn't—I was—Here I am!"

"Get those goddamn hands up!"

Dortmunder turned sideways, arms up so high his sides hurt. Peering sidelong to his right, he called to the crowd across the street, "Sirs, they're talking to me inside now." Then he peered sidelong to his left, saw the comparatively calm robber crouched beside the broken doorframe and looking less calm than before, and he said, "Here I am."

"We're gonna give them our demands now," the robber said. "Through you."

"That's fine," Dortmunder said. "That's great. Only, you know, how come you don't do it on the phone? I mean, the way it's normally—"

The red-eyed robber, heedless of exposure to the sharpshooters across the street, shouldered furiously past the comparatively calm robber, who tried to restrain him as he yelled at Dortmunder, "You're rubbing it in, are ya? OK, I made a mistake! I got excited and I shot up the switchboard! You want me to get excited again?"

"No, no!" Dortmunder cried, trying to hold his hands straight up in the air and defensively in front of his body at the same time. "I forgot! I just forgot!"

The other robbers all clustered around to grab the red-eyed robber, who seemed to be trying to point his Uzi in Dortmunder's direction as he yelled, "I did it in front of everybody! I humiliated myself in front of everybody! And now you're making fun of me!"

"I *forgot!* I'm sorry!"

"You can't forget that! Nobody's ever gonna forget that!"

The three remaining robbers dragged the red-eyed robber back away from the doorway, talking to him, trying to soothe him, leaving Dortmunder and the comparatively calm robber to continue their conversation. "I'm sorry," Dortmunder said. "I just forgot. I've been kind of distracted lately. Recently."

"You're playing with fire here, Diddums," the robber said. "Now tell them they're gonna get our demands."

Dortmunder nodded, and turned his head the other way, and yelled, "They're gonna tell you their demands now. I mean, *I'm* gonna tell you their demands. *Their* demands. Not *my* demands. *Their* de—"

"We're willing to listen, Diddums, only so long as none of the hostages get hurt."

"That's good!" Dortmunder agreed, and turned his head the other way to tell the robber, "That's reasonable, you know, that's sensible, that's a very good thing they're saying."

"Shut up," the robber said.

"Right," Dortmunder said.

The robber said, "First, we want the riflemen off the roofs."

"Oh, so do I," Dortmunder told him, and turned to shout, "They want the riflemen off the roofs!"

"What else?"

"What else?"

"And we want them to unblock that end of the street, the—what is it?—the north end."

Dortmunder frowned straight ahead at the buses blocking the intersection. "Isn't that east?" he asked.

"Whatever it is," the robber said, getting impatient. "That end down there to the left."

"OK." Dortmunder turned his head and yelled, "They want you to unblock the east end of the street!" Since his hands were way up in the sky somewhere, he pointed with his chin.

"Isn't that north?"

"I knew it was," the robber said.

"Yeah, I guess so," Dortmunder called. "That end down there to the left."

"The right, you mean."

"Yeah, that's right. Your right, my left. *Their* left."

"What else?"

Dortmunder sighed, and turned his head. "What else?"

The robber glared at him. "I can *hear* the bullhorn, Diddums. I can *hear* him say 'What else?' You don't have to repeat everything he says. No more translations."

"Right," Dortmunder said. "Gotcha. No more translations."

"We'll want a car," the robber told him. "A station wagon. We're gonna take three hostages with us, so we want a big station wagon. And nobody follows us."

"Gee," Dortmunder said dubiously, "are you sure?"

The robber stared. "Am I *sure?*"

"Well, you know what they'll do," Dortmunder told him, lowering his voice so the other team across the street couldn't hear him. "What they do in these situations, they fix a little radio transmitter under the car, so then they don't have to *follow* you, exactly, but they know where you are."

Impatient again, the robber said, "So you'll tell them not to do that. No radio transmitters, or we kill the hostages."

"Well, I suppose," Dortmunder said doubtfully.

"What's wrong *now?*" the robber demanded. "You're too goddamn *picky*, Diddums; you're just the messenger here. You think you know my job better than I do?"

I know I do, Dortmunder thought, but it didn't seem a judicious thing to say aloud, so instead, he explained, "I just want things to go smooth, that's all. I just don't want bloodshed. And I was thinking, the New York City police, you know, well, they've got helicopters."

"Damn," the robber said. He crouched low to the littered floor, behind the broken doorframe, and brooded about his situation. Then he looked up at Dortmunder and said, "OK, Diddums, you're so smart. What *should* we do?"

Dortmunder blinked. "You want *me* to figure out your getaway?"

"Put yourself in our position," the robber suggested. "Think about it."

Dortmunder nodded. Hands in the air, he gazed at the blocked intersection and put himself in the robbers' position. "Hoo, boy," he said. "You're in a real mess."

"We *know* that, Diddums."

"Well," Dortmunder said, "I tell you what maybe you could do. You make them give you one of those buses they've got down there blocking the street. They give you one of those buses right now, then you know they haven't had time to put anything cute in it, like time-release tear-gas grenades or anyth—"

"Oh, my God," the robber said. His black ski mask seemed to have paled slightly.

"Then you take *all* the hostages," Dortmunder told him. "Everybody goes in the bus, and one of your people drives, and you go somewhere real crowded, like Times Square, say, and then you stop and make all the hostages get out and run."

"Yeah?" the robber said. "What good does that do us?"

"Well," Dortmunder said, "you drop the ski masks and the leather jackets and the guns, and *you* run, too. Twenty, thirty people all running away from the bus in different directions, in the middle of Times Square in rush hour, everybody losing themselves in the crowd. It might work."

"Jeez, it might," the robber said. "OK, go ahead and—What?"

"What?" Dortmunder echoed. He strained to look leftward, past the vertical column of his left arm. The boss robber was in excited conversation with one of his pals; not the red-eyed maniac, a different one. The boss robber shook his head and said, "Damn!" Then he looked up at Dortmunder. "Come back in here, Diddums," he said.

Dortmunder said, "But don't you want me to—"

"Come back in here!"

"Oh," Dortmunder said. "Uh, I better tell them over there that I'm gonna move."

"Make it fast," the robber told him. "Don't mess with me, Diddums. I'm in a bad mood right now."

"OK." Turning his head the other way, hating it that his back was toward this badmooded robber for even a second, Dortmunder called, "They want me to go back into the bank now. Just for a minute." Hands still up, he edged sideways across the sidewalk and through the gaping doorway, where the robbers laid hands on him and flung him back deeper into the bank.

He nearly lost his balance but saved himself against the sideways-lying pot of the tipped-over Ficus. When he turned around, all five of the robbers were lined up looking at him, their expressions intent, focused, almost hungry, like a row of cats looking in a fish-store window. "Uh," Dortmunder said.

"He's it now," one of the robbers said.

Another robber said, "But *they* don't know it."

A third robber said, "They will soon."

"They'll know it when nobody gets on the bus," the boss robber said, and shook his head at Dortmunder. "Sorry, Diddums. Your idea doesn't work anymore."

Dortmunder had to keep reminding himself that he wasn't actually *part* of this string. "How come?" he asked.

Disgusted, one of the other robbers said, "The rest of the hostages got away, that's how come."

Wide-eyed, Dortmunder spoke without thinking: "The tunnel!"

All of a sudden, it got very quiet in the bank. The robbers were now looking at him like cats looking at a fish with no window in the way. "The tunnel?" repeated the boss robber slowly. "You *know* about the tunnel?"

"Well, kind of," Dortmunder admitted. "I mean, the guys digging it, they got there just before you came and took me away."

"And you never mentioned it."

"Well," Dortmunder said, very uncomfortable, "I didn't feel like I should."

The red-eyed maniac lunged forward, waving that submachine gun again, yelling, "*You're* the guy with the tunnel! It's your tunnel!" And he pointed the shaking barrel of the Uzi at Dortmunder's nose.

"Easy, easy!" the boss robber yelled. "This is our only hostage; don't use him up!"

The red-eyed maniac reluctantly lowered the Uzi, but he turned to the others and announced, "*Nobody*'s gonna forget when I shot up the switchboard. Nobody's *ever* gonna forget that. He wasn't *here!*"

All of the robbers thought that over. Meantime, Dortmunder was thinking about his own position. He might be a hostage, but he wasn't your normal hostage, because he was also a guy who had just dug a tunnel to a bank vault, and there were maybe 30 eyeball witnesses who could identify him. So it wasn't enough to get away from these bank robbers; he was also going to have to get away from the police. Several thousand police.

So did that mean he was locked to these second-rate smash-and-grabbers? Was his own future really dependent on *their* getting out of this hole? Bad news, if true. Left to their own devices, these people couldn't escape from a merry-go-round.

Dortmunder sighed. "OK," he said. "The first thing we have to do is—"

"We?" the boss robber said. "Since when are you in this?"

"Since you dragged me in," Dortmunder told him. "And the first thing we have to do is—"

The red-eyed maniac lunged at him again with the Uzi, shouting, "Don't you tell us what to do! *We* know what to do!"

"I'm your only hostage," Dortmunder reminded him. "Don't use me up. Also, now that I've seen you people in action, I'm your only hope of getting out of here. So this time, listen to me. The first thing we have to do is close and lock the vault door."

One of the robbers gave a scornful laugh. "The hostages are *gone*," he said. "Didn't you hear that part? Lock the vault door after the hostages are gone. Isn't that some kind of old saying?" And he laughed and laughed.

Dortmunder looked at him. "It's a two-way tunnel," he said quietly.

The robbers stared at him. Then they all turned and ran toward the back of the bank. They *all* did.

They're too excitable for this line of work, Dortmunder thought as he walked briskly toward the front of the bank. *Clang* went the vault door, far behind him, and Dortmunder stepped through the broken doorway and out again to the sidewalk, remembering to stick his arms straight up in the air as he did.

"Hi!" he yelled, sticking his face well out, displaying it for all the sharpshooters to get a really *good* look at. "Hi, it's me again! Diddums! Welsh!"

"Diddums!" screamed an enraged voice from deep within the bank. "Come back here!"

Oh, no. Ignoring that, moving steadily but without panic, arms up, face forward, eyes wide, Dortmunder angled leftward across the sidewalk, shouting, "I'm coming out again! And I'm *escaping!*" And he dropped his arms, tucked his elbows in and ran hell for leather toward those blocking buses.

Gunfire encouraged him: sudden burst behind him of *ddrrritt, ddrrritt*, and then *kopp-kopp-kopp*, and then a whole symphony of *fooms* and *thug-thugs* and *padapows*. Dortmunder's toes, turning into high-tension steel springs, kept him bounding through the air like the Wright brothers' first airplane, swooping and plunging down the middle of the street, that wall of buses getting closer and closer.

"Here! In here!" Uniformed cops appeared on both sidewalks, waving to him, offering sanctuary in the forms of open doorways and police vehicles to crouch behind, but Dortmunder was *escaping*. From everything.

The buses. He launched himself through the air, hit the blacktop hard and rolled under the nearest bus. Roll, roll, roll, hitting his head and elbows and knees and ears and nose and various other parts of his body against any number of hard, dirty objects, and then he was past the bus and on his feet, staggering, staring at a lot of goggle-eyed medics hanging around beside their ambulances, who just stood there and gawked back.

Dortmunder turned left. *Medics* weren't going to chase him; their franchise didn't include healthy bodies running down the street. The cops couldn't chase him until they'd moved their buses out of the way. Dortmunder took off like the last of the dodoes, flapping his arms, wishing he knew how to fly.

The out-of-business shoe store, the other terminus of the tunnel, passed on his left. The getaway car they'd parked in front of it was long gone, of course. Dortmunder kept thudding on, on, on.

Three blocks later, a gypsy cab committed a crime by picking him up even though he hadn't phoned the dispatcher first; in the city of New York, only licensed medallion taxis are permitted to pick up customers who hail them on the street. Dortmunder, panting like a Saint Bernard on the lumpy back seat, decided not to turn the guy in.

His faithful companion May came out of the living room when Dortmunder opened the front door of his apartment and stepped into his hall. "*There* you are!" she said. "Thank goodness. It's all over the radio *and* the television."

"I may never leave the house again," Dortmunder told her. "If Andy Kelp ever calls, says he's got this great job, easy, piece of cake, I'll just tell him I've retired."

"Andy's here," May said. "In the living room. You want a beer?"

"Yes," Dortmunder said simply.

May went away to the kitchen and Dortmunder limped into the living room, where Kelp was seated on the sofa holding a can of beer and looking happy. On the coffee table in front of him was a mountain of money.

Dortmunder stared. "What's *that?*"

Kelp grinned and shook his head. "It's been too long since we scored, John," he said. "You don't even recognize the stuff anymore. This is money."

"But—From the vault? How?"

"After you were taken away by those other guys—they were caught, by the way," Kelp interrupted himself, "without loss of life—anyway, I told everybody in the vault there, the way to keep the money safe from the robbers was we'd all carry it out with us. So we did. And then I decided what we should do is put it all in the trunk of my unmarked police car in front of the shoe store, so I could drive it to the precinct for safekeeping while they all went home to rest from their ordeal."

Dortmunder looked at his friend. He said, "You got the hostages to carry the money from the vault."

"And put it in our car," Kelp said. "Yeah, that's what I did."

May came in and handed Dortmunder a beer. He drank deep, and Kelp said, "They're looking for you, of course. Under that other name."

May said, “That’s the one thing I don’t understand. Diddums?”

“It’s Welsh,” Dortmunder told her. Then he smiled upon the mountain of money on the coffee table. “It’s not a bad name,” he decided. “I may keep it.”

Acknowledgments

Grateful acknowledgment is made to the following for permission to reprint their copyrighted material:

"Breakfast Television" by Robert Barnard. Copyright © 1987 by Robert Barnard. First published in *Ellery Queen's Mystery Magazine*, January 1987. Reprinted by permission of the author and his agent, Jane Gregory.

"Keller's Therapy" by Lawrence Block. Copyright © 1993 by Lawrence Block. First published in *Playboy*, May 1993. Reprinted by permission of the author.

"Spasmo" by Liza Cody. Copyright © 1990 by Liza Cody. First published in *A Classic English Crime*. Reprinted by permission of the author.

"Old Friends" by Dorothy Salisbury Davis. Copyright © 1975 by Dorothy Salisbury Davis. First published in *Ellery Queen's Mystery Magazine*. Reprinted by permission of McIntosh and Otis, Inc.

"Grafitti" by Stanley Ellin. Copyright © 1983 by Stanley Ellin. First published in *Ellery Queen's Mystery Magazine*. Reprinted by permission of the author and his agent, Curtis Brown, Ltd.

"Mefisto in Onyx" by Harlan Ellison. Copyright © 1993 by the Kilimanjaro Corporation. Reprinted by arrangement with, and permission of, the author and the author's agent, Richard Curtis Associates, Inc., New York. All rights reserved.

"There Are No Snakes in Ireland" by Frederick Forsyth. Copyright © 1982 by Frederick Forsyth. Reproduced by permission of Curtis Brown Group Ltd., London.

"Scrimshaw" by Brian Garfield. Copyright © 1979 by Brian Garfield. First published in *Ellery Queen's Mystery Magazine*, December 1979. Reprinted by permission of the author.

"Prisoners" by Ed Gorman. Copyright © 1990 by Ed Gorman. First published in *New Crimes*, 1990. Reprinted by permission of the author.

"McIntyre's Donald" by Joseph Hansen. Copyright © 1992 by *South Dakota Review*. Reprinted by permission of the author.

"The Most Dangerous Man Alive" by Edward D. Hoch. Copyright © 1980 by Edward D. Hoch. First published in *Ellery Queen's Mystery Magazine*. Reprinted by permission of the author.

"Nine Sons" by Wendy Hornsby. Copyright © 1991 by Wendy Hornsby. First published in *Sisters in Crime 4*. Reprinted by permission of the author.

"Challenge the Widow-Maker" by Clark Howard. Copyright © 1990 by Clark Howard. First published in *Ellery Queen's Mystery Magazine*, August 1990. Reprinted by permission of the author.

"The Last Spin" by Evan Hunter. Copyright © 1956 by Hui Corporation. Reprinted by permission of the William Morris Agency, Inc., on behalf of the author.

"Moment of Power" by P. D. James. Copyright © 1968 by P. D. James. Reproduced by permission of Greene & Heaton Ltd. This story has also appeared under the title, "A Very Commonplace Murder."

"One Hit Wonder" by Gabrielle Kraft. Copyright © 1992 by Gabrielle Kraft. First published in *Sisters in Crime 5*. Reprinted by permission of the author.

"The Reluctant Detective" by Michael Z. Lewin. Copyright © 1984 by Michael Z. Lewin. Reprinted by permission of the Wallace Literary Agency, Inc.

"Ride the Lightning" by John Lutz. Copyright © 1984 by Davis Publications, Inc. First published in *Alfred Hitchcock's Mystery Magazine*, January 1985. Reprinted by permission of the author.

"Do with Me What You Will" by Joyce Carol Oates. Copyright © 1973 by Joyce Carol Oates. First published in *Playboy*, June 1973. Reprinted by permission of the author.

"Incident in a Neighborhood Tavern" by Bill Pronzini. Copyright © 1988 by Bill Pronzini. First published in *An Eye For Justice*. Reprinted by permission of the author.

"The New Girl Friend" by Ruth Rendell. Copyright © 1983 by Kingsmarkham Enterprises Ltd. First published in *Ellery Queen's Mystery Magazine*, August 1983. Reprinted by permission of the author.

"Mary, Mary, Shut the Door" by Benjamin M. Schutz. Copyright © 1992 by Benjamin M. Schutz. First published in *Deadly Allies*. Reprinted by permission of the author.

"The Imperial Icehouse" by Paul Theroux. Copyright © 1979 by Paul Theroux. First published in *The Atlantic Monthly*. Reprinted with the permission of Wylie, Aitken & Stone, Inc.

"Too Many Crooks" by Donald E. Westlake. Copyright © 1989 by Donald E. Westlake. First published in *Playboy*, August 1989. Reprinted by permission of the author.